THE
SEXY LIBRARIAN'S
BIG BOOK OF
EROTICA

THE
SEXY LIBRARIAN'S
BIG BOOK OF
EROTICA

Edited by

Rose Caraway

Published in the United States by Cleis Press, Inc., 2246 Sixth Street, Berkeley, California 94710.

Printed in the United States.
Cover design: Scott Idleman/Blink
Cover photograph: Dimitri Otis/Getty Images
Text design: Frank Wiedemann

First Edition.
10 9 8 7 6 5 4 3 2 1

Trade paper ISBN: 978-1-62778-065-0
E-book ISBN: 978-1-62778-077-3

TABLE OF CONTENTS

vii **Foreword** *Bix Warden*

ix **Introduction**

1 **Book Swap** *Rachel Kramer Bussel*

17 **Sensate Silicone** *Lillian Douglas*

35 **Three Legs in the Evening** *Janine Ashbless*

55 **The Contest** *Michael Lewis*

69 **The Secret Game** *Chase Morgan*

81 **POW! It's Shibari Girl!** *Tamsin Flowers*

93 **Vivi and the Magic Man** *Kristina Wright*

107 **Second Look** *Heidi Champa*

117 **Taped** *Kay Jaybee*

133 **Lauren's Journey** *D. L. King*

145 **A Perverted Fairy Tale** *Emily Bingham*

159 **The Skilled Technician** *Kate Maxwell*

169 **Shades of Desire** *Allen Dusk*

189 **Moonshine Ballad** *Salome Wilde*

197 **Cherries in Season** *KD Grace*

215 **The Perfect Massage** *Olivia Archer*

225 **Full-Frontal Neighbor** *Lynn Townsend*

241 **The Whole of Me** *Katya Harris*

263 **Notes on a Scandal** *Kelly Maher*

279 **Appetizer** *Sommer Marsden*

291 **Mikhael** *Angela Caperton*

309 **The Mating Chamber** *Rose Caraway*

329 **About the Authors**

335 **About the Editor**

Foreword
Bix Warden

Libraries are full of endless possibilities. Each book contains worlds within it where we can lose, or find, ourselves. We can discover things we didn't even know existed, or follow our wildest dreams and most deeply held desires. And, as Jo Goodwin said, "A truly great library contains something to offend everyone." Librarians are on the front lines of our freedom to read, to think and to look at anything and everything the printed word, the digital word and the Internet have to offer. They fight the good fight every day, to ensure that you can access whatever you wish, without judgment or censorship of any kind. Is it any surprise that Batgirl was a librarian by day? Barbara Gordon, head of the Gotham City Public Library and superheroine fighting crime by night. Librarians in the real world these days are as likely to have pink hair and tattoos as they are to fit the stereotype of sensible shoes and a cardigan.

The best thing about being a librarian is that you don't have to know everything, you just have to know where to find it. And for those who believe there's no need for librarians in the age of Google, I give you this quote from Neil Gaiman: "Google can bring you back 100,000 answers. A librarian can bring you back the right one."

No wonder librarians are featured in the sexual fantasies of so many people. After all, the brain is the most important sex organ in the body. You don't have to be a sapiosexual to recognize that, yes, intelligence is the sexiest attribute. Librarians, in my experience, are often both smart and sexy; they read widely and across many genres, from horror to science fiction to literary fiction and nonfiction. If it's well written and thoughtful, a librarian is likely to enjoy it.

You hold in your hands a volume that invites you to let your fingers stroll through an enticing virtual card catalogue. So much variety is on hand, so many different tales that all celebrate the erotic in a way that is indeed both intelligent and arousing. When you've finished these, if you still find yourself craving more, look no farther than the shelves of your local library. Erotica holds a proud place in our collections, and books of erotica are among the most popular items in circulation. Just tell them a sexy librarian sent you.

Bix Warden
San Francisco

Introduction

A short story is a different thing all together—a short story is like a kiss in the dark from a stranger.
— Stephen King

I can't tell you how much this very sentiment appropriately describes the erotic fiction found within my private library. Every story I have ever collected over the years—read and reread—is, indeed, a very special kiss, although by now I don't think we are exactly *strangers* anymore. It seems I never have enough, however, and like a honeybee to nectar off I go, hunting for more stories. I'm *dedicated* one might say, ever on the prowl. Fearlessly expanding my search to wherever my carnal nose may lead. Until I'm finally honing in on the next incredible erotic tale—that special kiss in the dark.

To be honest, it actually makes me a little giddy when I know deep within my bones that I have located the perfect story for *you*, my darling patron. Much of my careful research is directed by your vast and varied tastes. While this journey of scouring the globe is my calling, I am your favorite Sexy Librarian and consider it to be an honor and a wonderful privilege to provide you with twenty-two stories taken from my own private collection in *The Sexy Librarian's Big Book of Erotica*. Each story brings exciting new fantasies with every turn of the page. There aren't words to describe the tremendous energy born of responsibility and respect that coursed through my veins during this quest as I sometimes made very difficult decisions to select the tales I felt you would enjoy the most. The truth is, I want to please you. I want you to smile, because once you begin the first story, that shiny little twinkle that suddenly appears in your eye...will be priceless. And I will get to say, *I did that*.

Yes, finding stories for your enjoyment is my job, but it's also my passion and it makes me feel good to feed your passions. Your joy is my joy and I am humbly at your service. I know that some days you want nothing more than to fall into a steamy *Romance*, a nostalgic *Classic Fiction* or a *Fantasy* because it helps you relax and discard the day's stress like a used shirt. I also know that your mood changes and you don't only want *Fairy Tales,* because your tastes and desires differ from day to day. It is no secret to me that some nights, nothing can get your blood pumping faster than reading a chilling *Erotic Horror*, a *Supernatural Thriller* or an explicit *Sci-fi*. And, on rare occasion, I know that you desire to be challenged to the very brink of ecstasy, teased and tweaked more than usual—you are a beautifully diverse being, complicated even at times. The only solution for untangling your intricate self is through reading a story with a well-disciplined, healing dose of *BDSM* that will help guide you into character and allow you to vicariously receive your very own overdue *Spanking*.

It is impossible to ever just pick one kind of erotic story; there are too many delicious adventures just waiting to be had! So don't worry, all of these stories are yours now, take them. Enjoy. These adventures will not simply sit on the page, they want to *be*. To prove that they can exist within *you*. They will get your juices flowing, make you grip the edges of the book with an irrefutable urge to read *what happens next*.

On behalf of all of the wonderful authors that have contributed their time, talent and creativity to help build this library, I thank you. Thank you for simply picking up this book. We appreciate it more than you will ever know.

I wish you well, darling patron, and of course happy reading.

Your Sexy Librarian,
Rose Caraway

306.7
Bus

Book Swap

author: Rachel Kramer Bussel

category: BDSM

subject:
1. Cougar   2. Airplane   3. Spanking

Book Swap

Rachel Kramer Bussel

As a start-up owner and type A personality, I believe in efficiency, technology and innovation. I am always on the go and love any apps or devices that will help me work smarter and faster. I've been called a "tech goddess" and am the ultimate early adopter—except when it comes to books. I know, it's a weird quirk, but even though I've tried every e-reader out there, when I sink into the glorious pages of a book, I prefer one with a cover that sparks my imagination, lush print on sleek paper, an object to hold and behold. When it comes to books, I'm low-tech. Lo-fi. Old school. I'm a completist, the type who arranges her books by author, buys first editions and hates creases on her pages. I read everything, from the acknowledgments to the dedications to the copyright page (you learn some surprising pseudonyms that way). Even in my office, which is otherwise ultramodern, my bookcase is a paean to my love of the classic written word.

It's why, even though I had plenty of work I could be doing on my flight from New York to Charlotte, I wasn't planning to use the airline's wireless service. Instead, I'd packed three beloved books, with room in my bag for more (even on a short trip, I like to have choices). Part of the joy of travel for me is visiting a new bookstore and reveling in its quirks and charms, plus asking for recommendations. I've found some of my most cherished books that way.

I settled into my window seat, smiling to myself as I pulled out my battered copy of one of my favorite novels, *A Concise Chinese-English Dictionary for Lovers* by Xiaolu Guo. I'd discovered it on a staff pick table in a London bookstore and been intrigued by its red cover featuring a naked woman turned to the side, decorated by artful green leaves that evoked, to me, Eve in the garden. It took me a while to get into the first time I read it, though, but it had been well worth it. Sometimes the best books, like the best sex, require a little extra effort. Now I reread it every year to remind myself of that London trip, and of narrator Z's discovery of language and love and passion. To transport myself. I actually look forward to flying for some solo time, away from beeping gadgets and urgent emails. I thanked my lucky stars, and the airline, that the seat next to me was empty, and settled in with my book. I never wait until the plane takes off to start getting lost in the story.

So I was swept up in the scene where Z goes to a peep show, when a man settled himself into the aisle seat. That I didn't mind, as long as he didn't take the middle one and infringe on my personal space. I was about to bury my head back in my book when I actually paused to check out my seatmate. He was ripped and tan and young looking—I pegged him for college age, or just out of school. He had a tribal armband tattoo, visible above his white V-neck T-shirt, and sexy blond stubble along his chin. More than any other characteristic, stubble is what does it for me. I was a goner then and there, grateful for the first time in months that I was single. Even if nothing came of it, I could still look. Yes, I'm forty-two, but to me one of the joys of middle age is being able to sample men from a range of life experiences, younger, older or my peers. I'm not picky about age, as long as a guy can keep up with me—in bed and out.

When he smiled at me, I just gave him a little grin in return. I've learned over the years that I have the best luck when I let the guy do the talking. If he didn't chat me up, I'd be more than happy to revel in my reading material. Which is exactly what I did, consuming those beautiful words as if they were a chocolate mousse melting on my tongue. They satisfied me in almost the same way. Once I finished that chapter, I shut my eyes as we coasted at cruising altitude, placing the book on the empty seat next to me and resting my eyes for a moment to relive the vivid imagery. I've been to strip clubs, but never to a proper peep show, but I feel as if I have from Guo's words. I adjusted my seat as far back as it would go and relaxed fully, letting all the tension of the workweek melt away. That's when I felt a tap on my shoulder.

"Excuse me, sorry, I know you're resting, but I wondered if you wouldn't mind swapping books for a few minutes. I'm reading this for school"—he made a face, indicating that *The Fountainhead* wasn't exactly his cup of tea—"but yours looks like much more fun. Could we trade for a few minutes? I'm Joel, by the way." My face burned for a moment, because if he were to flip back past my bookmark, he'd know the scene I'd just read had been more than simply "fun." Did I care? Well, yes. Sure, I wasn't above reading even risqué books in public, but even when you're on the subway or in a café or on a plane, reading is still one of the most private and intimate pleasures a person can enjoy. The times I've read racy passages out loud have been with lovers who I specifically knew would appreciate the words. This young man was someone I was forced to sit next to, and no matter how hot he was, he was about to know exactly what I'd been absorbed by.

Still, I wasn't about to say no; not only would that make him more curious and probably pester me, but also it really wasn't a big deal. So he knew I was reading a scene featuring a woman watching another woman at a peep show. It's a free country, right? Plus, maybe I'd be pleasantly surprised at his reaction. "Brianna," is all I said before passing over my tattered paperback. While he dug right into Z's story, instead of reading Ayn Rand's classic novel, I let my eyes dart over to him. He'd flipped ahead to the passage I'd just read. I couldn't help but smile when I noticed his eyes bulge; I'd bet he'd never been to a peep show or strip club. Maybe he was even a virgin, but that would've meant he'd surely turned down many a girl, because he was mesmerizing. I turned my head so I wouldn't be able to see him as closely; I know nothing makes me more nervous than someone watching me read. Instead, I stared out the window at the beautiful clouds below us, but rather than simply wishing we were there already, I savored the moment.

I must have shut my eyes, because I felt another tap on my shoulder. "Fascinating. I'd be interested in reading the whole book." He smiled at me, his deep-brown eyes probing mine. He didn't say a word about the erotic scene I'd been reading; he didn't need to—his eyes spoke for him, although I couldn't quite translate his desire. I often try to figure out what a guy will be like in bed well before we're headed there; it's a little game I play, but Joel wasn't cooperating. I couldn't tell at all whether he'd be selfish or selfless, a top or a bottom, the kind of guy who likes to fuck fast and hard or one who wants to take his time. As I smiled back, I realized that not knowing was drawing me to him as much as his stubble or strong arms or beautiful skin. I wanted to find out what was happening behind that gaze.

He handed the book back to me, and I returned his to the empty seat between us. Joel kept his hand in my lap, silently asking whether I wanted company. Part of me wasn't sure—he was so much younger than my usual bedmate. I didn't want him to fall for me, or to be with someone who fumbled around between my legs rather than giving me exactly what I wanted. "Have you ever been to a strip club?" is what I asked Joel. I was curious; his answer could tell me a lot about him.

"Once, but it wasn't really my thing. The women weren't, anyway. I'd rather get a lap dance from a woman I can touch and taste and smell than someone who's doing the same thing for every guy with twenty bucks in his pocket. What about you?"

Guys my age would have surely stumbled through an answer, whether they'd done it or not. I know because I've asked a few times—either they're too embarrassed to fess up, passing it off as a bachelor party thrill, or they know more about their favorite stripper's moves than their last girlfriend. Joel was direct and unassuming as he parried my query back to me.

"A few times. You get treated a little better if you're a woman who's really into it."

"And you are? Into it?" He leaned closer to ask, though it wasn't so much a question as an excuse to move closer.

"Yes, when there's chemistry. That's the most important thing to me—chemistry. But I bet you're too young to understand that." I couldn't resist, plus I was half-sure it was true. How could he get what I was talking about?

"I know more about chemistry than you might think. You're just too chicken to find out exactly what I know. I dare you—when we land, I dare you to try my chemistry." He made "chemistry" sound like a dirty word, a synonym for "cock," practically. I looked down and saw that his was hard, pressing against his jeans.

"You want it, don't you?" Joel continued. "Or maybe you want to watch me get a lap dance, want to watch a naked woman strut her stuff for me."

"Maybe," I managed, even though the answer was more along the lines of "definitely."

Suddenly I had a vision of Joel getting more than a lap dance; what flashed through my mind was a woman down on her knees, sucking his cock, while I licked her from behind. I couldn't help the sigh of longing that escaped my lips. I've never had a great poker face, which sometimes takes away from any cool, calm demeanor I'm trying to project.

"Or maybe she should give us both a lap dance. I know we can't touch her, but maybe if we go in a back room, I could spread you open for her to watch. She could tell me what to do to you while you just sit there and take it." Where had young Joel learned such things? His words weren't innocent, but they warred with that gorgeous, baby face. "Do you have any toys with you?" he asked, the words landing like silk against my skin. He was technically still in his seat, but he'd lifted up both armrests and leaned as far over as he could. "I want to use one on you."

I stared back at him, unexpectedly speechless. I'm not a woman who's often lost for words. "Don't you have a girlfriend or something?" I asked.

"I did, but we broke up a while back. For the record, she dumped me. I've been waiting for the right woman to come along."

"How long is a while?"

"Two months."

"You're seriously telling me a guy who looks like you hasn't gotten laid in two months."

"For that, I'm going to spank you."

"You're going to spank me for complimenting you?" I was amused, but also very turned on. I love men who throw off my center of gravity, who look sweet and almost innocent and turn out to be secret sadists (or ones who look tough and stern but not so deep down want to be tormented).

"I'm going to spank you for rubbing it in. And then I'm going to make you suck my cock. And I'm going to have *you* dance for me rather than a stripper; I don't want to wait to feel you across my lap."

I didn't have a snappy comeback, because I was no longer in charge. "To answer your question, I don't have any toys on me."

"But you do have this," he said, picking up the paperback. "I'm going to spank you with it, and maybe if you're good, I'll use the belt I have packed in my bag. And you're going to call up room service and ask if they have any adult toys you could purchase."

Somehow, in swapping books, it was like we were swapping roles, like I'd transferred every hint of erotic power over to this wunderkind. Whether we actually did those things or not, I was in. All in. It was so unexpected; I just sat and stared at him until he placed the book back in my lap and whispered, "Now close your eyes and think about how it's going to feel to have my hand on your ass and my cock in your mouth."

I did just that, trying not to squirm too much in my seat. I jumped, startled, when the flight attendant came by to take our final drink orders. Joel ordered a beer, while I asked for an orange juice. When it arrived, I took a few sips, but was so jittery I worried I'd spill it. "Drink up," he ordered me. "You need all the energy you can get for what's about to happen. I won't have you conking out halfway on me."

I loved the way he immediately took control, but I also loved that he'd waited to see if I'd responded to him taking charge. I have plenty of bratty sub in me, but I don't just let that side out for any guy, especially not ones who think all women should immediately bow down and take orders. That's the opposite of hot. Joel—Joel was everything I look for in a lover, and my body was already primed to respond to his every word. Sometimes, it's that easy—and I'm that easy.

He left me alone for a little while. I'd just settled into a daydream about kneeling on the floor with my hands bound behind my back when we started our descent. Joel grabbed my wrist, his fingers locked tight. He kept it there the whole ride, which earned us a knowing look from the female flight attendant who came around to make sure our seats were in the upright position and our seat belts were buckled. As we hurtled to the ground, Joel leaned over and whispered, "Show me your panties. Just for a second. Don't make a scene, just show me what color they are."

That made my red panties very, very wet, a fact I was pretty sure Joel found out in the brief moment I showed him what lay between my legs. I blushed fiercely, not because I'm shy, though—I was just amazed that in such a short time span, Joel had managed to have me at his mercy, ready to eat out of the palm of his hand, if he ordered me to. "Do you have checked luggage?"

"No," I replied.

"Good, because if you'd made me wait even longer you were going to get punished for it."

I had a feeling whatever punishment he'd concoct would be more pleasure than pain, but I smiled back. We landed smoothly; Joel opened my seat belt before I had a chance to, running his hand briefly between my legs. Not for the first time, I wondered if we'd have struck up a flirtation—or whatever this was—if someone else had been seated between us. I had a feeling the answer would've been no, unless we'd managed an airplane ménage à trois, which even for a hottie like Joel might have been a challenge.

I let him lead me along, grateful to simply follow. I shut off my overactive mind so I could focus on what my body was telling me, which was that I was ready for whatever Joel threw at me. That was good, because he started in the cab, after giving the cabbie the name of his hotel—he didn't even ask mine, but I realized quickly that they were both downtown, so it wasn't an issue. No sooner had the driver begun our journey than Joel was cornering me in the backseat. His fingers pinched my lower lip, making the rest of me sing with excitement.

"I'd try to find a strip club but all I want is to see the parts of you I couldn't make you show me on the plane," he muttered as he teased my lip. Joel shifted his hand from my lip to behind my head, pulling me close, but not close enough. When I tried to bridge the gap between us for the kiss I was dying to feel, he pulled back. "You have to earn a kiss, Brianna," he admonished. "Show me those wet panties again." He managed to say this in a much louder voice, one I was pretty sure the cabbie heard because he swerved slightly and quickly righted the vehicle.

I hiked up my skirt as briefly as I could, but he wouldn't let me pull it back down, instead leaving my panties on view for several seconds, though they felt like several minutes. He rubbed his fingers against my panties, pinching me for a moment before letting the skirt fall over his hand, which then rested against my hip. He'd moved so he was sitting right next to me, while I simply waited to see what he'd do next. I didn't have to wait long before he was tugging on my lip again, this time with his teeth. By the time we reached his hotel, I was swollen, aching, putty in his hands.

I was so aroused I could barely carry my shoulder bag. Seeing this, Joel managed to carry my bags and hoist me in his arms and into the hotel. "You need your energy, remember, to be my slut for the night." Who knew four little letters could be so charged? It wasn't so much the word, though, as the way he said it, like "slut" meant a magical princess who'd be treated to all sorts of sexual delights, if only she behaved. He ceremoniously placed me on a couch in the lobby, told me not to move and went to check in.

It would've been humiliating—if it wasn't so exciting. I couldn't remember the last time a man had treated me with such certainty that I was his, through and through. Of course I wasn't *really* Joel's—I barely knew him. We weren't in a love story like Z's, but I knew I wanted him. I knew that for however long we were together—an hour, a day, or possibly more—I truly *was* his, and I wanted him to treat me this way. Thankfully I'd managed to convey that to him on the plane, and now my job was simply to sit and obey orders. I was far enough from home that I didn't care if anyone caught on to what was happening between us.

Joel returned and pulled me up, tugging me close enough to feel the hardness beneath his jeans. "I'm very tempted to drag you into the bathroom right now and make you take care of this, but we have a whole suite waiting for us. I'm going to carry you to the room, and you're going to let me. Think about what you're going to do to my cock." No sooner were the words out of his mouth than Joel had picked me up—both our bags in one hand, the other wrapped around my ass—and carted me to the elevator. In this position, I could focus properly on his erection; being so close to him was making me unbearably aroused. So I shut my eyes, a necessity in case anyone was watching me and wondering what a woman my age was doing draped over this man's shoulder, and thought about how hungry I was for him—all of him, not just his cock.

If we'd managed to get it on while en route, I think ultimately, as hot as it might have been, I'd have been disappointed. Making me wait for him gave me extra time to let my imagination roam. As the elevator rose, an image of me kneeling, naked, with my hands tied behind my back, flashed into my mind. Joel was holding his cock in his hand, but he wasn't feeding it to me—no matter how much I begged, stuck out my tongue and even drooled at his command. Instead he was slowly sliding his fist up and down, letting me see exactly how hard he was.

I was so lost in my fantasy that when we exited the elevator I had to remind myself where we were. In my head, I was already poised to do anything for a taste of that precome tempting me from the tip of his cock. We entered the room and Joel threw me roughly onto the bed. While normally my first thought upon entering a hotel room is figuring out where the nearest outlet is located to plug in my phone, I barely even remembered I had a phone. I had more urgent devices to turn on. "I don't know whether to rip your clothes off or make you dance for me."

Wisely, I didn't say a word, letting him mull over his options. Instead, he brought my fingers to his zipper. "Slowly," he cautioned. I moved as slowly as I could, but it was a challenge. I'm used to getting what I want, and he'd already denied me for so long, but I knew if I tried to rush him, I'd only provoke the opposite effect. I shifted my gaze from what my fingers were about to reveal to his face. He offered me a sensual, wicked smile as his fingers covered mine and, together, we eased the zipper down.

"This what you wanted?"

The gorgeous hard cock that greeted me certainly was, but when I started to place my hand around it, he batted me away. "I'll tell you when you can touch me. Right now you're going to give me a lap dance. Hurry up." Joel slithered out of his clothes, pulled the covers back and sat on the bed, completely naked, his erection proud and inviting. I stood on shaky legs. "No music, just you dancing for me," he coaxed in a quieter voice. My heart was pounding a beat loud enough to guide me as I started with my skirt. I faced him, hands at the zipper, before simultaneously tossing my head back so my breasts brushed his face as I popped the button and let the skirt fall to my feet. I turned and bent over, baring my ass to him, getting into the spirit of it, especially when he pulled me gently back toward him and let his cock rub against my slit.

Emboldened, I stepped right between his legs as I undid the buttons on my blouse. They're more decorative than anything—I only needed to undo one to slip it over my head, but I chose to take the long route. Our faces were inches apart by the time I wriggled out of the top, my nipples almost peeking out from my bra. I tossed the blouse unceremoniously onto the bed, then shook my hair against his face as I unhooked the bra. I shimmied out of it, my hard nipples passing by his lips. I was glad he'd given me this assignment, because it helped sate my desire for his cock for a few minutes. I was thinking about him admiring me, wanting me, touching me, kissing me, rather than me devouring him. When I moved to take off my panties, his hands met mine and together we pushed them down to my ankles.

"Leave them there," he said as a finger brushed against my wetness. I stood, trapped between Joel's firm, muscular thighs, trembling as he acquainted himself with my wetness. "Put your hands on my shoulders." I did so, grateful for the support as Joel's fingers sought out my clit. I'd been watching, but shut my eyes when he sank those wet fingers inside me. I tightened around him, my nails digging into him as he was soon fucking me hard. I didn't know how many fingers he was using, but I felt full, tight, hot and ready. "Go ahead, show me how much you want me," he said, answering my unspoken plea to come.

My body responded instantly, nails digging deeper into his back, thighs shaking against his, as my climax drew his fingers deeper inside me. I'd thought I was ready, but the shock of it had tears racing to my eyes. My orgasm was a comet racing through me, exploding loud and hard and beautiful. His other arm wrapped around me protectively as it subsided.

I was shaky, but the energy whipped back into me when he said, "Now fetch me your book and get across my lap." I rushed to retrieve the novel, handing it to him gingerly before climbing across his lap. There's nothing to take the years off like settling into such a submissive pose. Whether he was going to "punish" or "pleasure" me with my spanking, I felt far younger than the face that stared back at me in the mirror. "I'm going to spank you the way I was thinking about on the plane. I so wanted to take you over my knee right there, let the passengers behind us get a view of this beautiful ass. So we'll just have to pretend we have an audience." I could picture it, easily, as the first blow from his bare hand landed. He knew exactly where to strike each cheek—clearly he wasn't the innocent virgin I'd imagined at first.

"If it's too much, say 'ground.' Okay?"

"Yes," I sobbed as he pinched my ass while waiting for my reply. Then the spanking resumed in earnest. I noticed that if I tensed my ass and tried to prepare for it, he just did something else—pinched my inner thighs, massaged my anus, trailed the back of his hand along my slit—until I relaxed. Then he let me have it. Joel made each smack count, the consecutive blows making my pussy so tight I wanted to scream. When I did, in fact, let out a yell, Joel said, "If you make so much noise that security pays us a visit, there'll be no more spanking, and you won't get my cock inside this very wet pussy." I shut up, letting the sound of each blow echo in the room and in my ears.

I'd have thought the book wouldn't have that much of an impact—after all, I've been spanked with paddles and floggers and rulers and the like. But Joel had a magic touch, or maybe I was just so sensitive from his hand, because the spanks from the book made me whimper again. With one hand holding my lower back firmly in place, he slammed the book against the fleshiest part of my ass until I was shaking. Finally, he dropped the book on the bed and delivered two of the hardest spanks I've ever received, using what felt like every muscle in his body to make my asscheeks sing with pleasure and pain.

He lifted me up so I was back between his legs, even more wobbly and aroused than before. "Now you get this," he said, finally placing my hand on his cock. When he said it, for a second, I didn't even want him inside me; the orgasm had been that good. But my hand around his hardness reminded me that I did still need to feel him there. He fetched a condom from his jeans and guided my fingers once again as I unrolled it onto him. Joel dragged me to the end of the bed, hoisted my ankles onto his shoulders, and speared me with his cock.

A moment before, I'd almost refused him—not because I wasn't turned on, but because all my senses were overwhelmed. I'd never been taken to such an erotic extreme, then made to wait. Joel probably could have gently licked between my legs and made me come again, so the blunt impact of his hardness, combined with the way he grabbed my ass and fucked me for all he was worth, had me spasming again almost immediately. Maddening tears formed in my eyes—tears of lust and desire, but even more, tears at finally having met my match in a lover. Joel fucked me the way I'd dreamed of being fucked—not just with his cock, but with his whole body, his mind, his soul. He didn't just pull out and ram back into me—although he did plenty of that. He offered me something more than just the promise of our airplane-flirting; he gifted a part of me back to myself I hadn't realized I was missing, a part I'd found in books and fantasies, but never completely in the flesh.

I wanted him closer, next to me, as near as he could get, but I didn't want to pull away or tell him what to do. I sat up as much as I could in that position, and he pressed down, the sweet ache in my thighs causing another ache where he was buried deep inside. "Open," he commanded, though I already was, open to him in every way. He pushed my thighs apart and bent over me, moving close enough to bite my lip again. With my lip trapped between his teeth, Joel came with a final, forceful thrust.

I didn't want to let him go and break the spell. Instead I looked up at him through filmy eyes. He stared right back, that beautiful face softened by what we'd just shared. He eased his cock out of me, but immediately replaced it with two slow-moving fingers that knew just where to go to make me come again. This time was quieter, but just as intense.

The bathtub was big enough for both of us. He filled it with strawberry bubble bath and sank inside. "Wait," he said before I got more than an ankle in. "Bring the book. Read me a story." So I fetched the novel that had brought us together, settled into the tub next to him and picked up where we'd left Z, not minding when the pages got dusted with bubbles. I planned to slip the paperback into his bag, with my phone number, before we parted. But first, we had a tub—and each other—to enjoy.

Sensate Silicone

Lillian Douglas

A medical miracle. Researchers taking home paychecks from the DOD found a way to link the human nervous system to the electrical pulse of a computer. It figures: life-enhancing technology brought into the world by an outfit trying to build better bombs. There was no way of telling how long they kept it under their helmets, but once out the news splashed across the news magazines. No such thing as lost limbs anymore. No such thing as cerebral palsy, MS. Neurological disorders were headed for a rout. Headlines shouted possibility from every street corner.

Some glorious people out there were aiming slightly lower. Amid the excitement about long-sought cures for terrible diseases, LiveVibes hunkered down, their minds in the same gorgeous old gutter. Down in the muck, they produced a miracle of their own.

This is where I come in. Jane Isley, porn star and sexpert, known to my friends in and out of the adult industry as the Dildo Queen. I'd done some work for LiveVibes in the past—strictly R&D, but certain circles pay premium for my endorsement—and we'd come away mutually satisfied. Me in the literal, sexual sense; their fake cock-skin is top of the line. And their money's plenty green. So when the phone rang Thursday noon, I was on a plane Friday morning out to Portland.

Business class and a limo waiting on the other end. Live-Vibes had come into some more substantial funds than I remembered. In the limo waited a suit and a lab coat, the suit under strict orders not to leak product specifics until I'd signed a nondisclosure and the lab coat dying under her professional veneer to burble and gloat.

"You've never seen anything *like* it," the lab coat promised gleefully, her inner third-grader surfacing for a romp, which I minded none. She had perky little almost-tits and a wide-open smile; a bit of a fox. I got a little growly between the legs stealing glances down her shirt (*Why the bra?* I wondered) and had to swear to myself I'd use her during the session as brain-fodder. Small girls can be so vicious—and who's hotter than the chick working to build the better dildo?

Forms signed and my lips tightly zipped, we strode down the hall from legal to development. The lab coat led and chattered. We attracted loose blue jeans and khakis until we'd snowballed into a respectable procession. Throw in some office equivalents of the pitchfork (staplers?) and it could've been a revolt.

"You've never seen anything like it," the lab coat promised for the thirty-seventh time, just as she pushed open a door at the end of the corridor.

The buildup, as I knew was inevitable, left me disappointed. It took a modest helping of self-control to avoid breaking the enthralled silence by telling the assembled crowd that I actually *had* seen something very much like it. It was just an average-sized fake cock. In fact, worse: an albino cock with varicose veins and blackheads.

I suppose I did not look sufficiently impressed, so the lab coat's face went somber as she delicately (as if the thing could feel—as if it were connected to some invisible albino man) lift-ed the dildo from its tastefully rumpled bed of white terrycloth and held it up for my inspection. It still looked like another fake cock. Except for the thick wire attached to a small suction-cup looking thing dangling from the base.

"What's this?" I asked very seriously, indicating the bit that didn't seem to belong.

She deliberately misunderstood me. "This is the next gen-eration in phallus substitution." How euphemistic. "A break-through. A quantum leap."

I tire of marketing without information, so I bent slightly at the waist, bringing my nose to its silicone head and taking a whiff. "Smells like a dildo," I said. Our audience of khakis and blue jeans (mostly male, some of whom were hot enough to glance at twice) chuckled at this, and the lab coat very nearly snatched the Great White Dick away from me.

"It is to a dildo what your skin is to a leather jacket," she announced triumphantly. I was still confused. She sighed and sacrificed grandiosity for clarity. "Sensate silicone. It can feel."

"It can...*what* can it feel? Like it knows how to touch me?" I wasn't playing anymore. I really just did not understand.

"No, like you can feel *it*," she said, exasperated. Her dra-matic unveiling, clearly strictly scripted in her own mind, had been thoroughly destroyed.

But I finally got it. And immediately disbelieved. The impli-cations were far too sci-fi for my little brain to swallow without choking a little. So I did what comes naturally in such a situa-tion.

"Of course I'll be able to feel it. What *else* is it for?" I tried to play it as deadpan as possible, and the overflow crowd chuckled appreciatively; I know the sort of jokes a sex-industry corporate culture spawns. The poor lab coat stood silently, playing the adult. I relented. "Nerve extenders."

"Exactly. The same technology that allows people to..."

"How does it work?" I interrupted. For a tech she sure liked pitching.

"Well," she said condescendingly, "that's a little complicated, but..."

"I meant, how do I put it on? How do I connect?"

"Oh. Sorry," she blushed slightly. "You wear it in a standard harness and attach the interface to your..." The blush deepened. But she was a professional, and it was a matter of pride to beat back childish embarrassment at such a vital word. "Clitoris."

"The interface?" I asked, indicating the suction cup. I caught it on its nearest pendulum pass and inspected its interior. She nodded. "And that's it?"

"Yes. The clitoris has as many nerve endings as the entire penis. It was simply a matter of extending each as best we could."

"Wow," I wowed, impressed but still a bit incredulous. "When do I get to try it out?"

LiveVibes had kept the room nice and warm, so disrobing was rather pleasant. As usual, I fought back a slight remnant of old shyness as I turned to face the mirror. Somewhere behind it lurked the eyes of the lab coat, a couple of extras and a camera, all certainly watching intently. To solidify her victory, my exhibitionist self licked her lips slowly. And then pinched my right nipple, just for effect.

I stepped into the harness with that odd-looking white cock dangling in place. They'll have to do something about that—don't want the world's first bionic cock to look like the Borg. It might remind people what it really is, which is a little creepy. I stared pointedly into the mirror, trying to give the lab coat her movie moment, and then crammed my hand down into the harness and connected the interface.

Something changed.

Not drastically, no epiphany. Just...different. Like during puberty when you crash into lamps and door frames because your arms and legs weren't so long yesterday. Like…well, I had to give the lab coat that: like nothing else. I drew the moment out, wetting my fingers from a bottle of lube they'd thoughtfully provided on a small metal table. Thinking again, I slipperied my whole hand. Widening my legs, performing for myself in the mirror, I made a bad-girl face, reached down and grabbed my cock.

And *holy shit*.

It was like a cool mouth had stretched my clitoris like a piece of saltwater taffy and swallowed it whole. *This* is what it felt like? But then ideas with words attached were pushed aside by something much larger.

I proceeded to treat myself to the best hand job I've ever given. The sensations were so *subtle*. So drawn out, with so much extra space. Like being fucked gently with no direct clitoral stimulation, except more tactile, more real. I swore like the Virgin Mother. The softest, most awed *fucks* you can imagine. I traced myself (for that's already how I thought of my android dick) up and down with two fingertips. I caught the head in the ring formed by my thumb and forefinger and squeezed a one-two beat. I played and played until all I could do was pump myself exactly as I've seen guys do, my hand a hard, purposeful cunt pushing back, back, back around my hard cock…

And I came for the first time as a faux-man, my free hand pressed up against the mirrored glass, bucking my hips in a wild frenzy, my face taut and rigid (as the tape would later reveal), grunting like a gorilla. I collapsed back onto the cot in the corner, which thankfully was more comfortable than it looked.

"Jane," came the lab coat's voice through a small speaker on the table. "You okay?" I flashed a tired thumbs-up her direction and laid my head back down.

I jerked off three more times that day. All for the camera, all in different ways. These extra orgasms were hard to finagle; the lab coat had been so thrilled by my initial assessment (*"Uhh-hgnhh!"*) that she was set to declare victory.

"You should have seen yourself," she gushed when I'd dressed sufficiently for her to enter my small heated sex chamber. "You really went nuts."

"Yeah," I agreed. "I suppose I did. But there were problems, too. Like the nerve tips go too far down the shaft—I can feel the harness chafe." Which was true, but I definitely had ulterior motives. "I think I should try again without the harness just to see how it would work."

She relented and the next orgasm was on my back, holding my beautiful new dick in one hand while I stroked with the other. No thoughts, no heavy fantasy, nothing but the sensation. That's rare for me; I tend to have so many orgasms that I generally need an active brain to get all the way there.

I dressed again so she'd come back, and came up with another excuse. I hadn't tried it without lube. She couldn't see why this was a problem—in her experience, I suppose, guys never beat it without some sort of slippery. I related a few choice stories, and she allowed me more time with what I had by now decided was *my* new toy.

Obtaining a second day of testing was more difficult. I had to play a little hardball, threatening to withhold my five stars from LiveVibes's packaging until I'd *really* tried it out. "Jacking off is well and good, but do you really think that will be the best use your customers find for your little device?" I said, trying to make the cock sound diminutive and controllable.

"Well, no, I guess," she wheedled.

"Damn right. It's going to be dykes fucking their girlfriends, straight chicks banging their boyfriend's asses, stuff like that." When trying to intimidate a woman who can watch a naked woman please herself through mirrored glass but can't walk into the room when she's still undressed, nothing works like a little vulgarity. LiveVibes allowed me to call in a couple of associates from Portland and invited me to stay in a fancy hotel on the company dime. I declined and slept on the cot, guarding my faux phallus like a mother bear.

In the morning it became clear that the majority of the males in the building had seen my prior work. On the way to the bathroom to use my toothbrush and wash my face, I heard several glowing commendations for this or that blue film. One kid—twenty-two at most—was bold enough to compliment my cock-sucking technique specifically. I suggested he be in the men's bathroom when I was finished with my morning toilette to gain firsthand knowledge whereof he spoke.

When his eyes had rolled back down into the normal position and with the tang of semen in the back of my throat, I walked back to my room to await Alyssa and Damien. I wasn't too careful leaving the lavatory and an older man with a substantial belly caught me on my way out. It didn't bother me much to think of the kid being sacked for fraternizing on the job—the cheeky little fuck deserved it, talking to a movie star like that.

My Portlandish pals arrived just after noon. I'd just finished some pretty good Chinese takeout, so their timing was as good as it gets. We greeted with the usual hugs: Alyssa's warm and lingering, Damien's crushingly hard, mine in return as lascivious as I could manage.

The suit brought back his releases and nondisclosures while the lab coat made trebly sure that they were comfortable being filmed, my repeated assurances that we'd been through this together several times notwithstanding. Finally, the flurry pushed out the door and behind the mirror, we were alone.

"So what is it?" Alyssa asked nonchalantly. "What's this *amazing* product we're here to help you sell?"

"You've never seen anything like it, sweetie," I replied. I took my pants off. I'd been hiding the dick along the inside of my left thigh, fully harnessed, interface clipped to clit, ready to go. I imagined I could hear a cry of dismay through the glass.

Alyssa had seen me pack heat enough times the sight left her unimpressed. "It looks like a dildo," she said.

"It *is* a dildo," I said.

"Makes sense it would look like one, then," Damien piped up, never one to leave an unnecessary joke unmade.

"But not just any dildo," I added with a wink before pulling off my shirt.

Damien gave me the same obvious up-and-down he gave me every time. "God, you look good with a cock," he breathed. Alyssa chuckled at the weakness of her man. "Don't mind him, he's just easy," she said.

I was now horny enough to be through with the preliminaries. "Alyssa," I said firmly, "I want you to suck my cock."

"Yes ma'am," she replied with a joke in her voice, and sank to her knees before me. Damien knew when he wasn't needed, so he stood and watched. I tried to be stoic about it. When she grabbed my dick like a microphone and looked up at me smiling, I think I managed to act like a woman whose dildo was being manhandled, a woman playing a role. No sensory involvement.

But when her full, soft lips slid over my head and started down the shaft, I couldn't help but gasp. Alyssa withdrew, gazing up at me with a cocked eyebrow. I was shaking, but I didn't say anything. Still watching my face, she very seriously stuck out her tongue and ran it from the base of my dick to the head. I made noise again, through clenched teeth.

"If I didn't know better..." Damien began.

"You can feel this," Alyssa stated.

"Yes," I managed with difficulty, because on the word 'this' she'd clutched my mottled white member with more intensity than was really required.

"Holy *shit!*" she hooted, laughing. Damien joined in. When

she'd recovered her poise and remembered my request of several moments ago, he joined in as well, dutifully finding my nearest nipple with a soft tongue.

"That's just...what *I* said," my voice finally eked out. Alyssa's oral abilities, at least where male anatomy is concerned, put mine to shame. Not only has she mastered tricks and skills I've never tried to learn (like taking a man deep down her throat), but she genuinely *likes* the activity itself. I enjoy the power and the feeling of pleasing someone; she likes having the actual dick in her actual mouth.

That translates to quite the ride for the man. Or, in my case, the technologically-enhanced woman. She dotted my T's and crossed my eyes, repayment in kind for the numerous thrashing, kegel-squeezing, yelling-out-for-mother cunnilingual orgasms she'd gotten from me over the years. (Now *there's* something one does with one's mouth that I can get into.)

I came with Damien holding most of my weight, flopping about like a Raggedy Ann-or-Andy. I'm sure on the tape it looked fake, I was so melodramatic.

"Shit," Damien breathed.

"Shit indeed," I managed, stumbling weak-kneed back to my cot. Alyssa stood and gazed at me intensely. We were silent for a moment. Alyssa shook her head.

"I've got to try that thing."

"Buy your own," I teased, then put my serious face on. "Are you wet, girl?"

She shrugged. "Not sure," she said as if the question were beneath her.

"Check her," I directed Damien. He reached over with his middle finger, ran it slowly up her clean-shaven cunt. "Not enough for what you have in mind," he replied, licking his finger. "Change that," I said. "Give me a second to recover and turn me back on."

Damien dutifully did as he was told. Kneeling on the floor,

her left leg supported on his broad shoulder, his tongue working her clit, he got Alyssa trembling. I found myself stroking my cock without thinking.

"That's good enough," I said. "How do you want it, Lys?"

"Mmm," she replied thoughtfully, extricating herself from Damien's clutch. "From behind, I think. That's always seemed like the most masculine way to fuck a girl. Now that you're built like a man you should fuck me like one." She strode over to the mirror, placed her hands low on it, bent at the waist. Stuck her ass in the air and gyrated lewdly.

"You want me to be your man, huh? Damien might feel a little threatened." I tried to disguise the effect her little dance was having on me.

"I don't mind," he murmured, as entranced by the show as I was.

"Don't try to pretend that this is about me being satisfied," Alyssa taunted. "It's you that wants to get her pole wet for the first time."

"Yeah," I said, placing the head of my dick at the opening of her pussy. "Yeah, it is." And then I fell into her.

How did I not know? With all the experience I've had with cunts, my own and others', you'd think I would've known, but I had no idea that such softness existed. Softer than velvet or silk, more slippery than soaped skin. The inside of Alyssa, where my fingers had been so many times—how did I not know?

I moved very gently, very slowly, locked in the sensation. Alyssa groaned as I have heard her groan before, a collision of satisfaction and increased need. I realized that this was no different for her than the many times I'd fucked her with silicone.

But it was day-and-night different for me. Within three strokes I felt myself careening close to the chasm. This is why men have such trouble, I thought. I looked at Damien and found his gaze fixed on my face. He looked away, suddenly shy.

"Sorry," he muttered. Then, by way of explanation, "I can see everything you're feeling."

I turned to my own reflection, saw eyes wide in wonder, brow sternly crinkled in pleasure. To Damien's reflection, I managed, "is this...really...what this is like for you...?"

He smiled nostalgically. "Not anymore."

Alyssa lifted her face so I could see it in the glass. "Would you two mind cutting the chatter so I can get properly fucked?"

Damien chuckled, made a *yes, dear* face, and moved to stand behind me. "Go ahead," he whispered in my ear. "There's no reason for you not to come. You have the best of both worlds— you'll never go soft, you'll keep wanting more. Go ahead." He reached around and held my breasts very tenderly, as if they were his own. "Go ahead," he whispered again, biting my ear-lobe gently, as I began to move more quickly.

"Yeah," echoed Alyssa, watching my face in the mirror. "Go ahead and come inside me." She dropped a hand from the mirror to finger her clit, keeping her eyes locked to my face.

I was skirting the edge. All I needed was to decide, to dangle a foot out in space and hang for a moment before the plunge. I could feel Damien's real, warm cock against my ass, his fingers on my nipples. He squeezed them, hard, just the way I like. I felt myself go over.

I shouted and thrust deep into Alyssa, the orgasm tearing its way through me. My legs went weak and I might have fallen, if I hadn't been sandwiched between lovers. "My god," I breathed.

Alyssa withdrew from me. "I guess so," she chuckled. "Mind if I give it a whirl?"

My immediate reaction surprised me, and I bit it back. Tried to be diplomatic. "Um, yeah, I sort of do mind. Sorry. I think you'll have to buy your own."

Lys was a little taken aback—it's not like me not to share— but seemed to understand. "You're attached to it," she quipped.

Then, tactfully changing the subject, she pouted her lip. "And I'm rather attached to the idea of myself as a woman whose man satisfies her. So far you've had two and I'm still at zero." Damien cleared his throat slightly, indicating his presence in that same boat.

I laughed. "All right, *greedy*. How would you like your orgasms this evening?"

The couple exchanged a look. "I think," Damien began slowly, as if pondering the question deeply, "that we should fuck you."

"Both of you at..." I began to ask, but then I got his meaning. "Oh. Hmm. That does sound interesting, doesn't it?"

After a bit of finagling, we had our system down. Damien lying flat on the floor, his cock in my cunt. Alyssa astride me, *my* cock in *her* cunt, her legs supporting most of her weight as to not crush poor Damien.

"Sure you're okay down there, lover?" she asked.

"Fantastic," he breathed.

I was happy she did not ask me for a status report, as I couldn't speak. I was at sea. I was impossibly lost in a soft wet desert of sensation. *Am I this soft to Damien?* my mind kept repeating. My lovers found a perfect rhythm, Alyssa receding as Damien thrust inside me, Damien pulling out as Alyssa fell back onto my cock. I was a very small boat buffeted by enormous swells. And the wind was picking up.

I heard my voice drift from my throat. *There's the wind,* I thought. "Jesus," Alyssa breathed. She put more weight on my chest, her left hand's fingers knotting around a nipple, hard. Her right hand moved frantically over her clit. Damien's breath came short and hard in my ear, and his hands pulled roughly at my hips with every thrust. They sped forward, each revolution coming more quickly than the previous. My sigh became a moan, became a croon.

"Oh Jesus, oh fuck, wait for me," Alyssa sputtered. "You

two fucking *wait* for me, oh fuck, fuck, fuck…" And she came, her inner muscles pulsing and squeezing me. Damien took his cue and thrust deep inside me one last time, shuddered and cried out. Heat enveloped me, like the gush of air from an oven door just opened. My song went ragged, turned half scream, half bellow, and my limbs clutched and quivered. I rolled off of Damien and out of Alyssa and we ended sprawled over cold tile, shaking and exhausted.

"Fuck," Alyssa whispered.

"Fuck is right," I answered. "Help me get this thing off."

The lab coat beamed at me all through the ride to the airport. I'd persuaded the suits to stay behind. A headache, I said.

"Hope you feel better," she said between proud-parent smiles.

"I feel fine," I reassured her. "Happy to be getting back."

"Good," she said. "You *certainly* did your job. We have so much footage we'll never be able to use it all. And the six-star review made the marketing department's whole year."

"Well, it's a killer product. Anyhow, that was my bargaining chip."

The lab coat looked confused. "Bargaining chip?"

"You know," I said. She shook her head. "So they'd let me keep my cock."

Her eyes blazed. "My prototype? They let you…"

"Yes. As Lys said, I've grown attached. Anyhow, it's not like they'd let it be used for anything else—unhygienic, you know."

She deflated somewhat. "I suppose. I'd hoped it could be saved…for posterity or something."

"Oh, it will be," I said, patting her knee. "Saved for posteriors. I promise that every time I use it I will think of you." She turned her face in embarrassment at that—the kid was in the wrong industry. I stared at her intently. After long seconds, I said, "Speaking of which. Have you tried it?"

Her head snapped to look at me, then away again, her gaze trailing out the window. "No," she finally said, her voice very flat. Disappointment? Regret?

"Well," I said, reaching into my bag. "I really think you should. Like you said, it's your prototype, your baby. If anyone should get to try this particular dick, it's you. I've thought about it a lot, and though I'm very...protective of my new body part, you're the one person I can imagine using it. I really think you should."

The lab coat looked at me, what, wistfully? "I can't," she said.

"Sure you can," I soothed. "There are motels near the airport. I'll get the room. Driver?" I rapped on the glass. "Driver, take us to the first motel you see."

"No...that's really..." the lab coat tried to break in. But she quieted once we made an immediate shift onto an off-ramp. She sat back in the limo's leather, nervously twisting her hands.

She'd been locked in the bathroom for almost twenty minutes. I tried to control my impatience. What's so fucking hard? Just clip the damn thing on...

"Jane?" her plaintive voice wafted through the door. "Jane, I need help."

I knocked quietly and entered. She sat naked and primly cross-legged on the edge of the tub, covering her very small breasts with one arm. "I can't..." she began, her lip quivering. I lifted her soon-to-be cock from the counter and squeezed the clit-clamp, opening it for her. "It's pretty simple," I said, trying to keep the exasperation from my voice.

"No, it's not that part, of course I know that part," she bristled. Her eyes indicated a tangle of black on the toilet seat.

"Oh!" I exclaimed. "The harness. Of course. Those things are a bitch if you don't know what you're doing. Here, give me your leg." In a few deft movements, I had her mostly trussed, but left the straps loose. "The dildo has to go in before you tighten," I explained, fitting her cock-to-be into the harness-hole. "There," I said with satisfaction as I pulled the last strap tight. "You're almost a man."

"Almost," she mused, staring down at herself. She had removed her arm from her breasts and stood naked and seemingly unashamed. She gazed at herself in the mirror above the sink. "I don't look it from the waist up," she said with a chuckle.

"Below the belt's what's important," I stated, and knelt before her. With one motion, I gathered the clit-clamp and parted her labia. She gasped slightly, but didn't pull away. "Ready?" I asked, looking up at her.

"Ready," she said firmly, clearly steeling herself for the moment when she...

...stretched, elongated, grew.

"My god," she whispered.

"My god is right," I replied. "You done good, kiddo." And then I couldn't resist. A job well done should be its own reward, but a little icing never hurts. Besides, how could she tell how well she'd done without a little proof? I put her cock all the way in my mouth.

"Gak," she gurgled, and tried to push me away. Then she cooed and smoothed my hair. "God god god," she said. "God. I don't...go for women really."

I pulled her out of my mouth long enough to ask, "Make an exception?" before drawing her back inside.

"Um," she said. "Um."

The third time was the best. As I'd thought, she needed a little acceleration time, but she was a ferocious little tiger after her second crashing, brain-bending orgasm. I had been on top, riding her hard and fast until she cried out and beat the sheets with her fists. She then unceremoniously threw me onto my back and proceeded to fuck me missionary like the coarsest, roughest male porn-star you've ever seen.

"Fuck fuck fuck fuck fuck fuck fuck," she said, one "fuck" per thrust, until her whole body went rigid and straight as a board, her cock deep inside me.

As the hard manliness left her, she curled up soft and pliable on my belly, her fingers tracing my face. She stayed inside me, inside my warmth so soft. I smoothed her hair as a mother would, or as the first girl you fuck really ought to.

"Fuck is right," I said, and checked the clock to see if I'd make my plane.

883.8   **Three Legs in the Evening**
Ash
      author: Janine Ashbless

      category: Literature, Greek Mythology

      subject:
        1. Oedipus   2. Breasts   3. The Sphinx

Three Legs in the Evening

Janine Ashbless

She found him among the tombs in the Grove of Colonus, outside Athens. The search had taken longer than she'd anticipated because it was so hard to ask people about him directly, but she had time on her side, and determination. She discovered him, in the end, amidst the arum lilies and the gnarled trunks of the ancient olive trees, sitting with his back to a sarcophagus, picking at the strings of a lyre.

He was no great musician, she thought.

She stopped in the dappled shade cast by the glaucous leaves, studying him. He seemed to be alone, for which she was grateful. He wasn't young—of course not: hadn't he left behind two grown sons and two daughters of marriageable age?—but his wavy hair was still brown, though his beard was striped with silver. A well-built man, as far as she could tell, and what she could see of his face was handsome, though most was masked by a strip of linen bound several times about his eye sockets. As to what lay beneath the bandage...she knew the stories. He'd gouged his own eyes with his wife's cloak-pin, in horror at his crime. It was merciful of him to hide the ruination beneath from visitors.

She stepped out from her tree trunk into the open ground. At once a prick-eared dog jumped up from where it had been resting next to its master, and ran toward her, barking.

"Agrius?" The man rested his hands on the lyre strings. "Is that you?"

The dog fell silent, but she didn't answer him.

"Agrius?" He tilted his head sharply, listening. "Who's there?"

She wasn't used to conversing with men. She ran her tongue nervously across her lips.

"Who's there?" he repeated defensively, lurching to his feet. "If you've come to stare, show some courtesy and declare yourself. I'm no beast in a cage, to be gloated at." He put his hand to his hip, searching for a sword-hilt that was no longer there.

Yes, she'd been right, she thought: he was tall, with the frame of a well-muscled man growing leaner with age. He wore a long chiton, the robe of a free man. Behind his obvious wariness, there was a dusty pride to his stance that reminded her he'd been a king once. King of Thebes.

"Come back and gawk tomorrow," he told the air about him. "I want to eat, and I've had enough of strangers today."

"Are you sure about that, Oedipus?" she asked.

Her voice revealed her gender, of course, and the stiffness dropped out of his shoulders. His mouth pulled awry as he turned toward her. "How many of you?"

"Just me."

"On your own?"

"Well, you hardly present a threat to my virtue."

For a moment his jaw tightened, but then he shook his head. "Well, that's true enough," he muttered. "I'm no danger to anyone now, maid or man. I'm...nothing."

"You are a legend."

He grimaced. He'd kept in contact with the stone of the tomb as he stood, so as to orient himself. Now he turned away and laid the lyre carefully upon the slab of the lid. "I'm expecting Agrius with food soon," he said. "Have you seen him? Just a boy—so high—I pay him to fetch things from the market for me and light the hearth fire at night." He gestured in the direction of a makeshift hut set back among the trees.

"I saw him down at the bottom of the hill—he was playing in the stream with some friends. So I brought your food up here myself." She hefted the bag she was carrying, though he couldn't see the gesture and she instantly felt a little foolish. "Where would you like it?"

Oedipus shrugged and patted the flat top of the tomb, and she came forward with her small burden.

"You're not afraid to eat among the dead?" she wondered. "Or live out here?"

His head tilted. He was working out exactly where she stood, she could tell, from sound alone. He was trying to picture her just from the timbre of her voice. The tiny flare of his nostrils betrayed him inhaling the fugitive perfume of her skin.

"Who else would have me, except the dead? At least they don't bother me with questions, and if they stare at me by night, well, I do not notice." He smiled. "Besides, they're centuries old, my neighbors. If there are any tattered fragments of curses left among their bones and dust...what would I have to fear? How could I be cursed more?"

She smiled too, sadly. Laying the bundle upon the stone, she unwrapped the contents. "Here. Cheese and bread. An onion. Some dried meat—ham, I'm guessing. A little flask of wine. Some walnuts, I see. Your Agrius has done you proud."

"I pay him," Oedipus muttered, but added, "He's a good lad," as he groped with uncertain hands across the repast. His fingers were long and strong with blunt square-cut nails. She found them curiously enticing.

"Shall I crack the nuts open for you?"

He hesitated, nodded, then tilted his head. "Is that rain?"

"What?"

"That noise. Sounds like rain."

She smoothed a hand across her hair. "I don't hear anything," she said, finding a loose stone and beginning to smack the shells.

"You sound young," he observed. "Your voice is very pleasant."

"I'm not that young." But she smiled, pleased.

"Would you care to share my food? The cheese here is salty; not as good as Thebes cheese, but not bad."

"Thank you."

"Help yourself." He turned away, a piece of bread in his hand. "Here, Apollo." He whistled. "Come get some dinner!"

"You name your dog after a god?" she asked, astonished.

"The gods tooled me over from birth. What can I do in return, except insult them?"

"You're brave." She was impressed, despite herself. She'd never dared to curse the gods.

"No. I just have nothing left to lose. My name is shit under every sandal. Even children too young to be told what I *did*, know to laugh at me... Where is that dog?"

"You'll find him eventually. Be careful, Oedipus: the gods are a vindictive lot."

"You think I don't know that? Did I ever do anything wrong, knowingly? Did I blaspheme or break the law or abuse my position? And yet...it was all the Oracle at Delphi, you know. If it hadn't spoken those *warnings*"— he almost spat the word—"none of it would have happened."

She separated out kernels from shell pieces carefully, and heaped the nuts next to the block of cheese. "Tell me, will you?"

"Ahh." Oedipus curled his lip, his voice growing colder. The piece of bread in his hand fell back upon the cloth. "You want to hear, do you? All about my...humiliation? Of course, what else should I have expected? Why else come and goad the freak?"

"I didn't call you a freak."

"You don't have to. I've heard it often enough before. You think you are the first person to come here and beg for my dirty story? You think you're the only one in Greece with a voyeur's itch?"

"How dare you," she hissed softly. "You know nothing about me, Oedipus."

"I know you're getting wet at the thought of how disgusting I am."

For a moment she was speechless. The horrible thing was that he was right, to a point—she could feel a slick warmth in her core, unexpected and sly. It wasn't the thought of his transgressions that did that, though. It was simply being able to stand close and converse with a handsome man, to look into his face and watch the play of his expression, to let her gaze rove his body—all without fear of being seen herself, all without consequences. It was such a novelty. But she couldn't confess to that. "You," she snapped, "are very arrogant, for a man who needs help to check for shit-stains on his clothes."

Oedipus laughed, softly. "Oh no—on the contrary: I have no pride left at all. I have to make a living somehow, don't I? I'll tell you my story if you like; I'll tell anyone, man or woman, priestess or whore." He swung his hand out, inviting the whole world. "Come feast your ears on my shame. Wallow in my iniquity. Despise and pity me all you like. It will cost you two obols."

She laid her hand out over the stone and dropped two small silver coins. "There."

For a moment he seemed to stare at her through his bandages. Crows called in the trees. He sucked his lips.

"It's usually men who come and ask, you know," he said

with insincere amiability. "They want to know the intimate details. What it was like fucking Queen Jocasta. Was she still beautiful when I married her, or as soggy as an overripe apricot? Did she feel at all *familiar* when I stuck it inside her? Did she not look at me and recognize her dead husband's features, or did that only thrill her? Did I take her first before, or behind, or in the mouth, on our wedding night? Did she beg me for more?" He smirked. "So...is that the sort of thing you want to know?"

"I want to know," she said, "about Phix."

He almost took a step back from the tomb. Instead, he caught himself and went very still. "How do you know her name?"

"I'm the one who asked for a story. And I want to hear the things you *don't* tell other people."

"Really." His neck was taut and now his hand curled, almost to a clench. He was taller than her, and if he had been sighted she would have been within easy snatching distance. Respectable women never came this close to a strange man, not on their own. Certainly not when the man had such an obscene reputation. "The things I don't tell other people?" he wondered. "That won't be hard. They're only interested in the end of the tale."

"But everybody knows how it ended. I didn't have to come find you, to hear that bit of the story."

"Huh. Well. If you like, then. You're not frightened of a story from a man's point of view?"

"*All* stories are told from a man's point of view," she sighed.

"I meant..."

"I know what you meant. Go ahead. I want to hear."

He nodded, and moistened his dry lips. "Very well. Not the end, then. The beginning. You have to understand it from the beginning, or you'll not believe." He leaned back against the sarcophagus. "I was brought up as a prince of the palace of Corinth. Son, so far as I knew, of the king and queen there. Ignorant that I was a foundling, adopted—because everyone who remembered had been instructed to keep silent upon the subject. And there was a girl there— Is this the beginning? I'm not used to telling this part. There was a servant girl there in the palace...a Libyan...who had the most beautiful breasts."

He paused, and tilted his head back, as if seeing the long-lost girl with his empty eyes.

"She was older than me, of course. I used to follow her around the palace when I was a youth, just to stare at those breasts. They were the color of pine honey, deep-clefted and firm and *big*, you understand, really big, swelling against her dress. And I wanted nothing in all the world so much as to lift those ample globes in my hands and suck upon her nipples and bury my head between them and suffocate there." He smiled wistfully. "Don't get me wrong—she was pretty too, with a big smile and a waist like so"—he shaped it, tiny beneath his masculine hands—"and a fine rump as round as the full moon that waggled when she walked. I liked all of her, but oh...her breasts had me in thrall.

"You know, even if I weren't blind, I don't think I'd ever see a pair so perfect again.

"All the servants sniggered at me. 'Here comes your puppy-dog again, Clio,' they would tell her: 'wagging his little tail as he follows you.' And she laughed at me too, but gently. She liked me. The day she caught me by the hand and pulled me into a storeroom and said, 'Time to do more than just stare at my tits, Prince Oedipus,' as she pulled open her clothes and laid my hands upon her... I think that was the happiest moment of my life. I felt like a man must feel touching a goddess. I felt like I was holding the sun and the moon in my hands. I felt like all the mysteries and treasures of the earth had been given to me.

"You know what the greatest wonder was? Her nipples *stiffened* as I touched them. They rose up, and their areolae puckered to the drag of my fingers, and she sighed and giggled. Her parts *reacted* to me—and I knew for the first time that a woman's body felt pleasure just as my own did. Nobody had ever told me that. She loved me touching her."

Oedipus shook his head in reminiscence. "Her *tits*. That's what she called them. A low word for such glorious things. 'Tits' and 'cunny' and 'ass' and 'clit,' those were the words she used, and she taught me all about them, over many months.

"And I was a diligent scholar, keen to master every lesson and put my learning to the test. I prided myself on the skills I developed under her tutelage. When, for the first time, Clio straddled me nose-to-tail and said, 'Make me fall first, Prince Oedipus, and I'll suck your cock until you spurt down my throat,' I made her come three times before I let her finish me off.

"This is the secret I learned from her: a woman's pleasure does not come, as almost every man thinks, from her being filled and stretched and pounded by the biggest cock possible, like a pestle banging away in a mortar. Oh, it's far more subtle than that. And far more complex. A woman's body is a labyrinth to be solved.

"I took the skills my Clio taught me, and practiced upon other women. Beekeepers and dancing-girls and weavers and potters... My reputation spread through Corinth like spilt wine, and couldn't be stopped. Through giggled confidences, they learned from one another. They came to my chamber by night and lured me into barns by day. They wanted to know if I was all I was rumored to be, and I delighted in confirming the tales. That was my pleasure—my obsession if you like, for it became like a yearning for wine or opium. I lusted to make women come. My own fist upon my cock was good enough for me, though I'd no objection to the hotter embrace of a mouth

43

or cunny. But what I really wanted, what I could do for hour after hour, was to lap the nectar between a woman's legs, and make her arch and swear and blaspheme. To take the shy and gentle maid and make of her a raving maenad. To have the lissome creature astride my face beg for more and more and more, and then weep with joy and thank me and kiss my cock like it was a god. I took delight in pushing a woman to so many climaxes that she would beg me for mercy out of sheer exhaustion."

"And were you merciful?"

Oedipus smiled. "Oh, eventually."

She bit her lip and was glad he couldn't see her flushed cheeks.

"It became a point of pride for me that no woman was immune to pleasure, under my hands. I would rise to any challenge: young or old, fair or plain. An ambassador of the Amazons, corded with muscle and scar-tissue, who had never had any use for a man, laughed at my reputation—but she'd changed her mind by the next morning and confessed publicly, blushing, that I had proved her wrong.

"After that I trod closer to the edge of propriety. I took two priestesses of Artemis to my bed and sent them away the next morning reeling and wide-eyed and debauched—but still technically virgins despite the throb of their licked and well-fingered winks and the taste of my semen in their mouths. Married women threw themselves in my path—but who could make an accusation of adultery, when my cock never went near the forbidden shrine of their marriage? *My* preferred site of oblation was across the pillowy expanses of their tits."

He smiled, fondly, then shook his head as if he were waking from a dream. "Eventually I provoked too many complaints from confused and outfaced men. To get me out of Corinth and give the pot a chance to stop boiling, the king sent me on a mission to the Oracle at Delphi. Some question about the siting of a new temple. So I went, with a dozen companions."

His smile had gone now. His mouth was a hard line. "There, in the dark of the cave, the Pythia breathed in the fumes from that crack in the floor that leads to the Underworld, and then slipped from her high stool into the priests' waiting arms, thrashing and gibbering. All very holy. It made my skin crawl, if I am honest. They carried her forward to where I waited, and she looked straight at me with pupils wildly dilated. And then she said it... You know that bit. Everyone knows that bit."

"*'You will kill your father and marry your mother.'*"

He dipped his chin. "The same thing my true father had been told at my birth. What worse abomination could be pronounced on any man among the Greeks? Patricide and maternal incest—an affront to the gods themselves! I had no choice. No choice at all. I couldn't ever risk going back to Corinth, and seeing again the father and mother I loved. So I sent my men home and exiled myself. I chose the road to Thebes, at random. And on the road I met—"

"Your real father, King Laius," she finished for him.

Oedipus would have cast her a reproving look if he'd been capable. "I met a peasant driving an ox-cart," he said coolly. "The wheel-pin had fallen out, and he was blocking most of the track. I stopped to help him unload, and reset the wheel, and while we were working a man drove up in a chariot and tried to push past. He nearly ran his horses over us."

He paused for a moment. "How was I to know he was a king at all? He wore no crown and had no retinue—he was just an arrogant middle-aged man in a hurry, driving from Delphi to Thebes. Well, I was arrogant too; I was a prince of Corinth by upbringing. I caught the bridle of the nearest horse as it crushed up against me and I brought his chariot to a halt, cursing him for being such a reckless piece of shit. He cut at me with his whip—I still have the scar, I think."

Oedipus ran his hand up his bare forearm, displaying the

thin white line imprinted there.

"I drew my sword then, and he drew his and jumped from the chariot. I slashed his forearm, disarming him...and then swung at his head. But with the hilt. I meant nothing more than to knock him senseless and so teach him manners; I had no idea that men's skulls could be so fragile. He fell and knocked his head on a stone, and when I bent to look, he wasn't breathing. It was just an accident. Even the cart-driver agreed."

He took a deep breath. "We threw the body in the ditch and left the horses to wander. We didn't even rob him—that would have been beneath me, I thought. And when we'd finished righting the cart I went on my way and thought little more about it. It's several days' walk to Thebes."

"Where you met Phix," she prompted him, when his silence stretched across the moments.

"You're an impatient woman. I met—I was captured by— a band of Theban soldiers, as I walked through their barley fields. They were on the hunt for lone strangers, it turned out, though I didn't understand at the time." He nodded to himself. "Thebes was a strange place, not like other Greek cities. They worshipped the gods, somewhat, but they had their own goddess too—a living one, who dwelled in a cave in the hills nearby and accepted offerings of fruit and sheep, and kept their enemies away. The Sphinx, they called her." He paused, significantly. "Are you intending to interrupt?"

"No."

"But now their goddess had gone crazy. Not content with mutton, she was hunting men: carrying them off sometimes, on other occasions just cornering them. Always the biggest, strongest men. And people said that before she killed, before she gorged herself on their corpses, she demanded that they answer her riddle. When they could not, she grew enraged and slaughtered them. Nobody understood why she was acting this way."

"I do."

"As do I, now. But at the time, all I understood was that the soldiers seized me, and looked me up and down, and asked if I was any good at the riddle game. 'Get it right and you'll be the hero of Thebes,' they told me. 'Even the king doesn't know the answer, and he's a cunning one. He's gone off to Delphi to ask the oracle what the answer is.'"

"Ah."

"Ah, indeed. In the meantime, while they waited for their king to come home and save them all, they were offering hand-picked sacrifices to their goddess. Slaves mostly, but foreigners and stray travelers were good too, in their eyes, so long as they were strong young men and had some wits about them. It kept the losses among their Theban champions to a minimum. I was just the next in a long line.

"They took me to the place of sacrifice—and those soldiers were as nervous as little girls, I can tell you; being a man armed and armored just made them targets for the Sphinx. The altar was a stretch of sandy hillside outside the city, a barren place. They stripped me and tied me to stakes they drove into the earth, hands spread out, staring into the sun. Then they ran.

"When she came, I was grateful for the shade of her wings. It allowed me to open my eyes again. She was..."

"Go on."

Oedipus bowed his head for a moment. "You know, I've never told anyone this before. People want to know about the monster, of course, but that's just a prelude to the stuff about Queen Jocasta. I've never told them about me...and Phix."

"You can tell me."

He sighed. "She was beautiful. Terrifying, of course—huge—but beautiful. The body of a lioness, the wings of an eagle, the head and breasts of a woman. I've seen statues and paintings that make her look Greek, but that's wrong. Have you ever seen a woman of Upper Egypt?—she looked like that.

Dense, long black ringlets of hair, and great dark eyes lined with kohl, and golden earrings that hung almost to her neck. I wondered—later—how she went about adorning herself, but it turned out she had thumbs that were almost human, on those great big paws.

"It wasn't her paws I was thinking about as she stood right over my helpless body, though. It was her canine teeth, and her breasts. Oh gods, her breasts... She was bigger than any human woman of course, and those orbs of hers hung over me like the mountains of the gods. The cleft between them was as dark and deep and rich as the Nile Valley, and her black nipples were bigger than the tops of my thumbs.

"Oh how I wanted those tits. Death seemed an irrelevance in comparison. Don't get me wrong—I was afraid. But my cock filled and lifted too.

"'Now answer my riddle,' she growled. 'What is it that walks on four legs in the morning, two at noon, and three in the evening?'

"I can understand why no one had answered her correctly before. Imminent death is not conducive to clear thought. But I couldn't stop looking at those incredible breasts. My mouth should have been dry with terror, but it was watering at the sight. As she crouched over me, not quite touching but mantling me with her wings like a feeding hawk, I realized I could smell her sex. Spice and musk and female lust: it went to my head just like the fumes of the Underworld filling the Pythia's skull, and drove me nearly as mad.

"'Well, I have a third leg right now,' I said hoarsely. 'And I am a man.'

"'Are you?' she boomed. 'Are you?' She looked down my body, at the rigid cockstand pointing right up at her. 'Maybe you are,' she said: 'at last.' With the razor-edge of her claw she slashed through my bonds. 'What will you do now, clever little man?'

"'This,' I said, grabbing her nipples and pulling them—together and down, and toward my lifted mouth. I got my lips around the tips of those ambrosial breasts and I chewed and sucked and nuzzled my face between them and kneaded with my fingers...and I damn near spent my load there and then, I tell you." Oedipus's hands were crossed over his groin now, in an attempt to hide the obvious. "The Sphinx seemed no less pleased," he added, clearing his throat. "She yowled like a cat in heat and arched her back, and lifted her rump in the air while she lashed her tail from side to side. But I couldn't reach any of that. I just had her wonderful tits in my face. That was all I could do...until she snatched me up and rolled over onto her back, taking me with her. I'm very glad she kept her claws velveted. Wings spread in the sand, legs open, she pushed me down her body.

"Her front was human—two breasts and no more, a hairless belly, and between her lion's legs a sex that looked entirely human to me, pink-hearted and wet and open like a blown rose. The smell of her was intoxicating.

"'Fill me!' she ordered, showing teeth like bronze daggers. And it was clear what she wanted, what was driving her mad with frustration—but how was any man supposed to satisfy her? I was sporting an erection of heroic proportions, but she was bigger than any woman, bigger even than a lioness, and I doubted she'd even feel my shaft."

Oedipus paused, breathing deeply. "She was the kind of challenge that made my blood sing."

She shifted her weight from one thigh to the other, feeling the impatient slickness between them. "Go on!"

He turned his face to her, a habit left over from his sighted life. "Do you really want to hear?"

"Yes!"

"You want to know how I fucked the Sphinx?"

"Yes," she repeated, her voice all twisted up.

"Then come closer."

She was sure he could hear her unguarded breathing, fast and shallow. "You would try to force me."

"Never." He smiled. "I would swear that, but what would I swear it on? The gods? My father's grave? My mother's honor?" His laugh was lightly bitter. "No force. If you want to hear, come closer."

She came round and stood in front of him. He cocked his head and smiled, and crooked his right arm.

"This. I fucked her with this." Speaking low, he made a spear-point of his fingers. "Like so, at first. She was tight, and slippery, and I worked it into her slowly. I used my mouth—the whole of my face, my other hand too—on her clit, and she opened to me with mews of pleasure." He closed his fingers into a fist. "Then like this, when I was inside. Building up the motions until I was using all the strength of my forearm. She took me to elbow."

She put her hand on his raised fist and drew her fingers down, over the broad wedge of forearm muscle. She felt him shiver. Her own heart was banging like a war drum.

"I want to touch you," he said hoarsely. "It's been two years since I lay with anyone."

"It's been longer for me. Much longer."

"Are you old?" He said it gently, without rancor.

"Older than you, Oedipus."

His lips were softly parted. "Let me touch you. Please."

She took his other hand and brought it up slowly. His fingers were warm under hers. Both of them held their breath as she laid his palm to the swell of her breast—and then he exhaled shudderingly. His thumb found the point of her nipple and circled it in wonder.

"Oh yes..."

She bit her lip, overwhelmed by sensation.

Gently, he slipped his hand under the thin linen of her peplos and traced the curves of warm skin. His fingers felt like cool water, like music, like flame.

"You're not old," he murmured. His other hand joined its twin, and she arched a little as he cupped and fondled both mounds, teasing her nipples until they were swollen like ash-buds in spring. "You're not old at all."

One hand slipped upward, caressing her neck, reaching for her face.

Mistake. Her half-closed eyes snapped open. She grabbed his wrist and her voice cracked: "No!"

"Apologies." He seemed a little stunned.

"Tell me," she commanded, pushing the errant hand back down. "Tell me about Phix."

He tried to concentrate. "I...I fucked her. I grabbed the base of her tail to brace myself, and I mashed my mouth over her clit, and I fist-fucked her. Oh gods...the grip and the heat of her...I thought she would pulp my bones. And the noise of the wet of her, and the kick of her pelvic girdle... She dug her rear claws into my leg and I could feel the blood running, but I didn't stop. I didn't stop until she screamed and I felt her come on my fist, the muscle spasms nearly crushing my forearm. Then I pulled out enough to get my cock in alongside my hand."

She was almost panting. "I'd have thought you wanted to spend on her chest."

"I did—but I knew what she needed. Oh, I'm sure she never even noticed my length, but I put my seed inside her never-theless. She purred afterward, like a great cat. She lay on her back, limbs sprawled, purring like thunder, pressing my face to her beautiful gash."

"Did you kill her then?"

"What?" He'd drawn her loosened dress off her shoulders by now, baring her from the waist upward. His hands were all over her, exploring the span of her waist and the flare of her hips. "No!"

"The story is that when you answered her riddle, the Sphinx killed herself in rage."

"That's not true either. She lived. They said I had tamed her, and they came out to her cave and made me King of Thebes. They gave me the widowed queen to wed. You know all that."

"Yes, I know."

Oedipus sank to his knees, burying his face in her cleavage, kissing her bare skin, licking at her nipples. "I was a good king. Do they say *that*? I ruled justly and in peace. Nineteen years. Does anyone remember, or only the way it ended?"

She groaned as he tugged her nipple between his teeth. "But what happened to Phix?"

Oedipus paused, and moistened his lips. "She had cubs."

"Children!"

"Yes. A boy and a girl. That's what she was after, all along. Seed."

"Your children!"

"Yes. They were shy; they hid whenever I went to visit her. But I saw them."

"You...visited?"

"I couldn't stay away. She was...those wonderful tits. You cannot understand. She was my goddess made flesh. I had to." His hand was up the inside of her skirt, caressing her thigh.

"Then what happened to her?"

"The girl-cub killed her. Fourteen years on, and nearly full grown. Phix didn't have the heart to slay her own, I think. I saw the fight, but there was nothing I could do. Then they both flew away...my children."

She pulled her belt free and her peplos slithered to the ground. The blind man made a noise of gratitude and delved between her legs with fingers and tongue-tip. For a moment she only gasped, and then impatience overwhelmed her and she pushed him backward against the sarcophagus. Getting one knee up high onto the slab lid, she slid her wet split over his upturned face and pressed down upon his mouth.

He hadn't just been boasting; he knew exactly what to do with his tongue, and his lips, and his fingers. He lapped and nibbled and slipped into her, pulled and sucked and stirred. It was a burning, exquisite joy, and a relief beyond words. She gripped his head with her hands and cried out, shuddering her hips. He ate her like she was the ambrosia of the gods. He drank her like she was nectar. Naked, wide-eyed, awash with flame, she passed from desire to apotheosis, pouring herself upon his face like holy oil.

And she felt, for the first time in years, like she was beautiful again.

In the after wash her trembling legs let her down and she sank to straddle his thighs. He'd pulled his robe aside, she saw, and his cock was hard and engorged and shiny under his stroking fingers. It looked delicious, she thought, pushing his hand aside and angling him into her hot and slippery grip.

Oedipus groaned, teeth bared. He did his best to hold back as she pushed down his length, but restraint was beyond him now; he bucked beneath her, thrusting up, filling her with his brine and his loss and his broken pride. She clenched about him, aftershocks of her own orgasm running through her along with his.

"I'm sorry," he gasped. "Too fast. It's been too long."

She wrapped an arm about her head to stop her hair falling onto his face, and—greatly daring—tipped forward to plant a kiss upon his mouth. She could taste herself.

"Hey." His hand clung to her thigh as she rose from him. "We needn't finish yet."

"We do." There were tears tracked down her cheeks, but he couldn't see those. "It's not safe." She grabbed up her clothes. "Thank you."

"For what?"

She didn't answer.

"Wait—how did you know Phix's name?"

She was already walking away, but she paused midstride. Near her feet, black lilies bloomed and the stone dog stared into space. "We were half-sisters. Keto was our mother."

"Then...what's your name?" he called, scrambling to his feet.

"Mine?" she asked, over her shoulder. "Medusa."

790.7
Lew

The Contest

author: Michael Lewis

category: Performing Arts

subject:
   1. G-string   2. Brick House   3. Happy Hour

The Contest

Michael Lewis

My first introduction to Nora came when she was sent to join
me for a campaign pitch in Phoenix. I wasn't thrilled with her
last-minute substitution for my usual copywriter, Kevin, but
things like that happen in the advertising business. Kevin had
succumbed to the monetary inducements of a rival agency that
needed to up their diversity quotient. In any other business,
you might think twice about an outrageous salary offer that
was predicated on the color of someone's skin, but ad execs
jump from agency to agency with less inducement than that. So
congratulations, Kev! *Hasta la vista!* Let me buy you a drink.
Touch any of *my* clients, and I'll put a knife in your back quicker than you can say *junior partner.*

Nora was new to the agency, fresh from her MBA studies
and still glowing with the suntan of a Cancun honeymoon with
her new husband. Her poise put me quickly at ease with her
status as my new colleague and pitch assistant. Granted this
was enhanced by the type of body most starlets have to buy at
Dr. Calabro's—shoulder-length blonde hair, green eyes, delicate neck, an ample (but not too ample) chest, narrow waist,

lovely hips and legs that made you forget about everything else. We hit it off almost immediately, and our success at bringing the Hinojosa Tortilla Company under the wing of the Bascom, Henry and Bascom Ad Agency solidified what would become a working relationship that's lasted four years now.

Since then, I thought that I'd learned everything there is to know about Nora; from the day she met her husband during his final year of med school, to her "three years of hell" working as an assistant product manager for a giant consumer company. She was rescued from the land of soaps and detergents through the largesse of Mom and Dad, who were willing to provide B-school tuition, room and board. The prospect of becoming the parents-in-law of a doctor seemed to make the investment worthwhile in their estimation. After two years of business school pursuing a graduate degree, she became the wife of an earnest doctor immersed in his residency, and the running-dog accomplice of a crazy ad man twenty years her senior.

If you're tracking through all of that, you might have deduced that there was a five-year gap between meeting the doc-to-be and getting that fabulous tan on the beaches of the Yucatan Peninsula. That might tell you more about Dr. Simon than any other description that I could put together. Let's just agree that there is a library somewhere on this planet that features a giant dictionary wherein next to the word *deliberate* there is a picture of Dr. Simon Hansen of Chicago. He invests more time in daily sock selection than most other people do in the purchase of a new car. You don't want him treating you in the emergency room following a car accident, but for long-term care, Simon's your dude!

It's not that Simon and Nora are mismatched in any significant or relationship-threatening ways, it's just that their styles for addressing challenges are different. In any case, it didn't seem to affect her seemingly spontaneous view of things, and thank god for that!

So there we were, almost four years after that successful mission to Phoenix, on a plane for Dallas to learn a little about the new marketing software that promised to "cut lead time, increase profits and boost creative opportunity to new heights." Essentially, we were traveling a thousand miles or so to drink lukewarm coffee, eat semi-stale pastries and listen to a geek whose world revolved around software that combined all the functionality of a word processor, graphics package and web design tool. Been there, done that, got the T-shirt!

I've lost count of the number of trips that we had shared together by this time. If you don't see anything wrong with friends enjoying a few drinks together, you would have never looked twice at our record...until the Dallas trip. We enjoy a comfort level that allows for the opportunity to be sarcastic, share dirty jokes or even make a lascivious comment about members of the opposite sex. By now I knew more about Nora and Simon's relationship than I cared to. Let's just say that Simon can be a bit stuffy and leave it at that. Nora's not exactly a free spirit, but she does like to kick up her heels once in a while, and the good doctor apparently cramps her style in that direction.

The seminar concluded early. It might have had something to do with the snores of the guy from Buffalo throughout the day and a half, but that offered Nora and me a leisurely afternoon and evening prior to the flight home the next day. I suggested we obtain sustenance at a nice little restaurant featuring hamburgers, hot wings, cold beer and busty waitresses. Despite her mild protestations of male chauvinism and salaciousness, Nora agreed to join me. Not that she was opposed to the place; her junior year of college had been partially financed with tips earned at one of the busiest locations this chain had in Denver.

Is there any better way to take nourishment than to be in the midst of big-screen TVs with twenty-four-hour sports and comely waitresses in tight tops? I don't think so, but then I've been free of my starter wife for five years now and probably have a fair amount of growing up to do before meeting my forever spouse. Not that she admires the waitresses in the same fashion I do, but Nora will tell you that sometimes it's more appealing to sip a cold beer and munch fries in front of an Australian Rules football telecast than to be balancing appetizers and a martini while making small talk about hospital politics.

The beer loosened our tongues while the 38Ds of our waitress loosened my imagination. By midafternoon, we had elected to move our conversation to a different location. It was Nora who noticed the Doll Factory as we drove past and suggested we take advantage of the happy hour twofers. This represented a new facet in our relationship, and one that certainly piqued my interest. So we parked the car and marched in, arm in arm. The girl at the door waved us in—something about a complimentary couple's admission—and we took a seat at a table. It wasn't a large club, but there were three stages, two empty during the late-afternoon slack time, with one currently featuring a fine-looking dancer of African American heritage. During the next two rounds I was treated to Nora's fascinating critique of each dancer's performance style. Most of the criticism ranged from faint praise to sardonic putdowns, with our waitress adding her two cents' worth from time to time—usually in agreement with Nora. I couldn't resist asking the waitress why she wasn't onstage, receiving the reply, "Not with my lack of rhythm, sweetie, but your girlfriend here could be a star if she put her mind to it."

Okay, backpedaling time! Too much information!

But while I tried to think of how to extricate myself from this exchange, Nora came out of nowhere and exclaimed, "You think so? I've always fantasized about that."

"Well, sugar," our waitress said, "you should just bring yourself back here tonight for the Amateur Contest and try it out. You never know what might happen."

Nora demurred, and shortly thereafter, my heart started

pumping with a regular beat. One more beer and we decided that dinner was a viable option. But she seemed a bit pensive throughout the meal. As we neared the end of dinner, she finally looked up with a grin of lustful determination and announced, "I'm going to do it! Are you with me, or are you going to wimp out and hole up in the hotel?"

"What the hell are you talking about?" I stammered, knowing damn well what she was talking about.

"Amateur Night...I'm going to dance! Why not? We're out of town, no friends or relatives to stumble in and ruin my reputation, or go squealing back to Simon...correct?" The look in her eye promised physical mayhem if I even contemplated telling her husband. My leering smile answered her without the need for any further assurances.

Why not indeed? We gathered our things and returned to the hotel, with a stop at Shannon's Sensuous Toys and Fashions on the way to obtain the correct apparel for such a performance. Watching Nora shop was an experience in itself. She passed on my suggestion of the pink-lace teddy; or should I say she demurred at my suggestion that she model the pink lace teddy? But she did pick out a tiny G-string with red sparkles that would glitter like crazy in the stage light. Mentioning a red blouse back in her hotel room that she could adapt, she finally decided that the only additional requirement for her performance ensemble was a tiny black leather microskirt. She didn't actually do a runway number with it, however she did strut a short distance out of the changing room to get my (enthusiastic and supportive) opinion. We made a slow pass by the dildo assortment, during which she looked just a tad wistfully at the various motorized cumbots, then paid for the skirt and G-string and hurried back to the Loew's Anatole Hotel.

At precisely 8:15, I left the elevator and met the sluttiest looking bundle of energy I'd ever seen. "Thank god, you're not late," she said, "the desk clerk keeps eyeing me like I'm some kind of hooker!"

"Well, my dear Nora, you do match the description somewhat."

"I know," she purred, "but I don't want to pass up an opportunity like this by getting busted in the lobby!"

We drove back to the Doll Factory, arriving to find the parking lot a little more crowded than it had been during the afternoon. "Sure you want to go through with this?" I asked. But there was no opportunity for an answer as my curvaceous friend was already out of the car and headed for the door.

The couples' admission policy was still in effect, though clearly there weren't a lot of patrons that had benefited from it. All three stages were in use now, showcasing some lovely dancers, one with marvelous moves on the stripper pole. Nora looked as determined as ever. Watching her sign the performance waiver was almost arousing in and of itself.

We had time for a drink. "A little Dutch courage," as she called it, then the manager retrieved her and the other contestants for their instructions, while I listened from nearby. They could go completely topless but there had to be at least a thong or G-string on the bottom. Removal of that bottom coverage—both fully or partially—was not condoned by the club, and could result in the arrest of the dancer if the cops were in the house. However...wink, wink...it could also generate greater enthusiasm on the part of the audience, resulting in more points. In other words, a flash of gash just might be what it took to win.

The number of contestants wasn't great, but the quality was better than I would have expected. As gorgeous as Nora was, winning would not be easy. At that point in time, I didn't realize that winning was even on her mind, having been treated to an almost professorial lecture from her on the "naked in front of an audience" fantasy she'd always savored. But, as the first girl stepped up to the stage, I couldn't help but notice an expression on Nora's face that reminded me of those moments before a business preparation.

"Omigod…she's in this to win," I thought to myself.

There wasn't a great deal of diversity in the contestant pool that night; four blondes (including Nora) and one spectacular brunette. The judging criteria called for the awarding of points based upon three factors: noise generated, tips earned onstage and the vote of a panel consisting of the manager and two customers. During the introductions, I might have been inclined to give the nod to the brunette (introduced as Molly from Grapevine) just for her singularity, but I reminded myself that I had to be partisan and true. My initial reaction proved insightful, as Molly seemed to gather the most enthusiasm during the introductions. Nora only looked at me with a sense of lustful purpose that made me uncomfortable in more places than one.

The first two performers went through their sets with enthusiasm, but with only borderline talent at best; a *little* dancing ability was needed. Nora and another competitor watched them closely. But I couldn't help noticing that Molly the brunette was nowhere to be found. It may have been just a coincidence that the bartender was on break at the time, replaced by one of the waitresses.

The third dancer raised the bar considerably—to almost 36DD inches, if you know what I mean—and it was obvious that she knew the difference between the rhythm of dance and the rhythm of contraception (did I mention dancer Number Two's bikini scar?). She was also far more relaxed and clearly more approachable than the others were. Following the same three-song format as the regular dancers, she avoided the novice trap of not pacing herself. Contestant Number One had apparently been in a rush to get down to her G-string, leaving her with too much time to deliver the goods to the stage-side denizens. Number Two might have suffered an attack of modesty, taking forever to remove the bikini top she'd brought with her, and not doffing her miniskirt until the very end of her set, a terrible faux pas—she should have stripped off the skirt first and then the top. Amateurs!

Nora was up next, so I replaced a skinny guy sporting a *Dungeons & Dragons* tattoo (what's up with that?) on his arm when he left his seat at the stage in search of the john. The difference between Nora (introduced as Sabrina from Arlington) and the rest of the field was immediately apparent. With a face flushed with sexual excitement, she pounced onto the stage to the driving beat of Robert Palmer's "Addicted to Love." After four years as business associates, I had probably begun to take her looks for granted. But seeing her onstage, wearing the black leather micro with red blouse loosely tied in front, accessorized with her favorite Chicago-style leather boots, was tantamount to a revelation. The blouse barely contained her boobs, making her a certified jiggle queen. Damn, she looked good!

She used the Palmer song to demonstrate surprising dancing ability, managing to flirt with every guy in the joint in the process. Near the end, she allowed one lucky guy to unzip her skirt, with him copping a brief feel of vulva in the process. By the time that the skirt slowly slithered down her legs there wasn't an empty chair at or near the stage. The way it rode the curve of her hips made her legs look even longer. Of course the black boots didn't hurt either.

The next musical selection, "Brick House" by The Commodores, kept the energy level up, but allowed her to get up close and personal with her new fans along the stage, and the tips started to pile up. New decibel levels of crowd noise were reached when the red top practically melted off of her, releasing two of the most perfect tits I'd ever seen.

More than one paying patron was delighted to experience the perfumed valley between her tatas, and I relished the look on her face when the first guy sucked a nipple into his mouth, lingering and savoring it longer than I ever thought she'd allow. She was enjoying this!

As she moved toward the end of the second song, we gave a brief demonstration of that typical Bascom, Henry and Bascom Ad Agency commitment to teamwork; Nora enlisted me in the removal of the thong, leaving her with only the G-string as the final barrier between her and the indecent exposure ordinances of Dallas. Hmmm...now that I think of it, the thong must have come from her suitcase. I know she didn't purchase it with the G-string and micro-skirt. Our level of eye contact as I pulled it down her legs with my teeth gave me the first real hint of what was to occur later in the evening.

Tom Jones provided the final bit of musical inspiration, "You Can Leave Your Hat On," a slinky classic if ever there was one! Prior to now, she had been shaking her ample bosom in front of the paying customers, in varying degrees of proximity, and showing off every other delectable body part she could. It was my turn again for some special attention. She leaned over, conveniently allowing her breasts to fall into my open hands as they lay palms up on the stage and kissed my ear, pausing long enough to say, "I have *never* been this turned on...*never*." Then, spinning around on all fours, she presented her world-class rear for my personal viewing enjoyment. This was the rear that had been parked next to mine in so many airline and lobby seats, and now here it was in all of its naked glory, just inches from my lips. Peering down between her legs, she reacted to my enraptured smile by reaching around and inserting her middle finger two knuckles deep into her pussy. It practically dripped with lust syrup, offering no visible resistance to her probing digit. She followed this by sucking the glistening fluid from her finger, staring so deep into my eyes that I temporarily forgot my name, location, and...well...I forget what else I forgot...

As the waitress replaced my empty beer bottle with a full one, she bent down and noted, "Your little blonde is enjoying this entirely too much! She's going to burn out, get arrested or make you jealous before all this is over." I didn't have the heart to tell her that "Sabrina" was actually an MBA ad exec, with a doctor husband at home in Chicago and more societal propriety than George W. Bush (insert your own political punch line here).

Nora was now past the point of no return. So much so that I would wager Dr. Hubby had never been treated to the labial views that the patrons of the Doll Factory now enjoyed. And when one of the regular dancers rolled a twenty dollar bill into a straw and, using her mouth, daintily placed it where the G-string would normally have been, the crowd went wild. I was now officially, irretrievably in lust! One guy got a little too carried away with his effort to study her vaginal perfume, an effort that earned him an assist to the parking lot, courtesy of Mongo the bouncer. Meanwhile the dancers on the other two stages had taken to shouting suggestions, giving Nora even more encouragement than she probably needed at this point. She finished the set in a prone position, her legs resting on one guy's shoulders with her ass and pussy almost too close to his face to be legal.

It would be good at this point to say that Molly from Grapevine didn't stand a chance, however the fix was in. Oh, her performance onstage was every bit as enjoyable as Nora's. I don't know if her costume was supposed to be a swimsuit, or whether she had just taken a couple pieces of maroon cloth and tied and wound it between her legs and over her neck, but the effect was awesome. My personal highlight was the flash of bald beaver that she shared with me and the geek to my left (hey...I was being true to Nora; I only tipped a dollar with the intent of delaying her from earning more). I should also note that I wasn't the only one at the stage to discern that Molly knew how to use a razor in intimate places.

It was at about this moment that I became aware of the subtle little edge that probably put Molly over the top. First there was the bartender's satisfied smile, followed by his whispered message to the manager and each of the judges. The excited look on their faces didn't require an educated mind to determine what would happen after the winner was announced. I suspect Miss Molly had been a busy little thing backstage! Sure enough, Molly was announced as the winner by "a razor-thin margin." She celebrated by flashing that expertly shaved vulva to everybody on one side of the stage.

After the awards ceremony, I had no idea what to expect from Nora. She graciously received her new fans, bestowing a few kisses, demurely rebuffing a couple of offers for the remainder of the night and rejecting a job offer from the management. At the first opportunity, she whispered in my ear, "If you don't promise to fuck my brains out tonight, I'm finding someone who will." That was enough for me! I grabbed her wrist and spirited her out of the club, into the car and back to the hotel.

During the return, she treated me to a full account of her emotions on stage as my mind raced and my khakis got more and more constrictive; she described the rush that she had experienced with the emergence of her nipples, and the mini-orgasm prompted by her brief finger-fuck in front of me.

Do you have any idea how difficult it can be to drive under those conditions?

We somehow managed to collect ourselves enough to rush through the lobby of the Anatole and into the elevator. There I was treated to a full-blown body press, hand grope and tonsillectomy all in one. It was ardent enough to scare off an elderly couple waiting at the next floor, and I'm pretty sure I caught sight of at least three or four people watching in awe as our glass-walled elevators passed each other.

In no time, we were in her room, conveniently located at the corner facing the other tower of the hotel. By now it came as little surprise to me that the windows were wide open, leaving our every move open to the prying eyes of at least a hundred or so of the hotel guest rooms. "Leave the lights on," she breathed, "the better for others to see us." Hell, by this point she could have invited the Dallas Cowboys to watch, accompanied by a film crew from *60 Minutes*, and I wouldn't have said no!

She was phenomenal, stripping off her clothes, removing mine and smothering me with kisses all the while. I was making up for lost time, sucking nipples, fingers, toes...anything my lips could get close to. I quickly made a mental note to check the seat of the car in the morning; if the passenger side was as wet as I expected it to be we'd better have a decent story to explain it. Nora was beyond soaked, and she nearly drowned me when she pounced on my chest and slipped up for my first sincere taste of Nora nectar.

How does Dr. Simon B. Boring deserve such a hot piece of ass? How does he keep her? Those were questions to ponder at some other time. By this time I had been able to find the answers to two of the questions that had dogged me for the duration of my association with Nora. Yes, she was a natural blonde. And if those tits were enhanced at all, the surgeon had pioneered a new and exciting no scar/no stretch method. I was busy licking and playing with the sweetest-tasting clit I'd ever encountered. For the rest of my life I'll be dreaming of the view I had, looking up from between her legs, past the neatly trimmed blonde thatch of her pubes, watching her moan as she pulled and extended her nipples.

Things quickly morphed from good...to great...to...*I can't believe this,* as the night wore on. With her on top, we savored my favorite sixty-nine position. I've never had any complaints about my ability to deliver face-to-pussy action, but if time to orgasm counts for anything, we set some kind of record. When she came, my cock was deep within her mouth stifling her screams and sending overload signals to the priapic node of my brain. My load left her with a foamy mouth that totally enhanced her newly acquired super-slut image.

We rolled over and switched into transitional kiss and grope mode, during which she began to pour out all of the performance fantasies she'd ever had. Repressed by Dr. Dull's fear of community scandal, she'd buried them in her head only to have them released tonight. As she said while I gave her left nipple some quality attention, the timing, setting and (I'm extremely pleased to say) the partner, were finally just right.

Now with naked, horny me to validate her moves—not to mention an unknown number of the guests watching from the other hotel tower—she began to dance and move with abandon. She treated me to moves I'll never forget. It was by sheer force of will that I avoided instant ejaculation when she perched doggie-style on the bed, looked between her legs and whispered, "You're not going to make me use my finger this time are you?"

Thank god our flight wasn't until noon on the following day. We fucked until sunrise.

A quick visit back to my room allowed me to collect my bags, but not before a steamy shower had given her the opportunity to demonstrate the effect that one long and talented soapy finger can have on the male prostate gland.

By the time we arrived at the rental car return, we had returned our outward appearances back to business mode, Nora looking almost prim in her moderate-length skirt ensemble and me with my khakis and sweater. We shared idle chat on the bus to the terminal, but as we settled into the seats at the departure gate, I noticed her leafing through her briefcase.

"Looking for something?" I asked.

"Yeah, I could swear that I had a brochure for a trade show in Las Vegas next month."

The gleam in her eye was unmistakable, as was the renewed stirring in my pants.

813.8
Mor

The Secret Game

author: Chase Morgan

category: Romance

subject:
1. Sexting   2. Married   3. Fantasy Swinging

The Secret Game

Chase Morgan

"I want to fuck you senseless," he said, leaning over to whisper into her ear. No other diners within earshot of them seemed to be paying attention. The warm glow of the lights in their favorite restaurant masked her flushed cheeks. John had been teasing his wife all night; an innocent little game of cat and mouse shared between the two of them. To him, she was ravishing. In an earthy, free-flowing skirt and a dark-brown tank top that outlined every beautiful curve of her body—she had been driving him crazy since they left their house. Tonight's "secret game," as they liked to call it, started when John opened the restaurant door for Kelly. With their friends in sight, she casually whispered, "I am not wearing panties," and then without missing a beat she walked right past him to hug their waiting friends. It was only fair that he got to make the next move; playing dirty was how this game went.

The couples ordered their second round of drinks as the waitress cleared the remnants of their appetizer. The mood was light and the laughs came easy with their dear friends Mike and Tami, who were blissfully ignorant of John and Kelly's secret game. As Kelly recounted a funny story from earlier in the day she let her hand rest on John's leg; she could feel his bulge against her pinky when she discretely slid her hand toward his inner thigh.

"Right, honey?"

"Huh, oh yeah, I couldn't believe that she said that either," stammered John trying to catch up with the conversation.

Recognizing her move, John slid his arm around Kelly and began rubbing the back of her neck. Kelly had a special spot and John knew that letting his fingers slide up and down lazily behind her ear would have the desired effect. He knew that with every trace of his finger behind her ear he was building a mental image in Kelly's mind of his fingers exploring her moistening pussy. There was no doubt in John's mind that she was wet and getting wetter, which was in turn making him harder.

The waitress returned balancing a tray of drinks, providing the horny couple with a brief moment of distraction from their friends. Jumping at the opportunity, they slyly utilized their phones as a part of their sexy strategies. Kelly beat John to the punch when a quick text hit his phone: *I want to shove your rock-hard cock in my mouth*. John smiled and quickly responded with, *I want to put a finger in your ass while I fuck you with my tongue*. Before returning her attention to Mike and Tami, Kelly squeezed his leg and looked up from her phone wearing a smile.

"Can you believe it took us an hour to reel it in," Mike rhetorically asked the table while recounting a recent fishing trip. "I am telling you, it was the biggest cobia any of us had ever seen!"

"Yeah, the tuna can put up quite a fight," John stammered.

"No, it was a cobia."

"Oh, yeah, that's what I meant." John tried to regain his composure but could not get the image of his gorgeous wife's pussy from his mind. His cock was thick with blood at the thought of his tongue parting her smooth lips.

The conversation quickly shifted focus as Tami began talking about a new shop opening in the local area and John seized the opportunity, excusing himself from the group to use the restroom. Sliding into the well-lit stall John quickly unbuttoned his pants with a mischievous smile on his face.

"Ooo!" Kelly's phone vibrated between her legs, sending an unexpected shock through her body. Tami was still engaged in her story and didn't seem to catch Kelly's quiet gasp. She looked down at her phone and was greeted with a picture of her husband's thick cock. He was not erect in the picture, he was at that semihard and thick stage; the stage that made Kelly salivate. She loved to take him into her mouth and let her tongue wrestle with his girth, craved feeling him grow harder and thicker with her lips.

"So I really think you would enjoy it."

"Huh? Oh yeah, I will definitely check it out," Kelly said, regaining her composure. She often wondered if Mike and Tami were at all aware of their tawdry little game; they didn't play it every time they were out with them, but this certainly wasn't the first time. Not wanting to be rude, but needing a little diversion, Kelly asked, "Have you heard from Becky lately?" The question had the desired effect and sent Tami into another lengthy diatribe. Kelly stared intently at Tami, listening to her response about Becky, while discretely sliding the tip of her finger under the top of her skirt and into her wet pussy.

John returned to the table to find their dinner had just arrived; he looked at Kelly with a wicked grin and winked.

Kelly's pussy moistened even more with the wink. He was winning the game, but not for long.

"Looks great as usual," Tami said as they began to eat. Slipping the fork from her lips with a slight moan Tami smiled and said, "This place has the best grilled chicken in town."

"Mmmm, these cherry tomatoes are so fresh," Kelly said

turning to John. Before he could protest Kelly pushed one to his mouth while deftly slipping her pussy-moistened finger to his lips. "See, isn't it fresh?"

John immediately recognized her familiar taste on his lips, forcing more blood to his cock. *That sneaky little shit,* he thought. Kelly had just upped the ante.

Mike and Tami were wonderful people but appeared to be the most vanilla couple on the face of the planet. Tonight, John looked like he had stepped from the pages of an LL Bean catalog. Wearing his typical khaki pants and button-down shirt, he was a well-built man with a full head of neat brown hair, but would easily blend into a crowd unnoticed at any function.

Tami was wearing a khaki skirt. Her long brown hair fell over her petite shoulders onto a button-up shirt concealing what John and Kelly had decided must be beautiful, ample breasts. They had long debated over the course of their friendship with Mike and Tami as to whether they still had sex at all, or if they were closet freaks; the jury was still out. Regardless, judging on outward appearance alone they were a stark contrast to John and Kelly.

Vastly different from vanilla Mike, John was a well-built man with a closely shaved head and neatly trimmed beard. Eyebrows that denoted warmth in his soul and a contemplative air when he was quiet perfectly framed his bright-blue eyes. His arms and back bore colorful tattoos, and he was almost always clothed in a comfortable pair of jeans and a T-shirt.

John's bride of twelve years was in her midthirties like everyone else at the table, but had the smooth, soft skin of a teen. Raven-black hair fell to her shoulders, which were also covered in tattoos extending down her right arm. Kelly's almond-colored eyes were set under dark eyebrows and beautiful long lashes. Tonight, her tank top was cut low enough to reveal ample cleavage without being offensive but still score her points in their secret game.

They had all met at a school function for their children several years ago and became fast friends. Despite outward appearances, the couples had many of the same interests and there was never a quiet moment amongst them. They regularly shared dinners, lunches and even camped together as families, but in all the years that they'd known each other, Mike and Tami remained a mystery to John and Kelly. "They are almost too vanilla," said Kelly. "I can easily see them in separate bedrooms, coming together only once or twice a year for some sexy time."

Mike and Tami were regulars at church; he was an usher and she played the organ. Their daughter was a Girl Scout and their son was the captain of the middle school chess team, a chip off the old block as Mike saw it. They hosted a monthly couples' book club and were regulars at the local golf course. Neither John nor Kelly could ever recall hearing a profane syllable escape their friends' lips during conversation. The two couples couldn't be more different if they tried.

Conversation continued to flow easily through dinner until the check came. There was never any of the usual banter over the check; the couples had long ago developed a nice rhythm, and tonight was John's turn to pick up the tab. The four walked to the door where hugs and handshakes were exchanged before they headed in the direction of their cars.

John slid his hand down Kelly's lower back as they walked to the car. His touch electrified her skin; She knew the anticipation that had been building all night was about to end. Kelly leaned over and kissed John quickly as he opened the door. Looking into his deep-blue eyes, she got into her seat and deftly slid her skirt up, revealing her plump, wet pussy. John felt the blood immediately rush to his cock as he closed the door and hurried to the driver's side. He tried to play it cool getting out of the parking lot in case Mike and Tami happened to drive by, but he barely had the car in gear before Kelly leaned over from her seat and unzipped his jeans.

His cock sprang out of the zipper as fast as Kelly unzipped it. She ran the tip of her thumb back and forth, from tip to base. "I want to put this fucking cock in my mouth," she said in a sexy whisper. "Do you want me to suck your cock? Do you want to feel my tongue up and down your thick shaft? Maybe rub your balls while I fuck you with my mouth?" she teased.

Kelly noticed a small drop of precum glistening on the head of John's dick. She felt her pussy flood and her mouth water at the sight of his sweet, clear fluid. She wanted to devour every hard inch of him, but in keeping with the spirit of their game, she needed to tease a little more. She slid her right hand down to the bottom of his shaft and pulled the skin tight around the base of his cock. For a quick moment she admired her husband's virility, then bent toward him and began the intimate act of consuming his erection.

Kelly unbuttoned his jeans for better access, then cupped her tongue against his balls and let her lips pull them into her mouth. She softly rolled them around for a moment before releasing them and then ran her tongue up the length of his massive rod. She savored the taste of his flesh as her tongue slid up his rippled shaft. He was intoxicating and addictive. When she reached the thick head of his dick, her prize awaited. The one little sticky drop of John's arousal was still perched so nicely at the tip, taunting her. Kelly put it to her lips, feeling its stickiness, and then rubbed it around like her very own naughty lipgloss, created just for her. With newly glossed lips she brought her mouth up to John's for a quick kiss. She made sure that he could taste himself on her lips and tongue before diving back down and burying his entire cock in her mouth.

John let out a deep moan when he felt Kelly running her tongue up and down his rod as she sucked his cock. She held the base of his shaft tight with one hand and followed her wet lips with the other, twisting and squeezing as she worked his full length. She let her hand slide down and massaged his heavy sack as she continued to work his shaft with her mouth. Kelly continued this ritual for several minutes while John did his best to concentrate on not climaxing in his wife's mouth. He had other plans. This was war after all.

With her head in John's lap drinking his cock in, Kelly hadn't noticed that they weren't heading back to their house. Her husband had found a secluded area in a neighborhood that was filled with empty lots and enough trees to conceal their parked car. He pulled in and turned off the lights. Kelly felt the car stop and sat up for a moment to see where they were.

"Now it's my turn," John told her as he opened his door and walked around to her side.

He opened the passenger-side door and Kelly immediately turned sideways in her seat and took his cock back into her mouth. She was at the perfect height to cup his balls while running her mouth and hand up and down his shaft. She could taste more precum on her tongue every time she paused at the top for a tease. She rubbed her palm across his balls, cupped them and then pressed the area where his sack met his body. Her fingers brushed over his ass and then quickly moved back to massaging his balls.

John was about to explode but felt the overwhelming need to taste his wife's pussy. He pulled his cock from her mouth; she fought a little, but he kept away from her and pushed her back in the seat. John winked at his wife before kneeling down outside of the car and pulling her hips toward the edge of the seat. He wasted no time in flipping her skirt up. Kelly kept a small tuft of dark hair on top of her otherwise perfectly shaved pussy. Her clit piercing twinkled under the car's dome light, and John began to salivate as he moved his face toward her soaking wet pussy.

He was too fucking aroused to tease and pushed his tongue as deep into Kelly's pussy as it would go and began to slowly work it in and out. He reached up and pushed her legs farther apart. Kelly's right leg was now perched over the back of her seat while her left leg hung partway out of the car. He let his hands slide down to her drenched pussy lips, and then he pressed three fingers in immediately. As his fingers entered, he slid his tongue out of her hole and used it to work her throbbing clit. He sucked hard, pulling blood into her clit and charging it with electricity. John allowed her clit ring to bounce back and forth over his tongue as he fucked her harder and harder with his fingers.

Kelly felt John's fingers filling her slit, thrusting in and out while his tongue played on her clit, but she wanted to get fucked. She didn't want his fingers; she wanted his big cock buried deep in her pussy. "Fuck me," she ordered. She knew he'd heard her, but he wasn't listening. So she reached down and grabbed his head, pulling his face to hers. She started to say something but he buried his pussy-drenched tongue deep into her mouth. She could taste herself. Her pussy flooded again and began to ache. "Fuck me right now," she ordered. "I don't care; you win, I just need that cock inside me!"

John smiled as he pulled his wife out of the seat and sat down in her place. Her flushed face wore a mischievous smile as she hiked up her skirt and backed herself toward him. She reached between her legs, grabbing the base of his raging-hard cock, and slowly guided herself down until she felt the head at the edge of her soaking slit.

Kelly loved the feeling when John's cock first pressed past her engorged lips; she savored it every time they fucked. She sat down very slowly, feeling the tip spreading her, inching down farther until she felt herself envelop the head, then she lowered herself the rest of the way down to his balls, filling her entire pussy.

When the tip of John's long dick hit the back of Kelly's pussy she began to grind; she felt every fucking inch of him filling her soaked cunt. She pushed down harder and harder while squeezing her inner walls, devouring every bit of his girth. The juices from her drenched hole ran freely down John's shaft as she rode him up and down. His thickness spread her lips with each pass and she leaned into his palms while he caressed her tits and squeezed her nipples from behind.

Visions of what they must look like flashed in her mind. Seeing her skirt pulled up as she sat on him reverse-cowgirl style, she could visualize her stretched pussy lips on display as John's thick cock disappeared and reappeared like magic, causing her juices to run down his shaft and drip from his balls like fat drops of rain off a fruit. The scene playing in her head set in motion the freight train that would quickly become her orgasm.

This was no marathon sex session; John and Kelly were fucking and ready to climax. She felt the train leaving the station; she grabbed the dashboard with one hand and her clit with the other. She settled in for her finale as she switched from grinding and slipping to slowly bobbing up and down the length of her husband's thick shaft. She sensed that John was about to explode too; she paused on the bottom of every stroke, writhing around like a slithering snake so the deepest parts of her pussy could feel the pressure of his cock.

Kelly worked her clit harder and harder as she picked up the pace, fucking John faster and faster. The freight train inside her body was at full speed and at this point, there was no stopping what was about to come. Her clit throbbed between her fingers as she rolled it into a little ball. The vision of him spreading her pussy coupled with the fullness of him inside her flashed in her mind one more time. Kelly's body froze as the freight train rumbled from her toes and up through her clit. Her pussy clamped down on John's shaft and she moaned loudly as the orgasm pulsed through her sweaty body.

After the shock subsided and her clit recovered, Kelly writhed around on John's cock a little more. Then she slowly rose up, letting his slippery cock fall from her pussy. Her vacant slit ached for cock, but she quickly lost thought of that as she turned around and kneeled down next to the seat just as John had earlier. She took his pussy-soaked cock into her mouth and slid her tongue along his shaft while taking hold of the base with her hand. Pulling the skin taut she worked his dick in concert with her hand and mouth. She knew how close he was and began fucking him with her mouth at a more rapid pace. Kelly paused long enough to look up and say, "I want you to cum in my mouth."

John watched as his wife's beautiful lips spread around his shaft, and his cock disappeared down her throat. Her dirty talk and the sight of her lips around his thick shaft pushed him past the point of no return. His balls drew up and his orgasm began to build deep within his core. With one final stroke of her warm tongue and tight grip, John erupted into Kelly's mouth with a loud sigh of relief.

When the first hot load hit her tongue she swallowed then opened her mouth to give her husband the show she knew he loved. Kelly milked each rhythmic pulse of hot cum, both into her open mouth and onto her chin, knowing that John loved watching it spill from her mouth while she pumped him dry. Once he was empty, she slid up his body and kissed him with a cum-soaked tongue.

Meanwhile, on the other side of town...

"Can you see John's big cock stretching my tight little pussy as I ride it?" Tami asked seductively. Her hands pressed down on her husband's chest caused her plump tits to squeeze together and kept them from bouncing as she rode his thick shaft.

Mike stared into his wife's seductive brown eyes before letting his vision drift down past her tits to the perfectly shaved pussy engulfing his cock. "I would love to watch him fuck you while Kelly sat on your face and sucked my dick," Mike moaned.

The vision raced through Tami's mind. She salivated at the thought of John pressed deep inside her while Kelly's wetness coated her face. She quickened the pace on her husband's rod. "I want to kiss her after she's taken your load in her mouth. I want to taste you on her tongue!" Tami's pussy clenched down as electricity raced through her body and her husband filled her pussy with his hot, white lava.

Tami collapsed down on top of Mike; feeling his spent cock still inside her she kissed him. "I am telling you, I totally get the vibe from them," she whispered. "And they were definitely fucking around under the table tonight."

Mike sighed as Tami rolled over and onto her back next to him. "They are definitely a very sexual couple who can't seem to keep their hands off each other, but that doesn't necessarily mean they would be into the book club..."

POW! It's Shibari Girl!

Tamsin Flowers

So, in case you were wondering, yes, superheroes do have sex. Often as not they have sex with the man-or-woman-on-the-street type that they've just rescued. Ugh! I know you're thinking that smacks of exploitation, but it's not, really. When you save someone, they frequently get a thing for you, you know, in the same way people get a thing for their doctor or their teacher. It would be mean, or just plain rude not to give them what they wanted, right? We've all been there: Superman, Cat-woman, Kick-Ass...and me.

Me?

By day I'm Mallory Majors, second violin in our third-rate city orchestra, college coed, dog lover and Mexican food aficionado. But by night, I'm Shibari Girl! Or Japanese Knot Girl, as *The Daily Bugle* sometimes refers to me, though that causes confusion because I'm not actually Japanese at all. Before I came here, I used to live in Baltimore. Anyway, my special power is capturing villains and tying them up in knots, real fast, and then I leave them hanging from city landmarks for the cops to clean up in the morning. I'll admit to wearing silver spandex,

I'll admit to stalking the bad guys through the night and, yes, I'll admit to getting down and dirty with the good guys I've rescued. Like I said, it would be rude not to.

But now I'm going to let you in on a little secret I've just discovered: it's actually far more fun to have sex with the bad guys than the good guys. How did I discover this? Here's what happened.

I was sitting at home one evening last week, minding my own business and putting the finishing touches to a term paper on the use of hessian as a wall covering by 1970s interior designers, when the Shibari! phone started to ring.

Dring-dring, dring-dring, dring-dring.

"Moshi, moshi," I say, by way of greeting. (My way of getting into the persona.)

"It's Commissioner Thomas, Shibari Girl! The city needs your help."

Doesn't it always?

"What can I do for you?" I say.

"It's Crabman. He's taken a side swipe at Jimmy Jack's Jewel Warehouse on Main Street and got away with $22.5 million's worth of rough diamonds."

It's the third time Crabman has struck in a month. He scuttles down the city side streets in his orange disguise, breaks in the side entrances of jewel stores and cracks open the safe with his hydraulic claw. I've come close to tracking him down once or twice but I've failed to catch him so far.

"Okay, Commissioner, I'll get right over there."

"And Shibari Girl!..."

"Yes?"

"He gouged out a message in the steel door of the safe."

"What did it say?"

"Get knotted!"

Now this is getting personal.

I pull on my silver spandex catsuit, grab a couple of coils of

Shibari rope and swing down the fire escape. Fifteen minutes later I arrive at a scene of total mayhem outside Jimmy Jack's warehouse: fifteen police cruisers are blocking the road to traffic, eight journalists have broken through the cordon and are firing off flashbulbs like the Fourth of July and Commissioner Thomas, his deputy and the store manager are standing flummoxed inside Jimmy Jack's huge, but now empty, walk-in safe.

"Shibari Girl! Thank god you're here," says the store manager.

I give him a curt nod.

"Would you fellows mind waiting outside while I check for clues?" I say to them.

"There's nothing here," says Commissioner Thomas, "apart from a small trace of blood on the twisted metal of the safe door."

"Get it analyzed," I say.

As they scurry out, something sparkling on the floor of the safe catches my eye. I bend down to pick it up and find that it's not a diamond dropped in the raid as I first suspected but a small gold token. Holding it up to the light, I can see a symbol embossed on one of its faces: a peach. I recognize it immediately. This is a cloakroom token for the Peachy Club downtown, the only other place in the city where you'll find anyone able to execute proper Shibari ties.

"Any of you drop this?" I say, holding it up in front of the three men who were in the safe.

They all three stare at me, wide-eyed and open-mouthed.

Time to get out of here.

The Peachy Club's heaving but no one bats an eyelid as I wander around the floor in my silver catsuit. If anything, I'm a little overdressed, considering that most of the clientele are naked. However, there are always people dressed up to play out their superhero fantasies and I can't help but hide a smile as I count three other Shibari Girls! grinding on the dance floor and getting into scenes in the public playrooms.

I head for the bar, hoping to find my man Tobi mixing the drinks.

"Mallory," he says, cracking a smile as I climb up onto one of the red-velvet bar stools.

"How d'you know it's me? There are at least three other versions out there."

"Easy, babe," he says. "I'd know your walk anywhere. Those other girls just don't got what you've got inside that spandex." He puts a shot of tequila on the bar for me.

I have to laugh. I've known Tobi for years, even had an affair with him for a short while, and he's one of only two people in the city who know my real identity.

He serves another customer and then comes back to me with a serious expression on his face.

"Say, I heard on the radio that there's been another crab attack," he says.

I nod and throw back the tequila.

"I'm on a crab hunt," I say, "and the trail leads here. Any ideas?"

He shrugs.

"It's busy tonight, a lot of faces I don't know."

I roll the gold token across my knuckles, wondering where to start looking.

"Where'd you find that?" says Tobi.

I glance up at him and notice a small cut on his left knuckle.

"It was just here on the floor in front of the bar," I say. "How'd you cut your hand?"

"On a beer cap."

He takes the token from me and puts it in his pocket.

"Cheers."

"When are you off, Tobi?" I ask.

His eyebrows shoot up.

"For you anytime, babe. I wasn't actually rostered on for tonight. Just bored."

Or creating an alibi, perhaps?

"Come on," I say. "I want to play."

I lead him up the stairs to one of the private playrooms but as soon as we're inside he slams me up against the wall.

"So how'd you know it's me?" he says.

"How'd you know I know?" I counter.

It would be like a game of chess if we were both a bit brighter.

"Because I know you," he answers, relaxing his grip on my throat. "If you're on hunt and you bring me up here, it means I'm your quarry."

"Are you?" I say, sliding a hand down to my belt and surreptitiously detaching one of the coils of rope.

"We had some good times, Mallory," he says, and suddenly his mouth is on mine.

For a second I'm caught unawares by how good his kiss tastes, but then the superhero in me takes over. As I work my tongue into his mouth, I push back against him and hook one of my legs behind his knee. He goes down onto his back with a grunt, pulling me with him, but I'm sitting astride him now and I still hold the advantage.

"They were good times, Tobi, but you got greedy."

I peel his Peachy Club T-shirt up his chest and he wriggles out of it. It's evident he's been putting in the hours at the gym and if circumstances were different... I lick my lips.

"I'll split the diamonds with you, Mallory. We could get away somewhere secluded, just the two of us. Things could be like they were before."

Am I tempted by his offer? Not until I flip him over and see the small tattoo of Shibari Girl! on the back of his shoulder. It looks fresh.

"You became Crabman to attract my attention?" I say.

"It was the only way. You usually look right through me. But now..."

He smells so good but then I remember the looks on Commissioner Thomas and the store manager's faces.

"Tobi, you broke the law and you're going down."

I grab his arms and although he struggles I'm too quick for him. In six simple knots I have him trussed and naked in a classic Shibari tie. His wrists are bound to his ankles and a corset of rope work holds him in a fixed kneeling position. He grunts and struggles as I work on him but as my fingers run up and down his back and across his chest, the grunts turn to moans and I can't help but notice his burgeoning erection.

"God, I've missed this," he whispers.

The memories flood back: Tobi swinging in a rope cradle with my mouth on his cock or the two of us, bound hip to hip in pneumatic motion. I'm not supposed to be getting turned on but I am. My breath hitches and his cock twitches in response. I clip a D-ring into the nest of knots at the small of his back and winch him up off the floor.

"Come on, Mallory," he moans. "For old time's sake before you turn me in?"

I look at how the red ropes bite his tanned skin, knowing the marks will remain for days and suddenly I know I've got to have him. Commissioner Thomas and his denizens can wait. Tobi won't be getting anything like this for a long time where he's going and, for the sake of a shared past, I can lend him a couple of hours. I secure the main rope to an iron ring set in the wall and then I take half a dozen more ropes and work up a cradle around him. The result is that now Tobi is swinging gently, several feet above the floor, in an armchair position. He watches me intently as I work, but he doesn't speak.

"Where are the diamonds?" I demand roughly, not wanting him to guess what's coming his way.

"Mallory, baby," he says. "This isn't about the stones. This is about us."

"For Jimmy Jack, it's about the stones."

I twist him round and round and then set him spinning.

"I need to know where they are before I can let you down," I say.

I love to watch Tobi spin on the ropes. He's a beautiful specimen of a man, long, clean limbs dusted with tawny gold hair, and a face so handsome you could cry. But the sheer beauty of him doesn't mean I'm not going to make him suffer for his pleasure. I take a riding crop from a rack on the wall and put a hand on the ropes to make him still. Tobi hates corporal punishment and his eyes widen in fear as my practice swipe slices through the air.

"Mallory, wait," he says.

I step back.

"You haven't asked for my safeword."

"Let's make it *diamonds*," I say. I take another practice swipe and then drag the tip of the crop across his chest.

"You can have the diamonds, babe," he says. "Like I said, we can share them."

I drop the crop and move in closer.

"I've missed you, Tobi," I say, cupping a hand between his legs.

His cock rears against the pressure of my touch and I feel a flutter deep inside me.

"That's it, Mal, I'm here for the taking."

I work his rod with my hand and latch my mouth onto one of his nipples. His hips buck and he tries to arch into me but the ropes keep him steady in the sitting position. I use my teeth on the tender pink bud, making him yelp.

"Where?" I whisper, plucking a chest hair with my free hand.

"No way!"

"Where?" I say, biting his bottom lip.

He pulls away, shaking his head.

"Where?" I mouth, as I peel off the silver spandex to reveal my naked body underneath. (It's far too tight for underwear; I'm too vain for panty lines.)

Tobi groans softly in his cradle of red rope.

I pull myself up to sit, legs splayed, on his lap. The ropes loop up behind me, giving me something to lean back against. Tobi looks down at my reclining body, practically dribbling with desire, but his hands are firmly bound so he can't touch me.

"Like what you see, Crab Boy?"

"Crabman," he says.

"I think I'm calling the shots, Crusty."

I lick a finger and then stroke it gently across the soft folds between my legs. A few inches away, Tobi's cock is throbbing with his need to be inside me.

"Where?" I say, using my fingers to open myself up. I'm wet and the earthy aroma of my desire suddenly hits my nostrils. Tobi breaths it in deeply, a small whimper escaping his lips.

"Where are they?"

I reach forward and tug on his cock. All his muscles tense beneath me.

"Mallory…"

"Tell me where they are and you'll find release."

The double meaning of my words leaves him guessing.

"I can release you," I say, caressing him, "or I can let you go." I glance toward the door.

I slide forward until I'm able to nudge the tip of his cock up against the entrance of my vagina. Tobi moans. I know which form of release he needs. Letting go of his piece, I reach my hands up into the ropes behind my head. By pulling down on them rhythmically and shifting my weight, I'm able to set us both swinging. Once I've built the momentum I turn my attention back to my trussed-up crab. I maneuver carefully to put my legs around his waist and then, at last, I lower myself onto his waiting cock. He slides in as easily as a hot knife through butter, and a thrill courses through me as I stretch to accommodate him.

The swinging movement angles our hips backward and forward against each other, allowing him to slide up and down, in and out, even though he has no control of his movement. I cup his face in my hands and lean forward to kiss him. But as my lips approach his, he twists his head to one side to bring his mouth to my ear.

"The ice is in the big ice bin, behind the bar," he whispers.

I kiss him. I nearly loved Tobi a couple of years back, but I thought then that superheroes couldn't afford to have love in their lives. Look what happened to Spider-Man. Now, though, I don't know. The rush of heat that blossoms up through me as his tongue slow-dances with mine feels, at this precise moment, more precious to me than the ice-cold haul of diamonds downstairs. I remember how much I used to want Tobi when I wasn't with him and how hard I had to work to suppress that feeling when I forced our breakup.

What a bloody little fool I was.

But that doesn't solve the current crisis. Our grinding hips make the cradle swing even higher and with each arc, Tobi's cock pushes deeper inside me. My nipples find friction against his chest, our teeth clash as our kiss becomes ever more passionate and his balls feel hard and ready beneath the soft rounds of my buttocks.

I know he's on the edge of coming, so I drop a hand down between us to find my clit. It's pulsing, a hot, hard pleasure button, and as my fingers work it with a familiar expertise, I'm able to time my orgasm to coincide with his. With a roar, he climaxes and I feel the heat of his cum jetting up inside me just as my own orgasm pulls my muscles tight. I clasp myself around him as he surges farther into me and we stay locked in rigid ecstasy until the swing slows down to a gentle sway.

"Babe, you are awesome," Tobi sighs.

His cock slides out of me on a wave of spent semen and pussy juice, flooding onto his stomach.

"You too," I say, clambering down from the rope cradle somewhat awkwardly. "I'd forgotten how good we fit."

I pull on the silver spandex.

"Where you going, babe?" he says, his voice worried.

"To get some ice, hot stuff," I say. "Got to check if you were telling me the truth."

I pad downstairs with bare feet, smiling at the thought of Tobi, hanging helpless in the swing with his jizz drying on his stomach. The club's pretty quiet now, just a few stragglers winding down their scenes and chilling out before heading for home. When the bar girl goes to deliver drinks, I slip behind the bar. I find the ice bin and rummage through it. At the bottom my hand lights on something hard and plastic. I pull out a rectangular Tupperware box and snap off the lid. $22.5 million in diamonds looking like a couple of cocktails' worth of ice chips.

Choices.

Hand them in to Commissioner Thomas? Run away with Tobi and live a life of wealth and privilege? I've always been partial to the taste of crab.

Or...neither of the above?

Superhero? Antihero?

What's a girl to do?

823.0
Wri
Vivi and the Magic Man

author: Kristina Wright

category: Fantasy/Horror

subject:
1. Bloodlust   2. Gypsies   3. Demon Orgy

Vivi and the Magic Man

Kristina Wright

She was watching him. Across the bonfire that licked up to touch the stars and warmed the silent group of freaks and misfits, dreamers and schemers, he saw her watching him. She shouldn't have been able to see him, not until he was ready to be seen. The others were oblivious to his presence; they rubbed their dry hands together and smacked their lips around tender bits of animal flesh. They were all but writhing in the delights of warmth and food and companionship. But not her. She seemed neither cold nor hungry, though she wore only a thin white blouse with an open bodice, hinting at a slight frame with generous feminine curves, and a long, ruddy skirt that seemed to be an extension of her body rather than an ill-fitting garment.

They called it Port City. A joke, since they were as landlocked as a desert and just as isolated. But it was a port city, a different kind. One that brought the outcasts and the vagrants from faraway places, in a quest for hope and escape, longing for a paradise they dreamed about when their rickety old wagon made off for some true port city, hawking magic cures and sensual delights until they were turned out and forced back here.

Home. Planning and scheming for the next adventure, rattling their bottles and indulging in their vices. But not this time. Oh no, this time they were coming with him. All but one.

She watched him knowingly, long dark hair lifting away from her face to stream like a banner over her shoulder. She had a hand tucked in her pocket, her fingers worrying something in its depths. An arch of an eyebrow, a dip of a shoulder and she was away to one of the wagons in this ragtag caravan. He followed her; he really had no choice. She was why he had come. She was the reason for this unplanned visit.

He circled the group to follow her, knowing instinctively which wagon would be hers. Brocade fabric, once ornate and expensive but now faded and worn, hung from a frame that creaked and sighed as he climbed the steps. The squawk of a bird greeted him as he dipped his head to enter and the hair on the back of his neck bristled at its human-like words.

"He brings death, ack! He's the one!"

"Hush, little one," he heard her coo in the dimness of the wagon. She bent down to feed the creature, an oddly colored bird about two hands high. Cerulean feathers gleamed with gold highlights, the broad head dotted with a tuft of orange fur. Instead of a beak, it had the muzzle of—what?—a dog, he supposed. Coyote, perhaps?

"Where did you get that—thing?" It wasn't what he'd intended to say to her first, but it seemed innocuous enough.

"Xerxes? He came to me in my dreams," she whispered, turning her steady gaze to him. "Just as I conjured you."

She was delusional, of course. All the strongest ones were. Even from a kneeling position, he could sense the power in her. The bird-thing had it wrong, he wasn't the one; she was. She was the maiden who blessed the barren, healed the Earth, made dead things grow again. Their little queen, a lesser prophet and savior. It was...sweet. He could indulge her for a little while and he would.

She was what he needed. What they all needed.

"You are the Magic Man," she said. "I knew you would come."

He'd been called many things, most of them unkind, few of them untrue. Magic Man was as good as any and better than most.

He nodded. "That sounds a bit...ostentatious. You may call me Dio. And you are Vivi."

"Vivianna Magdellana Riestto Tyluchia," she said with a curtsey, as if he were royalty come to visit. "But yes, they call me Vivi."

"Victorious, virtuous, valiant," he said, ticking off the other things they called her.

He deftly twirled a gold coin between his fingers, trying to remember from whence he collected it. Past or future, he couldn't remember. North or south, east or west, it didn't matter. He tossed the coin in the air, watching the gold wink in the light of a brightly colored lantern. She stood and crossed the narrow wagon while the coin still turned end over end. She snatched it from the air before he could catch it, slapping it into the palm of his hand with a sting and a smile.

"Vicious, violent, vile. Verily," she said, her crystal blue eyes going dark, so dark, as her pupils expanded to take over the blue of her irises, then the whites of her eyes, until she was all dark hair and bottomless black eyes. Eyes he knew too well for he saw them reflected in every shiny service.

He felt as if he was falling, spiraling downward into those depths. Few things surprised him anymore, but this did. This sense of being off balance, out of breath, helpless. Lost. When was the last time he felt lost? Had it ever been so?

He put out a hand to steady himself, grasping her arm that felt hot to the touch. So hot.

"They do not say those things of you," he managed finally, his voice a gasp of shock and pain.

Her eyes returned to normal, blinking at him with awareness and clarity, but not fear. "No, but they say them about you, Magic Man." She shrugged and laughed. "Magic Man. Dio. You have other names, yes? Diablo. Devil. Death. Evil. Magic Man is the nicest of them all, and it suits you. You look like a man of magic, of hope. A promise of the future."

He knew it was true. He'd styled himself that way. His hair, a rich chocolate brown rather than the clichéd black, was long to the point of being feminine, matching his narrow face and delicate features. The burgundy waistcoat fit his angular frame like a second skin, the matching felt hat was crisp and sharp edged, the charcoal trousers had been tailored for long legs used to walking slowly, deliberately. His calf-high boots were polished and shined, the unusual color of the leather from an animal not of this world. Spurs on their heels—gold from yet another forgotten tribute.

There was no need to dispute the truth, but he felt the urge to say something in his own defense. That in itself would have been amusing if it hadn't also been troubling. "I serve a purpose."

"As do I."

Whatever he might have said was lost in the sound of raucous noise. The group gathered outside was drunk—not on spirits, though certainly he'd seen a bottle or three being passed amongst them—no, their minds and emotions were altered by something else entirely. Music started, the twisted mechanical notes of an ancient calliope starting up, followed by an accordion and something stringed, a mandolin, perhaps? No, something more ancient. Voices raised, uneven, discordant, but singing, ever singing.

The night comes to take us away
This is the night we shall pay
Our lives for one

Our lives for her
This we become
Go into the earth
Away, away
Away

The instruments played carnival music, dancing music, but the words the freaks sang were eerie and haunting. Death was here.

She took his hand, her fingers long and surprisingly strong, calluses on each pad. "Come on," she said, her eyes flashing lavender and gold amongst the blue. A trick of the light or something of her own true nature, he didn't know. That truth was difficult to admit. He knew everything. Saw everything. Had experienced past and present and future at once, but he did not know the truth of her. For a moment, no longer than the flutter of an eyelash, he was afraid.

He had only time to ask, "Where are we going?" before they were out from under the canopy of her wagon and down the uneven steps and into the fray of the fire and the music and the drunken, hungry crowd.

She laughed, a breathy, musical sound. "To dance! To dance our lives away!"

It was a silly thing to say, for if he knew nothing else of her, he knew she could not die. Neither of them could. But he was caught in the web of her hair and her skirt and her strange and mysterious spirit, and he let her whirl him about in a crusty dirt cloud kicked up by boots and bare feet and long skirts. A need for something hungered in him just as surely as it hungered in these citizens of the fringe.

He spun, recalling the last time he'd danced like this. A dance to the death, not his own. He blocked the memory from his mind as best he could and followed her lead, dizzy from the heat he knew too well, dizzy from her aroma wafting from her dampening skin. He was becoming drunk and that was a dangerous thing, dangerous for all of them. But he didn't care. He didn't care for he was here, with her.

Her too-long skirts swirled around her like a desert dust devil, the color of hay left too long in a pasture, the sequins and bits of glass stitched into the rough-hewn panels winking in the firelight with a gaiety that her own expression did not match. She wasn't like the others, oh no, this one was different. She was special. In a circus of gypsies, outcasts and ghouls, she was uniquely special.

Vivi was not special in the way of Penwal, she of the angular face and serpentine tongue, with her long misshapen tentacles tucked beneath her own rotting skirt, the slippery tips swirling about in the dust, swiping at the others, capturing a bit of silver or perhaps a bauble in a moment of inattention. It would be returned later, or so she thought, for these were her brethren and to steal from them for real and true would be punishable by excommunication of a most painful sort. Now her tentacles tickled the narrow buttocks of a farm woman, plain except for the aura that hovered around her, blue and gray and mauve, darkening as she hiked her skirt up to midthigh, showing off flesh ravaged by age and disease and demon claws.

She wasn't like Blaskana, who whispered obscene things in an obscure language while she fed her milk-white breasts into a lover's mouth and used her hands, all five of them, to bring ecstasy and death. Blaskana took a different lover every night, but would only bleed one dry each month. Her erotic skills were such that many were willing to play her version of Russian roulette for the chance to bed her. He recognized Lebba, she of the multiple genitalia, writhing on the ground before her mistress. The two were well matched, he thought with a nod.

There were the twins, Buu and Onett, who told fortunes and granted wishes. The fortunes they proffered were always dire, which led their patrons to request wishes of health and wealth. For a few bits of silver, the industrious twins would offer a perfume to turn the nose of the most fickle conquest or a handful of fool's gold to line the pockets and attract true wealth. Their real talent was in telling the needy and desperate what they longed to hear—something exciting and dramatic to offset the dullness of lives led quietly and obediently in chains. They swayed in unison, two halves of a whole, their beautiful violet-tinted bodies with long, hanging phalluses that could woo a ship to the rocks—if there were a ship to be seen for a thousand miles.

There were the others, more names crowding his mind than he cared to recall, all of them different from Vivi. Nightmares. Monsters. Ghouls. His kind. Finley and Harris, tricksters and thieves who seduced everyone and each other alike, with a wink and a smile, and used knives to carve up the lot in sacrifice. Elenna, queen of the night sky and reader of the stars who could conjure erotic thoughts with just a thrust of her hip was now being serviced by Manitou, he of equine descent, heir to a throne of madness. Across the way and dangerously close to the flames was Jahone, who could swallow swords and spit fountains of fire. He swallowed other things too, Dio recalled with a shiver, his own arousal becoming thick and heavy in his trousers. Jahone crouched amid the dancing bodies, mouth open to receive a sword fed to him by Hillia, her rolls of ample flesh wriggling with delight as Jahone took the sword, his hands working between her plump thighs as he did. He watched them all with disinterest, knowing they were his for the taking when he chose. But it was Vivi who had brought him here; she was the reason he had been called to this place. She was not like the others. She was so much more.

The air was filled with the smell of arousal and burning things. Wood, fabric, bits of paper tossed into the flames. Seared flesh of animals, sacrificed and consumed, hungers fed but not sated. Not yet. That's why he was here. He served a purpose, as he reminded Vivi. Whatever they said of him, however much they feared him, he served a purpose. He was needed. Without him, they were little more than secondhand demons, bad dreams conjured by naughty children and banished in the light of day. Oh, but he made them so much more. He gave them bodies, made them flesh and bone. And now it was time to claim what was his.

There were more of them arriving in the camp. Legions of his followers, called from all corners of the universe to pay the price of their existence. Some he knew from centuries past, others only from their energy that fed him. The fire flashed and licked at bodies, voices shrieked in excitement, not fear. Limbs entangled—fleshy appendages multihued and textured, entwining arms and legs and tentacles and tails, vulvas pulsing and open and rubbing together, penises growing and stretching to fill bodies that welcomed them. Creatures of the night and of nightmares, less human now, but more real. More true. More *his*.

He could feel his hunger rising as he followed the twirling Vivi. She was bordering on manic, head thrown back, long bare neck pulsing with a life force unlike any he had ever felt. He ran his tongue over his teeth, stifling the urge. Tamping it down for now, at least. But it wouldn't be long, not long at all. And she would welcome it, as they all did.

"Dance, Magic Man, dance!" she screamed over the cacophony of music and screeching voices.

He danced. For her, he danced. His spurs jangled, incongruously loud amidst the noise. His heels beat out the time like the rhythm of a heartbeat, and the earth responded, awakening and stretching, shifting beneath their collective physical and spiritual weight. They undulated with their need, stretched by it, flesh nearly bursting open in an effort to release it. Mouths wide, fingers and talons clasping at air, at flame, at the bodies around them. The smell of earth and fire and sweat mingled with another odor—sex. He felt his own need roar to life, tearing lose from the confines of this humble body, craving what they offered. Sex and blood. The substance and weight of sacrifice.

Vivi pressed her body to his, her curves molded to his angular planes as if by design—but of course it was. This was their fate, their destiny. The sacrifice of many to appease the two and set the world to balance again. They would give themselves for her, willingly, gladly, throwing themselves into the flames, onto the knives, into the darkest of wicked nights. For her, they would die. And he would receive them as was his right. They would go to their deaths with her name on their lips, but with his mark on their souls.

He grasped her to him, knowing at last he had found his match. The weight of his cock pressed against her, large, full and beautiful—a vanity he indulged like all his vices. He was not the creator of these grim devils, he was the mirror—enhanced, more pleasing to the eye, but dark and dead beneath the surface. For the moment he was as alive as he would ever be, his body aching for the release the others around him sought as well. Vivi rocked against him in encouragement, her face shrouded by a veil of hair, her beauty obscured but not muted, for it seemed to hum in the air around her. It didn't matter; her image was seared into his mind like every deed he'd done and every soul he'd claimed. She was his, as much as this gypsy circus existing at the very rim of Hell itself.

"You may have them," she said, her lips pressed to his ear, her hands working the buttons on his trousers, freeing him as he would soon free her minions. "But I will have you."

"And so it will be," he promised, rending her blouse to useless shreds, the ancient fabric screaming as if alive.

Bare to the waist, her skin darkened from alabaster to ebony, rippling and dimpling as if something pulsed beneath the surface. He followed the transformation from her narrow waist to the fullness of her breasts and up, to the column of her neck, the delicate bone structure of her jaw, across her gently arched brow and down to her eyes. Her eyes, once blue with flecks of celestial color, were once again black as the night sky. They remained that way for a moment and then seemed to implode into a searing white light that nearly blinded him with the intensity.

She was stroking his arousal, bringing him along to the culmination of this event like a lover anxious to be penetrated, or impregnated. He reached for the waistband of her skirt and found it tied with a scarlet ribbon. No, knotted. End over end, little knots of fabric kept the skirt tight around her hips. He growled in frustration—a sound that was peculiarly human among the sounds of animal-like copulation, flesh slapping together roughly, wetly, voices torn from throats bubbling with possession. He was surrounded by an orgiastic tribute to him, to death itself, and he was undermined by a simple bit of knotted ribbon.

She laughed, stroking a nail along his cheekbone, drawing blood. "Oh Dio, you are so ready for me." The words were seductive, but their meaning...he sensed there was something he was missing. Bloodlust had dulled his senses, made him skip over some important part of this erotic feast. He felt like he was forgetting some bit of etiquette, and she was chiding him for it.

"I need you," he said.

There was no measure of love contained within his existence, but he understood his own need. And here she was, in her nearly naked glory, her skin fading back to alabaster, a network of purple veins beneath the surface, her dusky nipples drawn taut with her own arousal. He tugged at them now, drawing her close by these delicate bits of flesh, feeling his way up her thigh, bunching her skirt in one hand at her waist. He wanted—needed—to be inside this body. To fill her as he was being consumed by the need for her. He could not claim her as he claimed the others, he could not destroy her. But he could take her, fuck her, use her, deplete her. Possess the body she inhabited and brand it as his. The hunger to do just that was so strong, he sank his teeth into the muscle of her shoulder, drawing blood and more—her existence—into him. She only gasped and pawed at him ineffectually, helpless now, passive, his. *His.*

He barked out his triumph, his head thrown back to the night sky, inky black and void of warmth, of life, of compassion. Like him. He was the night and he had precious few hours to enjoy his reign. The fire had doubled in size and he heard the cries of those who had been too close and were now consumed in flames, still coupling like their very souls depended on it, which of course they did. They fucked each other senseless, this mass of ghoulish humanity, driving themselves into oblivion and release even while he captured them in a net of eternity, forever at his command.

He looked at his prize, the woman they died for—the creature they did not know, and neither did he. He only knew he'd been drawn here, to this place, to her, like a curious feline sniffs the trail of an injured mouse, thrusting a paw into a gap of wood and darkness and claiming a succulent morsel. He was here to do his job, serve his purpose, and she was the prize. She was his greatest conquest. He looked to the curtain of hair that hid her face and felt—not sympathy, never—a moment of compassion. She was weak, trapped, a victim of circumstance. Poor, poor Vivi. They loved her so, but it was not enough.

He bent her back toward the ground, his hand creeping up the inside of her bare thigh, finding heat and wetness bubbling like a long-forgotten well beneath the earth. Her smell was familiar, primal and earthy. He knew her, sensed something about her in that moment, felt the warning in his head and between his own thighs even though it was too late to turn back. He was already pushing himself into that warm, wet, dark space he had felt, that place that he knew was untouched by any before him, empty since the dawn of time and waiting for him, taking him in, making a home for him. His rightful throne, nestled in the welcoming, pulsing flesh of this woman-creature who drew him down to her, cradled his head to her breast and crooned to him in wordless singsong, the melody as familiar as her scent and her body, though he knew he'd never experienced either.

He was absorbed into her, filling her even as she opened him up and filled the vast darkness inside of him with white-hot light. This was what it meant to be accepted, to be loved. For one brief flicker in time, he knew life. Then, like an ember winking out and going cold, it was gone. And yet he was still being pulled downward, into her, into the earth, his cock still hard but encased in ice, the coldness penetrating every opening of his body, his being. It hurt, oh but it hurt, and the pain was all the more shocking because it was so unexpected. This was not how it was supposed to be, this was not the king claiming his throne. This was rejection, anarchy, rebellion.

He cried out, tried to pull away to look at her. Around them, the gypsies had shrunk in number, consumed and melted by the fire. Those that remained were bestial and wild in their need, tearing at flesh, flinging themselves into the flames, shrieking as they went, down, down, into the depths and the darkness, doing it for her. Always for her. He raised himself on his hands, staring into the white light of her eyes that was spreading across her face, the glow so bright it was like looking into the sun. He arched up, his gaze shifting down their bodies, his consumed by hers, gone into a darkness that pulsed and hummed at the juncture of her thighs, expanding to take him in, draw him down. White light above, blackness below, he could no longer feel the pulse between his thighs, could no longer control the thrust of his hips. He was slipping down into her, the white light beckoning as strongly as the darkness he knew so well.

"Look at me, Magic Man," she whispered, though her

mouth was gone, absorbed by the light. "Look at me, know me. We are one."

He wanted to deny it, but the truth thrummed in the veins he had left, the ones that were now entangled with her, a part of her existence, her essence. He looked at her, where her face had been, stared at her, though it hurt his eyes. Watched the white light spread, downward, downward, until the place where they joined had gone from darkness to light and his body, what had once been the body he claimed, was now pure white light, engulfing him like the flames took the few remaining members of their death party.

"You," he said, as if that answered it all. Perhaps it did.

He should have known her reputation was the most real thing of all about this night. He should have heeded the warning that crept along his skin like bugs seeking warmth. She was different, special, his match. At last. A wolf in sheep's clothing, this one, but he had been careless in his pursuit, smug in his victory. He was not the victor here. He was the final victim of a mass sacrifice in the name of light and earth.

All that is good comes at a price. All that is light has consumed the darkness and been made stronger for it. He crossed the threshold and was devoured, her name on his lips like all the rest as they sunk down, down, down into the warm earth. Victorious Vivi. Virtuous Vivi. Valiant Vivi. Vivi, the giver of life, the keeper of souls, the mother of all. Vivi.

Verily.

651.4
Cha

Second Look

author: Heidi Champa

category: Office Services

subject:
1. Pearl Buttons   2. Sign Language
3. Unlikely Love

Second Look

Heidi Champa

"Jon, I don't have time for this right now."

"Let me guess, you've got a million things to do, you're busy and you have to go. I know. I've heard it a thousand times. You know, Jules, someday I'm going to get tired of hearing it."

"Jon, what do you want me to do? It's my job."

"Nothing. Don't do anything Jules. At least now, I know where I stand."

I heard the click and the line go dead, my mouth still open, ready to retort. He hung up on me. I put down the receiver, pinching the bridge of my nose in irritation. How often could two people have the same argument? Ever since the merger, Jon and I fought nonstop. Nothing seemed to placate him. The latest argument made my head ache, the pain shooting through the back of my brain and down my neck. I reached into my desk drawer and fished out more pain reliever. Just as I pulled the cap free, I saw Keith round the corner and walk down the hall. He paused when he saw me, leaning in the doorway with a concerned look on his face. His hands started moving and I forced my brain to kick into gear, trying to read his words through the pulsing pain in my head. He was so sweet, always looking out for me.

"Not again? Jules, how many of those are you up to a day?"

His too-long brown hair hung in his eyes, no matter how many times he pushed it aside. Every time he brushed the strands behind his ear, the hearing aids that were mostly hidden by his shaggy locks came into view. I managed a weak smile, flexing my hands in a vain attempt to make my signs less rusty. I had learned to sign years ago, but hadn't used it much until Keith came into my life. My fingers began to move, but each gesture made my hands hurt even more. He could read lips, but I always signed, too. Even when it was the last thing my head could take.

"I don't even know. Isn't that sad?"

"Don't tell me. Jon's at it again?"

"I can't get it through his head how important this stuff is. He just hung up on me. I give up."

"Don't do that. You're great at what you do, and he should realize how important it is to you. He's not worth it. No man is worth this many headaches. You should be with someone who appreciates you."

"I know you're right."

I looked at him, like I had so many times before. The slope of his nose was too severe. His eyes, while a pretty blue, were a bit too close together. His height advantage over me was a mere inch. But he was sweet and loyal and one of the best workers to come from the merger all those months ago. At first, I was skeptical of the new people in the office, but Keith stood out. He actually had a sense of humor. Most of the newbies had come and gone. Some had been laid off due to cutbacks and the rest quit over policy complaints. Keith hung on and now was a valuable member of the staff. Plus, he brought donuts every Friday. That alone made him invaluable to me.

He gave me one last smile before shuffling away down the hall. The tail of his dress shirt stuck out of his pants; his shoes were worn out and unpolished. I shook my head, comforted by the fact that some things in my life hadn't changed. Since the first day he walked into the office, Keith was exactly the same.

As the time ticked down to five o'clock, I dreaded going home to my apartment, and to Jon. The last thing I felt like doing after a long day was fight. He hadn't called back after hanging up on me, and I refused to call him. I picked up my purse, but put it right back down again. My feet seemed nailed to the floor. Keith strolled by, his briefcase partly open and overflowing with folders. A trail of rumpled papers followed him down the hall. I followed him out into the hall and tapped his shoulder. He spun around quickly, finally noticing the mess he'd made.

"Keith, you're leaving a few things behind."

"God, I'm sorry. I guess I have a bit too much in here."

"You know, we gave you a desk here for a reason. You don't have to take so much work home. Trust me; it will all be waiting for you tomorrow."

"I was just trying to get ahead. Clearly, it's not working."

He sat down in my office, stuffing the papers into his briefcase, which was now closed but bulging. He stared at me, giving me a puzzled look before he spoke. As much as I wanted to look at his hands, I found myself sneaking glances at his face.

"I thought you'd be gone by now. What are you still doing here? It's not like you to hang around after five."

"The truth is I don't really want to go home. I can't face another fight."

"Why don't we go and have dinner? It will keep you out of the house for a while."

I looked up at him; his expectant smile melted my heart a little. He really was a sweet guy. I wished, for the millionth time, that Jon was more like him.

"Thanks for the offer, but I might as well get it over with. I'll see you tomorrow."

"Sure, no problem. It was just a thought. Have a good night. If you need anything, you know where to find me."

Keith shuffled down the hall with a wave. I sighed as I picked up my bag, resigned to my fate. As I headed down in the elevator, my phone buzzed. Apparently Jon didn't want to wait until I got home to fight.

Nearly two weeks had gone by since the breakup. Jon was almost completely out of my life and my apartment. I had avoided telling everyone, our busy work schedule making my secret a lot easier to keep. But people were starting to notice the change in my demeanor. One person in particular.

My door had been closed all day, but I saw Keith walk by at least a half a dozen times. Finally, I got tired of seeing him wearing a hole in the carpet and motioned for him to come in. He pushed the door open tentatively, his eyes filled with concern and what looked like fear. It was as if he was afraid I'd break if he said the wrong thing. He sat down, his hands gripping the arms of the chair. I just stared, waiting for him to say something. His hands left the chair and raised slowly, his signs so familiar I could almost guess them before he started.

"So, how are you Jules?"

"I'm fine, Keith. Thanks for asking. How are you?"

He sat back in the chair, clearly not believing me.

"You don't look fine."

"Is that a nice way of saying I look like hell today?"

"No. God, no. I just mean, you seem upset. Not just today either. You haven't been yourself in a while. You're not even eating the donuts anymore. I was wondering if something happened with Jon."

He spelled out Jon's name, his expression angry and sour. He made it clear how he felt, and I couldn't blame him.

"That depends. If you consider fighting for days followed by a protracted breakup something, then yeah. Something happened."

"God, Jules. I'm sorry."

"Don't be. It was a long time coming."

"Still. Hey, if you need to beg out of the overtime tonight, I understand."

"No. I'll be here. I just have to run home and let the dog out. By that, I mean I have to get my key back from Jon. He's picking up the rest of his stuff tonight."

Keith looked like he wanted to say something more, but he didn't. Reaching for the door handle, he smiled sheepishly as he walked out. He turned to me one last time, before he left. I looked up and felt my stomach flip as he spoke again.

"I'll leave you alone, Jules."

"Thanks, Keith."

I pulled into the parking garage, feeling strangely empowered. Jon had tried to turn a simple exchange of things into a nightmare. But I refused to let him get to me. It took every ounce of strength I had not to give into his baiting. He left befuddled and angry, but I got to leave peaceful and calm. I walked into work with a lightness I had been missing for the last two weeks. When the elevator opened, the floor was all but dark, the quiet cut only by the hum of computers and fans. The only light that was on was coming from my office, but it seemed dark and distant. No one was around. There were no fingers clacking keyboards, no phones ringing off the hook. Something was definitely up. Slowly, I made my way through the dark, until I reached my door. I stopped dead in my tracks from shock.

The whole office was illuminated by candles, flickering from every shelf. Music rang out from the tinny speakers attached to my computer. And, in the middle of it all stood Keith. His hair sliding down his forehead as he held out a single rose to me. The whole thing seemed out of a storybook, and I couldn't help but chuckle as I looked around. I took the rose, but set it down so I could ask him the one question that was burning in my mind.

"Keith, what is all this?"

"I wanted to cheer you up. I thought you might need it after dealing with Jon tonight."

"That's very sweet, but it actually went just fine. Is that really the only reason you did this?"

He stepped closer to me, his stiff body relaxing a bit. His hands were close to my face, his movements smaller than usual.

"All right, I admit it. I have my own selfish motives. I was trying to find the perfect way to tell you that I like you. Is it too much?"

Surveying the scene, I couldn't help but nod. He dropped his hands, looking dejected and sad. I immediately regretted my reaction.

"Keith, I mean, this is all very nice, but..."

"Stop saying I'm nice or sweet. I'm not as nice as I seem, you know."

"Keith, I didn't mean to insult you. It's just that you're not really my type. I like you a lot, but I just don't think we have any chemistry."

"No chemistry, huh?'

Keith took another two steps forward, his arms wrapping around my back before I could pull away. His face hovered right near mine. His eyes were filled with something I had never seen before. His hands dug into my lower back, grasping at my blouse with more force than I was used to. My body reacted before my brain could, my hips pushing forward against his. I felt my face grow hot, the proximity of his body to mine playing havoc with my senses. With him right in front of me, none of the little flaws I pounced on before seemed to matter. The fact that we saw eye to eye no longer bothered me, in fact it only made his piercing stare more potent. His hand slid up to the back of my neck, pulling gently on my hair. My mouth parted in a sigh, and he took advantage of my position and kissed me hard.

Never had a single kiss had such a profound effect on me. My body leaned against his for strength, his arms literally holding me up. When his tongue made its way into my mouth, I couldn't help but moan around it. Releasing me all too soon, he pulled back, still embracing me there in the dim light. His hands took on a whole new meaning, now that I had felt them on me.

"You know what, Jules, you're right. I don't feel a thing. Maybe we should just call it a night."

"That's not funny, Keith."

"I know. And, it wasn't very nice either."

I couldn't help but smile. His mouth dropped to my neck; the tug of his lips and teeth ripped a gasp from my throat. I clutched at Keith's shoulders as he continued kissing my throat, his fingers coolly moving the pearl buttons of my blouse through their holes. He pulled me toward my desk, pushing aside papers and files we were supposed to be working on. I perched on the edge, throwing my shirt across the room in haste. He stood between my legs, sliding his hands up my thighs. My bra was still on, my nipples hard and aching for his touch. I looked at him, his hands tentative for the first time. I reached for both of his hands and pulled them up to my chest but he stayed motionless. I smiled at him as I signed.

"It's okay, Keith. I want you to."

I urged his hands to move, my barely covered nipples slipping easily between his fingers. After a few seconds, he didn't need any more guidance. The fire he set off between my legs shocked me, my body reacting quicker than it ever had before. Reaching behind me, I flicked open my bra, Keith moving his hands long enough to let the flimsy fabric drop. I watched his face, his mouth slightly open, his eyes shining. As his thumbs ran over my tight, hard nipples we both gasped in stereo and I noticed his hard cock pressing into the zipper of his black pants. Wrapping my legs around his hips, I started yanking at his shirt. His hands dropped to the button on my pants. He moved slowly, too slowly. I got his attention and said the only thing I could think of.

"Keith, don't be nice."

Pulling me from the desk, he turned me quickly, forcing my hands down onto the fake wood surface. There would be no more talking for a while. He slipped my shoes off, and I heard them softly thud on the carpet. Yanking my pants and underwear past my ankles, he pushed me forward, spreading my legs apart. As his fingers teased my swollen lips, his tongue ran up the back of my thigh, meandering all over the place, but not the one place I wanted. Finally, Keith's tongue hit me right in the hot spot, his tongue thrusting into my wet, open pussy. His fingers played with my clit, strumming it in a steady rhythm. I was practically screaming, pushing my hips back against his face. I could feel my orgasm bubbling up inside me, the pressure of his fingers almost too much. Suddenly he stopped, turning me back toward him. His pants were sliding down his legs, his impressive cock standing tall from his body.

It looked too good not to suck. Sliding to my knees, I wrapped my lips around the full, flushed head. Keith whispered out my name, the first time I'd heard his voice in so long. His hands, the usual form his voice took, caressed my head. My mind swam, every sense full of the new, sexy Keith. I had been so oblivious to him and all that he was. But no more. Grabbing his ass, I pulled him deeper into my mouth. But he didn't let me stay in control for long. He pulled me to my feet, his hands fervent as he made a request.

"I want you, Jules."

I sat back on my desk and fished in my top drawer for a moment until I found what I was looking for. He stepped toward me and I took him in hand, slowly sliding the condom down his cock. He guided himself inside me, sliding easily into my cunt as I put my legs around his back. His hands cradled my ass, pulling me to him, keeping me close. My teeth pulled at his bottom lip as I whimpered and moaned into his mouth. He swirled his hips as he fucked me, my clit bumping against his pelvis with each stroke. It was enough to tease me, but not enough to push me over the edge. He moved quickly one minute, the next slow and deliberate. I couldn't resist looking between us and watching him pump in and out of me. Reaching down, I rubbed my clit, moving two fingers in small circles. I tightened my legs around him, knowing I wouldn't last much longer. Keith moved his hands to my face, our eyes locked as I let my pleasure wash over me. I fought the urge to close my eyes, coming hard as he thrust into me over and over. Finally, he broke the stare, his head nuzzling into my neck as his own orgasm ripped through him. I felt him pulse inside me, his body going slack against me.

When he finally looked at me, I couldn't help but smile. His transformation was complete. The old Keith I knew, the reliable, sweet coworker, was gone. He had been replaced by the man standing before me, the man who gave me more pleasure than I had ever known. I smoothed back his wayward brown hair so I could kiss his sweaty forehead. His hands told me everything I needed to know.

"So, Jules. Would you call that chemistry?"

"No, Keith. I'd call that sweet."

306.7
Jay

Taped

author: Kay Jaybee

category: Kink

subject:
1. Floral Van   2. Living Mattress
3. Special Order

Taped

Kay Jaybee

Flinging the back doors of his transit van wide open, Ryan called to his girlfriend as she unlocked the industrial-sized greenhouse where they worked. "Are you still up for helping me do the deliveries today, Beth?"

"Sure am." Beth began to box up some plants ready for loading.

Ryan's lips curved up suggestively as he took the first tray of flowerpots from her outstretched hands. "Good. A bit of company could be fun."

Beth couldn't help but smile back when she saw the mischievous glint in his mahogany eyes. "No need to look so excited, I'm only going to be carrying boxes of flowers in and out of your van."

The *That's what you think*, stare Ryan gave her in reply sent a mild stirring of unease tripping down Beth's spine.

Holding Beth's gaze, Ryan picked up three thick blankets. "You can start by helping me lay these blankets on the van floor."

The memory of the fantasy Ryan had shared with her the

night before, as they'd rolled around, limbs entangled, on his king-sized bed, suddenly loomed large in Beth's mind. "You aren't serious?"

Not sure she wanted to hear Ryan answer her question, Beth busied herself with wrapping extra strips of bubble-wrap around the bases of the flowerpots, giving herself time to remember how to breathe properly. She knew precisely what that dangerously sexy expression on Ryan's face could mean.

Two months ago, while walking along a beach, he'd shared a seafront fucking fantasy with her. The next minute Beth had been on her hands and knees, her lover's beautiful cock easing in and out of her, while her nub was tickled with the tip of a hermit-crab shell. The memory of how scared she'd been of someone spotting them while they rutted in the sand, and how aroused the thought of discovery had made her, sent quivers of confused longing through Beth's chest. The look he'd given her then, and the one Ryan was giving her now, were almost identical.

"You know I'm serious."

Trying and failing to keep her voice as steady, Beth protested further. "But we can't! The chances of being spotted are huge!"

Carrying on as if Beth hadn't spoken, Ryan layered the rugs over the metal floor. "You said the same thing when I stripped you in your kitchen window and flicked your nipples until you came. You went all paranoid about your neighbors spotting you, but you didn't move away."

"I was scared stiff they'd see! I would've had to move house."

"Rubbish. You're gorgeous; they would have enjoyed the view."

Beth's chest tightened at the thought of how Ryan's rough gardener's hands had reduced her clothing to nothing but her oversized shirt in seconds. He'd even managed to thread her bra through her sleeves without removing her top. All the time, her head had nagged at her that it was insane, but she'd been too caught up in pleasure to stop him, even though her heavy chest had been on show to anyone who happened to be passing.

"You are an exhibitionist, Bethany Parker, and don't you forget it!"

"I am not!" Beth felt strangely indignant, especially as she had a horrible feeling that Ryan was right.

Satisfied with the placement of the blankets, Ryan began to secure the trays of plants to be delivered into the special crates strapped against the van's right side.

Beth swallowed. Ryan usually balanced his crates on either side of the van. Today he was leaving one side free.

When the last tray was in place, the space on the left side of the van's floor remained horribly obvious. Beth didn't dare ask why. Her eyes frantically scanned the greenhouse in case there was a pile of compost sacks ready to put on, to balance out the van's load. There were none.

The lack of conversation between them was beginning to get to her, and Beth finally braved the question she'd been afraid to ask. "What goes there?"

"You already know the answer to that."

Taking a step away from the van, Beth nervously wiped some soil from her hands. "Come off it, Ryan, that was just a fuck-time fantasy."

Her boyfriend didn't answer, but continued to double-check that the stack of plants was secure and wouldn't fall in transit. Then, brushing past Beth as if she wasn't there, he picked something off his workbench.

"Oh good grief, I haven't seen one of those for years! Where did you get it?" Beth felt her unease drop a fraction as she stroked the old black cassette recorder he was holding with nostalgia.

"I've had this since I was a child." Ryan popped open the

tape holder. "I used it all the time, poor thing had a right bat-tering." Slotting in a worn-looking blank cassette, he snapped the lid shut.

Thinking that perhaps he'd just been teasing her with the whole fantasy thing, Beth began to breathe more easily, un-til Ryan carried the antiquated machine into the back of the van. She watched in fascinated horror as he took two lengths of extra-strong packing tape and used them to stick the cassette recorder into place on the floor next to the plants.

"What's that for? You'll never hear anything from it in the front of the van."

"It's obvious isn't it?"

"Obvious? I know you've lost your iPod, but does that thing even still work?"

"It does indeed. I want it there so that I don't miss any of the noises you are going to make. As I'll be in the cab and you'll be in the back, I'm bound to miss out on hearing some of your lovely moans and groans. I figured we could listen to the tape together later."

Beth's mouth opened and closed as her boyfriend strode to-ward her. Engulfing her in his arms, Ryan soon had his lips on hers, eating her protests away before they had the chance to escape from her mouth.

The night before, she'd been able to picture every moment of Ryan's fantasy as they'd playfully discussed it. Now she could see the possibility of it right before her—with the addition of a tape recorder.

"You'll love it." He spoke softly in her ear.

Beth said nothing. She knew he was right, but she wished he wasn't.

"I will keep you safe."

"How? I'm bound to be seen!" She raised her voice, half in panic, half because she realized by asking the question she had just agreed to go through with this. Suddenly, every nerve in her body felt as if it was attached to a piece of string that was being sharply tugged toward her twitching crotch.

Cupping her face, Ryan tucked Beth's chestnut hair behind her ears. "Don't worry babe, I love you, and I will protect you. Any entertainment we might provide for others is just a delicious bonus."

Beth's stomach did an internal backflip. He'd really thought this through. She was barely whispering as she asked, "But how?"

Ryan returned to his bench. A heavy-weave fabric ground sheet sat neatly folded. "We'll use this." He lifted it up by one of the short ends, and flapped it open.

"Oh my god!" Beth stared at the doctored sheet before her. Three rectangles had been cut out of it in salient places; if this had originally featured in his erotic dream, he had neglected to tell her.

"Anyone who might catch a glimpse of you won't know who you are. Now, get undressed." Ryan spoke as if refusal was not an option, but Beth couldn't move. Her feet felt as if someone had super-glued her to the floor.

Reaching out a hand, Ryan cupped Beth's groin through her jeans. Her sigh gave her away. "I know you want to. You know you want to. Let's just get you into position before I'm late for my rounds."

Beth's fingers came to her shirt buttons. She fumbled clumsily, struggling with the small white fastenings as her hands shook. The memory of the climax she'd had when Ryan had told her how his fantasy went made every fiber of her being buzz with erotic expectation. "But what if...?"

Ryan cut her off. "I told you, I'll be very careful. Just get undressed, baby."

Her clothes fell to the dusty floor. It wasn't cold, but Beth shivered anyway.

Ryan's expression spoke more about his approval of her

naked body than any amount of words would have managed. Taking her hand, he helped a turned-on but trembling Beth into the back of the van, without failing to notice the slight glisten that had started to form at the top of her thighs.

Lying down, her back to the mattress of rugs, Beth's hands felt restless at her sides. Even though her knowledge of the fantasy meant she knew it was coming, the zip of the packing reel made her heart drum faster. Then without a word, Ryan taped her right wrist down onto the top rug, before repeating the move over her left wrist, and then over each ankle.

With a lingering look into the lustful yet uneasy hazel eyes of his girlfriend, Ryan threw the prepared sheet over her, lining up the holes, so that her tits, pussy, and mouth were all on show, but her face was carefully hidden. He then climbed up next to Beth, pressed RECORD on the tape player, and retreated before he gave up on his plan and jumped directly on top of her instead.

The shake and noise of the engine as Ryan switched on the ignition reverberated through Beth. The stale compost-smelling air of the van's interior rippled over the rectangles of exposed flesh as she lay, unable to move.

Even though her mouth was free, the heavy cloth over her body, and the sensation of being captured in the confined space of the van sent a wave of claustrophobia over Beth, and she found she had to concentrate on breathing. She wondered if the sound of her loud rasping breaths would be audible when Ryan played the recording back later.

There was an abrupt jerk, and Beth yelped as the van began to move. As its speed crept up, Beth's fingertips gripped into the rugs beneath her. The sensation of swaying from side to side and yet being kept perfectly still made Beth feel as if she was on some sort of kinky roller coaster. As Ryan took a corner, the flower pots, rocking in their stacks, showered a fine rain of loose soil onto her, its dampness adding to her arousal as it spotted her chest with muddy freckles.

Desperate for the van to stop moving, but nervous about what Ryan would do when it did, Beth's imagination went into overdrive. *How is he going to get the plants out without anyone seeing me? What will happen if someone does see me? Will Ryan let him touch me? Will Ryan fuck me in the van like in his dream?*

As she continued to think, Beth's chest swelled to fill up more of the cutout rectangle. The edges of the doctored hole chafed at the tender undersides of her breasts, and Beth couldn't stop thinking how good it would be when Ryan kissed her sore flesh better.

Even though the sheet prevented her from seeing, Beth's eyes were open. Each time she blinked her eyelashes scraped on her shroud, a sensation that would normally have been annoying, but at that moment was simply an insubstantial touch against her naked body.

As the surface beneath the wheels changed from smooth tarmac to rough gravel, Beth's ample tits wobbled, and her body vibrated with the engine. Even in her disorientated state Beth knew that they must have turned into a garden center's driveway.

When the van finally came to a stop, the stillness and quiet after the noise and jostling of the motor felt almost spooky. Beth couldn't begin to think what the tape recorder might have picked up as they'd traveled. Perspiration dotted her body, making the sheet cling to her, and the sticky surface of the parcel tape that tethered her began to itch. Beth didn't care about that though. Every inch of her was tense, frozen; waiting for the moment when the back doors of the van opened.

The slam of the driver's door sent an extra dose of uncertain desire through Beth. *Is Ryan really going to open the doors while other people are about and act as if I'm not there at all? In his fantasy he did, but surely in reality he wouldn't risk losing his business just so he gets the thrill of letting others see how far his girlfriend would go for him?*

Ryan was talking to someone outside. Beth thought she heard the name Ian, which meant they were at the Summertown Garden Center. Hoping Ryan had parked at the back entrance where the deliveries were supposed to take place and hadn't just pulled up by the public entrance, Beth totally failed to relax. Of all the people they could have met today, Ian had to have been on the top of her *I hope he isn't working today* list.

She'd seen the way Ian ogled her when she was fully clothed. What he'd make of her like this Beth didn't even want to guess. He was so sure of himself, so cocky and—a treacherous voice at the back of her head reminded her—so fit!

Beth found herself slipping into fantasy mode. She couldn't stop herself from wondering what it would be like to have Ian's hands on her chest as she lay there. *After all, I couldn't do anything about it could I, so Ryan could hardly complain...*

The laughter of the men from outside, and the rush of air that flooded across her body as a back door opened, bought Beth back to reality. Clamping her mouth closed, trying to make her breathing as quiet as possible, Beth squeezed her eyes shut. She was fairly sure Ryan had only opened one of the van's back doors, as the draft from outside was stroking her side rather than stroking her pussy, so for now at least, she wasn't on public show.

"You wanted six dozen trays of violas and twenty-four individual giant geraniums?"

The voice that replied to Ryan's order check was definitely Ian's. "Sure do, mate. Plus the special order if it's still on offer?"

Special order?

"It is, I sorted it specially, but we'll leave it until the end if that's okay."

Ian's laugh was deeper as he replied, "I'll look forward to that."

Beth went hot from top to toe. She wasn't sure how she

didn't cry out and give herself away as the stacks of plants were untied, and then passed to Ian's waiting arms. It was only when she heard Ryan call, "One more tray and we're empty," that the nerve-heated perspiration on her body turned abruptly to cold sweat.

If the van was already empty, that meant this was the only garden center they were visiting today. If Ryan was going to do anything to her, it was going to be here. And if Beth had gauged the tone of Ian's laugh correctly, the special order wasn't a plant at all. It had to be her. Which meant Ian had known this was going to happen before she had.

Caught between shame at how easily she'd allowed Ryan to put her in this position, and confusion at the fact that, in spite of the knowledge, her body felt inflamed and extremely aroused at the idea of more than just Ryan's hands falling on her, Beth's throat turned bone dry.

Beth tried to remember precisely what Ryan had said during his fantasy talk last night. He'd mentioned hands running all over her as she lay, taped in the bed of his van, like a living mattress. At the time she'd assumed he'd meant *his* hands. Now she thought differently.

The unloading had finished, and Beth was aware that the voices outside the van had faded away. The door was still open, but she wasn't sure if there was anybody there. Her legs were beginning to feel cramped from being strapped in one place for so long, but she was too scared to flex them and risk being seen. Straining her ears, convinced she was alone, Beth risked a slight roll of her neck. Her movement made the sheet above caress her flesh, causing her to sigh far louder than she intended to.

"I'm not sure that sigh was loud enough to be picked up by my old tape recorder, baby." Ryan's voice made her jump. "When I come to play the cassette back to you later on, I think it would be nice if there were more interesting noises to listen to, don't you?"

Beth was too busy thinking to reply. *Are we alone, or is Ian still there?*

"I asked you a question." Ryan's tone was firm, and this time Beth found herself answering.

"Yes, Ryan."

"Good girl." With the plants gone, there was room next to Beth, and she felt the van rock as someone climbed into the van and sat by her head. It was Ryan. "I can't tell you how amazing you look."

His hand came to Beth's stomach, smoothing the sheet over her. The frustration of the cotton's presence between her and the touch she longed for was overwhelming, and Beth failed to hold in a groan. "That's more like it, baby. Nothing like a grunt of frustration from a bitch in heat, all hot and ready to be serviced."

Beth's pussy rippled with lust as she recalled him saying those very words to her the night before. They hadn't seemed strange then, just sexy as he'd share his erotic dreams. Now they really meant something. She felt every bit his bitch, and Beth couldn't have denied the heat if she'd wanted to as warm cunt juice flowed from her.

The other back door opened. "I promised no one would see you to the extent where you could be recognized, didn't I?"

"Yes, Ryan." Beth's mind raced. She knew Ian was looking at her, and wondered if his dick was stiff, and what he was thinking.

"I didn't say I wouldn't let anyone else touch you though, did I?"

She swallowed carefully, her reply barely audible, "No, Ryan."

"Louder for the tape!"

"No, Ryan!" Beth shouted, biting back the temptation to tell them to get on with it. If someone didn't touch her chest soon she was going to explode.

"That's better. Now, I have a lovely surprise for you." The van rocked again as someone else clambered inside. "I can see from your nipples how keen you are to have a good seeing to, and so I've asked a friend to help out. If you're good and make lots of lovely sounds, I'll let him touch you wherever you ask him to. If you don't ask for something, it won't happen." Ryan bent down and kissed his girlfriend's mouth through the hole, before adding, "The louder you are, the more fun you'll get, baby."

Beth found herself pulling at her tethered wrists and ankles, desperate to be able to touch her companions, but the tape was industrial strength, and she had no chance of escape. Then, suddenly, she was pinned further in place by a body sitting astride her legs. Beth could picture Ian staring straight down at her neatly trimmed pussy.

She lay there waiting for his next move, imagining Ryan's cock trapped, flagpole like, inside his work clothes, but nothing happened.

Impatient, Ryan snapped, "If you don't speak soon, then I'll take you home again without so much as a finger being laid upon you."

Beth licked her lips and, her need for a fuck greater than her self-consciousness, cautiously said, "Suck my tits."

A foreign mouth was over her right teat in less than a second. An agile tongue lapped over and around her nipple, making her groan, and her left teat feel poorly neglected.

Already bolder, she added, "Touch my other side as well." Again the response was instant, and Beth felt infused with a combination of physical relief and ever-growing desire.

Now it was her nub that felt left out, and she yelled out, "Finger my pussy!"

The mouth came away from her right nipple, and a hand dived to the lower opening in the sheet. Beth's voice became huskier as her unseen lover swirled and flicked his fingers over her nub. Still it wasn't enough. "Stick a finger inside me!"

Her silent suitor did just that, his slim digit at once blissful and yet unsatisfyingly narrow as it pumped in and out of her.

Feeling utterly wanton, revelling in her role as the object of Ryan's voyeuristic pleasure, Beth hoped her boyfriend was enjoying watching another man service her. Raising her hips, she begged for a second finger to be added to the first. Even though her request was instantly granted, she craved more. She needed to feel a dick in her mouth, to be kissed on every part of her flesh. She was long past caring if she was recognized or not. Ian knew she was Ryan's girlfriend anyway, so he must realize she was the one beneath the sheet. In a haze of lust, Beth started to call out for everything to happen to her at once.

"Pinch my tits, let me suck your cock, lick my clit, kiss me and FUCK ME!"

In that moment life became a whir of sensation. In less than ten seconds, Beth found a shaft between her lips, hands molding her breasts and fingers tugging at her nipples as if her handler was seeing if they might be detachable. As her moans of ecstasy escaped louder and louder from the corner of her full mouth, her requests granted, a tongue came to her clit, and Beth's butt began to lift again, this time in her urgency to thrust more of her mound toward the face that was lapping at her.

She deliberately became noisier still, slurping and growling against the length down her throat, confident now that with each fresh sound she made she would get more rewards.

Gasping, Beth suddenly pulled back her head, resting the taut muscles of her neck that had been lifted to give the blow job properly, and virtually screamed, "Get that cock between my legs NOW!"

The rip of a condom packet being opened ricocheted around the van as the man that had been in her mouth headed south. "Oh no you don't, you stay here," she called out, "There's two of you in here. I want one of you in my mouth, and one of you in my cunt. Do it! And make sure you touch my clit at the same time!"

Never had she felt so full. The penis plunged back down her throat so hard she nearly gagged, while the man between her legs pumped like a thing possessed, his fingers dancing over her snatch. His comrade, who Beth imagined on all fours over her gobbling face, rubbed the tips of her teats until they felt as if they had been hot-wired.

Her climax, which had been building ever since Ryan had parked his van, erupted within her with a force that took her breath away. With a primeval howl from her semi-gagged lips, Beth's body jackknifed until she collapsed exhausted against the soft rugs.

The cock in her mouth withdrew, and Beth could hear the spatter of spunk over the sheet, while the pronounced shudder and bitten-back groan of Ryan as he orgasmed informed her that it had been her boyfriend's dick wedged so beautifully within her channel.

Two hours later, Beth listened in shock. The voice of the woman on the tape was so certain, so secure in the knowledge of what she wanted, and so loud. "That can't be me yelling like that!"

Ryan, his naked body pressed against hers, brought his lips to the sore patches on her wrists where the packing tape had been ripped away. Kissing her, he murmured, "It most certainly is you, baby. I could listen to you giving orders like that all day."

Beth still couldn't believe she'd let Ryan do that to her. She asked, almost shyly, "Did he enjoy it, the other guy?"

"You do ask some stupid questions!" Ryan laughed as he tickled a finger over her chest.

"I was so wrapped up in how I was feeling; I didn't even know which cock belonged to you toward the end!" Beth spoke as if in disbelieving awe of her own behavior. "I was surprised you chose Ian to help you though, seeing how full of himself he is. You don't think he'll tell people do you?"

Ryan looked confused. "Ian? He only collected the plants. He was long gone before the action started."

Beth frowned. "But, I thought...what about the special order? Who was it then?"

"The special order was some seedlings Ian's been after for ages; I had them in the cab. My helper was someone you don't know, and who doesn't know you. I promised I'd protect you, keep you safe and keep you anonymous."

Beth smiled with relief, nuzzling into Ryan's neck.

"But now I know you're the brazen hussy I always thought you were." Ryan's eyes shone. "I might well get Ian to help me out next time..."

Lauren's Journey

D. L. King

The *Perspicacity* would be delivering colonists and equipment to a new home in the Alpha Centauri system. All things considered, in the great vastness of the universe, the trip wasn't all that long. At just under light speed, the journey would take a little over five years. It was, however, long enough to place the precious human cargo in stasis. The amount of energy needed to manufacture life support and artificial gravity for spaces large enough to accommodate the 500 colonists, not to mention storage space for the food required, would be staggering. That's why they always put the passengers to sleep shortly after leaving Earth.

Leah Malone, the ship's captain, along with two other crew members and Rajit Harrison, the ship's doctor, and two med techs would make the journey awake. Leah would be able to pilot the ship, should anything happen to the AI. She and her crew would also keep an eye on the systems and make any necessary repairs. Rajit's job was to monitor life support and to see to the colonists' general health and well-being. It was also the doctor and his assistants' job to place the passengers in stasis and to wake them up a few weeks from their destination.

Psychologists had long since discovered that the human psyche fared better during long space flights if people were allowed a brief period of adjustment to being in space and to their fellow passengers before being put to sleep. Allowing for a waking period before arriving at their destination was also beneficial.

The colonists were healthy young adults. Emigrating to another star system had been their choice and they had jumped through hoops to get this posting. They had filled out applications, participated in several interviews and been subjected to many and varied medical tests before being chosen. Intellectually, they knew how the trip would work. They knew they would be spending the majority of their time asleep. Most of them had never been in space before and had no personal point of reference as to what the next five years would be like.

After takeoff the passengers spent some time exploring the common areas of the ship and began the task of getting to know one another. After dinner the first night out, Dr. Harrison called everyone to the Great Hall to explain stasis and answer questions.

"As you know, you will all spend close to five years in stasis. You will be housed and cared for all together in the passenger hangar. General life support and artificial gravity will be shut off everywhere in the ship except the bridge and living quarters of the few of us remaining awake, in order to save energy reserves. Let me assure you that I will be keeping careful watch on your monitors in my office and I will spend at least five hours every day in the passenger hangar, seeing to each of you personally."

"Now, in order to keep your muscles from atrophying, they will be constantly stimulated and exercised. When you are awakened, you should exhibit no ill effects from your weightless confinement. You may actually be in better shape than when you went to sleep."

A young woman toward the front of the auditorium raised her hand. "Doctor, will we be aware? I guess what I mean is will we dream?"

"Although I have never experienced stasis personally, I have been told by other travelers that they do dream. They say their dreams are very vivid and become their reality while they are asleep. The dreams tend to be centered around their body's activity."

A man in back said, "It's a little scary, isn't it; to dream for five years. What if the dream becomes a nightmare?"

"I'll be monitoring your brain waves and I will be able to tell if you become agitated. Don't worry, in that case I'll guide you into something more pleasant. I'll be meeting with each of you privately, to get a sense of what makes you happy and what frightens or upsets you so that I can vary the activity. I haven't had any complaints yet.

"Because there are so many of you, I'll be putting you to sleep one at a time, over the course of about a month. A random order of your names was generated and put on the lists, posted outside the hall. Mail has been sent to you, in your quarters, giving you the date and time you should report to me for your presleep consultation. Office appointments will begin tomorrow. About a month after that, you'll begin your sleep journey. I'll give you the date and time to report to the passenger prep room for your consultation. In the meantime, enjoy the ship and each other's company."

Lauren thought about her consultation as she got ready to meet Dr. Harrison in the prep area. Who would have ever thought the prospect of going to sleep for five years would be exciting, but here she was, excited. She had received her message the day before, telling her not to eat anything twelve hours before preparation.

Dr. Harrison had begun by asking her what kinds of exercise she preferred. Was she a runner? Did she like to swim, play tennis, lift weights? She had told him she liked swimming, rock climbing and skiing. Then he had asked what she found sexually stimulating. She was a little taken aback by the question. He assured her that whatever she said would remain confidential. He told her she would find her dreams more fulfilling if she could be honest about her sexual proclivities with him.

He explained that she would be stimulated sexually while she slept. Every muscle in her body needed to be stimulated and exercised, and as time wore on, this exercise would need to be more and more constant.

The longer the body remained weightless, the more exercise it needed to be able to function in Earth-type gravity. This is why long periods in space before the advent of artificial gravity had been so dangerous. Astronauts were unable to exercise as much as was necessary and still get any work done. Some people came back from flights lasting several years and needed the same amount of time just to recuperate back on Earth. Some even ended up with their muscles so badly atrophied that they never regained use of them again.

He explained that all her involuntary systems would continue to work, but the rest of her muscles would need to be maintained through exercise. That included her vaginal muscles, her colorectal muscles, her sphincter, everything. He said he could stimulate these muscles for her and she would derive some pleasure from it, but psychologists had discovered people were happier and enjoyed their sleep periods more when they were stimulated sexually, allowing their own bodies to create the exercise these particular muscles needed.

She thought about her discussion with Dr. Harrison as she hurried through the ship, making her way to the passenger preparation area. She had already become slightly aroused by the time she arrived.

Dr. Harrison greeted her then asked when she had eaten last. Satisfied with her answer, he led her to another, smaller room.

"You'll be wearing a tight-fitting suit and it must make good contact in order to work properly so we need to remove all your body hair, or at least the hair below your neck. This cabinet will remove the hair with sound waves."

He opened the doors to a small box-like cabinet and Lauren saw a stool inside.

"Now, if you'll remove all your clothing, you can step inside and have a seat on the stool."

She sat down and he closed the doors around her neck, leaving her head sticking out of the top. As he flipped a switch, she felt a tingling sensation, which built in intensity and quickly cycled back down to nothing. The whole process was finished in less than two minutes.

Dr. Harrison opened the doors, and as she stepped out, the first thing she noticed was her missing pubic hair. That was a shock. She couldn't help touching herself. Her mons felt so smooth. She noticed the doctor waiting for her and began to blush.

"That's all right. Practically everyone has the same reaction. Now, if you'll follow me into the next room," he said. "Have a seat in the chair and put your feet in the stirrups. I'll be giving you a douche and an enema."

Lauren noticed that the seat was horseshoe shaped. When she sat down, only her legs made contact with the chair. She put her feet in the stirrups and the doctor strapped them in and spread her legs apart. After placing a basin underneath her and donning gloves, the doctor opened her labia and inserted a nozzle. He opened a clamp, allowing the liquid to flow inside her. It was body temperature and felt good. She felt a steady stream of fluid running out of her body as more entered her. He removed the nozzle and let the rest of the liquid run out of her into the basin below, then blotted her dry.

"I'm going to tilt the chair back now, Lauren. Don't worry, you won't fall. You'll be lying flat on your back."

He pushed a button and she felt the chair begin to tilt backward. She held on to the armrests until it stopped, then found it was more comfortable to put her arms across her chest, just under her breasts. She found it a little disconcerting to be lying on her back with her legs apart and her feet up in the air. As she was thinking this, she felt a lubricated finger prodding her anus.

"I'm going to give you an enema, Lauren, then put a device inside you to keep the solution in while I take Jim Carson to his place in the hangar."

She felt his lubricated finger enter her then withdraw to be replaced by a nozzle pressed against her anus. It slid inside her, and she felt the liquid begin to fill her bowels. The doctor continued to talk to her while working.

"You may have noticed he was the passenger right before you on the list. Well, it's like an assembly line around here. He's just been through the same thing you are doing now, minus the douche, of course."

She felt the doctor remove the nozzle from her rear end and slide something else inside. Her nipples had gotten hard from all the attention. She realized that she was becoming aroused from the doctor's ministrations. She hoped he hadn't noticed; it was embarrassing. At least he hadn't said anything.

"I've just put a small plug in your anus to keep the solution inside while I get Mr. Carson situated. I'll be back in about fifteen minutes. Just relax."

As he left the room, she felt the pressure of the fluid in her abdomen but it wasn't uncomfortable. Her hands went instinctively to her pubic area. She explored the clean, smooth, hairless skin. Her stroking and gentle prodding was beginning to get her hot. She let her fingers delve between her lips and explore her moist slit. As she touched her clit, she felt her juices begin to flow more copiously.

Lauren hadn't planned on this. She had only wanted to feel her hairless mound, but now she couldn't stop herself. She brought one hand up to her breast and began to alternately pull and rub her already hard nipple. Although it had started out lazily, the finger rubbing against the side of her clit had picked up speed. Her nipple play now matched in speed. She felt herself climbing up to the edge, as her breathing became shallow and rhythmic.

The climax rolled over her like a wave. When the quaking subsided, she opened her eyes to find Dr. Harrison smiling down at her. She froze, and a blush suffused her entire body.

"Don't worry about it," he said. "It's normal. Just about everyone does that while waiting for me to come back. I'm going to bring your chair back to an upright position and help you to the bathroom."

Lauren held on to the armrests as the chair slowly brought her to a sitting position. Dr. Harrison removed the straps from her feet and lowered them to the ground. He took her hand, helped her up and walked her to the bathroom. He placed her hand on the plug.

"Just sit on the toilet and pull out the plug. You can leave it in the sink. When you're finished, I'll be waiting outside."

After cleaning herself up, she returned to where Dr. Harrison was waiting.

"Just follow me. Your suit is waiting by your station," he said as he led her into the passenger hangar.

The site was overwhelming even though there were only about a hundred people, as yet, in stasis. The room was large and the stations were situated closely together. People wearing tight black bodysuits were lying prone in midair, suspended in slings about three feet off the ground. Wires and cables, attached to the suits, were gathered together and plugged into several towers throughout the room.

Even though artificial gravity and life support were still on and would remain on until the last passenger was put to sleep, she could see a lot of movement. Feet were being flexed, arms and legs were being bent and heads were being rotated on necks. Occasionally, she heard gentle noises coming from the sleepers.

They stopped at an empty station. A suit had been placed over a cart by the sling. She noticed some devices on the cart. The aforementioned Jim Carson was in the neighboring sling. Jim, unlike the other passengers, appeared to be lost in the throes of a rather intense orgasm. She could see his cock straining against the fabric of his suit and his hips were pumping up and down as much as his sling would allow. His fingers were grasping, his legs were stiff and his toes were pointed. He was breathing hard and she could see his pulse pounding in his neck. She turned to Dr. Harrison to ask what was going on but before she could say anything, he started to explain.

"It's the suit, you see," he said. "He's just getting used to it. The suit, itself, is very stimulating. You'll understand when you put it on. Because he was aroused while he was still awake, the suit is bringing him to climax. Climaxing just after one loses consciousness seems to put people into the most relaxed state possible. It also starts their dream off with a bang, so to speak."

He unzipped the suit and held it open for Lauren to see. There were wires and thin metal plates everywhere. There were also concentric silicone rings on either side of the chest. The suit interior looked a little like a computer chip. She reached for it.

"First there are appliances that must be installed," he said as he draped the suit over the cart again.

Dr. Harrison donned a pair of gloves and began to spread lubricant on a large black plug he picked up from the cart.

"Okay, Lauren, turn around with your back to me, spread your legs, bend over and put your hands on your knees. I'm going to insert a plug into your anus and then another into your vagina. No, no, don't worry, you'll like it, you'll see," he said soothingly as she started to tremble.

He spoke reassuringly to her, telling her to take deep breaths, as he deftly inserted the anal plug. Nerves had gotten the best of her but once the plug was in, she relaxed.

"Let me put the vaginal plug in, and then you can stand up. After that, there's one last appliance to install before we can start putting you into your suit."

There wasn't any need for lubrication, as Lauren was already quite wet. She sighed as he inserted the remaining plug into her opening. With a hand against the small of her back and against her upper chest, he helped her stand up and turned her around. She was smiling and her eyes were half closed.

"See, I told you it would be enjoyable. I think you're really going to like this next piece." He held up an item shaped like a large flattened arrowhead. One side was smooth and flat, but the other side had a small cup cut into it. He knelt down in front of her and with his lubricated, gloved finger between her labia, he began stimulating her clitoris. She gasped and started breathing erratically. When her clit was erect, he placed the shield over it. Her clit just fit inside the cup. He smoothed her labial lips back over the shield to help hold it in place.

He helped her put her feet into the suit then smoothed the tight material over her legs. As he pulled it up over her buttocks, she could feel both plugs lock into ports in the suit. She placed her arms in the sleeves, and Dr. Harrison pulled the suit up over her back.

"I've just got two more pieces for your breasts," he said.

He showed her two more shields. They were small. Only enough material to cover her nipples and areolae. They also had cups cut into them. He put lubricant inside the cups and used his lubed fingers to stimulate her nipples. When they were hard, he placed the shields over them, fitting her erect nipples into the cups, and then closed the front of the suit and zipped it up, keeping everything in place.

Lauren felt a bit antsy. The stimulation was constant, but not intense enough to cause an orgasm. Dr. Harrison adjusted the sling around her body. She barely realized what was happening when suddenly she felt her feet leave the floor as her body was placed in a prone position in the air. She felt completely supported. When she had first seen the other passengers suspended in slings, she wondered how it would feel. Surprisingly, it was extremely comfortable.

She could feel him plugging wires and cables into the back of the suit. Cables were attached to the anal and vaginal ports, where they protruded from the suit. He plugged more wires into the front of the suit, including a cable over the clitoral shield and a cable over each breast shield.

The first piece to wake was the clitoral shield. She felt the cup grip her clit and begin massaging it. A surprised yip came out of her mouth. She felt the anal plug undulating inside her. Soon the vaginal plug began the same undulation. She felt muscular contractions building in her anus and rectum as well as her vagina as she began rocking her hips back and forth. She felt the nipple shields grip her erect nipples and begin squeezing them gently while the silicone rings on the inside of the suit began to knead her breasts.

"Oh, wow," she murmured as her body began to buck.

Dr. Harrison stood beside her, smiling. "I'm going to put you to sleep now, Lauren. Sweet dreams."

398.4 **A Perverted Fairy Tale**
Bin
author: Emily Bingham

category: Fairy Tales

subject:
1. Little Red Riding Hood 2. Wolf
3. Wicked Intent

A Perverted Fairy Tale

Emily Bingham

Little Red skipped to the outskirts of town in her short gingham dress, delighting in the red-and-white pattern that hugged the womanly curves of her buxom breasts and shapely behind. It matched her hair and danced in the breeze, floating just above her kneesocks and Mary Janes. As her walking took her farther from the village she tired of the wind making hurricanes of the abundant waves about her face and took a set of sateen ribbons from her pocket to tame her locks. She put one flopping braid on each side of her head and began to skip her way into the woods feeling the braids sway in time to her steps.

The woods were dark and it was rumored evil beasts resided here, but Little Red hadn't a passing hint of fear; the darkness fascinated her. Secretly she hoped to find one particular creature she had heard thrived in these enchanted woods. Wearing such an irresistibly impish outfit, she knew she could lure him out of hiding. She did love an adventure.

Breathing hard from her long journey, she sat on a nearby flat rock to rest. She leaned back, sunning herself in the beams of light that pierced through the trees. Popping open the first button of her thin dress she realized how nice the warmth felt on her skin. Little did she know that in the nearest burst of bushes her dangerous visitor already watched.

It had big eyes gleaming with wickedly growing intent. It was strong and powerful. The hypnotic intonations of its speech could lull and elicit desire from anything that crossed its path. These spells were especially useful on scrumptious women like the one it was gazing upon. Thankfully for Little Red, the voyeur was, however, powerless in the light of day. Darkness was the only time it could leave the shadows. The full moon made it even more dangerous. He was, though, a patient Wolf and had every intention of getting his paws on this red-haired morsel.

Drooling, he watched as Little Red fingered open several more buttons on her dress, exposing her delicate neck and chest to the sun. He noticed new freckles appear on her white skin as she rolled about on the rock deep in sleep. By the time the sun was tracing the edge of the horizon and Little Red was grinning her way through the end of a dream, the Wolf was shivering in anticipation. He counted the moments on his claws until he could leave the thick grove of trees and make his way to the lady in the sunny clearing. The deepening shadows were already strengthening him.

He watched as the pools of blackness spread across the rock Little Red lay upon. Dusk first tickled the edge of her stocking toes—her shoes long since tossed aside in the dirt—then it moved up her strong legs. The dark also played across the pale bit of thigh peeking between the edge of her socks and the lace of her crinoline. The Wolf tongued his jowls at the sight, suddenly hungry and thirsty at once. Soon the shadows puddled together so that only Little Red's hair was kissed by daylight. The angle and color of the setting sun cast an extra crimson shade to her long braided locks.

Now the Wolf left the protection of the trees to get a closer look, savoring the scent of flesh as he shortened the distance between them. She would be dinner eventually, but first he would play. It had been too long since he had come across something this lovely. The stray lumberjack or farm animal that he was accustomed to were nothing but food to fill his belly; this girl was a treat. He wanted this to last.

Proceeding in silence, the Wolf tiptoed to Little Red's sleeping rock. He waited until the moon took over the sky to get close enough to disturb her slumber. He blew hot mouthfuls of rancid meat-flavored bursts over her neck, the earthy musk of her sweat making him dizzy. It wasn't long before the tickle of his breath began to wake her.

Still wrapped in the fog of sleep, she thought herself at home in her room being roused by the family dog and instinctively reached out to pet the Wolf's tangled coat. This was going to be easier than he had imagined; she already had a fondness for his kind, and was all too happy to stroke the harmless dog lost in the forest.

It took all of his self-control to stifle a toothy grin and not reveal himself as something other than an ordinary wolf. He delighted in her first moment of heart-quickening surprise when she was jolted fully conscious. Humans were such a joy to toy with. Her realization that she had awoken outdoors far from home, alone with her hand near a strange creature was priceless.

She curled her knees to her chest and slid on her behind to the farthest edge of the rock, falsely comforted by the space between them. He remained still, enjoying her fear. The concern in her wide eyes sent bolts of electric lust through him. He breathed in deeply the smell of what he thought was fear, savoring the beauty of this moment, his control over her. From here he also had the benefit of the view her folded legs afforded him.

Her skirts hung so loosely she might have purposely done

nothing to cover her thin linen bloomers. He assumed that thinking only of the danger she was in, Little Red had momentarily forgotten her modesty, which suited the Wolf just fine. He had a perfect view through the fabric as it clung to her sun-moistened skin. Each fold of her flesh was outlined in nearly transparent cloth, hinting at the intricacies hidden between her legs.

The Wolf stiffened at the sight. As he looked into the sky he became aware that Little Red and her tempting underthings were not the only reason his skin was tingling electric. He was going to have to act quickly. Though he wanted to hear her scream and beg, first he wanted to gain her trust. If she saw what was about to happen the shrieking would begin far too early.

The Wolf glanced at the full moon again, before creeping closer to Little Red. She was braver than he would have expected, not letting out a peep as he laid his chin on the rock next to her. She smiled, taken in by his puppyish behavior. Before she could contemplate reaching out to touch his head, however, she met his orange eyes. In an instant her lids became heavy and she was seemingly unable to look away. Her limbs relaxed, causing her legs, suddenly heavy as stone, to fall out straight in front of her limp body.

He began soothing her without speaking a word, communicating using only his thoughts. These powers came in handy at times like these, since humans didn't ordinarily understand wolf speak. He explained to her that soon he would change out of his wolf suit and she wasn't to be afraid, that she should trust him because he was a kind wolf. She nodded her understanding.

With the task of subduing her complete, he fell to the ground, moaning and howling the primal belly-rattling noise of an animal evolving into something more. He stared into the glowing orb in the sky and felt himself change in a series of convulsions he could do nothing to control. When he was done flailing about in the dirt he was as much man as he was wolf. It felt good to rise on two legs, naked except for the abundant dark hair covering him. Thankfully he still had possession of his claws and sharp teeth, in addition to this half-man body, which he was going to enjoy putting to use. It was the best of both worlds.

The Wolf reached to cup Little Red's chin in his hand, pulling her face to look in his direction. It was then that Little Red appeared to take in the waking dream she found herself in. A statuesque naked man stood over her. And though she had no idea where she was or how long she had slept she wasn't the least bit anxious; instead she was incredibly turned on. She examined the man standing before her and smiled up at him playfully.

"Hello little girl," the Wolf sneered in his man voice. "What might your name be?"

She didn't respond so he decided to call her Red. He snorted in a heady dose of her smell, reading the simple human needs on her scent. With as much mock compassion as he could muster, the Wolf inquired if Red was hungry. Slowly Red lifted her shoulders as if she were the wrong person to ask. It was then that the Wolf remembered he hadn't given her permission to speak. He sighed deeply at this oversight before realizing the game would be much more exhilarating this way.

"I know how to remedy that. Come with me and we'll find you some dinner." He reached out his paw-like hand and beckoned her off the rock to follow him.

Little Red let him pull her up onto her shaky legs. Forgetting her Mary Janes, she walked in stocking feet behind the Wolf, barely able to keep up. He led her deeper into the woods, trees engulfing them and snapping at her bare arms as they passed. The Wolf waited until they were a distance from the clearing before he stopped.

Dense trees surrounded them; there were no sounds save those of insects and smaller creatures that didn't have the good sense to scamper in the other direction. No one and no thing would hear them in this place.

The Wolf watched as Red's eyes strove in vain to focus in the darkness; eventually she gave up and tightened her grasp on his arm. He grinned as Red pressed her warm body against his, her scratchy dress brushing roughly across his naked skin, causing his prick to harden. If only she knew he was the thing in the forest she should be most afraid of, perhaps she wouldn't have been so eager to get closer to him.

"That bush over there straight ahead has the best berries in the woods." The Wolf pulled his arms from her grasp to point in front of them, knowing full well she couldn't tell one bush from another in the dark. This was just as well as there wasn't a bush, tree or picnic basket in the forest with anything edible to humans.

He watched with glee as Little Red's hunger overtook her and she let go of the Wolf to grope her way forward. Arms stretched ridiculously in front of her, Little Red tried to feel her way to the promise of food. Vines scratched at her arms as she pawed at bushes, hoping to feel something she recognized as fruit but finding none. Thinking she had reached for the wrong plant she pouted then continued feeling at others.

The Wolf watched from a safe distance, drooling at her struggle and the scent of her blood in the air where thorns had cut into her soft white skin. But above that, another scent crossed his palate: a stronger, demanding scent. He allowed a paw to wander down his body and stroke his hardness, savoring the moment, this calm before his evil fantasies came to fruition. He waited until she was kneeling in the bushes, her behind swaying out from under her red-and-white dress, practically presenting itself to him. He couldn't imagine controlling himself any longer.

The bushes Little Red had been rooting around in made a perfect cushion for her face, as he took one of her braids in each hand and forced her onto the ground. The smell radiating off of her was almost overpowering, permeating their surroundings until he became breathless. His actions seemed beyond his own instincts. With her cheek lying against the cool earthen padding, arms folded beneath her at an odd angle, she made such a pretty picture. It was nearly too easy to have his way with her.

And so he did. Her thin underthings offered no resistance; he wrenched them from her body in one rapid swipe, expecting Little Red to protest. In the next movement he brought the torn garments to his nose to sniff them greedily, stiffening even further at the intimate, earthy scent of her before tossing them to the ground.

He fumbled next with her petticoats and crinoline, eager to finally get past the layers humans insisted upon wearing, until he got to the parts of her that interested him—that seemed to direct him. She was a sight with all the fabric around her shoulders and nothing but her exposed bum framed in front of him. Her frenzied half-untied hair he continued to use as a handle. The misplaced clothing also conveniently worked to confuse Little Red, who couldn't seem to figure out how to dislodge herself from the situation or her frock. He quickly dismissed the suspicious idea that perhaps she was merely putting on a show for his benefit; he was too excited to contemplate such ridiculous things. Never would such a beauty freely give herself to him.

Finally he could no longer deal with the anticipation. His rock-hard staff was inches away from her hole. Her only response to his inevitable penetration of her was a small noise that the Wolf mistook for distress but was in fact quite the opposite. It was hard to tell if it was of acquiescence or discomfort, but he of course assumed the latter. However, Little Red's enthusiastic grunting perked his ears.

Half of him was disappointed with his decision to keep her under his trance and he assumed that the fighting and screaming would be in abundance soon enough. Now, however, he would be a total fool not to revel in the simple pleasure of having his way with her.

While pounding into her, he thought briefly about keeping her around awhile, extending the game a couple of days before he made her into dinner, of course. He could drag her to his cave and listen to her enchanting voice as she cooed and begged, all the while using her however he wished. It was a lovely idea to consider. In reality he knew that as soon as the moon left the sky what little self-control he maintained would leave him along with his half-man body. In the daylight, when he was back to being fully wolf, Red wouldn't stand a chance.

With this strange notion newly solidified in his mind, the Wolf threw himself fully into the mindless abandon of having Red. The way the Wolf pounded into her tiny frame it was a wonder he hadn't yet split her in half. Women weren't exactly built to accommodate wolves under the influence of the full moon. This only further added to his fun.

Grabbing at her hips, leaving dirty claw marks imprinted against her skin, while animal howls and grunts escaped his throat, his greedy lust took over for his body and brain. The Wolf panted and thrashed against the pliable, rag-doll body of Red. He lashed at the remains of her shredded crinoline, pulling it from around her waist with a tortured final snap. Without that tulle barrier blocking the way the Wolf was allowed his first view of Red's face since he had begun fucking her.

Her hair was no longer bound but splayed out at all angles in chaotic tangles around her head. When he stopped howling into the voyeuristic sky he could hear her making noises into the trampled ground. Addicted to the rush of power her stuttering breath created within him, he wanted a closer audience to any sounds that were desperate enough to escape through the bindings of the trance she was in. Such lovely music were the cries from her parted lips. Grasping a thick tangle of her red locks, he tugged her head back from the ground so that he was now looking at the side of her face and hearing her no longer muffled grunts. She was a ravaged mess of mud from the grassy rut where her head had lain and her tears or drool—he couldn't tell which—had mixed with the earth to make a disheveled mess of her. The strange mumblings, the sweaty sheen on her forehead despite the chilly air, and her hopelessly sullied body excited him to near bursting.

Before he allowed himself that release, he took more of her hair in his other hand and forced her head back farther still to pull her tiny frame into an impossible arch to study her while he fucked her. Though he thought it impossible, this new angle allowed the Wolf to force himself even farther into her body. Into that space of her cunt no decent lass would allow anyone to enter. Overcome, he felt himself thrusting so deep and so hard into Red that he was forcing her open in the deepest, tightest, most forbidden limits of her body. That was when he allowed himself release, spasming messily into her.

Accustomed to conflict rather than calm after such exertions, he chose this moment to break the trance he thought she was still under. He wasn't just a beast to be teased, after all. Red would have to face her consequences. He breathed hard against her back, feeling himself soften inside her but only momentarily; the immediate recollection of what had just occurred made him stiff again. When he had a good grip of her head and could see the strain in her face from the tightness of his hold, he knew this was the perfect time to wake her fully.

He was rather logically expecting any manner of screaming, begging or crying, particularly looking forward to any variation on the words *no, please, stop,* or *you horrible beast!* Any or all of them, in any combination. This is what he was accustomed to hearing. In anticipation he tightened his grip on her hair.

So the Wolf was more than a little surprised when Red calmly turned her eyes to him, and said as plainly as if asking his name, "Silly Wolf, why did you stop? I was just starting to enjoy myself."

His shock jolted him into dropping his hold on her, giving her a chance to rise up on her hands and turn her head fully to him so that she could enjoy the wide-eyed and aghast expression on his face. His look was pained, as if she was the one who had just finished roughly having her way with him.

It was almost a shame to ruin his plan, but he deserved the jolt. Over were his days of taking advantage of women who were foolish or naive enough to wander into his realm in the dark. He had met his equal this time. Red knew all about this dark creature and had sought out the Wolf whose ravenous appetite matched her own.

After a full minute of her looking back at him, the Wolf still seemed to be struggling to make sense of the situation. He was so focused on his usual course of things that he had no clue what to do. She hadn't fought back. She wanted to be used? This was absolutely unheard of.

Red tried to get him to snap out of it and continue where he left off. As they were still connected at the hips, she moved hers against him hoping to suggest that he carry on the rhythm of his thrusts. Even with the confused look on his snout she couldn't help but notice he was still firm inside her, yet he continued to pitifully rest against her, unmoving.

It was then that she remembered she had just now made the mistake of making eye contact with the Wolf. Poor thing, it was embarrassing how much more powerful her magic was. He ran around thinking he was the king of the forest, so powerful, so scary, so dangerous, so fierce. In reality she didn't need any of his boring old mumbo jumbo to create a trance. Recently she had gotten so talented she could just look at someone with the intent of silencing him and it was done. She was still getting accustomed to it.

She was also bright enough to know where to find the Wolf and protect herself easily from his lame hypnotic suggestions. The sweet, innocent girl lost in the woods act was just a lure, and it had worked perfectly. He had never suspected, so full of lust that he hadn't bothered to notice the alluring smell of trickery wafting off of her the entire time.

She had been quite lucid and enjoyed every thrilling moment of his game. Red couldn't quite decide what part she liked the most; the experience of fornicating with a magical creature or beating the Wolf at his own insidious game.

She looked over her shoulder at the Wolf again, careful this time not to make eye contact. "Well, if you aren't going to fuck me I'll have to do it myself."

Red lifted herself off of his rod and crawled away from him a bit, pitying him just enough to give a show as she straightened herself out as much as was necessary, taming the stray hair that had been tickling her face and spitting out the grass she had been chewing to muffle her pleasure. When she was done, Little Red pushed him over with the touch of one finger. She watched him fall from a kneeling position to lying supine and vulnerable on the ground. It would have been comical to watch if it hadn't been so easy.

She was talented but the trance she had put him in held no element of control over his stiff member, which continued to point up at the sky. Red had to admit she was impressed with his contribution. Grinning, she threw a leg over, straddling his midsection, and slowly eased her way onto his cock.

Taking her time to ease every little bit of him in, she lifted herself all the way up again before she started the long journey in the other direction, never fully allowing him to penetrate her and careful to never totally stop touching him. She did this over and over again patiently, never changing her speed or rhythm, continuing to tease him, enjoying his grunts of frustration.

When Red suddenly broke the routine and drove herself onto his cock until it was in her to his full extent the Wolf realized how much trouble he was in. She was bucking around on his member in a manner that made him concerned that she might break him in half with her enthusiasm. Instead of worry, however, all he felt was lust more all-consuming than anything he had experienced before. He watched her thrash with her long hair occasionally coming to rest over her face, making a lush curtain over her features.

The last bits of her gingham dress were filthy and falling over one of her freckled shoulders exposing part of her ample breast with her bouncing motions, though her areola never managed to break free into his view. The Wolf was suddenly very sorry he hadn't torn the dress from her body when he had the chance.

Under the weight of her rocking mechanizations the Wolf managed to break his gaze away from her to notice the ever-brightening sky. It would only be a matter of moments before the sun broke, the clouds retreated and the formerly black nook in the forest where they lay was pierced by a new day. The power of her young agile thighs engulfed him, pressing hard against each of his legs, holding him down and grinding his back ever farther into the ground.

He alternately looked at the sky brightening and at her in awe, wild haired, eyes closed, gasping as she rocked in a primal, ageless rhythm. So beautiful. So dangerous. So be it if she should be the last thing he saw before losing his man-body or perhaps losing his life altogether.

Dawn began to settle in as the Wolf realized he had never bothered to test the boundaries of the rules set for him when he began his life in the dark and otherworldly woods. He had no idea who would be in more trouble when the sun fully appeared. Red, who would find a none-too-patient Wolf locked in her loins, or him, melting in the sunlight.

When she opened her eyes fully and focused them on his, her grin made him think she knew exactly what was about to happen.

629.2
Max   **The Skilled Technician**

    author: Kate Maxwell

    category: Maintenance and Repair

    subject:
      1. Muff   2. Snatch   3. Bearded Clam

The Skilled Technician

Kate Maxwell

Confiding in her therapist Laura postulated, "I think I'm a woman of extremes...I've gone from celibate to sex addict in the span of three months. Seriously, it's all I think about anymore. I find myself fantasizing all day long about a good fuck. Usually the thoughts kind of hop around inside my head, but if I actually allow myself to focus on the fantasies, I'm literally in a lather within moments and ready to jump on the next guy I see. *This isn't me!* I never used to even think about sex. It was like I knew it existed for other people, but it just wasn't a part of my life anymore. A few months ago I didn't engage in sex at all, nor did I give it any thought. Now I do both. Like, all the time. I downright *fantasize* and find myself obsessing about getting laid, and then acting out those fantasies when I find a guy who interests me. And lots of guys interest me these days. Honestly, I don't even know who I am anymore."

The female therapist, in a rather clinical voice, asked, "Do you masturbate?"

Laura grinned, rolled her eyes and almost exasperatingly replied, "Uh, yeah! I have to relieve the pressure somehow!"

"Well, then you are handling things appropriately."

"Appropriately? I'm *way* out of control. See, you have to understand, this is not me. I'm not a nymphomaniac, or an animal, or some slut. I'm a good girl who doesn't do these things. I've never been like this before, and I'm not sure if I like being this way now"—Laura let out a sarcastic twist of a laugh and went on—"but I don't want to do what I have to do in order to stop."

"What do you feel must stop?"

"The sex!"

"And what do you feel you must do to stop it?"

Laura paused, thought for a moment, then answered honestly, "Go to confession, repent and pray that God will help me be strong enough to stop."

Expressionless, the therapist attempted to clarify things for her patient. "God gave us our natural sexual desires, Laura. Embracing what is natural is not wrong. It is what our bodies were made to do."

"My body wasn't made to go around fucking strangers."

The therapist tilted her head to one side in a gesture of significant thought, and said, "That is certainly an unsafe behavior, and one which I would not recommend to any of my patients. However, sexual activity is by no means unnatural or unhealthy. Sex is a biological need."

"It's *not* a need. It's definitely a desire, but no, it's not a need." Laura had been raised in a strict religious home and her upbringing showed.

"Laura," the therapist gently asked as she leaned forward in her chair, "do you think that you would be behaving like this now if you had not deprived yourself for so long?"

Laura was silenced as she considered this notion. Several moments went by before she was able to give an honest answer. "No."

Her therapist smiled gently at her and patted Laura on the knee. "You must free yourself to experience your own sexuality, and that is exactly what you are doing right now. Yes, your behavior is a bit extreme, but in time, after you have relieved your pent-up frustration and inhibitions, it will all even out and you'll be comfortable in your own sexual expression. This is an experimental phase of reawakening everything that you repressed since you split from your husband five years ago. Now let go, relax and enjoy the ride." With that the therapist winked at Laura, and the session was over.

An hour later, Laura was at the automotive repair shop adjacent to the shopping mall. Her car had been making an odd clanking noise every time she turned a corner, and since she took the entire afternoon off from work for her therapy session, it seemed like a good time to get it fixed and do a little shopping while she waited. After she'd explained the noise to the kid behind the counter, he suggested the mechanic take a test-drive with her to diagnose the problem. Although she was annoyed at the delay this posed to her trip to the mall, all aggravation abated when she got one look at the mechanic. He stood about six feet tall with dark and thick wavy hair, a scrumptious and well-trimmed matching goatee, solidly muscular arms and piercing green eyes the likes of which she had never seen before. His chiseled jawline and angular nose made him a near-perfect male specimen, and Laura was instantly attracted to him.

Her mind went into overdrive as she simultaneously carried on a normal conversation with the automotive repair professional, all the while entertaining fantasies about the numerous ways she wanted to fuck him. He asked her questions like, How often do you hear the noise? And, When was the last time your car was serviced? Although she answered appropriately, her mind was racing with questions of her own such as, How big is that cock? What would one of those thick fingers feel like inside my pussy? Or, even better, What would that tongue be like lapping at my clit? With such important questions on her mind, it was difficult to focus on her vehicle's service history.

Moments later they were both inside her car, she in the passenger seat while he drove. There was something indescribably magnetic about him, and she sat there silently drinking in his masculine presence.

She wanted him.

No, she had to have him.

She wanted to rip into his shirt and run her hands over his bare chest, push him down in the seat, then unzip his pants and play with his cock. Numerous glances at his crotch indicated there was something very nice hidden within, but these glances only served to fuel her curiosity. What would he do if she leaned over and reached into his pants for a nice feel of what he had? Would he be offended? Frightened? Disgusted? Or would it turn him on and drive him into the same wild frenzy to which she was rapidly escalating?

He drove her car down the service road that wound back behind the mall while she gazed at every part of his body. His manly scent filled the interior of her car and intoxicated her as the fantasies played out in her mind, one after another. She visualized taking charge of him and mounting his cock like a ravenous whore, thrusting her hips back and forth on top of him as his manly hands rubbed all over her body.

There was a nearly deserted side road coming up ahead, and she mentally debated whether or not she should ask him to turn down it. Almost too late, she gestured left and said, "Turn down there." With lightning fast reflexes he immediately did so.

Once they drove several yards down the wooded road, she asked him to stop the car. He glanced at her in a combined expression of confusion and curiosity, but he did exactly as she asked. As he moved the gearshift into PARK, Laura took particular note of the movement of his arm muscles that ran from his wrist to his elbow, and when he turned to face her she ran the fingers of her left hand up along his forearm, tracing those very same muscle lines.

Clearly a little surprised by this physical contact, he looked into her eyes and asked, "Yes?"

Laura smiled mischievously. "That's exactly what I want to hear from you."

"Yeah?" he asked. "What else do you want to hear from me?"

Laura shook her head. "Nothing."

The next instant she had her mouth up to his and their tongues were gently becoming acquainted with each other; warm and wet, they danced together inside the open mouths of the mechanic and the woman so newly awakened from her sexual coma. And awaken she had. Lust and arousal had now taken Laura to the point of no return, and her animal instincts took over.

Breathing more heavily, she maneuvered herself around so that she was kneeling in the seat and leaning over the object of her desire. She unbuttoned her blouse and the front snap of her bra, exposing her full and beautiful breasts to him. "Suck them," she commanded.

He looked up at her for an instant, smiled eagerly and immediately took the hard nipple of her left tit into his mouth. While his tongue playfully teased the one, his hand gently fondled and caressed the other. Laura tilted her head back and groaned with pleasure, which intensified to bliss, and at once she could feel the moisture welling up inside her pussy. Her panties were quickly soaked with all the juices of her arousal, and she hiked up her skirt to her hips, latched both thumbs on either side of the elastic band of her red lace underpants and pulled them downward. Consequently, the interior of her car now filled with the effervescent aroma of her profoundly wet and passionately worked-up, cavernous rosebud. *Hole. Vag. Pussy. Muff. Snatch. Cunt. Bearded clam.* All the terms she could think of for her vagina danced through her head like a series of primary flashcards for porn, and she giggled at the mental imagery it produced.

Startled, he asked, "What?"

She smiled down at him, dangled her panties in front of his face and asked, "Can you smell me?"

He put his nose directly into the crotch of her panties and inhaled purposefully, as if he were sampling the aroma of a fine cigar, and replied, "Yes, even better now. But I've been smelling you almost since the moment we got into your car."

Laura's mouth opened slightly in surprise. "Excuse me?"

Eyes twinkling, the mechanic repeated, "I'm serious. I could smell this sweet aroma within moments of getting inside the car."

Laura stuffed the scanty red lace undergarment into the mouth of her newly discovered favorite automotive technician, reached around to the side of the driver's seat, adjusted it to fully recline and pushed her hot play toy down to a prone position. He offered no resistance. Immediately she opened the fly of his pants and reached her hand inside, his muffled groan adding to her excitement. Buried in his checkerboard boxers was a thick and sizable cock growing larger by the moment. She released his manly appendage completely, leaned down and licked the soft head as she wrapped her hand around the base of the shaft. The bulging vein pulsated in her petite hand as she gently stroked up and down his ever-stiffening cock. It was hers to play with as she pleased, and she was enjoying every moment of it.

His hands were thick and strong as he massaged them up and down her arms and back. Then he began to undress her, removing her open blouse and bra, then her skirt, until she was fully naked in the car. Laura felt exhilarated in the knowledge that should anyone drive by, her real-life fuck fantasy in progress would be visible to all. It made her even hornier, if such a thing were possible, so she straddled him and mounted his swollen rod. Slowly pushing her wet and salacious pussy down every inch of his cock, she moaned from the base of her throat in ecstasy. His cock felt phenomenal sliding inside her, hitting every sensitive spot along the way and satisfying the ravenousness she felt within.

Arching her back, she thrust her hips back and forth, slowly at first, then a little faster. Her long hair swept across the base of her back, adding another element of sensual pleasure to the moment. With her eyes closed she shifted the rhythm of her hips to form small circular motions that intensified the stimulation to her clit. At the same time he took hold of both her nipples and started gently massaging them with his fingertips. Within seconds she felt the rush of an orgasm beginning to build up inside her, and she whimpered. As she continued to ride him the sensation intensified, and a moan vibrated deep within her throat. His cock, solidly stuffed inside her warm and creamy cavern, was a perfect fit that indulgently gratified her insatiable pussy and stimulated every sensitive point within it. Suddenly, Laura felt the consuming eruption of orgasm overtake her entire body, and she let out a groan that grew to an animalistic howl at the moment of climax.

As she drifted back down to earth from her intense, inner-body experience, she panted, "Oh damn, oh damn that was great."

She opened her eyes just in time to see her fuck toy remove the panties from his mouth. He smiled broadly and said, "Yes it was. But after tasting the delicious appetizer you so kindly shoved into my mouth, I'm going to have to have a taste of the entrée." He sat up, kissed her deeply and said, "Of course my challenge now is to create a repeat performance of the climax I just witnessed you enjoy." He shook his head ever so slightly, then added, "But I do enjoy a challenge."

With a contented murmur, Laura replied, "Oh, no. I don't think I can. I don't think I have it in me."

The mechanic chuckled while caressing her shoulders. "No woman who does what you just did is done this quickly. Relax, beautiful, and let me handle this one."

He gently returned her to the passenger's seat and put the driver's seat back into an upright position. "Get in the back seat, sweetie, and lie down."

Now Laura took direction from him and happily did as she was told. As she climbed in back and lay down, he walked around to the other side of the car and opened the back passenger-side door. He knelt down on the ground, grabbed hold of Laura's thighs and pulled her pussy up to meet his face as he buried it down into her.

First he teased her by softly running his nose and goatee up and down her lips, tantalizing her with the thrill of what was to come, then he lightly blew several little puffs of air over her groin and the sensation made Laura shudder with delight. Then she felt him plunge his tongue right onto her clit and he stroked it with several deep, long licks that made her pussy surge and swell with more of the sweet creaminess that had engulfed his cock moments before.

An instant later Laura felt him begin to explore inside of her with one finger, then another. He gently curled his middle finger upward and hit her pleasure spot with precision-like skill, causing great waves of euphoria to travel up and down Laura's body. She shuddered in response. Alternating his tongue and finger between her clit and pussy, the skilled technician brought her to the edge of climax, relaxed his maneuvering just enough to bring her back down and then repeated his handiwork. He continued to repeat his technique over and over again. His only goal was to tease her orgasm to the edge of existence, then force it to back off until it could grow into a cataclysmic, body-rocking event. And he was quite successful. When he finally allowed her to achieve the climax he had been manipulatively teasing for what felt to her like hours, her entire body became engulfed in spasms. She reached her arms above her and clenched the door panel just over her head, her feet curled downward and her body shook so hard the car rocked in place. The explosion she felt within herself was literally felt by every nerve ending in her body, and she reveled in the lingering ecstasy for several blissful moments.

Covered in a thin, glistening layer of sweat, her skin shimmered in the tree-dappled late afternoon sunlight that poured through the windows of her car. He gazed at her beautiful body, spent from the pleasure she had experienced, and when she finally came back down to earth, she opened her eyes to see him watching her.

"Wow. Incredible," was all she could say.

"Yes, you are," he replied with a smile.

Smiling back at him, she responded, "I believe it's your turn now."

He shook his head. "Can't right now. We've been gone way too long as it is, and I have to get back. But I want to do this again very soon. Sound good?"

"Sounds delightful, but it hardly seems fair that I've cum so hard twice now, and you haven't at all. How about a quick blow job? You've gotta still be hard."

He leaned into the car, kissed her as he retrieved her clothes from the front seat and handed them to her. "I'm pretty sure I'll be hard right up until we can get together again for another round of fun. But there's one thing I know for sure, and that's that it will totally be worth the wait."

Smiling at his little bit of flattery while buttoning her blouse, Laura paused, and then looked back at him. Nearly blushing, she asked, "Um, what's your name?"

The mechanic threw back his head and laughed heartily. "Haven't we already been formally introduced?" he teased her. He stretched out his hand to shake hers and said, "My name's Greg; it's nice to meet you."

823.0
Dus

Shades of Desire

author: Allen Dusk

category: Steampunk/Horror

subject:
1. Witchcraft   2. Spectral Fingering
3. Ionic Psyclonic Field Intensifier

Shades of Desire
Allen Dusk

Coal dust befouled the skies above the great cities, reducing the mighty sun to a red smear behind perpetual chestnut haze. Aspiring astronomers climbed the highest peaks or traveled far beyond the urban sprawl for sanitary glimpses of the heavens through polished lenses. Around them in the dense woods others also gazed skyward while dancing beneath the moon. These were the covens of witches, who had learned the cycles of the stars many millennia ago, before any steam-powered engine ever spun its gears.

An owl perched amidst the twisted limbs of a dying tree, a silhouette of bare flesh centered in its reflective stare. It hooted once, ruffled its feathers against the brisk night and watched the ceremony unfold.

Adora stood in the exact center of the pentacle traced with lines of salt. An obsidian rune dangled between her supple breasts from a hemp cord strung about her neck. Winds howled through rattling branches, but the air inside the protective circle stood still.

Her hair was perfect, parted straight down the middle, one

half stark white and dusted silver, the other half raven black and powdered cobalt blue. Lengthy bangs were held back from her face by bobbins of lace. Hours of tedious waxing ensured smooth caressing of pale flesh.

Biding time, she waited with her head tilted toward the heavens; patience was the only virtue ever learned through trials with the coven mothers. Fine scars from their lashings crisscrossed like fine lace across her bare bottom. No matter the depth of her concentration, her gifts never matured at the rate they'd desired. Then, soon after the *Fever* consumed her, everything changed. Aether bent at her whim, and the mothers concealed their fear when anger burned inside her eyes.

"Guardians of the Spirit Realm," she spoke loud with a hint of her old French accent. "When the witching hour rings true, bring my lover Alexandre back to me. Other souls may hear my call, but they are not welcome in this place. Only the one named Alexandre Malveaux, who has known my body more intimately than any other, may enter this sacred space."

Wormwood incense smoldered around her bare toes. The owl looked on in wait; Adora's chest rose and fell numerous times with her breath. She stood still, her patience waning.

Adora raised her arms; incandescent aether swirled about her fists. Her breasts heaved with a deep breath before she yelled into the night, "Oh, great and marvelous Guardians of the Spirit Realm, hear my plea! I have been a faithful servant, practicing my craft in ways only intended to please your will. I beg of you, on this anniversary of our proposal, that you bring Alexandre forth, so that I may kiss his lips, and feel his arms about me one last time."

Long shadows of curious spirits gathered around the circle, wondering who dared disrupt their slumber. To some blackened eyes her form was all too familiar.

"Please, I *beg* of you!" Frustration swirled in the centers of her crystal-blue eyes. "The fracture through my heart cracks deeper with every passing moment. I have asked for *nothing* in return while others use their gifts for only personal gain. After all these years of faithful devotion I fail to understand why my request is continually denied."

"Bring my lover forth, I *command* you, you stale shadows of grandeur passed!" Adora clapped her hands above her head. Rings of blinding light exploded outward from the circle. Shock waves scattered spirits, splintered trees, and blew the owl into a cloud of gore and feathers.

She searched for any vestige of her lover's form. Only the wake of destruction surrounded. Her lips jittered, tears misted her eyes, yet she refused to utter even a sob. Renewed burden weighed down her shoulders. She gathered her supplies, wrapped herself in a wolf-skin cloak and cantered into the night.

Adora twiddled her thumbs; her eyes traveled between vendors of the Barton Hill Marketplace. The poultry farmer sat on the edge of his wagon with his expression stretched long. He sighed twice in the same minute; a positive indication the morning had started slow. Even his crated chickens appeared bored. She needed a fresh flow of revenue after exhausting her savings on the airship venture out to the Crimean Battlegrounds. Perhaps a niche market would arise for her peculiar talents. She angled her sign to allow passersby a better read. FORTUNES TOLD, fancy letters proclaimed without listing a price.

Families passed in laughing groups. Lovers strolled by holding hands. Nobody offered her a second glance. Twice she caught herself glancing beside her to find only an absence within her shadow. Envy taunted with evil whispers, snickered how she'd die old and alone.

Muscles stiffened down her back. Steady pressure built in her bladder. The itch to stretch her legs persisted until she yielded, though there was the possibility of missing a potential customer. She slid her divining bowl beneath the table and cloaked it with a spell. She spun her sign to display the message, WILL RETURN IN 15 MINUTES.

Adora relieved herself, then wandered the market stalls to observe what others were selling, and to gather some goods on her shopping list. She was about to ask the price on a bushel of toadflax when a deep voice gained volume above the market chatter. Curious faces walked toward the crowd gathering in the center square.

"My miraculous Ionic Psyclonic Field Intensifier will not only soothe any aches, but I daresay many of my satisfied customers have reported that this amazing device also abolished the pox, diminished goiters and even mended a broken heart or two."

Adora waded past patrons for a closer view. A slender salesman wearing a stovepipe hat danced about a wooden stage folded out from a large-spoked wagon topped with billowing steam stacks. Electric lanterns flickered behind panes of colored glass. An automated calliope warbled in the rear. Long curls of waxed mustache jiggled over his smile as his narcotic gaze fixated on her location.

Warmth swept up Adora's neck; her nipples perked beneath her robes. She glanced at others around her, and when she looked back at the stage she found his eyes still glued upon her.

"Some have even described it as *witchcraft* in a box." A gold tooth gleamed in his grin while he raised a hand in a theatric gesture. "But I wouldn't let that discourage the God-fearing citizens of Barton Hill. What I have here is based on precision engineering, modern scientific advances and nothing more."

"Shenanigans!" An old lady booed. "I'll believe it when I see it."

Optimism twinkled in the salesman's eyes. "Step up here, and I'll prove to you that my device does indeed work as I have stated."

The old woman looked around, making certain she was the one being spoken to. She pointed a rickety finger at herself, and he rewarded her with a brief nod.

Men gathered around the woman to escort her toward the stage. Years of coal dust exposure had yellowed her spectacles. Her shoulders hunched over a broad crutch, which she leaned against during every hobble.

"What ails you, madame?" The man wound a lever on the side of a smooth copper cube measuring six inches square.

"A mule kick shattered my hip when I was forty-two, and I've been damn near disabled ever since."

"Mending bones?" The salesman laughed at the crowd. "A simple task for my miraculous Ionic Psyclonic Field Intensifier! Now, I need you to concentrate on your hip. Imagine the shards of bone, rearranging them as if you were assembling a puzzle."

Skepticism twisted her wrinkles. Reluctantly she pointed her eyes toward her hip.

"Focus my dear!" The salesman tapped the lone, smooth button centered on the lid. Vibrations from the cube trembled his hand. "This device will generate an electromagnetic field which will empower your body to heal itself."

Nonsense, Adora thought. *A simple potion would heal her hip in due time.* She examined every move the salesman made, anticipating the precise moment when he reached for the trick up his sleeve, or when the wig fell off the woman to reveal she was an actress in disguise. Her third sight peered into the aether amassed between their bodies, half-expecting nothing whatsoever.

Brilliant fractured rays of light swirling with rainbows radiated in every direction from the center of the cube.

She inspected the herd around her, reading only earthen-colored auras about them. Her sight reached farther out into the market, and made certain she was the only magical being around capable of viewing the unexplained scene unfolding across the astral plane. Her eyes darted back to the stage.

Silver tendrils stretched from the cube and wrapped themselves around the old lady's hips. A pain-stricken yelp bellowed from her. She stumbled backward, teetered against the edge of the stage. The crowd gawked silently, some patrons secretly wishing for her demise.

Vibrations ceased from the cube. Its colorful auras faded into filthy air. Slowly the old woman straitened her posture. She raised her leg while fighting not to grimace. Her scuffed boot twisted in circles; she wiggled her foot around.

"My God," the old woman gasped, sobbing immediately. "I can feel my toes." Her sobs evolved into high-pitched laughter. She danced about the stage and threw her cane out into the crowd. "I can *walk* again! I can't believe it."

The crowd erupted with cheering applause.

"How much is it?" somebody yelled.

"For you and everybody else here at the moment, I am offering this miracle of modern science for the unheard-of low price of only *five* shillings."

"That's less than a week's rent," somebody mumbled who stood beside Adora.

"I'll take one!" A hand flew up gripping exact coinage.

"Me too!" Other voices sang out in the crowd causing the salesman's smile to widen. He dashed about exchanging hard-earned currency for paper-wrapped enigmas.

Adora hadn't thought twice about buying anything frivolous in her life. Most of her wares she crafted by hand, her groceries never cost more than a few pence. Standing amidst the frenzied crowd she was overcome with the sudden urge to purchase a cube for herself. She reached for her coin purse and frowned at its light weight. Only a mere two shillings and a few pence jingled inside.

She returned to her table, exchanged many smiles, but nobody ever approached to learn their fortune. She held out until the last person waddled by with arms full of goods, and dusk's blood-red splotches stretched through murky gray. Slowly she gathered her belongings into her knapsack, hoping perhaps somebody would run up for a last-minute reading. She cinched her bag closed, waiting another bit longer.

Adora went out of her way to stroll through the market center on her path toward the exit. The crowds were gone; a group of young market hands swept their refuse into piles. The steam-driven wagon sat just where it had been before, its steam stacks cold, lights turned off, its stage folded away. She searched for a glimpse of the owner without getting too close.

"Can I help you, miss?" The salesman's bold voice spoke over her shoulder.

She jerked, screaming a bit from the startle. She turned and stared up at the man, whose hat and jacket were removed. Starch crisped the collar and seams of his white shirt. His presence all alone onstage had helped him appear tall, but standing this close she observed his height easily stretched near two meters. His slicked black hair was parted down the center, his waistcoat buttoned tightly over his broad chest.

Adora focused to read his aura and met resistance. *He knows what you're here for*, her intuition whispered.

"I'm very intrigued by that device of yours," she said smiling. "I witnessed your demonstration earlier, and still can't quite believe my eyes."

"Why yes, my Ionic Psyclonic Field Intensifier. I must admit it's quite a marvel of precision engineering." He flashed a grin that soon faded. "My apologies, madame. I'm Doctor Edward Vincent Ingram Longfellow, at your service."

"Adora," she said, her cheeks flushing.

"So, I can see by your expression that you have your doubts about my device."

"Anybody *can act* like a cripple one moment," she hesitated, not wanting to start a fight, then decided to continue anyway. "And walk perfectly fine another moment, especially when piles of shillings are on the line."

He chuckled, twirling the tip of his mustache with one hand. His teeth were perfectly aligned and a brilliant white. "I assure you it was no trick, only a feat enabled by modern technology."

"Well, I'd like to get my hands on one of those boxes of yours. Maybe I'll take it apart so I can learn how it really works."

"You're not the first person with that idea, but I would advise you against such action."

"Why is that?"

"The cases are assembled in a specially pressurized room by one of the finest watchmakers in Switzerland. Any tampering with the seal may throw its delicate parts out of alignment, thus distorting the field it creates. The results of such a careless action could turn disastrous."

"You're selling them to common folk for less than a pound. Surely something so sophisticated should carry a higher price?"

"That was merely a special one-time offer. The price has returned to its original five pounds. Surely a woman as well off as you could afford my regular price?"

"I don't have that much money on me." She bowed her head, ashamed of her dingy shoes. "I'm just very curious as to how it functions."

"It's quite simple, my dear." He wrapped a long arm over her shoulders. His other hand traced his talking points in the air. "There is a precisely tuned crystal secured inside, and through a series of my own patent-pending mechanisms, the device generates a field which intensifies the natural healing properties of the human body."

"Well, it all seems like flimflam to me. No offense, sir."

"My dear, Buddhist monks have used the power of meditation to perform healings for thousands of years." He nodded with a wink. "All I've developed is a mechanical process for harnessing that power and making it available to the masses."

"I see." Adora bit her lip. She knew all too well engaging in debate about magic versus science would only end with her temper lost. She'd already assembled the words to hex his hair away. Rather than utter them she pulled herself away. "Good day to you, sir."

"Wait." His firm hand grabbed her shoulder. "How much money *do* you have?"

"Not nearly enough."

"Possibly we can strike a deal then." His eyes gleamed over a wicked grin. His arm slithered around her shoulders as he whispered in her ear. "If you were to oblige a lonely traveler with a small favor, then in exchange I would provide you with one of my devices, completely free of charge, of course."

She should have walked away, but she'd approached the wagon already knowing full well in the back of her mind the extent that she would sacrifice to get her hands on one of his cubes.

"Of course." She forced a smile. Magic glimmered in her eyes. "Do you have someplace a little more discreet where we can conduct our transaction?"

"Why, yes I do."

The doctor led her through a door in the back of the wagon. After passing beneath calliope pipes they entered a small room with a humble bed and dresser built into the wall. Trinkets and photos from his world travels were tacked about in no certain order. Old vapors of smoke and sweat fouled the air.

"It's not much, but it's home for now," he said.

"This will do." Adora raised the hem of her robe and kneeled on the floor.

A bulge grew below her hands as she unfastened his trousers. His eager cock bobbed out, silently pleading for her affections. She stroked the shaft with one hand, fondled his balls with the other. She could care less if it was the biggest prick she'd ever seen, but the actress in her moaned with admiration. Her tongue swirled a slick coat of spit over her lips prior to sliding the doctor's cock into her mouth.

Memories of her dead lover rushed back to her. When last they made love they'd lain upon a blanket beneath a harvest moon, their bare flesh glowing beneath its light. Delight coursed through her from every caress, his mouth bedeviling her body inside and out, leaving her weak and trembling, but still longing for more. She could still picture the full moon reflecting in his eyes when she screamed his name through the night. Her thighs clutched his body against hers until climax stole their final breaths, then they lay in each other's arms until dawn warmed the horizon. She thought she had loved him before, but that moment was when she actually knew it. That was the night before he sailed off to wage battle in the Crimean War. Weeks passed without any word before an admiral had knocked on her door to notify her of Alexandre's death, and he presented her with a letter discovered in her lover's breast pocket. A bullet had blown through the center; shades of dried blood smeared the ink. Most of the words were easily read. The missing ones she penned with spilt tears.

Surely her lover would disapprove of what she was doing with this man, but there was no time to save up for the purchase, and she refused to resort to petty thievery. She would have to use her body to get what she wanted, just as when she needed safe passage from bloodthirsty bandits. After maturing into adulthood she finally realized the true potential of her talents. Then the industrial revolution swept magic's grasp away from the world. Nobody bought protective amulets anymore because they would rather holster repeating pistols. Perhaps if she were to combine her powers with a mechanical device like the doctor's cube, then her abilities would strengthen to a whole new level.

The doctor moaned. His frantic hands bore down on her shoulders. Warmth flooded her mouth, dribbled a bit down her chin. She swallowed every salty spurt and moaned as if she'd actually enjoyed herself.

"Oh my, that was most incredible." He wiped his cock off with a handkerchief before tucking it away. "Take any of those boxes stacked over there. You've certainly earned it."

Betrayal coated her tongue, its sour juices clotting into a brick deep within her stomach. Her guts buckled, then knotted from anguish, the urge to vomit spunk all over his shining boots seemed all but unavoidable. She gulped spite and bile down her throat, her volition feasting on the brew. Her cheeks cramped from forcing a smile while she walked over to claim her cube.

"Thank you very much, Doctor."

Cold air drew the black clouds close to the Earth that night, making for perilous navigation by airships dotting the horizon. Two collided without warning over the city center. Their fuselages erupted in flame and rained wreckage through crowded streets. Victims' screams carried over hills in the countryside where a flock of sheep scattered.

Adora looked back at the flaming skyline, the magnitude of the inferno muted by dense fog rolling in from the bay. She hurried along the cobblestone path toward the Necropolis. A pair of long hairpins made quick work of the lock on the wrought-iron gates towering over the entrance. Just inside the night watchman snored with a bottle of rum cradled in his arms.

An outstretched oil lantern guided her through swirling fog. Most of the tombstones she knew by name, having conjured their souls for wealthy mourners.

Adora struggled with the heavy gate securing the entrance to the Malveaux family crypt. Hinges squealed. Rust from last winter's rains crumbled free. She made sure to lock the gate behind her, then hung a thick tarp over the bars to muffle her incantations.

Her previous attempts to conjure Alexandre's spirit were on the battlefield where his body was recovered, and in the dark forest where magic still thrived. Now she stood upon the granite where she'd previously wept, wondering why she hadn't before attempted her spells where the bones of her lover lay resting.

The witch emptied out the contents of her knapsack and readied the tomb for her ritual. She fashioned a circle of pink salt large enough for her to lie in, and placed six pillar candles around the edge in precisely spaced increments. Inside of the circle she used chalk wrapped with red ribbon to draw a pentacle aligned with the Northern Star. She smoldered wormwood incense in a silver chalice scored with ancient runes. Gradually its smoky wisps filled the space with haze.

A clock need not chime the midnight hour approaching. Adora cast her eyes upward, and through the veil of aether she envisioned celestial bodies spinning past. She turned toward the moon, and smiled at the old man's face sketched from craters. She dropped her robe and stepped naked into the center of the circle.

"Guardians of the Spirit Realm," she recited calmly while winding the lever on the cube. She'd briefly studied its functions, daring not to open it as the doctor had warned against, and etched symbols across its surface that were meant to magically alter the focus of its mechanical effects. She pressed the button in the lid, felt it catch a cog, then trigger a spring. Small vibrations trembled gemstones in her rings.

"When the witching hour rings true, bring my lover Alexandre back to me. Other souls may hear my call, but they are not welcome in this place." Her eyes fell shut, her volume escalated. Memories of Alexandre's features appeared in the void behind her eyelids. Warm, brown eyes. Smooth cheeks. Tender lips kissing every intimate surface of her flesh. Ears she once whispered past and screamed his name when she came.

"Only the one named Alexandre Malveaux, who has known

my body more intimately than any other, may enter this sacred space." Warmth spread over her fingers. She cracked one eye to check her progress.

Tentacles of silver mist reached out from the cube. They read over names chiseled upon crypts, probed through cracks where only maggots had crawled before.

Adora squeezed her eyelids shut, focusing all good will on her one true love. Vibrations migrated through her arms, steadily chattered her teeth. "Hear my pleas, great Charon, ferryman of the dead. Row your boat across the Styx, and transport the soul of my lover to the shores of life so that we may embrace once again."

Granite creaked. Spirits whispered around her, their slow words muffled through the protected circle. Frost hung in the air, condensing her breath, puckering her nipples. Ice crystals shimmered across the floor, but dared not traverse the circle.

"Missing you does not even begin to adequately describe the hollow cavity left beneath my breast." Adora's words filled with weeping. "I was with child when you died, and the trauma of your loss purged our child from my womb. I have conjured so many souls for mere shillings a name without even breaking a sweat, yet the one I hold truest to my heart continues to elude my greatest efforts. No longer shall I walk alone! No longer shall I cry myself to sleep at night."

She set the cube in the center of the circle. Her voice echoed among graves outside as she spoke at the top of her lungs. "Alexandre Malveaux, I command you to stop hiding behind the shelter of Death's veil, and enter into this circle where I may worship your beloved body once more."

Silence befell the sacred place, save for the humming cube, and the beating of Adora's heart. Beneath the volume of her pulse she detected a second rhythm. Anxiety burning in her gut urged her to open her eyes; the fear of failing again taunted her to keep them shut. Unhurriedly, she raised her eyelids. Her throat clamped shut at once.

A phantom darker than pitch hovered mere inches from her. Gossamer shadows crafted a hooded cloak about its figure, a veil blacker than night hid its face. Aether burned sliver about it, symbolic of pure energy awaiting potential.

Excitement severed her words with a blunt edge. A squeak crawled through the stricture in her throat and dragged its sound from the tip of her tongue. "Alexandre?"

The spirit nodded. An arm formed from black mist, then reached up to press its slender hand against her shoulder. Uncontrolled shivering shook her body. Its freezing touch burned through her flesh. Alexandre's face materialized inside the cowl with two shiny pence hovering in his sunken eye sockets.

"Thank you!" Adora cried up at the heavens. She threw her arms around him—her expression echoing surprise as they passed through him as if nothing were there at all. "Alexandre, you are the only man for whom my heart has ever beaten. If only I could touch you once more, my love."

Darkness melted away to reveal his naked form. Beads of ectoplasm dripped down his flesh. A ragged bullet hole pierced his chest, offering a glimpse of his bloodless heart beating inside.

Excited thoughts boiled through her brain. *The strange cube was working exactly as she'd hoped for.*

"My beautiful Adora," his words resonated between her ears though his lips never parted. "When Death raptured my soul beneath his outstretched wings I never thought I would see you again."

She kissed him, bearing past the searing cold so her tongue could explore his mouth. Spectral energy crackled over her lips. Absinthe flavors flowed down her throat. His muscular arms encircled her, raising denser layers of gooseflesh wherever they touched.

"I don't want to waste a moment of our time." Adora's heart lurched inside her chest. Heat dripped along her inner thighs. "Make love to me, as amazingly as the last time we lay beneath the stars."

Alexandre said everything she needed to hear with his smile. The warmth of his soul burned through death's chilling veil, their mouths came together and their passion combusted. His touch transitioned to warmth while his hands explored her flesh, seemingly in multiple locations at once. His fingers slipped between her thighs, the sudden rush of pleasure buckled her knees. He swooped her against his chest and lowered her onto the floor.

Adora gently slid the cube beside their entwined bodies, making certain it didn't break the circle. Its vibrations transmitted through the floor, up through her ass, and teased her throbbing clit. Her pussy became increasingly sensitive with every passing moment. Anticipation glistened over its supple lips.

Alexandre feasted on her mouth, consumed her neck, drifted to devour her breasts. Adora clawed at the floor as his mouth glided down between her legs. His tongue bathed her slit with spectral warmth, and a jolt rippled through her clit. Lengthy digits slipped inside her next. Electricity from his touch tormented and excited her all at once. A finger wormed its way inside her ass, pressing the inner walls of her cunt against his tongue. She ground her pelvis against his face, further fueling the ecstasy coursing through her senses.

Adora came hard. All the tense years, all her grief, the absence of affection callousing her heart—it all splintered apart from her soul. Orgasm stole her breath, bathed sweat over her flesh. Ecstasy trembled through every nerve.

Her lover rose, easily pressing his cock through her slick pussy lips. Slow pops of static danced through her cunt, immediately refueling her climax. Unbearable bliss advanced until his cock swelled to fill every available inch of her depths. His hips rested against her, his taut scrotum nudged her ass.

Arms drew bodies close. Passion flowed freely between their lips, nerve endings savored the euphoria of their skin again connecting. Two lost souls finally joined as one.

Adora's hips slowly rocked against his. Their eyes locked on to each other's smiles. Alexandre's pace quickened, and though the stone flooring chafed her asscheeks, no other sensation existed at that moment than their fucking.

His delight melted into a concentrated stare. She sensed from the frenzy of his thrusts that his culmination loomed close. Her cunt clenched around his girth. Every voltaic thrust pounded her harder against the floor. She reached her arms up and grabbed his ass, pulling him deeper inside her body.

Lightning storms rolled through Adora's vision. She writhed about, her two-tone hair splayed over her face. Her quivering thighs clenched his hips against her body. Bliss stole away her gasps. Climax tore through her crux with all the ferocity of rabid wolves. Sweet juices oozed from her pussy, and smeared the pentacle drawn beneath her.

Ectoplasm beaded across Alexandre's brow. "Oh, my love, I'm going to come."

"Yes, my love!" She squeezed her body against his, softly chewed perspiration from his neck.

Warmth spilled through her cunt. A surge of voltage cramped her breasts. A coppery taste singed the back of her tongue. His body fell upon hers, his hips pumping every last drop of spectral seed inside her.

Tendrils of energy danced along their intertwined forms. Adora beheld a glimpse of the heavens, and for a rare instant, all time halted around her.

"I love you Alexandre," she whispered. Joyful tears trickled from the corners of her eyes.

He gazed at her; the intensity of his emotion pierced her flesh, and fluttered her heart. His lips parted, words of affection poised on the tip of his tongue. A metallic *PING* shook the cube; its vibrations ceased at once.

Every muscle in her body tensed. Abruptly she was aware of countless spiders watching their frolic from webs lacing above. Icy cold gnashed her fingertips as they sank through Alexandre's flesh without warning. His figure faded into shadowy mist flowing about her body.

"I won't let you go again!" Adora concentrated on her lover, straining every ounce of energy manifested by their union.

His face materialized once more with the coins still covering his eyes. She clawed at the mist to draw it closer against her. Their lips touched with a chill, then during the stillness between racing heartbeats her lover vanished.

"Alexandre?" She bolted upright, searching the candlelight for his presence. "My love?"

She dashed for the cube. Frantic fingers struggled for a secure grip. Metal clattered inside. Fingernails cracked away leaving bloody smears as she tore the lid open. Wide eyes scanned its contents.

A snapped spring lay on the bottom. Delicate gears appeared dislocated from their reels. Shimmering light faded from a white crystal suspended in the center.

"No." Adora whispered, attempting to shake away the disbelief setting into her bones. "Please, no."

She coaxed a gear back into position with the tip of a bloodied finger. A rod running through its center bent, and the crystal tilted out of alignment. "Oh, Sweet Mother Goddess. No!"

She rose quickly to her feet. Ghostly cum glowed down the insides of her thighs. All of her rage spewed forth with a blood-curdling shriek as she hurled the cube against the far wall of the crypt. Delicate gears and shattered crystal showered the dark with their melody.

Blackness churned within Adora's tears. Aether steamed about her naked flesh. Catastrophe smoldered in her glare. She screamed out again, struck the nearest wall and shattered every bone in her fist.

Temperature shifts permitted slivers of morning sunlight to peer beneath the haunted sky. Many of Barton Hill's residents took to parks and markets to delight in the rare occurrence. Forecasts for the following days warned that nobody should venture outside without a respirator as the Great Black loomed close to the shore.

Adora walked through the crowd, her arm suspended with a scarf she'd fashioned as a makeshift sling. Several more days would need to pass before her healing potion took full effect. For the time being, agony throbbed though the fractures with every step. In her good hand she clutched a cloth sack containing remnants of the cube. Every jingling piece reminded her of great failure.

She strolled through the market center where she last saw the doctor's wagon parked. Perplexity gripped her when she happened up to his empty stall. Her panicked glances fell on every passerby. Her silent prayers hoped she'd simply overlooked his move to another location in the market.

A young market hand sauntered by with a broom in his grip. His duties required that he smile at every customer, but he quickly looked away when he noticed the air shimmering around her.

"Excuse me, young man." She chased after him, her voice frantic. "I need to ask you a question."

"Be quick about it, toffer." He spun sneering, prepared to swing his broom as a bat.

"Did you work here yesterday?"

"Maybe. What about it?"

"I'm looking for the man who was peddling the boxes from his steam-powered wagon. The one who made the old lady walk again."

"No idea, ma'am." He shook his head slowly, almost nodded as if he knew.

"Would this stir your memory?" A shilling gleamed between bruised fingers in her sling.

His eyes widened in his dirt-smeared face. He pocketed the coin with a flash and a grin. "Oh, yeah, that man. He left just after the market closed yesterday."

"Do you have any idea where he may have headed off to?"

"I overheard him say something about a telegram, and how it was utmost necessary that he board the first ship bound for America this morning."

"Thanks, kid."

Adora rushed down to the docks. Panic propelled her every heartbeat. The silhouette of a steamship shrank toward the horizon. Tugs towed other ships into port. Crewmen bustled about loading and unloading cargo with mechanical lifts.

She scanned the aether for any hint of his direction, but the commotion around her clouded her efforts. Weeks would pass before she could afford the fare to America. Hell, she didn't even know which port the doctor had headed toward. He could have been sitting behind her sipping a whiskey for all she knew.

Angst paralyzed her until a bellowing foghorn shook her back to her senses. Adora stared out to sea, where whitecaps dotted swelling waves. Her mangled hand clutched her chest.

Surrounding clamor drowned out the whisper carried from her lips. "My dearest Alexandre, I swear to you that I will find the doctor, and I will learn the secrets behind his mysterious, mechanical cubes. And when we finally meet again, I will slash my throat so that we may spend the rest of eternity slumbering within each other's arms."

Moonshine Ballad

Salome Wilde

for Carson McCullers

Gotta laugh at them uppity bottles there, showin' off labels like
the cover's all you need to know about a book. They just stand
there on the shelf, proud as peacocks, tall an' clean an' shinin'.
Then, snap! They in a fella's hand an' he's puttin' up all he done
earned in a week's hard labor for fool's gold. High-class hooch
don't care what it costs a fella. Them bottles just waitin' to be
pulled down. They listenin' for the sound of crisp dollar bills
an' clankity change, spillin' sweet an' loud. Fella spills all he's
worth on the General Store countertop, just like he's gonna spill
his seed when he's bottle-drunk later on.

It ain't that I'm jealous—nary a bit. Yeah, I see what they got.
Fancy paper 'round the neck, waitin' to be torn by greedy fingers. Or a 'luminum crimp that makes a real nice crackle when
you twist it, tellin' the world they's important bottles, worldly-
wise whiskey. Makes the fellas feel worldly, too, I 'spect. That
potion they carry in those pretty glass bellies melts a man's
insides smoother'n butter on a biscuit. Them bottles gets waved
in the air an' then poured into shiny little glasses, sometimes
mixed with Coca-Cola for the girls faint at heart or aimin' to

act that way to keep control over mischievous boyfriends.

Fancy bottles fulla fancy liquor, they so pretty. *Smooth*, that's the word. Many a man an' plenty women swear they take a body on a mighty fine ride. (Depends on how you figure "fine," don't it?) Drink enough an' you don't rightly remember what you done come mornin'. An' that's prob'ly for the best. Ain't nice when you know what high-priced spirits done to you. Give you a good, hard fuck, that's what they done. An' I suppose that's what some folks want, even if they say otherwise. Still, ain't hard to be smarter.

Take Miss Mary Mae Murphy. Lots of folks call her smart. Pretty as a peach an' got her high school diploma, too. Everyone thought she'd find a good man an' settle down. Maybe even land a city fella. But she didn't show no such interest. Ended up movin' in with the seamstress, Miss Annie Bugg, takin' in laundry an' learnin' how to sew.

But if you wanna see stupid, take a gander at ol' Lou Abney, settin' yonder in the shade. Lyin' back against that big oak, snorin' like thunder, an empty bottle still in his hand. He's dreamin' high, just like he was doin' last night when he latched onto Miss Mary Mae. He didn't recognize her first off when he saw her at the barn dance. The girl had grown so much since she'd moved to the edge of town. Fine-lookin' woman she was now, he was thinkin' as he brought the half-empty bottle to his lips. He'd promised Sue-Beth, his plump spitfire of a wife, he wouldn't drink no more after she went home, complainin' that the hay was makin' her sneeze. But Lou Abney was a liar through and through. Most folks said he an' the truth ain't never even met.

Miss Mary Mae stepped out for some air 'round the same time, wonderin' why she'd let Annie talk her into goin' the dance on her own. Later, she couldn't rightly say why she'd let ol' Lou convince her to take a swig from his fancy bottle, but she did. An' a little while after that, she stopped wonderin' why she was doin' anything she was doin'.

'Course, while Lou moans in his sleep under that tree, Miss Mary Mae is long gone. She cain't recall much as she wakes beside Miss Annie. Not when nor how she got home or what she done to make her ache below. How was it that only a few sips from that bottle an' Lou didn't look so terrible bad to her, she wondered. Bulb of a nose didn't seem so big an' red. Bulgin' gut seemed smaller an' right soft to lean on as they sat together, listenin' to the fiddle playin' in the barn, far off. Miss Mary Mae was light-headed, watchin' the stars wink at her in the cool night sky. When Lou bent over to kiss her, it was like bein' kissed by the sky—dark an' soft an' distant. Nothin' seemed real.

Now, though, she's rubbin' perfume at her temples to chase away the head pain, knowin' she'll be late to church if she don't hurry. Miss Annie's already waitin' by the door, tryin' to convince herself she did the right thing in sending Mary Mae to that dance in the dress she made for her. Their bed was cold an' lonely until Mary Mae came back. Annie hid her face when the gal stumbled in, smellin' of whiskey an' sawdust.

If Miss Annie kept her peace, askin' not a single question of her lodger, Mary Mae had trouble just puttin' two words together. All she can manage is to wash up an' fix her hair. Her church-goin' hat with the veil hides her red, bleary eyes—another gift of that pretty bottle, the one that's helpin' Lou wake slowly to his own hurtin' as the hot, summer sun rises. Why'd he spend the night outdoors, anyhow? Was it a dream, or did he really bend that pretty slip of a girl Miss Mary Mae over the workbench in the shop where he makes porch swings an' rockin' chairs? An' did she truly say he was the first man she'd ever had?

While neither's quite sure yet of what all they done, their questions will have answers right soon. Lou, he'll groan with regret as he soaks his head in a horse trough an' fights away pictures in his mind of how he untied the rope that held up his pants with drunken, clumsy fingers an' pulled out his prick to stuff beneath Mary Mae's fresh-smellin' skirts. How he didn't even look, just felt his way until he pushed it in. Tight, it was, that's sure. Made him spill sooner'n he meant to.

His wife won't be told such details, though she's bound to find out he done her wrong. She always does. She'll regret havin' left the dance with just Lou's promise to behave. "Sow the wind an' reap the whirlwind," is what she'll say, in the end, pointin' an accusin' finger. Then she'll throw the "no-good, low-down, cheatin' skunk" out...again...until maybe she takes him back come Christmastime, forgives him when he brings 'round a fresh ham an' a hand-carved vanity he worked on all season, every chance he got, just for her.

Miss Annie, she won't be thinkin' on forgiveness, nor vengeance neither. Or, if she does, it'll be on the Lord's vengeance on *her*, not on poor, sweet Mary Mae. Annie loves that girl with all her heart an' soul—but it don't stop there, an' that's the trouble. Her love touches places she don't even let herself touch. So, it cain't be betrayal when Annie's always known that Mary Mae'd have to leave sooner or later, when the right man came a-callin'. Only, did it have to be that dreadful Abney fella? *Man's uglier than the south end of a north-bound cat*, Annie thinks, *an' just as sneaky.*

As the church bells chime their Sunday welcome, Lou an' Mary Mae are both rememberin' Lou puffin' away an' the rustle of Mary Mae's crinoline. But as Lou ambles home an' Mary Mae raises her voice to praise Jesus, they both find the same truth: Lou only tried an' Mary Mae only let him 'cause that costly liquor was doin' the drivin'. He was takin' all he had for granted, an' she was sure she couldn't have what she wanted. They twined together, stuck by glue poured straight from that bottle. Shame is its lastin' gift.

An' what if Miss Mary Mae starts showin' in a few months'

time? What then? That night'll cost 'em both more'n all the bottles in the General Store. An' I coulda saved 'em from such a terrible lesson, if only they'd let me.

By now, I bet you're wonderin' just who am I to talk against those fancy bottles, blamin' store-bought whiskey for bringin' people low? Must be I got somethin' 'gainst liquor, you think. Prob'ly just some old preachy teetotaler, you're guessin'. But that ain't me. I'm all for a good time. Got me a kick stronger'n any mule. An' from the first sip, my aim is true. Moonshine's my name.

Weren't born in no factory. Never had no label. An' ain't been aged in a barrel, given time to plot an' plan, figurin' the best way to worm into a body, fill it with foolish longin' an' send it off in the wrong direction. I ain't no good at deceivin' 'cause Moonshine burns all the way down. Only an underhand-ed, overblown bottle-drunk drives a woman-lovin' woman into the arms of a cheatin' man who barely remembers what he done or why he done it.

Used cannin' jar's good enough for me, don't even have to be clean. Still in the cellar brews me up fresh. An' Miss Amelia, with her strong, tender fingers, pours me careful-like into an old jar an' caps me tight. Coulda been Grandma's pickled rhu-barb or Aunt Molly's prize-winnin' blackberry jam inside once upon a time. An' just like a taste of home-cookin', Moonshine shows you what's real. Sears clean through lies an' fool dreams. When you tip me back, you cain't hide from yourself an' you don't wanna. You can see right through me like I see through you—strong an' cool as sulphur water from the town pump. I just cure a different kinda thirst.

Now, say the night of the barn dance didn't happen like I first said. Ol' Lou came 'round the *back* a' the General Store 'stead a' headin' for the front an' bangin' through that squeaky screen door with his week's pay. Say he held out his dollar an' wrapped his hand 'round somethin' real. Held me up to the night sky an' let the moon shine right through. "Hell with that old barn dance," he said, already sweet an' lazy-minded after the first swallow. Home he went, arm 'round his pink-cheeked Sue-Beth, to have the kinda good time a man don't have to regret an' a woman won't soon forget. Wouldn't even've seen Miss Mary Mae, eyes sparklin' as she sashayed down the road in her new dress, proud to be posin' in what Annie made so special for her, takin' in praise words with a "Thank ya, kindly" that she couldn't wait to bring home. Miss Annie shied from dances as well as the back porch of the General Store. Not Mary Mae, though, not this night. Now that she was of age, she just stepped up an' bought herself a little jar, then took it right on home. In the year she'd been stayin' in the pretty little cottage, it had come to feel more like home than the house she'd been raised in, an' Miss Annie was the best teacher she'd ever had. An' after a mouthful of Moonshine, Mary Mae knew it was time to do some teachin' of her own. The gal's heart was full, an' I made it fuller.

Walkin' down the dark lane, Mary Mae hummed to herself, hardly aware of her own voice, just feelin' it. When she arrived, she smiled big an' held out the jar. She didn't let Annie protest the drinkin', nor helpin' her out of her day clothes. Soon, they sat together on the bed in their short, delicate shifts, the ones they'd hand-embroidered together with sun-yellow stitchin' a few weeks back. For minutes that stretch to feel like hours under the influence of Moonshine, they just looked at one another.

Slowly, with quiverin' fingers, Mary Mae reached around to unbraid Annie's long, brown hair. Eyes down as she toyed with her neatly sewed hem, Annie couldn't stop grinnin'. Mary Mae was touching Annie with the hands of a woman not a girl, pressing her nose into the thick mass of chestnut curls an' beyond to the nape of Annie's neck beneath, inhalin' long an' deep. Annie shuddered, holdin' in a girlish giggle, an' Mary

Salome Wilde

Mae kneeled up to lay her back in the sweet softness of clean white sheets to spread her legs with poised hands an' honest kisses.

"What are you doin'?" Annie whispered, knowin' full well.

"Doin' what's right," answered Mary Mae, confident an' strong. "I love you, Annie," she said. An' before Annie could answer the same, Mary Mae was pressin' her mouth to the bloomin' lily between Annie's parted thighs. Safe an' Moonshine-drunk in the darkness of their little home at the edge of town, they knew themselves—every inch—an' they knew love.

An' that's what I do.

635.2   **Cherries in Season**
Gra
    author: KD Grace

    category: Horticulture

    subject:
      1. Cornucopia 2. Sticky Licking 3. Organic

Cherries in Season

KD Grace

My fruit sense tingles the minute I walk through the door of
Maggie's greengrocer. My mouth waters when I see them.
They're displayed center stage on the shelf between the plums
and the strawberries like round, plump little exhibitionists practically screaming *eat me*! I forget entirely about the cucumber
and tomato I'd planned to buy to go with the lettuce I'd grown
in my own little plot.

Maggie has cherries!

Cherries! That's what I want, and I'm not looking at anything else.

At least not until I hear *his* voice.

"They're really good this season." I look up into eyes the
color of toffee and the rest of the package is at least as edible.
The hair, that makes me wonder if he's just hopped out of bed
after wild sex, is that golden color of ripe, full summer, and
suddenly cherries are not the only thing I'm hungry for. I manage a thought for Maggie, wondering where she is. In the three
years I've lived here she's never trusted her shop, nor her exquisite produce, to anyone else. Then my mind returns to cherries
and the delicious bloke offering them.

Anyone into grow-your-own knows that just because something looks succulent and ready to eat doesn't mean it is. "It's not really season yet." I manage to sound like I'm not flustered, like the T-shirt hugging the hard geography of a seriously broad chest isn't interfering with my higher brain function, like those eyes aren't melting me like butter on hot toast. "These are early, and they're still a little too expensive for cherries in season." I shoot him a quick glance, then feel the heat rise and spread up my chest and over my throat as though just by making eye contact he might be able to read my naughty thoughts. I nod to the cherries that seem to be taunting me. "They may look nice, but how do they taste?"

He closes the distance between us in a heartbeat. There's no one else in the shop at this hour of the morning but us. He's taller than I thought, and I feel the warmth radiating off him and smell the delicious combination of good clean male sweat mixed with the early morning air.

Suddenly I want to eat him as badly as I do his cherries.

"Two words," he says, brazenly popping a cherry between my lips, an act that makes me blush like a schoolgirl.

"Two wo'ds?" I mumble around the cherry.

"Sun trap," he replies. "The orchard is perfectly situated to catch the best rays." A knowing smile crosses his full lips as the taste of the cherry hits my tongue and I catch my breath in a little moan that's only slightly less than orgasmic sounding. "I know the grower," he continues, eyes twinkling, "this year his contract with another shop ran out and voila!" He pops another cherry into my mouth just as I make an ungraceful effort to spit the pit of the previous one into my hand. "Location, location, location," he says and produces a pristine tissue for my pit, then adds, "These cherries are ripe and succulent and practically begging to be eaten two weeks, sometimes a full month, before any of the other cherries are. They're such little sun hogs that they absorb all the bright spring and early summer heat to arrive in Aunt Mags's store way before the others and tasting like the best sex ever."

Jesus! Did he just say that? Had he read my mind? I lay a hand against my chest, suddenly aware of the thin tank top I threw on this morning and my lack of a bra. I was just going to buy veg with Maggie and maybe a few early risers there. No one would notice or care how I was dressed, but right now my nipples were feeling as heavy and as plump as the cherries.

I spit the second pit into the tissue mumbling something incoherent, and we both laugh nervously. Maybe he's noticed my nipples too, I mean, I'm nobody special, and certainly not at this hour of the morning, unshowered, no makeup, dirt under my nails from my veg patch, my hair tied back in a careless ponytail. But there is something about eating cherries that's as close to good sex as you can get. And this time, he raises a third cherry with a look on his face that confirms it. Just as I open my mouth for the reward, he pulls it back ever so slightly, and I bite into it with my front teeth. An explosion of sweet ruby juice runs down my chin, onto my chest and onto the tight swell of my breasts. How the hell could one cherry have so much juice?

I yelp and, Jesus, I sound almost like I've just orgasmed. Suddenly I see that there's cherry not only on my tits but on his white T-shirt too, and fuck, if his nipples aren't as hard as mine! His tight little points rise in salute as mine return the favor. The sweet tart flavor, the jewel-red splash on white cotton, the 3-D definition of the flesh below has me seriously struggling to find my breath.

"Oh Christ! Oh god! I'm sorry, I'm so sorry," I hear him say, his breath is as fast as mine. His face is tinged a lovely shade of pink. I look down to check the damage all embarrassed and flustered and there it is—straining against his light summer trousers like the cucumber I originally came to buy. I've made him hard! I've actually made him hard. It's been a long time since I've made anyone hard. And my body remembers exactly how to respond. Suddenly I'm wet and tetchy and I feel as ripe and ready to be eaten as those cherries.

He's saying something about sparkling water taking out tough stains and, from somewhere, he produces a bottle and more tissue. He's just ready to hand them over to me when he catches his foot on a crate of potatoes and we both get a fizzy bath. My tank is suddenly see-through, and my nips aren't even trying to behave themselves. And neither is his cock, which has gotten its own splash of fizz.

I can't tell what he's saying because we're both yammering on at the same time, not making any sense as we try to be polite. I swear nothing like this has ever happened to me before, and I can't help wondering what the hell was in those cherries. But he's lovely, all embarrassed and befuddled when he offers me a handful of tissues. With the look of horrified contrition setting so charmingly on the strong lines of his jaw, how can I help myself? I grab him by the wrist and guide his hand right on down to a soft landing on my left breast.

"Oh god," he gasps, dropping the tissue. His eyelids flutter and a tremor runs through his whole body. There's a jerk of further expansion in the front of his trousers. "Oh god," he repeats.

Mortification and arousal are a bizarre mix, and I'm about to apologize and run for the door when I realize I'm no longer holding him against me, but he's cupping me, taking the weight of my breast into his palm, worrying my wet, chilled nipple to stretch and strain against cherried fabric.

"Oh god," I respond, stepping closer to his warm hand. "Honestly, I didn't …I never…I shouldn't have…" And damned if I haven't forgotten the English language in its entirety. Damned if I haven't forgotten my own name!

Our eyes are super-glued in a gaze that feels completely combustible, that feels as physical as his fondling of my breast. Then he steps closer and I feel his breath on my face, smelling of morning coffee and cherries, humid and labored, and becoming more so as he guides my hand to rest on his erection. I think I might have whimpered at the hot, tense feel of him beneath stressed fabric. At my first touch his reflexive action results in a near painful squeeze of my breast and a harsh grunt. For a moment I think he's come, but then he takes control, settles my hand and shifts against it, guiding my fingers with his own to show me what he needs, and I'm a quick study. I feel his breath hitch; I feel his hips shift closer to my touch. Even through trousers it's not difficult to tell that he's thick enough and long enough to scratch my itch, and fuck, my itch so needs to be scratched.

I become reckless and giddy stroking the cock of this man I don't know, stroking him hard, grinding my hips in empathy. I'm making subtle little squeezes and wriggles in my shorts, my pussy gripping and gaping and gripping again on the slippery seam, the rub exquisite in the absence of the panties I also didn't bother with this morning.

Our breath is tight and tense and spastic until it finally stops and there's no movement. We could be statues accept for the gaze that binds us and the heat that scorches us. How can so much lust be compacted into so little movement? How can the crescendo of arousal be so totally all consuming and yet focused and narrowed down to tight little centers of heat waiting impatiently to burst free and explode?

I come first, with no more stimulation than his hand on my breast and the rub and stroke of my pussy against my shorts— that and the knowledge that I've made this gorgeous man hard. He grunts and jerks and strangles a cry before it can escape those deliciously parted, cherry-scented lips. His grip on my wrist is bruising as his cock spasms inside his trousers, inside my hand, and I feel an impossible surge of liquid heat that keeps my pussy trembling and grasping against the drenched crotch of my shorts.

For a second we stand breathless, stunned, staring at each other in the honeyed sunlight streaming through the storefront window making his hair look like it's been showered in copper. And he leans in, all cherry-breathed and humid and smelling like summer heat itself and just as his parted lips brush mine, just as the very tip of his tongue flicks over my lower lip, Gemma Braynard bursts through the door with her three devil spawn who are all over the store like a bad rash, dirty little hands on everything. She's yelling for her darlings not to touch and to be good for mummy. We jerk apart like we're rocket propelled. I break for the door embarrassed, overwhelmed and horny as hell for more. As the door shuts behind me I hear Gemma ask about the cherries.

I don't live far and I can't get home fast enough, barely making it through the door before I'm stripping. I make it upstairs to the tetchy pleasure of the shower massage. There I sit sprawled in the tub, one leg over the edge, the other braced against the tiles directing the pulsing jets of water between my legs, down over my distended clit and up over the pout of my labia. The shower massage is good in a pinch, but it's not what I need. Not nearly what I need. I think of cherries and cucumbers and a toffee-eyed greengrocer with a cock that I made hard, a cock that I took care of, a cock that I want inside me.

I eat a cheese toastie for lunch, too embarrassed to go back for my cucumber and tomato and not about to waste the petrol to drive to the supermarket. As I settle in at my laptop to get a few hours of work done, I wonder where Maggie is. I wonder how long she'll be gone, and if maybe I *will* have to drive to the supermarket instead of having to face the man I practically attacked over a couple of cherries. And he did call her "Aunt Mags." If that's the case, if Maggie is his aunt, and she finds out I've gone all cougar on her nephew, I might not be welcome back anyway. Absently I wonder how old he is. Old enough for Maggie Kittredge to trust him running her shop, and old enough to know a thing or two about cherries, other than they're red and they taste good. And anyway, I'm not that old, I reassure myself, and I'm looking a whole lot younger these days after the divorce. Plus I have nice tits, so why wouldn't Cherry Bloke like playing with them?

It's early afternoon when I notice the note pushed through my mail slot. It's written on one of the small paper bags Maggie keeps on hand for produce. It simply says *Cherries are in season.*

With my heart racing and my pussy gripping in muscle memory, I open the door to find another paper bag filled with ripe red cherries and another note inside.

> *Cherries are in season—and on the house as an apology for my bad behavior. I hope you'll come back and pick up the things you originally stopped in for. And anything else you might need. I work until five.*
>
> *Hal*

I get to the shop just before it closes in case I need a quick escape, or in case we continue with the groping after hours. This time I wear underwear. After all, the free cherries might just be Hal's good business sense. He may not be looking for another encounter. But I still make sure plenty of cleavage is showing, and the skimpy summer skirt offers much easier access than the shorts did.

When I arrive Hal's waiting on two elderly ladies, and a third is fondling the melons near the back. He sees me and offers a smile that's almost shy, and the blush that climbs his slightly freckled cheeks goes straight to my crotch. I return his blush, and my nipples offer a stand-up greeting through the bra.

I wander around the store feeling up the produce and listening to snippets of conversation. Maggie's on holiday—first one in ten years, and Hal's filling in. The ladies seem totally enthralled by him. They take their time talking about the weather and their grandchildren and the horrid state the world's in. And Hal, like his aunt, doesn't rush them. He makes them feel like they're the most important people in the world. He recommends the most succulent fruit and the tenderest, most tasty runner beans. When the last customer leaves the store with a smile and a wave over her shoulder, he walks quietly to the door and turns the OPEN sign to CLOSED. My heart thumps as I hear the click of the lock, as I watch him pull down the shades, and then I suddenly find myself the center of his attention.

He looks at me from under thick lashes and heavy lids, and he's not smiling. My tummy jumps nervously. "You owe me," he says at last.

"I'm happy to pay," I say feeling a bit confused about the cherries, and I reach into my bag for my wallet.

He shakes his head and in two quick strides is standing beside me. "Not the cherries. Those were a gift. I'm talking about the hard-on I had all day thanks to you." He nods to my bag. "There's nothing in there that'll compensate for that. Do you have any idea how difficult it is to wait on customers with my cock leading the way? I spent the whole day thinking about your gorgeous wet frontage and fantasizing about the rest of the package." He rakes me with a look that breaks a sweat in the tight plunge between my breasts and makes my pussy quiver.

"Come on," he says, taking my hand. "I think we could both use some fresh fruit, and I know the perfect way to prepare it." He leads me to the back storeroom. I hardly notice as he slips my bag from my shoulder and drops it on the floor. He doesn't waste time with any more words. His mouth is better occupied entertaining mine, urgently pushing me back with darts of his tongue between my teeth, making me think of a predator pouncing. He laps at my tongue, teases and nibbles my lips, all the while maneuvering me back onto a stool nestled between boxes and crates of fruit.

"You planned that," I say with a little gasp as I half fall, half settle onto the stool.

"It worked out pretty well, didn't it?" He's practically on top of me. In my peripheral vision I can see the heavy press of his cock against the front of his trousers. His calloused fingers move up under my skirt, up the inside of my thigh, as his mouth migrates from my lips to my earlobe and then to my nape. One hand shoves down my tank top and bra strap until he can nibble and lick his way onto the swell of my breast. I lift my bottom as he pushes the skirt up and slides aside the crotch of my thong just as his mouth converges on the nipple he's nuzzled free from my bra, and we both gasp our appreciation.

"I was hoping for more cherries," I tease. "You were right, they do taste like the best sex ever," I manage as he wriggles two fingers to spread my labia and trace the wet valley in between.

"Saved back a few kilos for personal enjoyment," he mumbles through his efforts to tongue my stippling areola to a tense crinkly scrunch around the peak of my nipple. With his mouth fully occupied and me grabbing his hair holding him to my breast while I bear down on the slip-slide of his fingers, his other hand fumbles in the stacked fruit crates until he produces the biggest, most succulent cherry I've ever seen. The fingers that have been in my pussy slide under my shirt to undo my bra, and in the same instant I feel the release of the hooks, I feel the cool firm fruit, not unlike the head of a cock, pressing teasingly at my slippery hole. I cry out at the urgency of the press, and my legs fall open even further. Then he completely surprises me by pushing the cherry up into me as far as his finger will reach. When I struggle and try to protest, he kisses me into submission.

"Don't worry. I promise you'll enjoy fresh fruit prepared this way." His dexterous tongue probes my mouth deeply as if to reassure me that the hunt for the cherry is a challenge he's well up for, and I'm convinced.

I prop my feet on two convenient crates that he pulls forward so that my feet can rest on them for support, almost like stirrups in a doctor's office, then he upends an empty crate between my legs and settles onto it, not unlike a doctor about to give an exam. His face is close enough to my pussy that I can feel his hot breath. I clench tightly around the cherry, and I hear him grunt in empathy.

He takes a Victorinox from his pocket. I'm just about to panic at the sight of the shiny blade when he grabs a hefty melon from one of the crates and carves out a crescent moon slice like a pro. He offers me a bite from one end. I make a show of running my tongue along the underside, of slurping and suckling before I bite. His dark eyes are enormous as he watches, pupils dilated, breath catching, juice dripping down his fingers and onto his wrist. He takes a bite from the same end and offers his own tongue action that has me squirming and slickening the chair. Then he circles the cool sticky fruit around my hardening clit. Just as I begin to rotate my hips, finding the sweet spot against the melon's intriguing press, he shoves it into my pussy next to the cherry then bends and sucks the juice from my clit with a tight grip any hungry infant would envy.

I'm on the edge, so close that my pulse skitters in anticipation. He covers my mouth with a wet kiss that tastes of melon and my own juices. "There are so many wonderful ways to eat fresh fruit," he whispers into my mouth. I hear the zip of his fly and feel the heavy anxious warmth of him against my thigh.

He does the same deft carving job on a peach, sharing the first slice with me, kissing the sweet tart pulp into my mouth with his tongue before the second slice joins the fruit salad in my rapidly filling pussy. I don't know if it's peach juice or my own juice I feel leaking down my perineum onto the stool, but Hal dutifully licks and suckles up the excess while I squirm and grind. The slide of the fruit inside me makes me feel full and heavy and oh so needy, like I need to come, like I need to come urgently and like once I start I may not be able to stop.

"Mmm. Fresh fruit and the taste of a horny woman. The perfect blend," he says. I feel his filthy smile all the way down to my fruit-filled cunt. "And healthy too." He breathes a chaste kiss onto my clit and pulls back shaking his head. "Don't come yet. I'm not finished, and trust me it'll be worth the wait."

I'm scrunched down on the stool with my bum nearly off the seat and my weight supported by my feet resting on the crates. My stomach is tightening and tensing with the effort, and I feel the pressure of contracting muscles on my full hole. I know it would take only the tiniest shifting and just a little more squeezing, and I could come, and it would be so good. But there's something outrageously arousing about holding it, keeping it inside, feeling its weight, feeling its urgency, feeling its tetchy, distended, delicious discomfort. So I hold on.

All the while Hal's stuffing my pussy with more fruit, his cock is stretched solicitously, obscenely, through the open zipper of his fly, bouncing and straining with his every move. I watch as he inserts a fat strawberry and two blueberries up into me. He thinks about it for a second and then adds a couple of raspberries. Each time he fingers more fruit into my vagina, my inner muscles grip, and my opening sucks and clenches and pulls everything deeper.

The tip of his cock is now sheened with a soft glaze of pre-cum, which he strokes at absently as he fills my slit, and each time he does that, I clench and grip and feel the overwhelming need to bear down. When he inserts the tiniest tidbit of a Kentish plum, after drizzling its juices over my tits and licking it off, I'm sure he can't possibly fit anything else up into me. My whole body aches with the need to come, and the sounds that escape my throat are kittenish and desperate.

"Now just one more thing," he says. He takes one last plump

cherry, and I try not to writhe as he slides the cool skin of it around my clit and down between my heavy pout to my already stuffed snatch. Somehow, I don't know how he does it but, with the pad of his thumb, he pushes it up in me securely and then tugs slightly at the end of the stem, which still protrudes, and I gasp.

"Perfect," he says.

I breathe shallowly, in tight little gulps to keep from coming. I'm on the edge, the very edge, and I fear even the tiniest trickle of juice along my supersensitive slit will push me over. I'm intrigued, I'm fascinated. I want to wait for him. I want to come with him.

My eyes follow the bounce of his straining cock as from a cupboard on the other side of the crates, he finds a clean white tarp and spreads it down on the concrete floor, then kicks off his shoes and strips until he stands before me completely naked. I gasp my approval at elongated muscles with very little fat, at the tight half-domed buttocks, at the light splash of bronze hair across his hard chest. He doesn't notice my approving gaze as he concentrates on the plan he has in his head. He rolls his clothes up and places them on the tarp. "That should do," he says with a satisfied smile. Then he offers me his hand. "I want you there." He nods to the tarp on the floor.

Clenching as tightly as I can, I carefully lower my feet onto the floor and stand in front of him, feeling the heavy juicy press of the fruit threatening to expel itself as I walk, slightly knock-kneed, to the tarp. Before he eases me down onto the floor, he removes my clothes, a task with which I'm unable to help, shifting from foot to foot, clenching and gripping, full and uncomfortable and concentrating hard to hold off my orgasm just a little longer, just a tiny bit more.

He offers me a smile that's more wicked than reassuring and does nothing to ease the arousal I can barely contain. Then he guides me down onto the floor; all the while I'm whimpering and moaning and grunting with my load. "There now," he soothes. "Almost ready. Just a little bit longer and you can come, and I can come too." He settles his rolled-up clothes under my hips, and I gasp from the effort and the added pressure, fearing a fruitful, explosion-powered orgasm is imminent. My clit feels at least as big as the cherry he's topped me off with and just as ripe and ready to be eaten.

He sits on his haunches, one hand wandering to cup his balls where they rest on his thigh and then to stroke and tug at his distended cock. The flat of his other hand caresses my gape like he would a frightened puppy; his gaze is locked on my pussy so perfectly hoisted and displayed on the pillow of his clothing. And god, I want him to see. I want him to look, to touch, to taste how naughty, how needy I am. He offers a filthy little laugh and his eyes sparkle in the half-light of the storage room. "All this effort's made me very hungry." He raises his eyes to meet mine. "So I'm now going to enjoy my five a day, and so are you."

He arches over me and for a frightening second I think he's going to try and push his cock in right along with the fruit. Instead, he nibbles and kisses and licks, starting with my lips, moving down slowly to my neck and shoulders and breasts. All the while a splayed palm exerts just enough pressure low on my abdomen to keep me from squirming and yet make me more desperate to do just that as he forces more pressure against my stuffed vagina.

As his lips and teeth reach the bulging undersides of my breasts, his long middle finger curves over my damp pubic curls and rhythmically strokes and circles and presses my clit. He allows me just enough movement of my hips to push up into the heel of his palm, push up and grip, push up and clench. I swear I can almost feel the shape of each individual piece of fruit rotating and pressing and massaging, and oh god, it's exquisite agony to be so full and so in need of being emptied.

As he works his way down and plants a kiss on my mons, I know what's coming next, and I tense in anticipation. But before he begins, he looks up from between my legs. "I'm hungry, so hungry," he says.

He nips my clit and I yelp, which puts the pressure on my full vag, and I feel my lips part grudgingly, teased by Hal's tongue and the gentle tug of his teeth first on my labia and then on the stem of the cherry. I feel the tremor all through me, but hold it tight as he extricates the plump round tidbit and I clench down again. He arches over me and offers me the cherry, and as I rise up to take it, he clamps his mouth on mine, biting half of the fruit away as well as the pit and stem with amazing dexterity.

Before I can do more than gasp my appreciation, he goes down for more fruit, scooping out berries with the curved hollow of his tongue and placing them in and around my navel. "Hold still," he commands.

"I can't," I reply. "I can't hold still. Oh god, I need to come so bad."

He shoves a raspberry and a blueberry into my mouth with fingers that taste like pussy, and in spite of my agitated state, I moan my appreciation.

"There, that's better," he says, licking the trail of mixed fruit and pussy juice down from my navel, pausing to pucker my clit still further with a tight suckle. "You'll feel better after you've eaten," he says. His eyes darken and his breath catches in a little grunt that makes his cock bounce. "We both will."

And then he gets serious. I don't know how he manages, but it feels like he's crawling up inside me, eating his way to every last tidbit of fruit and sucking out every last bit of juice—an act that isn't even possible in the hyperaroused state of my pussy. He extricates and he eats and he shares. He sometimes offers me whole berries; he sometimes offers me what he's chewed. He offers it in kisses that make my mouth water and makes me lift my ass from his rolled clothes, lift it as though I'm making an offering of not just the fruit, but of the vessel holding it, the vessel that really doesn't want to be empty, the vessel that's aching to be filled again.

Sometimes he smears my breasts and belly with fruit softened and pulped and fragrant from my pussy. Sometimes he smears it on his cock and offers it to me, and I taste his precum with the same delight I might taste rich thick cream or custard. He watches me lick and suck; he watches with those eyes that make me want to eat, to devour, to slurp and taste and feast. Then he pulls away and goes down again. I'm beyond myself, insane with desire, wild with a hunger for fresh fruit served to me from his lips, from his cock, from my snatch. As he empties me one bite, one lick, one nip at a time, I'm desperate to be filled again, and I hear myself chanting over and over again, "Please Hal, fuck me, please fuck me, Hal. Please."

His breath is faster with each bite, and he becomes sloppy. Sticky juice and pulp dribble down his chest and mine. He slips and slides in it over my belly, on top of my body, teasing me with the cock he knows I desperately want. His fingers have found my anus, his tongue has licked cherry juice from my armpits, his lips have suckled sweat from behind my knees and his teeth have sent shivers up my spine tracing a path over my heel and up my tightened calf muscles. He knows my body, Hal does, and there's now nothing that I don't want him to see as he buries his face deeply, hungrily one final time to extract that last fat cock-tip of a cherry.

I'm keening and writhing and needing.

From a long way off I hear the rattle of a condom wrapper, and my vision is overshadowed by the man above me resting his weight on his arms and knees. He doesn't need his hand to guide his cock. It knows the way. He thrusts into me deep and hard, and I'm stunned to find that he can fill me even fuller than the fruit had.

I'm coming from nearly the first plunge, roaring and clawing and convulsing. But he doesn't stop. He keeps thrusting and thrusting and slipping and sliding across my belly, in the juice and the sweat and the blending of flavors that are us. He keeps humping and surging, and the room smells of fruit and sex and him, and me. I keep coming and raging and he's grunting and shoving until I think he'll break me, until I think he'll break both of us, until at last he explodes. The sound is raw and aching at the back of his throat coming up from deep in his belly, where I feel muscles grip like iron and release in tremors that shake me as they drive back up into me. When it's finished, when we've wrung all there is out of our bodies, I lie there beneath him stunned and amazed and giddy.

Later when we're bathed and have eaten a mountain of Chinese takeaway sitting on the floor of Maggie's flat, later when my body aches from sex I'm not used to, and my pussy is already twitchy for more, I ask, "So how long are you here for?"

"Aunt Mags is away for two weeks," he replies.

Two weeks, I think. Not very long. But then maybe it's long enough. Maybe it's just a fling. Probably just a fling.

He eyes me for a long moment, chopsticks trailing Singapore noodles over his bowl.

"The cherries," he says, "they were my deal."

When I offer a blank look, he continues.

"It was my way of proving I'll make a good partner. I negotiated the cherries. Oh she's tough, Aunt Mags is, but she isn't getting any younger, and she needs help around here. Plus the place has potential to grow that she can't realize on her own." He speaks around a mouthful of noodles. "She needs a partner who knows fruit and veg. Someone who knows how to get cherries in season."

"And that would be you."

His smile is broad, boyish, and it makes me smile back.

"That would be me. When she gets home I'll go back to Kent and get my things. She bought a nice little bungalow for herself not far from here. I'll live in this flat, that way I can take care of the heavier work and the longer hours." This time the smile he offers me feels almost physical. "If I didn't love the place already, I certainly do now. I'm definitely looking forward to getting to know the locals. Plus"—he scoots close to me, nabs a plump cherry from the bowl on the coffee table and pops it into my mouth—"I really am good with fruit."

I move to sit on his lap, feeling his cock rousing against my bottom as I share the cherry in a kiss. "As a real fan of fruit, and especially cherries in season," I say as I fumble with his fly making ready for round two, "I can't tell you how much that pleases me."

615.1 **The Perfect Massage**
Arc
      author: Olivia Archer

      category: Alternative Medicine

      subject:
        1. Mask   2. Ménage   3. Deep Tissue

The Perfect Massage

Olivia Archer

Armand is exactly what I need: a sexy man whose sole purpose is to give me pleasure. I find him just when my dating life has reached a standstill.

The first Monday of each month, I place myself in his able hands. Initially, I left my panties on, but he slid his warm fingers beneath the orange strings, liberating my hips to his touch, complimenting me on my womanly shape. I laughed and said that my friend who had recommended him didn't have these kinds of hips. His strong hands lingered beneath the straps of my panties, while he playfully told me that *this* was what a woman should look like. No masseur has teased me before. I liked it! Had the reception desk still been open when I left, I would have scheduled another appointment on the spot. But mine was the last of the night. I wandered out alone to relish the feel of my relaxed body beneath the beautiful, star-studded sky.

Massage was the one indulgence that I allowed myself. In my job, I dealt with a lot of stress and needed someone to rub the knots out of my neck. And with my unfulfilling social life, it seemed necessary to have the touch of another human being—hands on my skin—before I became too accustomed to my solitude.

Over the years I had tried many massage therapists, many styles, with just as many disappointments. I did not want that tiny glass of bad champagne served on a tray adorned with a plastic orchid blossom. I wanted relief. Someone who could find the source of my ache and make it go away. Really, it seemed simple. There were too many services that merely pampered superficially. Then I tried Armand, and from our first session, he had a way with my body. His hands found the areas in need, and he worked them until my muscles yielded.

In my subsequent appointments with him, I tried to draw him out, asking about his weekend, trying to find out what his life was like. He was respectfully responsive, but did not elaborate. I mentioned this when I met Liz, the woman who had told me about Armand; she said that he chatted with her. When I questioned what she knew about him, she couldn't remember anything specific.

The next time I saw Armand, wanting to know why he treated me differently, I asked, "I saw Liz and she said the two of you talked the whole time that you massaged her. Is there a reason you don't speak much with me?"

I was facedown and turned my head slightly to listen. He deftly pressed my palms while contemplating. "She likes to hear herself talk so I suppose that she believes we are having a conversation. You and I communicate on a different level."

Hmm. I pondered this as I let myself melt into his touch. My preference was for deep tissue massage, but I had been unsatisfied at other spas, feeling like I just paid someone to rub lotion on my body, and I could do that myself. When going to a professional, I wanted to feel someone's fingers pressing me to the edge of pain, digging in to release the troubles buried there.

This facility is attached to the country club's offsite gym. The massage rooms are remotely located in the back, with a separate entrance to avoid walking past the machines, aerobics classes and loud racquetball courts. By now I know the routine: I check in with the welcoming receptionist, and wander into the locker room to quickly strip off my clothes and snuggle into one of their plush white robes.

Armand uses Room 3; I wait inside on the bamboo bench, door open. He arrives, exactly on time, to greet me. "Good evening, Ms. Rollins. Please lie down on your stomach, under the sheet, I'll be back in a few minutes." When the door closes, I slide beneath the expensive linens, pressing my body into the heated massage table, and try to relax. I am accustomed to being in control and this part makes my heart race—surrendering my naked body to whomever chooses to open the door and walk in. Realistically, I know people are around, but for a moment I feel that spike of adrenaline when he knocks softly on the door, then enters. Armand's familiar voice asks me if I want anything different this time. I reply that I am confident he will find my aches.

In those moments when he greets me, I admire the features of his attractive face, knowing that soon I will only be able to see his interesting, tattooed feet while he massages my back. His soft pants sway as he shifts his weight; they are always a natural color, setting off the darkness of his skin, like espresso and cream. Then I carefully roll over and see nothing more because he secures a luxurious silk sleep mask over my eyes. No one has done this before during a massage, but I willingly acquiesce, content to let my mind wander in the darkness as his hands dance across my body.

He is very predictable—the songs on the CD, the way he moves. Facedown for eight songs, then I turn over for three more songs while he finishes up by relieving any lingering tension in my jaw and scalp. When the music ends he chimes the smallest bell and exits quietly, telling me to take my time, to open the door when dressed. Armand returns with a glass of water, to wish me good night, reminding me to soak soon in a saltwater bath since he worked me thoroughly.

After a couple of appointments, when I arrive home, I amend my prescribed post-massage routine, heading directly to my bedroom instead, while the scent of his massage oil lingers. From my assortment of sex toys, I select the eight-inch realistic dildo. Setting the vibration low, sliding the phallus in and out of my wet pussy, I fantasize that Armand is above me, fucking me slowly with his hard cock.

As the days near for my next appointment, I begin to worry that I will be too turned on when he touches me now. Just the thought of his hands firmly rubbing my skin gets me wet because his image has permeated my erotically charged dreams. Will this man, who knows my body so well, notice the difference in me? Do I dare don my panties again—perhaps, feigning menstruation—to not have to worry that I will leave a wet spot on those posh sheets? But I don't want to be untrue to him. After all, I trust this man with my deepest aches. I need to give my body to him honestly so that he can unravel my pain.

A decent hookup would help keep my horny mind in check. Unfortunately, my last date was another of the endless disappointments. I've given up on hoping for a soul mate. This encounter was another online dating disaster. We met at a bar— no points for originality there. He was too sexually aggressive for my taste, but I needed the touch of another human being. I went to his place and we had sex. Or at least we tried to. It was one of those embarrassing nights where his cock kept shriveling and sliding out of the condom. I shrugged it off as too many beers and kept sucking him until he was hard again. After we had three unused and sadly deflated condoms on the bed, I called it a night. And I did not return his texts, instead counting the days until my next massage.

When I arrive for my appointment, the receptionist seems a bit frazzled, telling me that Armand has not arrived, but that

I should go ahead to the usual room. As I sit on the bench and relax, the minutes pass and I begin to wonder if my session has been canceled. Just as I am about to give up, a tall, handsome blonde man rushes up to me, out of breath, and introduces himself as Lance. I have seen him around the spa, working out of one of the other rooms. He apologizes and says that Armand is detained. I can either reschedule, or he will gladly take Armand's place this evening.

Though the thought of not having Armand's expertise tonight is disappointing, I am here and might as well get a massage even if it is abbreviated since the facility is closing shortly. I tell Lance that it's fine; he nods and quickly exits. Since he has given me no instruction, I follow Armand's routine, disrobing and waiting facedown, nude beneath the sheet.

Moments later the door opens and I hear fumbling as the CD player starts up. It is Armand's music—or, maybe, this is standard issue for the spa. Either way, it relaxes me and I hope that Lance can soothe my body in a similar manner. I listen to his movements around the room, and finally his feet come into view below me—they are large, the skin pale.

"Relax," he whispers while standing at the head of the massage table. And he begins. I'm surprised that he doesn't ask about my aches and injuries. Perhaps he has conferred with Armand. Listening to the music, I can almost believe I am in Armand's sure hands. Then I smell that same musky oil and I give my body to Lance, to do with what he pleases. As he is working the knots out of my shoulders and forging a steady path down to the base of my spine, the door opens abruptly and we both jump.

It's Armand's familiar voice. "I apologize, Ms. Rollins. I had a flat tire driving over here."

Driving over here? I turn my head to try to read his face in this dimly lit room and ask, "Didn't you have appointments before mine?"

"I was not scheduled to work today," he explains, "but informed the club that I would come in for your appointment. I hope Lance was able to get you started sufficiently."

Lance has moved to the side of the massage table, but his hands continue to rub my lower back. I can hear Armand moving around, out of my sight line, then he applies pressure to the balls of my feet. Being touched by both of them makes my libido rev up even more.

"He's been great," I respond, "*This* is amazing."

"*This?*" repeats Armand. "You wish for Lance to remain?"

I laugh, embarrassed yet serious. "Two men rubbing me? Who could say no?"

So, instead of leaving, Lance begins to massage me intensely, moving lower on my back than Armand has before. The sheet had been pushed down and draped across my butt. Now Lance moves the sheet down farther, beginning to deeply knead my glutes. Most masseurs shy away from this area, but it contains powerful muscle groups and mine could use some release.

Meanwhile, Armand spreads massage oil on the backs of my legs and begins rubbing the muscles down there. He asks, "May I remove the sheet?"

"Yes," is the only word I can summon in this state of bliss.

The sheet is gone as both men attentively massage my body, their hands getting closer together until I can no longer distinguish Lance's from Armand's. My body is supple from their touch and alive with desire.

Hands slip between my thighs. Their steady rhythm causes my breath to quicken in anticipation. Time becomes fluid as I am lost in pleasure.

Normally the sheet is pulled up to my shoulders, then I discreetly roll onto my back for the final part of my massage. I feel hesitation from them. Someone starts the music again.

Armand asks me, "Would you like to continue?"

"Yes."

He instructs, "Lance, the mask." Lance's hands carefully gather my shoulder-length brown locks as he slips the silky mask on, and helps me roll onto my back.

I wonder how my body must look, bared on the table before them, but don't have much time to think about it because they both begin rubbing me again. I am so turned on, I fight the urge to spread my legs wide open to Armand, who is still at my feet.

Lance begins kneading a path across my shoulders, but soon is circling my breasts with his gentle hands, teasing each nipple with his slick fingers.

Armand asks from below, "Ms. Rollins, may I?"

May he what? I wonder, as I answer, "Yes!"

Hands are between my legs again, this time parting them as far as possible on the narrow table. My open pussy is fully on display to Armand. Deft fingers disappear into the folds of my labia, to probe my wet heat, revealing the strength of my desire.

Lance kisses my forehead, then my lips. His fingertips continue their amazing patterns on my breasts. My nipples are throbbing in sync with my crotch.

I hear rustling at the foot of the table, then Armand removes his hands. Lance stops kissing me, and I listen to the sounds of clothing being shed. My heart is thundering. I think that it must be as loud as my panting breath.

The table shifts slightly as a man climbs onto it, near my ankles. His bare skin brushes mine as he nestles between my legs. Again Armand asks, "May I?"

I arch my hips in response. His question gives life to my limbs, and I reach down to touch him for the first time. The pressure of my hands on his ass is the only consent that he needs. It is my turn to explore his body, finding it as solidly built as expected, defined with powerful muscles. I feel the tip of his cock probing, as he rubs it against my clit.

Now that I am awakened in all senses, I reach around for
Lance. He is still near my side and seems to be naked as well, so
I touch his cock, slowly exploring it. When Armand nudges his
way inside of me, I gasp, and tighten my grip on Lance's cock,
running my hands along his length.

The motions we use are deliberate, delicious. Though I'm
tempted to push the mask aside, I resist because without sight
my sensations are heightened. Armand continues to slide in and
out of me, while someone's hand stimulates my clit. A mouth is
on my nipple, then an eager tongue fills my mouth.

I cannot hold out much longer, the slow strokes tormenting
me as I hang on the edge of orgasm. Lance lets go, shouting,
"Oh!" as he erupts warmly across my stomach. Armand moans
while I ride waves of pleasure, firmly holding his ass and urging
him deeper, deeper.

When I pull Armand down on top of me, I can no longer
distinguish where he ends and I begin. I only feel him thrusting
inside of me and that sends me over the edge. Seconds later, Armand
kisses me passionately and loses himself to me. My pussy
clutches him tightly as his cock spasms within me.

Moments pass. The only sound is our collective heavy
breathing.

As Lance leaves the room, Armand gives me one last kiss,
then retreats from the table. He finishes the way he does in all
the previous sessions, by applying firm pressure to the arches of
my feet and telling me to take my time.

This has been an evening beyond belief. I remove the mask
and use a nearby towel to clean up a bit. When I am fully dressed
and seated, Armand enters, carrying a glass of water as usual.
He smiles and asks, "Same time next month, Ms. Rollins?"

808.8
Tow

Full-Frontal Neighbor

author: Lynn Townsend

category: Romantic Hero

subject:
1. Exhibition   2. Trauma   3. Curvaceous

Full-Frontal Neighbor

Lynn Townsend

"My goodness!" My real estate agent, an enthusiastic little woman with the fading remains of her Eastern-European accent hanging around her too-loud voice like Christmas lights, exclaimed. "That young man is stark naked!"

Well, that wasn't something I heard every day. I turned to look out the indicated window—a full bay enclosure situated in the dining room—and was nearly knocked over by the home inspector. *Gee, Skip,* I thought, straightening my tunic and glaring at his back, *I didn't know that was your thing. Next time, I'll book the Chippendale Dancers when I get my new house inspected.*

Technically, it wasn't my house yet. But if there was nothing really awful on the home inspection, it might well be. I nudged Friedel with one shoulder and she relinquished her spot at the window. The show was probably over already—the house had been abandoned for several years and the neighbor could be easily forgiven for walking around with the curtains up, but surely he'd noticed the cluster of gawkers in the window opposite him. Surely.

He hadn't.

The naked man—and Friedel was absolutely correct, he was just as naked as the day he was born—leaned against the gleaming counter in his kitchen. One leg was bent, the bare foot placed against the cabinet door. One arm supported him. In the other hand, he held a mug, from which he was sipping. He appeared to be gazing dreamily at something out the porthole window and I could only see his face in profile. Strawberry-blond hair, cut messy, spilled down his forehead. His nose was narrow and his mouth full and sensual.

I dropped my eyes lower. A sprinkle of cinnamon hair dusted his chest, drew a narrow line from his belly button to more interesting sights south of his waist. I smirked; if he was that interesting at half-mast, there was a squirming heat in my lower stomach that wouldn't have any objections to a glance with full sails. The flames spread farther, heating my breasts, bound as they were by an eighteen-hour bra. Nipples chafed against the too-firm, too-tight satin.

"Well, it's a nice view out the window," I said, too abruptly. Skip jumped nearly two feet straight up, and I turned a laugh into a quick cough. "What else is on the list?" I glanced down at the clipboard. "We've checked the water, the gas line, the windows?"

Skip snatched the papers away from me. I hissed; the searing, unbelievable pain of a paper cut put out most of the remaining desire. I stuck my finger in my mouth, glaring at Skip from over the knuckle. He mumbled an apology and consulted the list.

I couldn't help it. As real-estate agent and home inspector got back to the job at hand—which is to say, getting a fair chunk of money so that I could give an even larger chunk of money to a bank—I glanced over my shoulder.

Neighbor boy was still oblivious, mug still cradled in his hand, still just as naked and just as glorious as he'd been a few moments before.

Yep, I thought as I turned away, *I have a great view.*

"Jeez!" I exclaimed into the phone. "I need to get some curtains!" I fumbled the phone and almost dropped my coffee, but didn't take my eyes off the window.

Claire, owner and operator of Merlin's Pen Publishing, who happened to also be my best friend, laughed in my ear. "Seems like you shouldn't fix what ain't broke, Mal."

"This conversation is over." Despite that, I didn't turn on the dining room lights and I didn't move from the spot. Neighbor boy was fairly comfortable in his routine; apparently ritual nudity was somehow involved in his life. Like clockwork, every weeknight between seven and eight at night, he was in his kitchen, starkers, drinking coffee and daydreaming. "Tell me what you got for me."

"Well, I have three covers. How's your time? Can you do three in a month?"

"I have a couple in the drawer that I painted just for funsies. Maybe one of those would fit. Otherwise, I got time for two. I'm still knee-deep in the moving-in process. Stupid movers lost half my stuff and I'm just now getting it back."

"Sounds like a blast. Which reminds me, I saw your ex. He said he still had some things of yours and was awaiting your apology before he'd give them back."

"I can live without it. And him," I grumbled. "I had to move back East to get away from him." That wasn't entirely true, but I wasn't above blaming David for just about everything. It was one of my less attractive traits, but at the moment, I wasn't worried about it. Claire hated him almost as much as I did. Neighbor boy stretched magnificently, and I stood there, silent in the darkness, watching him in all his masculine glory. There was a delicate, not quite unpleasant, ache between my legs. At least David had been good for one thing.

"...And I've got one collection of short stories about shape-changers," Claire said. I drew my attention back to the conversation.

"Werewolves?" Great. I hated painting werewolves. Readers all had their own ideas of what lycanthropes should be, and inevitably, anything I painted would be all wrong for two-thirds of them.

"No, just shape-changers. Some of them turn into cats, or foxes. I think one of the stories has a guy who turns into a weasel."

"All men turn into weasels, eventually."

"You know it, girl," Claire said. "So, how 'bout it? Can I send you the specs?"

"Go ahead." Neighbor boy turned. He couldn't possibly see me, and yet I thought he did. Between two layers of glass and the distance of our postage-stamp-sized yards, our eyes met. I couldn't look away. I felt trapped, turned to stone, by that proud, knowing gaze. My breath caught in my throat, a rock-sized lump that I couldn't swallow. My entire body went up in flames. By all that was holy, that was a fine man.

He finished his turn, put his cup in the sink and allowed me a lingering, longing look at his muscular buttocks and lithe back. A dark scar twined up his hip and across one shoulder, highly visible against his ginger-haired, pale complexion. Interesting.

"Mal!" Claire snapped. Reluctantly, I returned my attention to the phone conversation. I had the feeling I'd missed quite a bit of whatever she'd been saying.

"What?"

"Take a picture?" She sounded wistful, which was silly. Claire was the hit of the party, never lacking for a man on her arm or in her bed, sometimes more than one. Not like me, only a few months out of an abusive, obsessive... I shook those thoughts away. I was free now, and that was all that mattered.

"Maybe I'll paint one," I mused.

"You know, you should just ask him out," Claire said. "This is an amazing piece. One of your best. Too bad we had to cut the head off."

"Yeah, well," I said. I eyed the cover art. Typical romance novel wrap, the hero lounged naked against a stone wall, firm chin lifted, abs well-defined, stomach flat, marked with a ropy scar. The ginger-colored cat with wise, knowing eyes, tail wrapped neatly around paws, sat on a tree stump, positioned just right to block the most interesting part of the painting. "He's not even going to look at someone like me."

"You don't give yourself any credit for being a wonderful human being," Claire said, firm and no-nonsense. But I knew *wonderful human being* was polite code for round and dumpy, short and plump. Dishwater-brown hair that never lay flat, not enough curl to be anything other than messy.

Sparkling personality.

You have such a pretty face.

Boring brown eyes, freckled complexion and a complete inability to use makeup.

I shrugged.

"I'm not dating any more pretty men," I said. "They're too much work."

"Your loss. I'd love to take a bite of this guy."

"I'll be sure to introduce you, next time you come to visit," I said sourly.

"I'll get that check overnighted to you. Let me know if you find out what the hell's been happening to your mail," Claire said. I had already faded from her attention; someone was yammering at her in the background. The time difference between East and West coasts; she was still working while I was wrapping up for the day.

"Thanks. Painting this one was fun, but a girl's gotta eat."

The doorbell rang. "I gotta go."

I still had the cover clenched under my arm when I opened the door to look at the subject of my painting. Why, why, why did I never look out the peephole?

"Hi!" I squeaked. My heart hammered and I fumbled with the book, trying to turn it around, dropping it on the ground at his feet.

"Hey," he said. My own full-frontal neighbor, right there on my doorstep. He was even more attractive close-up; his hawk-like nose cut a fine line down sculpted features toward a lush and kissable mouth. He grinned. "I'm Travis Elliot. We're neighbors." He offered his hand and I looked down to take it, saw the mostly naked painting just by his feet and dropped to one knee in front of him to fetch it. I snatched up the novel, turned the picture toward my stomach, and glanced up. Well, that had put me right on a level with his groin, no more than kissing distance away. I squeaked again and bounced to my feet.

"I know," I said, taking the offered hand. His skin was warm, the fingertips calloused, his grip firm but not crushingly so. "I mean, I've seen you." I blushed furiously at my own words. I was still clinging to his hand, and I dropped it hastily.

"And you're Mallory Ellis," he said. I stared and he offered the other hand, several letters held between two fingers. "I've been getting your mail by accident." I jerked my gaze back to his face; he only had the two fingers on that hand, while the others were nothing more than scarred stumps. A ginger blush spattered across his cheeks. Great, now I was making him feel bad? How did that happen? What the hell was wrong with my life?

"Thank you," I said. I held my hands out for the letters and dropped the book again. I swore under my breath and bent to pick it up yet again, and bumped my forehead into his chest as he moved to do the same.

"Could this get any more awkward?" Travis asked. He

picked up the book and turned it over. His breath hitched in.

"Just did." The ground wouldn't swallow me up and end this. I couldn't possibly be that lucky.

He stared at the cover and traced one of his battered fingers across the raised title print. He opened the book and scanned down the title page. *Cover illustration, Mallory Ellis.* "This? *This* is why you've been watching me?"

Shame flooded me, agonizing. "I'm sorry," I said. "I knew I shouldn't. I should have bought some curtains or something, but...you're right, you're totally right. I would be furious."

He brandished the book at me and I flinched, bringing my hands up to guard my face, mail scattering over the sidewalk.

"Whoa," he said. "Whoa, whoa, wait. I..." He touched my arm, brought it down. Those two fingers cupped under my chin, gently tipping my face up. Incredulous, dazed, amazed. "I'm not angry. I'm flattered. You...this is what you see, when you look at me? A romantic hero?"

"You knew I was watching," I whispered. Tears leaked down my cheeks, dripped over his fingers. I was helpless to contain them.

"I spent six years in Iraq and Afghanistan. I *always* know when someone's watching me." Travis gathered up my mail again, groaned and got to his feet slowly. He offered me his hand. I took it, and missing fingers or not, he was strong and lifted me up without the huff of air I was used to getting from David. "Look, can I come in? My leg hurts after I stand up for a while."

"Yeah, sure," I said. I stepped aside to let him pass, not being able to take my eyes off him. My god, was he really in my house? I could almost imagine that I was dreaming, having one of those awful nightmares where I showed up late for class without having studied for a test, or was running frantically from room to room trying to find a place to pee, except I could smell him, lingering coffee, soap, leather and man. My cheek and chin tingled from the warmth of his hand, and I couldn't figure out what to do with my hands.

He tossed the letters on the half-circle table and waited for me to lead him to my living room, although we had matching layouts and he probably knew where every room in my house was as well or better than I did. Travis walked slowly with deliberation, not quite a limp, but it probably would be if he was tired. He paused at the top of the stairs, looking out the window where I'd watched him so often.

"Why?" I twisted my hands together, hearing my knuckles groan and protest.

"Why what?"

"You knew I was watching you. Why let me?"

He eased himself into one of my living room chairs, a battered and comfortable piece I'd picked up at a second-hand shop; the people-eating chair. He stretched one leg with a pained groan.

"Don't laugh," he warned me, still looking down at the cover—god, the cover I'd painted of him.

"I don't see how I could possibly," I admitted. I wasn't comfortable enough to sit. I paced, trying not to look at him, trying not to look out the window, trying to figure out what the hell to do with my arms; locking them behind my back just made me look fatter, and damn, was I trying to look *pretty* for this man? Was I?

"It's part of my therapy," he said. "Although I don't think my therapist meant it so literally."

"Your therapist wants you to be an exhibitionist?"

Despite warning me not to, Travis laughed. "I have PTSD. Posttraumatic stress disorder. I..." He gestured with that crippled hand toward the right side of his body, where the scar was on his back, and the leg he limped on. "I was the only survivor of a street bombing. The other guys in the Jeep with me, they all died. I spent months in the hospital, learning to walk again. Getting weaned off pain meds. Came home. And I didn't feel safe. I didn't like people to look at me. I didn't like to be outside. I couldn't have the windows open, or the blinds up. I stopped feeling safe if I was undressed. It got really bad. I started wearing layers, as if more clothing would help keep out bullets. It wasn't logical; it wasn't sane. The guys in my unit, we all wore body armor, and look what happened to us. A jacket wasn't going to keep me safe and whole."

"My god," I said. "How awful."

"My wife left me. She took our daughter," he continued, his fingers absently rubbing the cover of the book. "I have to be in therapy so that I can see her. My ex portrayed me as being a dangerous lunatic. I'm allowed two-hour, supervised visits, twice a month."

"So you stand naked in front of the window," I said, "to prove to yourself that you're not afraid anymore."

"And then came you," he said. He put the book down. "And I could see you watching me. I didn't disgust you. You didn't flinch away. You kept watching. So I kept showing up, and you kept showing up. I can't tell you how it made me feel."

"I don't see how you could possibly disgust anyone," I said.

Wordless, he held up his mauled hand. I moved slowly, I knew something about trauma, and I knew I didn't always want to be touched, didn't always like human contact. He never wavered and I took his hand in mine, pressed my lips to each scar. "I think you're beautiful."

There it was, out there. The elephant in the room. Couldn't be avoided. Admiration and desire from a pudgy, plain woman whose only claim to being interesting was painting pictures for what were commonly considered pulp novels.

"Mallory," he said. His hand was shaking. "I shouldn't even be here. I don't want you to feel obligated. I have no right to ask you, to want you, to..." How did he sound so vulnerable, so uncertain, when I was the one who'd invaded his privacy, when

I was the one who was deeply, deeply in the wrong?

"And I had no right to watch you," I said. "I did it anyway. Because I wanted to." I leaned closer to him, feeling his breath against my cheek. "What do you *want?*"

No man had ever bent me over backward to kiss me, nor carried me over a threshold, nor littered my bedroom with hundreds of roses, the sorts of grand, crazy gestures I saw and read about in my daily work. Why would they? Love and lust and desire were for thin girls and pretty girls and girls with money who could make a man feel ten feet tall by batting their over-mascaraed eyelashes at him. No one ever kissed me like his life depended on it, like I was a combination of fine wine in the glass of the snobbiest connoisseur and a drink of water to a man in the desert.

Until now.

Travis devoured me, nipped at my lip, teased my tongue out and plundered my mouth when I opened to him. I maintained only enough of my sense and cynicism to engage in mental mockery, to notice where the coffee table was and twist us to one side so that I didn't break my back when we hit the floor. *Damn, I think too much,* I thought, while he continued to kiss me until there was nothing left except the body pressing against mine, his hand strong around the small of my back, the graceful arch as he lowered me to the floor.

My tidy-bun hairstyle disappeared under his hands, fingers tight against my scalp, pulling pins and scattering them everywhere until my hair was in my face, my mouth, in *his* mouth, between us like a living thing, demanding attention. Travis pulled my cotton T-shirt over my head baring the skin on my back to the soft wool of my new Pakistani carpet. He traced a line down my bare arm, raising gooseflesh. I shivered and he followed that line with the heat of his mouth, branding kisses down my shoulder, my arm, licking at the tender and sensitive nook inside my elbow, all the way down to my fingers. He planted a kiss in the center of my palm and then pressed it to his cheek. I stroked his face, feeling the rasp of stubble under my skin, watching his beautiful mouth turn up in a trembling, shy smile and even though this had to be one of the craziest things I'd ever done, I was going to do it nonetheless.

Make love to a perfect stranger—emphasis on perfect—right there in my new living room, naked on my new carpet and crazy with desire.

It was a bit of a fumble getting my bra off. Hell, the damn thing was probably built by a bridge architect and I always had trouble getting it off, even with daily practice and ten working fingers. Nonetheless, he managed it and my breasts sprung free from their satin cage. Ah, sweet freedom. I stretched mightily, feeling the cool air under my boobs. There was nothing quite like it. Travis shifted, resting most of his weight on his left hip, snuggled against my side and just stared at me. Unnerving, motionless. My jaw ached from clenching my teeth, from keeping my mouth shut, because damn it, I wasn't going to apologize again for how I looked. He knew I was a big girl before my shirt came off and if he had a problem with it, I might actually cry. And kill him. Which was going to get blood on my carpet. Sigh.

"I can't get over how radiant you are," he whispered, leaning close to press a kiss against my cheek, just under my eye. "Exquisite." He kissed the other cheek. "Lovely." The tip of my nose. "Amazing." He licked along my throat. "Ravishing." His breath was hot and eager in my ear.

"Horny," I pointed out, "and you're still all dressed."

"Well, let's do something about that," he said. He pushed up on one arm, gesturing to his buttons with his mangled hand. "You might need to assist."

"Happy to." I jerked the buttons out of their holes, brushing against his warm skin as I worked. I pushed the shirt open and bent to taste his flesh, tonguing a circle through the crisp ginger curls around his flat, male nipple. I pushed the fabric off his shoulders and licked at the scar that snaked its way, raw and red, along his chest, savoring the raised mark against my tongue.

Somewhere, the rest of our clothing disappeared as we explored and experimented. Travis found that ticklish, sensitive area along the back of my knee that sent me into gasping, clenching convulsions of sensation, played it until I was sweaty and out of breath. He had a similar, delightful reaction when I stuck my tongue in his navel. He squirmed so much that I knelt between his legs, pressing my heavy chest against his fully engorged cock, and then tasted the area around his belly button thoroughly, grinning through my ministrations as he bucked and then groaned under me, his dick rubbing hard against my breastbone, my nipples gently abraded by the curls of hair on his thighs.

"Oh my god," he gasped, reaching out. He pressed my boobs tight together, sweat on my skin forming a slick passage that he stroked and fucked as I nibbled at his belly and chest. He rocked against me, his breath staccato exclamations of lust and wanting. "That feels so good, so fine. Damn, Mal! My god. Stop, wait." Travis writhed away from me. "Not yet, and if you keep doing that, I'm gonna go off like a rocket."

He turned me gently onto my side, spooning up against my back. The hot length of him pressed into my buttock. He touched me all over, his mouth fastened on my neck, molten and sucking at the tender skin with bruising intensity. He circled my breasts, teasing the round flesh there, not giving my nipples ease until I was whimpering and bucking against him. One hand played with my boobs, first one nipple then the other. He tickled and teased over my ribs and belly, obviously enjoying every inch of my skin. He rubbed firmly against my legs, sliding his cock in between my full thighs. At the same time he pressed me from behind, and his maimed hand found the center of my pussy. There was a decided benefit: his forefinger and thumb pinched, circled, spiraled that tiny bundle of nerves and sensations without other fingers getting in the way, uncomfortable between my legs. I needed my thighs tight together to come, needed to be able to work those muscles in my lower back, my abdomen, to really feel it, and I'd never quite gotten this ease from another lover.

Travis rubbed his thumb and forefinger together, my clit the money between his *gimme* gesture. My toes curled up, calves aching as muscles ratcheted up another notch, then another until I was screaming with need, with heat. My scalp tingled and my forehead beaded sweat, dripping down my temples and along my throat. We slid together, lubricated by the heat between us, and just as I thought I couldn't bear it anymore—I had to come or die, black sparkles in my vision, the pounding of my blood in my temples—his cock slid home into my wet pussy. I felt him inside me, pushing forward, driving against his working hand, rocking me between his fingers and the strong rhythm of his hips and thighs.

I screamed his name, fingernails digging into the soft weave of my carpet. I went stiff with unspeakable pleasure, each nerve ending on fire, each cell in my body straining toward that single moment. Like thin ice, I cracked and broke apart. Almost too limp to move, I turned my head to watch him. Over my shoulder, his face framed by my crazy tangle of hair, I watched the play of emotions on his face, the curling of his upper lip, the set of his jaw, his cheeks flushed. He stiffened, breath coming faster, then releasing in a single exhale.

I let myself collapse on the carpet, overwhelmed. I'd never actually seen a lover orgasm before. All my experience was in the dark, hidden under covers, eyes closed and shame blanketing my perceptions. I shivered, sweat cooling against my skin. Travis shifted slightly, pulling out of my damp thighs. His come leaked down my leg. He pulled his shirt over my shoulder, then snuggled up against my back.

"I feel like I should say something romantic and wonderful right now," Travis confessed, "but I admit to being overwhelmed. That was amazing. Incredible. Thank you."

I laughed, feeling his body slick against mine. "You could welcome me to the neighborhood."

"Won't you be," he sang softly, "please won't you be my neighbor?"

"Hello, neighbor."

823.0
Har

The Whole of Me

author: Katya Harris

category: Speculative Fiction

subject:
1. Greedy Little Slut   2. Neural Implants
3. Voices

The Whole of Me

Katya Harris

2058

"Don't leave me." Shaun's voice hitched, thick with tears. "Please."

He had never begged for anything before, not once in his entire life. He begged now, the pain in his heart a vicious ache.

"Shaun. Don't." Clara's voice was so weak now, Shaun could barely hear it over the soft humming of the machines working so hard to keep her alive.

A sob of sound escaped him, a watery kind of humor. "I thought we agreed that you couldn't boss me around anymore. Not when it came to this."

Clara's bloodless lips stretched. Even as he looked at her, the skin of her bottom lip cracked, a bead of brilliant red welling on the parched surface. Picking up a tissue from the bedside table, Shaun blotted it away and then applied a thick slick of balm from the small pot in his pocket.

"I never agreed to that," Clara murmured against his finger.

Shaun couldn't help but smile at the echo of her usual mischievous tone. "Stubborn bitch."

Clara kissed the tip of his finger. "Don't you forget it."

He wouldn't. He wouldn't forget anything about her.

The idea had blossomed in Shaun's mind the night before as he'd sat in the armchair in the corner of Clara's hospital room. He'd been unable to sleep, terrified he'd wake up to find that she'd died in the night. It had given him time to think and then to plan.

Perching on the edge of her bed, Shaun stroked his hand down her right arm. His fingertips glanced off the port hidden in the underside of her forearm just beneath her elbow. His mouth dry, he reached for the dual-headed jack that sat coiled on the table. Luckily, he'd had one in his car.

"I can't let you go." His words were a rasp.

Clara's eyes were glazed, but for a too-brief moment the flame of her former vivaciousness flickered in their depths. "I don't want to go either." The light in her eyes died, eaten by the cancer that had destroyed her body. "Shaun, I'm so tired."

Panic squeezed down on Shaun's heart as he watched her eyes flutter closed. They had run out of time.

Peeling back the skin-plas that covered his own port, Shaun slid in one of the jacks and twisted it until it secured with a subtle click. A needle of cold pierced him in the shoulder, a metallic taste coating his tongue. He did the same for Clara, ignoring her restless shifting.

Shaun's right hand moved in a complicated gesture, the movement accessing his neural implants through the signals generated by his nervous system. Years ago, they would have been able to connect with a wireless connection, but there had been too many instances of people being hacked and wireless neural components had been outlawed.

"Shaun, wh-what are you doing?"

"Shh, shh," Shaun soothed her. Brushing lank strands of hair from Clara's face, he leaned over and kissed her cool forehead. "It will be all right, baby." His mind worked on bringing down her firewalls, the embedded tech still strong despite her body's weakness. "Just go to sleep. When you wake up, I'll be here." Information started to stream into his mind. "You'll be with me forever."

A year later

"Come on Shaun, don't you think it's been long enough?"

"How long is too long?" he shot back.

Concern darkened Peter's eyes. It was the only thing that kept Shaun from punching him out for bringing him here.

The bar was packed and it hadn't taken more than a minute after walking through the door to realize that everyone in here was looking for a hookup. Surrounded by a combination of prowling men and scantily dressed women, Shaun nursed his third beer and tried to ignore the flirtatious looks being cast his way.

"Shaun, it's been a year. A year. This is, what, the second time you've been out since the funeral?" Peter didn't wait for him to answer. "Clara wouldn't have wanted you to cut yourself off from the world like this. You know that."

No, his extroverted Clara wouldn't have, but she was dead and his own love of socializing had waned. The only way he wanted to spend his nights now was at home, where he could close his eyes and access the memories nestled safely in the center of his mind.

"So I should just, what?" Shaun asked. Anger thrummed beneath the surface of his skin. "Just find some woman and fuck her? Maybe then I'll forget all about my dead wife, yeah?"

Peter recoiled at his friend's vehemence, but then anger lowered his brow. Leaning into Shaun's face, he hissed, "You know that's not what I meant, you stubborn bastard. I loved Clara too. She was one of my best friends." The grief on Peter's face was genuine and seemed to douse his temper. "I know you miss her, Shaun," he said, his voice softer. "How could you not? But

Clara wouldn't want you to bury yourself along with her. She would want you to be happy again."

Yes.

Shaun frowned and looked around.

"Shaun?"

His head swung back to Peter. He struggled to remember what Peter had been saying. "I just, I just need more time."

"Look," Peter said after taking a swig of his beer. "I'm not saying to jump into a relationship or anything. Just..."

He floundered and Shaun saved him. "Find some woman and fuck her," he supplied with an amused smile.

Peter's expression was chagrined. "Yeah, I guess so. Come on Shaun, after a year don't tell me you aren't interested."

In fact Shaun's body was raging at him to get laid, a state not currently helped by the women that frequented this place. All of them seemed to be in dresses that revealed more than they concealed. A parade of barely covered flesh that had his cock standing at attention since they'd walked in.

"I dunno," he hedged. Pride wouldn't allow Shaun to admit that maybe his friend was right.

A glimmer of gold at the corner of his eye snared Shaun's attention.

A blonde walked past their table with a sidelong look from her smokily made-up eyes and a curl to her red, red lips. Her hair tumbled around her shoulders to her lower back, an artful cascade of glimmering curls in a hundred shades of gold.

Clara's hair.

"See, I knew I was right."

Peter's smug voice snapped Shaun's head back round. He glowered at him. "Fuck off, idiot," he grumbled.

Peter grinned at him unrepentantly before sliding his gaze to the blonde that had caught Shaun's attention. He went a little slack-jawed himself. "Jesus," he breathed, his eyes roving over the sweet curve of her ass as she stopped at the bar. "You should go talk to her."

Despite his earlier denial, Shaun found his gaze being drawn back. Christ, she was sexy.

More than me?

"No."

Peter snorted. "Dude, you are crazy."

Shaun jolted a little in his seat. Who had he been talking to? He frowned. "Why don't you take a run at her then?"

"'Cause I was balls-deep in a girl last night," Peter told him with a cheekily smug grin. "So I'd thought I'd let you have this one."

Shaun rolled his eyes. "God, you're a pig. How you get any woman is a goddamned mystery."

Peter laughed and admitted, "I'm gonna be seeing her later on tonight too."

"Really?" Shaun's eyebrow twitched up. Peter had always been a love-'em-and-leave-'em kind of guy. "Is it serious?"

The streak of red that suddenly colored the other man's cheekbones was telling. "Maybe. Kelly—" He sighed, his expression softening. "I know you're going to tease me unmercifully, but she's not like any girl I've ever met."

A shadow of grief passed over Shaun. He swigged his beer to cover it. He knew exactly what Peter meant. It had been that way with Clara.

At the bar, the blonde turned her head. Her eyes caught at his and the smile that pulled at her lips was a tease and an invitation.

She wants you.

Shaun's cock twitched. He talked to Peter, asking about his Kelly, but his eyes rarely left the blonde who kept giving him flirtatious looks as she talked to the friend beside her. Refusing to sit at the bar like her friend was, the blonde leaned against it instead. She knew exactly what she was doing. Just in Shaun's line of sight, he could see at least half a dozen guys eyeing the elegant line of her back, the luscious curve of her ass, the long lengths of her legs. Her painted-on dress, the exact scarlet shade of her lipstick, ended just beneath her bottom. If she leaned over any more then she'd be showing the entire bar what was hidden between her legs.

Do you think she's wearing panties, baby? I bet she isn't. I bet she's bare, in more ways than one. All slick and pink.

That voice stroked him, inside and out. He had either drunk too much or he was going mad. Shaun found that as long as that voice, Clara's voice, whispered in his mind he didn't care.

Look at her.

Shaun did. He even smiled and watched the heat in her eyes flare. Red lips parted, a dark pink tongue darting out to lick at the full curve of the bottom one. She turned her upper body a little toward him, displaying her undoubtedly augmented body to full advantage. Her gravity-defying breasts were barely contained by the low-cut neck of her dress, the valley between them a dark invitation. The image of sliding his dick there imprinted itself on his mind.

Fuck her Shaun. You know you want to.

"I love your place."

The blonde, Monica, threw her purse on the sofa as she looked around Shaun's apartment. The floor-to-ceiling windows that encompassed the living area caught her attention. Kicking off her stilettos, she sauntered over to them. The sway of her hips was mesmerizing.

Shaun prowled after her as she looked out at nighttime Seattle. His apartment was only a few floors shy of the penthouse and had spectacular views. Monica seemed entranced by the twinkling sea of lights.

Coming up behind her, Shaun braced his hands on the window on either side of her. He pressed the front of his body tight against her back, pushing her against the glass. Monica gasped as her body met the cool surface. Or it might have been because of Shaun's erection digging into the furrow of her ass.

"What are you doing?"

There was a tremor in her voice, but it wasn't fear. She proved that when she tilted her hips back, rubbing her butt against him.

Nuzzling his face into her neck, Shaun kissed and licked at the long line of her throat. "I'm getting ready to fuck you."

In the reflection of the glass, Shaun watched her lips curve upward. "Mmm, such a sweet-talker."

Shaun nipped at the flutter of her pulse making her gasp again. "You didn't object at the bar." It had taken surprisingly little conversation to get her to come back to his place.

"What can I say? I'm a girl who knows what she wants."

Capturing her hands, Shaun pressed them palm down on the glass. Skating his hands up her arms, feeling goose bumps roughening her silky skin in their wake, he touched the thin straps of her dress.

"And what is it you want?" he asked her, his voice a low murmur in her ear.

All the reluctance that Shaun had expressed at the bar was gone. Burnt away by the fire of lust raging through his veins. That whispery voice in his head had helped too.

Monica made a little hungry noise at the back of her throat, an adorably feminine growl. "I want to come."

Greedy little slut.

Shaun answered that amused observation in his head. *Like somebody else I know.*

A silvery laugh shivered through his brain.

Hooking his fingers around the straps of Monica's dress, Shaun pulled them down her shoulders. Monica's breath hitched and then a little moan feathered past her parted lips. He pulled the straps farther down her arms until her breasts popped free.

Large and round, capped with small dusky-pink nipples, Monica's tits were luscious. They overfilled Shaun's hands as he palmed them. Her nipples were hard little darts and exquisitely sensitive when he pinched them lightly. Monica's head lolled back on his shoulder as he teased her. Her hips rolled back, massaging his dick with increasingly frantic motions.

Shaun could smell the heated wetness of her pussy. He clenched his jaw to keep from groaning. He hadn't realized how much he had missed the musky-sweet perfume of a woman's arousal.

"Anyone can see you, you know?" They were high up, but there were other buildings overlooking them. With the lights on, they were lit up like there was a spotlight on them. "But I bet you like that, don't you? Thinking there could be someone out there watching you."

A ripple.

"Yes," she hissed. "I like it."

Moving his hands down to her waist, he pushed her forward onto the glass. She cried out as her flushed breasts squashed against the cool glass. Shaun's hands smoothed over her hips, gripped the hem of her dress and pulled it up. Instantly, her legs parted in invitation, one that Shaun took her up on. His hand slid between her legs.

See, I told you she wasn't wearing any panties.

She was bare too, the plump folds of her pussy waxed clean. Lust surged through Shaun's bloodstream, his cock trying to poke a hole in his trousers to get to the slippery, wet flesh between her thighs.

She was so wet, her clit a hard little pearl poking out from between her slick pussy lips. Shaun teased it with his fingers, glancing little touches that drove her wild.

"Please," she begged.

"What?" Shaun whispered in her ear. "Tell me what you want."

She moaned, tremors running through her body. Her reflection showed that her eyes were closed, her mouth slack as she gasped for breaths. "Touch me," she pleaded. "Please. I think I'll go crazy if you don't."

She's so hot for it, Shaun. Give it to her. I want to see her come.

Shaun speared two fingers deep into Monica's dripping wet pussy.

Monica screamed out at the sudden penetration. "Oh god yes!" Her hips gyrated wildly, helping Shaun finger her.

More, Shaun. Give her more.

Obediently, Shaun added another finger to the two already inside Monica. She was so tight there was barely enough room, but the slick juices that spilled from her compensated for it.

"So wet," Shaun purred in her ear. Curling his fingers toward his palm, he pushed them deep. He knew when he hit her G-spot. Monica's hoarse shriek reverberated off the glass. "That's it. Show all those people watching just how dirty you are. Come on, let's give them a show."

Monica's hands flexed on the glass. Her panting breaths misted the gleaming surface. A bone-deep shake jittered through her body, the movements of her hips becoming increasingly erratic. Whimpers and desperate whines squeezed from her lungs.

Shaun didn't know whether the woman's reactions were natural or something she'd learned from a porn flick, and he didn't care.

Insinuating his other hand between her breast and the window, Shaun pinched her budded nipple as he ground the heel of his palm against the throbbing knot of her clit. Monica came with a shrill shriek, falling forward against the glass as orgasm juddered through her. A flood of juices squeezed past Shaun's fingers. He could feel them shooting out of her, drenching his hand. He wondered if she'd squirted all over the window.

"Damn," Shaun breathed. Her cunt spasmed tightly around his still-pumping fingers and all he could think of was how good she was going to feel around his aching dick. He grimaced, lust a dark taste in his mouth.

Monica mewled, a kittenish sound of disappointment, when he slid his fingers free. It turned into a sharp cry when Shaun gave her ass a slap.

"Behave," he growled.

Turning her head, Monica pouted. The playful glint in her eyes tempered the spoiled princess nature of her demeanor. "I was enjoying that." Her voice was husky, roughened to a sexy murmur by her screams.

Stepping back a little, Shaun's hands went to his belt buckle. He undid it and then gripped the top button of his trousers. He paused. "Really? Maybe I should take my cock somewhere else."

"You're a hard-ass," Monica told him. "I like that." The brightening of the lustful gleam in her eyes showed it.

Taking a couple of steps back, Shaun started to unfasten his trousers with a leisure he didn't feel. "Bend over," he ordered her.

She obeyed eagerly, her hands sliding down the glass until her back was level. The lush globes of her ass parted as she canted her hips up, revealing the flushed folds of her pussy, glossy with her juices. Her asshole winked at him invitingly.

A flicker of movement at the corner of his eye. A flash of gold and cream.

Shaun stilled. He didn't look away from the blatantly exposed flesh of Monica's cunt, afraid of what he would see, afraid of what he wouldn't.

A whisper of sensation through his mind, a soundless hum.
I'm here Shaun. I'm always here.

Clara's voice sent a wave of lust crashing through him.
Do it Shaun. Do it. I want to see you fuck her.

Not bothering to undress more, Shaun roughly shoved his trousers to his thighs.

"Brace yourself," he rasped out hoarsely.

A second later, barely enough time for Monica to obey him, Shaun was pushing his cock inside her.

Pleasure ripped up his spine as he drove into Monica's scorching-hot pussy with relentless force.

"Oh god," she cried out, her entire body shaking as she stretched around him. She was so tight, her sheath swollen from her previous orgasm.

That's it, Shaun. Make her scream.

Monica did scream as he pushed into her to the hilt with one forceful shove. He didn't stop for her to get adjusted to him, immediately pulling out only to thrust into her again and again, hammering her pussy with near-brutal lunges. Their flesh slapped together, hard enough to leave bruises. Monica didn't seem to mind. She pushed back into his rough fucking. Words, hoarse and barely coherent, tumbled from her lips. Shaun blocked them out. All he cared about was the way her hot, silken, wet cunt gripped him as he pumped his cock into her. That and Clara's voice whispering through his head.

Does she feel good, Shaun? I bet you feel good to her. A flutter of pale fabric on the edge of his vision. *I remember how good you could make a girl feel. Your big cock filling me up, stretching me wide.*

He could almost feel her behind him, the material of her dress, his favorite, brushing against him. Closing his eyes, he imagined her pressing close to him as he worked his cock in and out of the woman in front of him. His lust surged.

Look at her Shaun. Look at how wet she is.

Opening his eyes, Shaun looked down, watched as his dick shuttled in and out of Monica's cunt, the blood-darkened flesh coming out streaked with the thick white cream of her arousal. He groaned, his pleasure heightened as much by Clara's voice as the sight of what he was doing to Monica. It was madness and he surrendered to it completely.

A shattered cry broke from Monica's lips, the delicate muscles of her pussy beginning to flutter and clench around his dick.

That's it. Harder now. Faster. She's going to come.

Orgasm convulsed Monica's body. Her cunt spasmed, squeezing Shaun tight. He yelled out as her greedy body milked his orgasm from him, his cock pulsing in heavy throbs of pleasure as his cum shot from him in knee-weakening bursts.

Ecstasy ripped Shaun apart, the intensity so great it felt like every nerve lit up in glowing radiance. Even his neural implants hummed, resonating with a bright-edged harmony.

Tension seeped from him as he exhaled a groan. His hands loosened on Monica's hips, and his cock, still semihard despite his spine-cracking orgasm, slipped from her pussy. In an instant, she was standing in front of him, her breasts mashed against his chest as she twined her arms around his neck. Her ruby-red lips caught at his, her tongue sliding deep into his mouth.

Drawing back with a little lick at his lips, Monica purred. "I like the way you fuck, Shaun." Reaching down between their bodies, she gripped his cock, still wet with their juices. It helped her jack him back to hardness. "Let's do it again."

Breathing hard, he smiled even as he tried to make sense of what had just happened. "You're going to be a handful, aren't you?"

Monica smirked. Keeping her eyes locked on his, she went to her knees in front of him. "And you're going to be more than a mouthful."

Shaun's spine bowed as Monica sucked him into her mouth. Her red lips stretched wide around the thick girth of his dick, and her agile tongue lashed at him. Fuck, she felt good. His hands tangled in her hair, guiding her head as she bobbed up and down on his length.

He groaned, his head lolling back on his shoulders, and froze.

There, reflected in the window.

Clara looked back at him and smiled.

"What the fuck is happening?"

It was morning and Monica was gone. She had left, a smile on her face and her hair still damp from the shower they'd shared half an hour ago. She'd kissed him sweetly, teasingly fondling his cock as she told him to call her. Now, he was alone. Sort of.

Do you think she enjoyed herself? The question that whispered through his mind was archly amused.

Running his hands through his hair, Shaun said distractedly, "Yes, I think she did." They'd barely slept last night, their energy and lust seemingly boundless. Monica, he thought, was simply insatiable. His own hunger was more complex. It had been more the soft voice whispering in his ear, the glimpses of his dead wife he kept catching in reflective surfaces that had spurred his lust to such gargantuan proportions. No sooner had he come than he was hard again. It had delighted Monica.

"How can I see you?" Shaun knew it had to do with the download, but the why didn't answer the how. What he had taken from Clara's mind were just her memories, remembrances that he could weave into his own whenever he wished. Shaun usually chose his dreams to access them because then his subconscious could fill in the blanks, create something new flavored with the old. Interaction like this should be impossible outside of sleep. She shouldn't have been able to talk to him, not as if she were actually alive.

Why not? Clara's voice whispered through his mind as he collapsed onto the sofa. *Our memories are what make us who we are. When you downloaded my memories, you took everything that made me, me.*

"So, what? You're alive in me?" His mind struggled to understand the enormity of that. If what Clara was saying was true and he wasn't going mad, Shaun had a whole other consciousness living in his head.

You don't sound happy about it. Shaun could feel her distress. *You said you never wanted to let me go.*

Contrition stabbed at his heart. "I do want you here. You know that. It's just a lot to take in." A thought struck him. "Why haven't you spoken to me before?"

The silence in his head stretched until he wondered if his delusion had ended as suddenly as it had begun. When Clara finally answered, he released a breath he hadn't even known he'd been holding.

I couldn't before. I needed time to—develop.

Shaun frowned. Even as a disembodied voice in his head, he knew the differing tones of her voice and what they meant. "There's something you're not telling me."

The sigh moved through his mind, a cool breeze scattering the leaves of his thoughts. The hairs on his body lifted in a prickling rush.

Does it really matter Shaun? I'm here. With you. A husky laugh, so familiar it made his heart clench. *It was good last night wasn't it? You liked that I was here.*

Just thinking of the past night, of Monica's willing body and Clara's sexy voice in his mind, made Shaun's dick start to harden.

Do you want me to go Shaun? Do you want me to leave and never come back?

Clara's words threaded through Shaun's thoughts, her hurt a pain he felt himself, and he gave in to the sweet madness of her presence.

"No," he said, a wild improbable joy beginning to bloom in his chest. "Don't leave. Stay." Undoing his jeans, he pulled out his erection. He couldn't stop himself. God, he'd missed her so much. Fisting his cock, he slowly started to jack himself.

"Talk to me Clara. Talk to me."

* * *

Shaun groaned as he struggled his way to consciousness. His head felt twice as big as it should be and throbbed with a rhythm that threatened to empty his stomach all over his bed. Clutching it in both hands, he lay on the crumpled sheets and tried to think.

"What the hell?" he croaked through a mouth that tasted like a brewery had died in it. "Clara?"

There was only silence in his head.

Rolling onto his side, Shaun sat up with a groan. His entire body hurt, phantom pains creating a patchwork of aches over his flesh. Christ, what had he been doing last night?

"Clara?"

She didn't answer.

After nearly a month of living with Clara existing inside of him, it was disconcerting to be so alone now.

Shaun's eyes snagged on the bedside clock. "Shit." The hissed expletive was vicious and heartfelt. He was late for work. Again.

His stomach roiled violently as he lurched to his feet. Staggering to the nearest wall, Shaun braced himself, willing the nausea to subside. He was tempted to call in sick, but his boss had already spoken to him about his poor performance lately.

Half an hour later and Shaun was showered, shaved and as decent as he could make himself look. Painkillers had solved most of his problems, but something nagged at him, something hovering just on the edge of his memory.

He was going through his front door when he noticed a voice mail on his cell. Distractedly, he listened to it, wincing as Peter's voice blasted into his ear.

"Shaun, what the hell is going on? I saw you last—"

He cut the message short, deleted it. He didn't have time to deal with whatever was up with Peter.

Going to the garage beneath his building, Shaun got into

his car. Inputting his destination into the car's navi-array, he engaged the autopilot. Usually he liked to drive manually, but today he needed the extra time to think.

He needed to cut back on the nights out. Lately, he had been spending more nights out than in, prowling through bars and clubs. Clara in his head and a lust that refused to be slaked. He tried though. A train of women had made their way through his bed.

Why had he woken up this morning alone then?

A flicker of memory darted through his mind. An impression of flesh and heat. A shadow of arousal that had his dick hardening. He hadn't been alone last night. Maybe they had snuck out before he woke up? It bugged Shaun that he couldn't remember her though.

And where was Clara?

The car stopped. Three beeps snapped Shaun back to awareness, an electronic voice telling him he had arrived at his destination.

Getting out of the car, he locked it and made his way inside his office building. He hadn't taken more than ten steps beyond the revolving doors when a voice called him to a stop.

"Shaun? What the hell are you doing here?"

Only by a Herculean effort did Shaun stop the blistering swear word that wanted to fly past his lips. Turning, he pasted a smile on his face and hoped he didn't look as sick as he felt. "Mr. Mortenson, good morning. I'm so sorry I'm late."

The older man frowned. "Late?" he repeated and then louder, "Late? You call not showing up for work for *four* days, late?"

Around them, the few people walking through the lobby stopped and stared at Mortenson's incredulous shriek. Shaun couldn't blame them, not when he could only stare himself. A sick chill crept up his spine.

"What are you talking about?" He could barely keep his voice steady. "It's Monday."

"No. It's Friday." Mortenson's frown deepened into heavy lines of disapproval. His face scoured him. Shaun knew what he would see. The rumpled suit. The dark circles under his eyes. His pale skin and hair still damp from his hurried shower. "Are you on drugs?"

Shaun heard the question, but didn't bother to answer it. A glance at his cell and the truth that he had missed was there: *Friday 24th.*

Ignoring Mortenson and his indignant cries, Shaun staggered back toward the entrance.

"Clara, what have you done?"

Nothing but an echoing silence answered him.

Chills swept up his spine as he stumbled back to his car. His hands shook so much he could barely unlock the door. When he finally managed to open it, he collapsed inside, breathing hard and on the edge of passing out. He programmed the car to take him back home.

Four days. Four fucking days when he had no idea what had happened to him. What he had done.

Shaun changed his destination.

It wasn't even ten o'clock yet, but he had to go back to the bar where he had met Monica, the last place he remembered being before this morning. Hopefully going there would spark his sluggish memory to life because Clara was still dormant.

"Why won't you talk to me?" he whispered to himself.

Was he really going crazy? Had her voice ever been real?

Finding a parking spot a little way down the street from the bar, Shaun got out and hurried toward it.

"Shaun. Hey Shaun."

The unfamiliar voice rocked him to a stop. Confusion swirled through his mind because he didn't know that voice and yet he did. Clammy sweat dampened his skin and chilled him to the bone.

Shaun turned around and found himself enveloped in a clinging embrace.

"I was so hoping to see you again." The man loosened his hold a little and grinned at him. "Naughty boy. You told me you'd leave me your digits."

With a wrench, Shaun broke free. He clenched his fists to hide the sick shaking.

The man, a handsome Asian guy in his twenties, frowned in concern. "Hey, you all right?" He reached out a hand to touch Shaun's cheek and Shaun flinched away.

"I don't know you." The words were choked out of Shaun's throat because even as he said it, he knew he did. He knew this man down to the taste of his cock and the noises he made when he came. The knowledge burst through his mind, the memory followed by another and another.

The other man frowned, hurt in his eyes and the shadow of angry suspicion. "You don't remember me? Come on, you weren't drinking that much."

Shaun knew it had nothing to do with alcohol.

Clara, what have you done?

Without saying a word, Shaun spun round and rushed for his car, ignoring the man shouting his name behind him.

Owen. His name was Owen.

He made it back to his apartment in a daze. Bursting through the door, Shaun slammed it shut behind him and screamed. The ragged cry echoed through his apartment. It hadn't faded before he collapsed on the floor, the strength gone from his limbs as he tried to understand.

He could remember, he could remember all of it. The lost hours, the lost *days*. All the things that Clara had tried to hide from him. Peter's message suddenly made sense.

"You stole my body." A pained whisper.

For the first time since he'd woken up, Shaun felt Clara move in his mind. She felt sluggish, like she was tired. Shaun guessed she had reason to be.

Only for a little while.

Fury rushed through Shaun, chasing away the chill of shock. "Four days," he hissed. "That's not a 'little while' and it's not the point. You took me over! You used my body!"

And she'd let others use it too. A barrage of images battered him, ghostly sensations sweeping over his body. Pleasure that even now made his cock surge to life between his legs. Fuck, no wonder he was sore. The things he had done, that he had begged those men to do to him. Shaun's cheeks burned.

I just wanted to have a little fun, Shaun.

He couldn't believe what he was hearing.

"You're not Clara. My Clara would never do something like this to me."

Oh, but I am. I am everything Clara was and all the parts that you never saw, never knew. Not just her memories, but her dreams, her desires, all the things she kept secret. Even from you.

"Clara didn't hide anything from me."

That velveteen laugh as familiar as it was strange. A glimpse of a face from the corner of his eye. Gone when he turned to look. *Shows how much you know.* A pause. *There was so much I didn't get to do, Shaun, so many experiences I didn't get to have.*

Sensation rippled through his mind, a caress. Despite his anger, his horror, Shaun's eyes slid shut, his head falling back on his shoulders.

I got carried away. I'm sorry. I promise I won't do it again.

A tear squeezed out the corner of Shaun's eye.

"You're lying."

Another pause. *How can you tell?*

Shaun laughed and it was as bitter as his tears. "Because you're my wife and there are still some things I know about you."

You wanted me to live, Shaun. I want to live.

Peter had been right. All his friends had been right.

Closing his eyes, Shaun moved his hand in a small, complicated gesture. It felt stiff, unwilling. Was it his reluctance or Clara's? He didn't even know.

Shaun, stop it.

"I love you Clara, I'll always love you, but I'm doing what I should have done a year ago." His hands fisted as he accessed his neural implants, selected his commands. "I'm letting you go."

No, Shaun, don't do—

"Good-bye."

813.8
Mah

Notes on a Scandal

author: Kelly Maher

category: Contemporary Romance

subject:
1. Masturbation   2. Library   3. Love Letters

Notes on a Scandal

Kelly Maher

The first note appeared with the photocopy of an article from
1853 discussing the fallout of an affair between an aristocratic
lady and a married minister in England's exchequer office. Pale
lavender pages scrawled across with dark purple ink were inter-
filed with the black-and-white pages.

> *It has been too long since I last saw you. You rare-*
> *ly notice me, but every time we meet, I find that*
> *I cannot tear my eyes away from your features.*
> *Each night after one of our timeless, and yet too*
> *short, encounters, I dream of you. I wonder what it*
> *would be like if our hands brushed. The electric feel*
> *of skin against skin, a physical connection not to*
> *be denied, the knowledge of what could be if more*
> *than a square centimeter of our individual bodies*
> *met together. Would it be glorious, this conjoining?*
> *Disappointing? Have I built you up too much in my*
> *own mind? To the point neither you nor another*
> *man could meet the high standards I have?*

Friends tell me I'm too picky. They don't know the true reason: I'm afraid. Afraid of my dreams being met and exceeded. Afraid of my dreams being too lofty. How would you counsel me? Your intelligence shines bright in your eyes every brief moment we have together. It is your quick mind and wit which first attracted me, I must admit. I've never understood the predilection of my friends for fine features without substance behind them.

My fondest dream is one where we meet, surrounded by other people, and you see me, truly see me and wake as if from an enchanted sleep. You clasp my hand in yours and declare the need to whisk me away from the crowd to learn more about me. We leave everyone behind, ignoring the whispers building around us.

We find a secluded room and there, we begin to learn each other. The soft touch of lips, fingers. Exploring, discovering, uncovering. Soon, the crowd refuses to be rejected and comes to claim us once more. We are separated, but all I can feel are your hands upon me. Learning my curves, my secrets.

Gasps fill the air around me as I cannot resist remembering, recreating the way your hands moved across my skin. I need more of you. More time. More hands. More cock.

Brandon blinked. The abrupt end to the handwritten note had him scrabbling through the other papers in the envelope trying to find the rest of the letter. There had to be more. No woman would end an intimate letter to a lover on such a note. He paused. That was such a bad pun.

"Argh."

He caught a few glares from the other students surrounding

him and flushed. Wincing, he acknowledged their silent rebukes and returned to his search. Nothing. Not one more scrap of paper. He read the note again and realized there was no way the paper was contemporary to the subject of the article. This was not a missive from between the parties involved in the scandal he was studying, as he'd first assumed.

Who, then, was it from? Who was it for? The language didn't strike him as particularly modern, but what did he know? It's not like he'd ever been the recipient of a love letter of any kind.

He packed his bag up and headed back to the access services desk. Lauren sat to one side, typing away at the lone computer on the service desk. She smiled at him.

Her dark-blonde hair was twisted up behind her head with what looked like chopsticks anchoring it. The dark-brown plastic rims of her glasses seemed to emphasize the chocolate brown of her eyes.

For some reason, he'd never noticed the specifics of Lauren's appearance. If pressed, he probably would have said her eyes were blue, because didn't all blondes have blue eyes?

"Can I help you?"

Thinking back to the content of the letter, he found his tongue tied.

"Brandon?"

He cleared his throat. "Sorry. I, um, found some papers in with the article I requested."

"Can I see them?"

He felt heat burn the tips of his ears. "Um, they're kind of personal."

She folded her hands and pursed her lips, but he saw the twinkle in her eyes. "As a librarian-in-training, I keep all requests and personal information about my patrons in the strictest confidence." She held up one hand and waggled her fingers. "Come on. Hand them over."

He gave her the whole packet: envelope, article, and letter.

She scanned everything and shrugged. "Sorry. All I can tell you is that we open the envelopes when they're received. If it's only a single request, we leave it in the original packaging and log it into the system. The letter was probably added here, but I can't tell you who did it. You don't happen to study forensics, do you? You could dust it for fingerprints."

"Nah, I'm studying economics."

"Cool. I'm graduating from the library school program this semester. When do you finish?"

"I've just started the hard-core research for my dissertation, so it will be another couple of years."

"Good luck with that. Anything else I can help you with?" She stood up and leaned her hip on the desk as she handed the packet back to him. He caught a whiff of a light floral scent.

He smiled. "I guess not. Maybe let me know if anyone's missing a love letter?"

"Want to leave it here?"

He probably should. He wondered why she had given it back to him. "Um, no. I'll take care of it."

She grinned at him. "I'm sure you will."

Two days later he was back at the library to pick up another request. This one had apparently come in with a batch of others as the envelope this time had their university's seal in one corner. Lauren was again manning the desk.

"How's that love letter treating you?"

"Uh, fine. Anyone come to claim it?"

"Not yet."

The person behind him in line, a prissed-up old lady, from the anthropology department if he remembered correctly, coughed and cleared her throat. Taking the hint, he said good-bye to Lauren. The twinkle was back in her eye as she shot him a quick smile and then composed herself to face the dragon.

He headed up a floor in the library and staked out a table. Opening the envelope, he dumped the contents of it onto the flat surface. More lavender pages fluttered out from between the sheets of the new article.

I dreamt once again last night. We had secreted our-selves in a bower filled with bouquets of lavender and braziers of a spicy scent I have few words for. I lay on the bed as you stood by the door. Unsure of how to comport myself, I offered myself to you. Instead, you became commanding. Full of yourself. Your masculinity. I wanted to submit to your every desire.

I wore a diaphanous silk dressing gown, and nothing else. Thin ties held it together in three spots down my torso. You demanded I leave the bed and come to you. As I did so, the gown billowed out beyond my body. I searched the dim recesses of the room for windows as I felt a tropical breeze caress-ing my skin. Between the flutter of silk, the tendrils of wind, and your hard gaze, my body dripped in readiness when I finally paused before you.

Your hand wrapped around my neck, fingers dig-ging into my hair, which had been arranged in some kind of knot. Slowly, ever so slowly, your head bent toward mine until micrometers separated us. Our breaths mingled as you held yourself apart from me. Heartbeat bled into heartbeat and yet you tortured us both.

Words yearned to break free of my breast, but fear I'd turn you away held them locked inside. I closed my eyes, unable to meet your gaze a moment more without breaking. I felt the air stir around my face as you laughed softly.

"Worship me."

Unable to refuse the command, I did so. My fingers grazed along your jaw as I imprinted the line of it onto my memory. I wanted, so badly, to caress your lips with mine, but instead, I slid them down your throat. At the base, I met my first barrier.

The shirt you wore was made of linen. Starched and firm, the collar scraped the tender skin below my own jaw. My fingers undid the buttons, and I spread the lapels wide to reveal the hardened muscles of your chest and the dusting of dark hair across the surface of your skin.

Have I ever told you how much I love the look of hair on a man? I only wish you hadn't shaved. I want to feel the rasp of your beard marking me, claiming me, all over my body. Next time, won't you?

Not once did you release your hold on my hair. You let me explore, but if I strayed from your ultimate desire—and mine, too, you must have known—you redirected me. Not even to fully remove your shirt did you let go. When I reached your pants, I undid the belt buckle and unzipped them. Inside, your cock waited for me. Eagerly. I barely brushed the cotton of your underwear and it jumped, craving my attention.

I pushed down both slacks and underwear, exposing you to me. I cupped your balls, caressing the wrinkled skin that nestled in a thatch of fur. You moaned as I wrapped my hand around your base and squeezed. I couldn't resist anymore. I had to taste you.

First, I kissed the tip of the head, and then eased my lips open as I pushed my head down and allowed you to enter me for the first time. As my lips encased you, I paused so they rested around the rim of the head of your cock, and sucked. Your fingers tightened in my hair, but that was your only response. I longed to have you shout and writhe under me.

I started squeezing my fingers around your base in rhythm. Hummed along with it as I stroked my head up and down your shaft.

While I played with you, I played with myself. I couldn't resist the pull your erotic magnetism had on my own body and senses. Soon, your grunts filled the air. Not shouts, but it would have to do. I watched as the muscles of your lower belly clenched and delineated themselves moments before you spurted into my mouth.

I broke away to allow the last moments of your orgasm to spray against my breasts as I worked my clit in a frenzy. As the last of your semen came, so did I.

Brandon headed for the rear study room of the fifth floor. He glanced around and saw no one around. Not even the sound of a page reshelving books could be heard. At the last moment, reality intruded and he thought to look for security cameras. None facing the room, and none in the room. That he could see anyway. He had to take the chance. His body wouldn't last long enough for him to run the mile to his off-campus apartment.

This was as private as he was going to manage.

He closed the door behind him and backed himself into the corner so no unsuspecting coed or librarian would accidentally see him jerking off.

The visualizations from the letter fired through his brain once again. Heated his blood to boiling. He jerked down his zipper and wrenched down his boxers so he could grab his cock. He fisted himself, pumping hard until the strongest solo orgasm he could remember having wrenched through him. At the last moment, he thought to yank down his T-shirt to catch his come.

Wrecked, he slid down the wall. Knees weak and cock hanging half-erect from his open fly, he heaved in breaths, trying to recover his mind.

The only thought he could muster was that he needed to find the sender of the letters and discover whether or not they were intended for him.

A week later his phone buzzed. He picked it up from his desk and saw an automated message from the access services department in the library. Another of his requests had come in.

He piled the papers he'd been working on together and tossed them into his messenger bag, slinging it across his body. He shouted a quick good-bye to the other grad students in the communal office and ran outside to his bike.

Five minutes later, and shocked some campus cop hadn't pulled him over for reckless biking, he locked his bike up at the library's rack.

He hurried inside and found Lauren helping some other student, or maybe a new faculty member, at the desk. No other staff member came out, so he waited his turn patiently. Even if he did want to snap at the other guy for nickel-and-diming Lauren on the ILL fees for his items.

When the ass-hat finally left, Lauren grinned at him. "Let me guess. You're here for your article?"

Blushing, he winced and nodded. What must she think of him? How many other grad students rushed over for new research? "Yeah. I just got the notification."

She laughed. "I haven't even had a chance to put them in the retrieval files. Hold on a moment and I'll get it for you."

Disappearing into the work area, she came out with a manila envelope in her hands. He wanted to yank it out of her fingers, but clenched his hands until she scanned it in the computer and marked it as picked up.

"The fees for this one ended up being ten dollars. We'll add that to your account, okay?"

"Yeah, sure." When she handed it to him, it took all he had to calmly remove it from her grasp and nod his thanks to her.

Forcing himself to keep to a sedate walk, he headed for the study room from last week. Only, when he got there, he found it filled with a pack of undergrads. They looked up at him, but he waved and headed back downstairs. Damn. The only place he could think of was his apartment.

He didn't want to wait, but he'd pushed his luck last week with that stunt in the study room. What the hell had he been thinking?

As he hurried back past Lauren's desk, she shot him a confused look. "Hot date?"

"Um, yeah. Forgot an appointment I had."

"Have a great weekend."

"Thanks. Um, you, too."

He noticed her eyes sparkled as she waved him off. She was seriously cute. Maybe he should ask her out one of these days. What better than a live girl who might be interested in him to get his mind out of the rut into which these letters had thrown him? He turned around to do just that and found her involved in a heated discussion with someone who looked to be a faculty member. Later, then.

The bike ride to his apartment did little to cool his blood or ease his nerves. He fumbled with his key at the door and finally closed it behind him. Locked it.

Ripped the envelope open and pulled out the papers inside. Breathed a sigh of relief as he found lavender sheets of paper nestled within his article.

We were back in the bower. All you wore were satin sleep pants. Your chest was bare, I wanted to reach for you and cuddle close. You lit candles and circled them around the bed. I lay there, waiting for you, clad once again in the gown. This time, it was only tied with one set of ties. You had untied the top set and bared my breasts, then the bottom set and framed my pussy with the edges of the gown.

"Perfection," you said. I feared moving would disturb the tableau for you and break the spell. I held myself as still as possible and wondered if a heart could beat through a chest wall. My breasts must have moved with every beat.

When the last candle was lit, you crawled onto the bed and lay down next to me. You traced the edge of the gown, down one side and up the other. When you brushed the sides of my breasts, I wished you would bend and suck the nipples. All you did was draw circles on my skin.

I bit my lip and tried to lock my muscles, but I could still feel twitches and knew you had to see. You didn't say anything.

Did I please you with my stillness?

Time stretched thin with want. When I couldn't bear it anymore, I let my breath shudder out from my lungs and reached one hand for you. You pinned it back on the bed.

"Are you a naughty girl?"

"Only for you."

"We'll have to do something about that."

You flipped me over. Slapped my ass. Shock careened through me. Desire. This is what I had wanted, though I hadn't known myself well enough to ask. When you next made contact, I arched my back to lift my ass into it. Your palm curved over the globe. Strike. Strike. Strike.

Then I felt your teeth on my neck. A nip.

"Do you require more discipline?"

Did I? Perhaps. Would it be against the rules to ask for it? Between my legs, I could feel wetness gathering at the entrance of my pussy. Would you punish me for the pleasure?

You lifted the skirt of the gown, cupped each globe and spread my ass, my legs. I heard your breathing deepen. "Maybe later."

The rough skin of your fingers stroked down my cleft, gathering some of the wetness before circling my clit. I moaned into the pillow. Never had I wanted anything more than I wanted you inside me at that moment. You ripped one of the pillows from my grasp, lifted my hips and placed the pillow below them.

As you shifted your legs between mine, I felt the scrape of the satin of your pants. Wondered if your cock would feel the same as their rough silkiness. Rather than entering me right away, you nestled your cock along my cleft and rocked against me.

"How does it feel?"

I tried to close my legs against you, wanting— needing—more pressure, but the weight of your body against mine limited my movements. "More. Give me more."

You chuckled against my ear, but continued rocking. I could feel a faint pulse begin in my clit. I shuddered, but it only teased me. As you did. I know you felt my reaction, but all you did was pump your body against mine. Promising, forever promising.

When the second pulse had my lower lips lapping

against you, you finally relented. Pushed inside of me. I sighed in relief at the glide of your cock. This. Fulfillment.

You planted your hands just above my shoulders on the bed, and I gripped your wrist as you pumped into me. I turned my head so I could take your thumb into my mouth. I had to have you fill me in every possible way.

Seconds? Minutes? Hours? Millennia? How long were we joined as one? Time lost meaning for me. All I cared about was the feel of you inside me. Claiming me as yours.

I tried to claim you as mine in return. I clenched down with my inner muscles, trying to keep you with me for as long as possible. Did I make you mine?

Eventually, neither of us could avoid the ultimate release.

I shouted your name, Brandon.

I want you to shout mine.

Meet me tonight at 9 by the Alma Mater statue?

In the throes of his orgasm, he almost missed the import of the last portion of the letter. Him. The letters were for him. The letter writer wanted to meet him.

Should he? She could be crazy. Who wrote—by hand—anonymous love letters these days?

He looked down his body to where his cock was cupped in his hand, jizz splattered against his lower belly. Well, maybe not love letters so much as lust letters.

God.

He wanted to. He really wanted to meet her. He'd never connected to someone like this before. Anonymous or not. What would sex be like in person? Yeah, he wasn't as inventive as she imagined him to be. But she sure as hell had an imagination. He'd be happy to play whatever role she wanted him to.

He had hours before the appointed meeting time, but his concentration for anything beyond his mysterious letter writer was shot. Finally, he managed to get himself showered and dressed. Even then, it was barely six-thirty.

Every time his phone rang, he let it go to voice mail. A few texts came in, both from friends wanting him to join them at happy hour, and from students wanting to know if he'd graded their midterm papers yet.

Flipping on the TV, he watched reruns of old football games. He knew most of the outcomes already, which made it perfect brain candy while he bided his time. When his watch finally showed eight-thirty, he booked it out of the apartment and headed for the statue.

With ten minutes to go, he spent the remaining time pacing up and down the walkways surrounding the statue. He encountered a few groups of people, but as he left them alone and steered out of their way as they approached, they passed without comment.

The bells of the school carillon chimed the hour. He glanced at his watch and saw they were a minute ahead.

In the distance he heard more footsteps. Lighter footsteps. One person's footsteps.

She emerged from around the building. Hair pulled behind her head with sticks of some kind poking out from around her head. Dark glasses framed her eyes. Familiarity tugged at his consciousness. She wore a hip-length leather coat, jeans and heeled boots. A scarf was tied so it framed her face along her jaw as it was tucked into the neckline of her coat. As she crossed under a lamppost, he finally made out who it was.

"Lauren?" He wanted to rub his eyes to make sure he wasn't imagining her. Especially since he'd been on the verge of asking her out before he read the last letter.

"Hey, Brandon." She grinned at him. "I was worried you wouldn't come." She winced. "Um, yeah, ignore the pun."

He knew if it had been light out, she'd have seen the tips of his ears glow stoplight red. "Sure. So. You wrote the letters?" He seriously couldn't believe it was really her standing in front of him despite the evidence his eyes and ears were conveying to his brain.

Her chest lifted as she drew in a deep breath. "Yes. I did. I hoped they'd get your attention, and if you didn't like them, no harm, no foul and no damage to our professional relationship."

"That's kind of..."

"Unethical?"

"I was going to go for ingenious. I'll skip the ethics discussion if you will." He smiled at her. "Want to go for dinner? We can talk about how to spend the weekend over a nice steak."

"You can have steak, and I'll go for a Portobello mushroom. But, yes, I'd love to discuss how to spend the weekend with you."

He held out his elbow and she slipped her hand through it. Feeling the press of her leg against his as they walked to a nice little on-campus bistro was only the beginning of what he was sure was going to be the weekend of his life. All thanks to a librarian who couldn't resist naughty letters to go along with articles on indiscretions of the past.

813.8
Mar

Appetizer

author: **Sommer Marsden**

category: **Romance**

subject:
1. Hotel   2. Oral Sex   3. Light Cuckolding

Appetizer

Sommer Marsden

I told Jamie the fantasy a million years ago. I had confessed one night after too much wine and too much laughter and that game you play where you spill your top-secret fantasies to each other. In a new relationship, that game can make you or break you. I knew we were meant to be together when he listened patiently to my most secret thoughts and then proceeded to bend me over and fuck me as if the world were ending and it might be our last time.

Then I'd promptly forgotten my confession.

It'd been five years since then and on the anniversary of our first date he'd decided to take me to dinner. To the big seafood restaurant by the harbor. The one we never could have afforded when we first hooked up. I had no money and he had no money and dates consisted of cheap wine and cheese platters in front of bad B movies or sitcoms.

I was nervous, and I had no idea why. Something in the air. An ozone smell that signified something big, maybe. Or a crowded thick feeling that made me think of anticipation.

Either way, I could feel something as I shimmied into my

little black dress. Underneath I had on a simple black bra. I've never been much for fancy lingerie and neither has he, given his most famous bedroom line is: "That's nice. Take it off."

I rummaged for panties but ceased searching with a gasp as his big hand came down over my much smaller ones. Jamie said, "Why not leave it to chance under that there black dress?" He winked at me and it went right to the center of me. I was already wet, just thinking really, about what would be the inevitable outcome of our night. But I went from wet to soaked when he grabbed me that way.

"What if my dress blows up?"

"What if it does?"

"What if people see?"

He grinned at me and another fine tremor of excitement shook me. "What if they do?"

I bit my lower lip. Torn. Wanting to protect myself but please him too. Turn him on. Fuck, turn us both on. In the end, the temptation of going bare was too great and I shut my underwear drawer.

"Stockings?"

"Nope. It's warm."

It was warm. Warmer than most Mays are. The heat had gotten into my system. Giving me a sultry feel all day long and into the night. I always felt as if the drumbeat of my heart was audible. We'd had sex every day this week and I doubted this night—given the celebratory nature of it—would be any different.

"I have a surprise for you," he said, walking into the bathroom to give his teeth a quick brushing.

"You do? Is it diamonds?"

He laughed.

"Rubies? Pearls? A beach house in the Bahamas?"

"Nothing quite that dramatic, Blair. Or expensive," he added. "But I think you'll like it."

He reached out to tweak my nipple through my dress and it brought me down to a sigh. His touch usually did that.

"I have something for you, too," I said, thinking of the framed concert ticket I had for him. It was the concert we attended the night we first fucked. I'd dug it out of his memento drawer and had it matted and framed. Silly, really, but something about it made me happy. "Do you want it now or later?"

He was on me in two big steps, his hands slipping beneath the hem of my dress and shoving the fabric high on my thighs. Since I was sans panties per his instruction, cooler air kissed my clitoris and brushed over my slit.

"Later," he growled. And then he started singing "Anticipation…"

I laughed. "Let's go before we just fall into bed and rut like animals instead of going for that nice dinner we could never afford until now."

He grinned and shook his head. "Damn. And here I was considering the rutting portion of our evening first."

"Later," I said and kissed him.

"The restaurant's the other way," I said as the car slithered down a typical one-way city street. "If we turn around—"

"Reservations for seven, not six like I said. This is the surprise." Jamie pulled into the private parking structure for the Charles Hotel.

"A hotel?"

"For the night. By the harbor. Water view from up where we are."

I smiled, floored by the nice surprise. "Wow. Swanky," I laughed.

"That's not all. Let's get checked in and I'll explain. We have a while before we have to leave for dinner."

"What will we do?" I asked.

"Oh, we'll figure it out."

My scalp prickled with excitement. I was sure we would figure it out. I was sure I'd like whatever we ended up doing. And
the fact that he was toying with me—which was clearly evident
now—only made the absence of panties more noticeable.

My pulse beat heavy between my legs, my pussy wet for him
before we even entered the lobby. Blush swept over my cheeks
because I felt like everyone could see and smell and sense my
arousal.

Jamie took my hand and squeezed. He led me to the counter and went through all the motions of getting us checked in
and up to our rooms. The ride in the elevator seemed to take
forever. We had one overnight bag that he'd had stowed in the
back of the car. So we were all alone, no porter to help us.

Right before our floor he moved me to the wall of the elevator, pressing one big forearm across my breasts to pin me. My
breath hitched, and I squeezed my insides tight to trigger a blip
of pleasure. When he kissed me, the little bit of air in my lungs
evaporated. I was suffocating on his kiss and it was the best
way I could imagine dying.

"I can't wait for this," he said.

"Me too." But I didn't really know what this was, did I?

Which became utterly clear when we entered the room to
find a tall, handsome man with a shock of chocolate-colored
hair and bright-green eyes. He was sitting on our bed and smiling.

"I...um—do we have the wrong room?" I stammered, back-
tracking to read the number on the door.

Jamie laughed softly and stopped me with his body. He put
his hands on my shoulders, turned me to face the man and said
in my ear, "Blair, this is Oliver. Oliver is your appetizer."

My tongue stuck to the roof of my mouth and I felt a little
light-headed. *This*. This was my fantasy. An appetizer before
sex is what I'd told him. A man to go down on me. Get me wet.
Get me juicy. And then the man I loved could swoop in and fuck

me. It was a fantasy I'd had for as long as I could remember.

"You hired me a hooker?" I whispered.

Jamie laughed and even Oliver joined him.

"Actually, no. I work with Oliver. We hang out at lunch. We both play basketball on the work league. We...*share* over beers sometimes. And he is a—"

"Oral slut," Oliver jumped in. He stood halfway and stuck out his hand. I shook it with a hand that was mostly numb. "I like to go down on women. It gets me off. A lot."

I felt my eyebrows go up of their own volition and a tiny squeak escaped me.

Behind me, Jamie was working my dress up slowly. He'd only raised it an inch or two but every millimeter was evident to me because cooler air caressed my legs. The tops of my thighs were wet with my own juices and I found myself fixated on Oliver's mouth. A pretty mouth. A pouty mouth. A mouth that almost—but not quite—belonged on a girl.

"So you want to..." I couldn't bring myself to say it.

"Eat you out," Oliver said with a nod.

"Go down on you," Jamie said, pressing his mouth against my neck and kissing me there. "While I watch. And then poof! He's gone. And I'm fucking you and then as promised...dinner." My dress rose up a little more. I felt as if he were drawing up a curtain to show off my recently waxed mound. That thought alone made me moan.

Once I did that, he planted soft kisses along the nape of my neck just below my hairline. Jamie kissed along my shoulders and lifted my dress at the same time. Filtered hotel air licked at my pubis. I pressed my thighs together, both shy and eager.

"Where would you like to be?" Oliver asked.

At the sight of me bare, his eyes had glazed over a little. As I watched, his wet tongue took a fast swipe over his lips. He stared at me and with every second that ticked by I felt my pussy grow slicker.

"Where do you want me?" I asked Jamie.

"This is your fantasy," he said. He stroked my asscheeks softly, moved his hand around to tweak my clit. Then a finger slipped inside me as easy as you please.

"That's part of my fantasy. You telling me where to be," I gasped.

"In that fancy chair, then. Legs spread wide so I can see. I'll sit on the bed. Oh and Blair..."

"Yeah?"

He added a second finger to the first, pumping them roughly inside my slickened cunt.

"You're dripping wet, baby."

He led me to the chair, and I stumbled a little on my heels. I dropped into the seat and my husband placed his hands on my knees and forced my thighs wide.

"There," he said. But he was addressing Oliver, now, not me.

I licked my lips and tried to sit still. My stomach was a knot of nervous energy; a lump of anxiety was lodged firmly in my throat.

Jamie took his finger and dragged it over the plump knot of my clit. I hummed low in my throat, my body moving softly under his ministrations.

"Come on then. You have to taste this pussy. Sweetest thing since Georgia peaches," he whispered. He was addressing Oliver.

My face grew even hotter at his praise. I watched Oliver, Oliver who was so pretty he almost looked like an anime character, move toward me. My skin erupted in goose bumps, my nipples stiffening almost painfully inside my no-nonsense black satin bra.

Oliver dropped to the carpet. It was so thick he barely made a sound. He moved toward me on his knees and I watched Jamie, grinning slightly, sit on the edge of the bed to watch.

"Remember now, Ollie," Jamie said. "Just tongue, lips, teeth. No fingers. No penetration. That's for me. Not for you."

"Got it," Oliver said. He sounded as breathless as I felt.

He looked me over slowly at first. My cheeks burned with embarrassment tinted with need. What did he think of me? Of this? Of us? But then I saw the hump in his khakis and realized he had an erection. A quite sizable one if I wasn't mistaken. I forgot all that when he bent forward, almost as if in prayer, and kissed my inner thighs. First one, then the other. He dragged his soft bee-stung lips up to the very top of my thigh where the skin was the most sensitive. He kissed a maddeningly soft line across my mound and then down the other side. When my hips lifted up to meet his mouth, to tempt him, he finally gave us both what we clearly wanted. His mouth clamped down on me, his lips soft and hot. His tongue parted me, slickening my already juicy pussy with his saliva. His tongue painted insistent swirls on my clitoris until I was gripping the arms of the chair and moving my body up to meet him.

Jamie sat and watched. His cock was hard, that much I could tell. His eyes were shiny, mouth set in a fine amused line. He was enjoying this almost as much as me, I realized with what bordered on shock.

It had never occurred to me that this fantasy of mine did anything for him. But clearly it did.

"Make her come," he whispered.

Oliver sealed his mouth to me, using the rigid tip of his tongue to nudge my clit over and over and over until I was panting for breath. Then he stopped. His mouth hovered near my pussy but he'd pulled back. He didn't touch me.

My head pounded with blood, and I shifted restlessly. I wanted to come. I *needed* to come. Desperately.

Oliver glanced up at me with his pretty gem-colored eyes and gave me a crooked grin. Then he blew warm breath across my damp sex. Before I could register this new tactic, his mouth was back on me, his tongue back at me. Working me.

I came with a rough cry and an eager thrust of my hips. Thrusting up with such a force I felt the bite of his upper teeth against the smooth skin of my mound.

I sank back and sighed. Then I began to laugh.

"Good?" Jamie asked. I could tell he was asking both of us.

"Good," I echoed, trying to catch my breath.

"One more?" Oliver said.

Before I could answer, Jamie nodded once and said, "Yeah, but after that first one she's really sensitive. So you'll have to hold her legs."

I blinked but had no time to react in any other way before Oliver had pinned my legs wide with his large hands. He had very long fingers I noticed, and I wondered wildly what it would be like if Jamie would let him stick one or two in me. What it would feel like if he fucked me with those fingers.

The sensation of his mouth back on me swept me under. As he lapped at me with a stranger's tongue, holding me with a stranger's hands, I felt like it was all too much. The pleasure bordered on pain, and it threatened to eat me alive. To crush me.

"Please, please..." I muttered.

Through my nearly shut eyes I saw Jamie nod with confidence. "Keep going. She always says that. And then you hit a point where—"

The next lick from Oliver sent a shiver through me. A steamy gush of pleasure filled my lower body.

Jamie laughed. "There it is. We always hit a point where the pleasure beats out the sensitivity."

I wriggled in the seat, feeling how plump and ready I was. How slick and willing. In my mind, I let Oliver shove those long, thick fingers into me. I let him play me like his own personal instrument. I let him fuck me with thick digits while eating my pussy as if his life depended on it.

"And there it is..." Jamie chuckled as I came for the second time, my voice a rough ghost of its former self. I clutched at Oliver's lush, dark hair as if I were sinking.

Oliver kissed the inside of my right thigh, then my left. He sat back on his heels and saluted Jamie. "Thanks, J. Mrs. J," he said, giving me a friendly nod.

I was too stunned and flushed and pleasure-drunk to do much more than nod and say, "Nice to meet you." As if that were in any way appropriate given the circumstances.

When he stood I noted the impressive hard line in his pants. I fought the urge to reach out and touch it just to feel the evidence of my appeal under my fingertips. Just for a fleeting moment. I wondered what he'd do with that cock. If he'd jerk off in the elevator or maybe his car. Or go home and fuck a wife or girlfriend with it.

Jamie caught me looking, and cocked an eyebrow. Before either of us could speak, Oliver was out the door.

Jamie held out his hand to me. "Come," he said.

"Twice," I teased. But I stood on wobbly legs and moved toward him where he sat.

Before he could say anything else, I dropped to my knees and worked his zipper with shivery fingers. I had his cock out and in my mouth before he could say anything. I was celebrating the fulfillment of my fantasy with one of my favorite things. Sucking his cock.

His fingers played through my short hair and then he tucked it behind my ears so he could watch me. He stroked the sides of my face gently as I drove my lips down to the very root of him. My eyes drifted shut from the sensation of his fingers on my skin.

"I can't wait anymore, baby," he said.

When I refused to stop, he tugged a hank of my hair just hard enough to get my attention and send a fresh rush of wetness to my pussy.

I moved up where he wanted me, his spit-slick cock standing

straight up. He held it for me and I straddled him, sank down on him slowly. Moving as gracefully as I could for a woman shaking so hard.

"That was the hottest fucking thing," he laughed.

"No, this is the hottest fucking thing," I said, moving like I had all the time in the world. I knew what I was doing to him. I felt how hard he was, how fast his heart was beating in his chest. I kept my hand over it as I moved my body languidly. He groaned.

"Blair—"

"I was just kissed down there by lips that have never ever touched me before."

Jamie groaned again.

"His tongue was on my clit," I whispered. "Inside me at times."

Jamie thrust up under me once, hard, but I forced myself to continue a slow, lazy rhythm.

"He held my thighs open with his hands," I said. "His fingerprints were on me."

With a growl, Jamie clamped his arms around me and turned fast. He trapped me under him, pinning me to the bed with his forearm the way he had in the elevator.

My head felt light and my insides turned to liquid. I laughed softly and simply said, "Fuck me, baby."

He did, his body moving in a wild rhythm. When he was close, so close his jaw was tight, his eyes were hooded, he rocked his hips from side to side and I came, his cock pressing deep inside me as I shuddered.

His forearms came down a bit harder, trapping the breath in my lungs, only long enough for him to drive into me once, twice more before the ending. He came with a bellow and dropped his head to my shoulder.

"Wow. Wow." I said it stupidly. It was the only thing I could think to say.

Jamie raised his head, looking very pleased with himself and our anniversary celebration.

"You hungry? Who's hungry?" He grinned. "I am."

"I'm starving." I whispered, touching his face. I couldn't help but laugh again. "After all that, yes, god, I could eat." I kissed him hungrily.

"That's what appetizers do. They provoke your appetite."

"Consider me provoked."

"I think we might need to get in touch with Ollie again in the future." He watched me think.

My face was hot with blush, but I nodded. "I think you might be right."

133.1
Cap

Mikhael

author: Angela Caperton

category: Supernatural

subject:
1. Scandalous Seminarian   2. Girls' Dorm
3. Voyeuristic Spirit

Mikhael

Angela Caperton

In the last moments of darkness, before the rising sun painted the window golden, Marcia dreamed she prayed. She had not actually prayed in many years, so the dream seemed silly, but she remembered the earnest craving when she woke, the hunger for forgiveness and God's favor.

How fucked up was that?

Marcia had taken the room at Elysium House because the rent was low. She knew two other grad students who rented apartments there, but after only a week, she regretted her six-month lease. The co-op dorm dripped quaint Victorian charm, but the old mansion also gave her bad dreams.

"Maybe some Sleepytime tea?" Amber suggested, just after midnight, as she settled in her bentwood chair at the little table in the kitchen of Elysium House.

Marcia put a kettle on the stove and joined her friend, other things on her mind besides Amber's herbal tea insomnia remedies. Amber had a fourth-floor room, directly above Marcia's on the third. "Does this place ever scare you?"

Amber took a bite of her leftover pizza and nodded, looking

away laughing, embarrassed, Marcia guessed, by the unspoken admission.

Marcia wanted a smoke, but Ms. Garrity would have a Hereford if she smelled it. Less than thirty minutes to curfew, so the old lady would be around to clear the kitchen soon enough. "Girl, you won't laugh when I tell you what I learned," Marcia told her friend.

Elysium House occupied most of a block in an old neighborhood north of the university. Betty Garrity, the landlady since 1969, rented rooms only to female graduate students and maintained strict rules about noise and visitation. A sweet old hippy, gray-haired Betty's moral values seemed at least two centuries out of date. Everyone said she'd had bad experiences with men, but no one knew the particulars.

"I did some research into this place's history," Marcia said. She was chasing a master's in public policy and had a guaranteed job in the state comptroller's office when she graduated. She had minored in history as an undergraduate and still knew plenty of people in that department. "Elysium House used to be part of a seminary," she said. "This house was next to a church that's gone now."

"Creepy! What church was it?"

"A weird branch of the Unitarians—technically the Oswald Unitarians. Some old books call it the Church of the Evening Star. They were big in the 1870s. Elysium was built in 1888. It's only been a rooming house since the 1960s. Before that it had been abandoned since 1926."

"Abandoned?" Amber asked. "You mean like haunted?" She giggled a little, a nervous sound that Marcia found oddly comforting. She wasn't alone.

"Yeah, that's exactly what I mean. I found two books of county history that have stories about our little home away from home. One story from the forties is about five destitute children breaking into the place for shelter during the

Depression. The author couldn't confirm it really happened, but she believed it. Two of the kids disappeared and the other three went insane."

"You're making this up," Amber accused her.

"There's an older one, a worse one, about what happened to the seminary, and this one isn't a folktale. It really happened. By 1910, there were only four students left—the church's leader got caught in some kind of scandal and the church was almost extinct. One of the four remaining seminarians...killed all the others. The police found him inside, in some condition they wouldn't disclose, but rumors said he was eating his fellow acolytes."

"You are so making this up! Next you're going to tell me the church was really a devil cult."

"No." Marcia shook her head. "Best anyone can tell they were just lapsed Unitarians."

The kettle whistled sharply and Marcia had the satisfaction of seeing Amber jump.

"Listen." Amber smiled and squeezed her hand before getting the kettle and pouring hot water into their cups, where the teabags waited. They shared the fragrant brew and the old house seemed very quiet and still as the Felix clock above the stove ticked toward curfew. "Mind if I sleep in your room tonight?"

"Mind? That sounds wonderful!"

In Marcia's bed, they listened to Betty Garrity make her rounds, the old wood creaking as she slowly moved up and down the stairs, the not-so-subtle pauses as she listened at doors. Lights out at midnight was another one of her rules. Marcia's jeans-clad legs entwined with Amber's and she ached for what would happen as soon as the landlady was gone from the third floor.

They kissed as Betty passed by, Marcia dying to have Amber undressed and lying against her, skin to skin. Amber was a dedicated lesbian and Marcia thought of herself as bi, but no boy had ever treated her so well in bed or brought her to mad orgasms the way Amber did.

When they were both naked, Marcia explored Amber's taut thighs, the stiff points of her high breasts, and lost herself in Amber's kisses. Sweat slicked the places they touched, and musk and perfume hung heavy as mosquito netting over them. They sixty-nined long enough for each of them to come and then embraced, face-to-face, pressing and licking. She stroked Amber's back, kneading the tight velvet muscle of her butt. They fucked, hands to clits, lost in each other's open kisses, Marcia trying not to scream when she came again, but Amber did, apparently not caring who heard her as she spasmed and bucked.

They tangled outside the covers. Marcia enjoyed the cooling air on her bare butt, her mind warm and fuzzy as she thought, *This must be how a guy feels after he makes a girl come.* She liked the feeling. A colder breeze blew across her bottom, almost like the stroke of a slender hand.

Beside her, Amber made a choking noise. So severe was the cry that Marcia rolled away, untangling their limbs, thinking she had somehow caused physical pain, maybe cut off blood flow to Amber's arm or leg, but Amber still gasped, the sound unmistakably now one of fear rather than pain.

Amber sat up, hugging her bare legs. "Damn it, Marcia. Don't you see him? He's right there! He's watching us. Oh god, he's dead and he's watching us."

She followed Amber's gaze and saw only a shadow, but her lover's frantic grab for a pillow, burying her face in it, convinced Marcia that she was not playing a joke. The room continued to chill unnaturally, as though a winter wind blew through an open window, though no breeze ruffled the curtains or rattled the blinds.

"There's nothing there, Amber, I don't see him."

But then she did, pale, wearing a dark robe, his ash-blond hair tousled and matted, sitting in the big chair by the window, as vivid and real as anyone Marcia had ever seen and he was, just as Amber had said, staring right at them.

Achingly conscious of her nakedness, Marcia scrambled for the sheet, but Amber's weight held it down. "Oh god," Amber cried. She had turned to look again and gripped Marcia's thigh hard enough to draw bloody little half-moons.

The tall, dead young man rose slowly from the chair, the depthless pits of his charcoal eyes fastened on Marcia. His robe came open but Marcia saw no body, only shadows where it gaped. As he approached, reaching out, then fading, she felt phantom hands, cold as wet cloth, run rough over her breasts, tweaking her nipples with ghastly play, and felt someone thrust against her pussy, smooth and icy.

Amber screamed. Marcia lost all control and screamed with her, forgetting what Betty Garrity would think, knowing only that, if the thing did not stop touching her, she would go mad.

"You think you know what it is," the landlady told them. "But you're wrong."

Marcia and Amber had dressed, but it seemed to Marcia the room still smelled like sex, and she had the sense that Ms. Garrity knew exactly what had been going on in the room before *he* appeared.

"It's one of the boys isn't it?" Amber asked. "The last student from the seminary."

"In a way..." old Betty said. She sat in the chair where the thing had perched.

"You know about this?" Marcia asked. *"How can you live here?"*

"This is the first time—that I know of, at least—that anyone else has seen him in almost twenty years. Oh, sometimes girls hear him or feel him, but to see him? That's rare." Betty Garrity clucked a little. She did not appear to be alarmed, only a little sad. "I don't think he'll hurt you."

"You expect us to sleep here after this, Ms. Garrity?"

"Call me Betty, dear. *I've* been sleeping here a long time. He watches me sometimes. It's flattering really, the way he still stares. I think you girls are making me a little jealous. Did he say anything?"

Marcia wanted to ask if she could move to another room, but she couldn't find words. She still imagined him—whoever he was—suspended somewhere between Betty's chair and the bed. The room had not warmed much at all. Amber still held her hand.

"He's the one who murdered the others, isn't he?" Amber persisted.

Betty's brow furrowed. "No, no, I don't think so. His name is Mikhael—you know, with a K. You girls were fooling around, weren't you?" Neither of them denied it, and Betty went on, "It's all right. I had girlfriends too. No one can get you off like your best friend can, right?" Not-so-old Ms. Garrity smiled knowingly.

"What does he want?" Marcia asked, inwardly reeling at the sudden insight into her landlady.

"Oh, tonight I think he just wanted what any man might, to watch two pretty girls making love."

"When does he visit *you*?" Amber asked, some of the mischief creeping back into her voice. The sound gave Marcia courage.

Betty demurred, but finally answered, "When I put on a show for him."

Marcia saw Amber grin. Marcia guessed Amber had found a new friend. Old Betty was quite attractive, when you looked past the years. She kept herself fit and her gray hair fell soft around high cheekbones and a forehead that hardly showed wrinkles. Her eyes were bright blue and lively.

The room grew colder.

Betty smiled at them. "He won't hurt you. I'll tell you something I've never told anyone. I've wanted Mikhael to...touch me all these years, and he never has. Just the cold and sometimes a breeze."

"Does he talk?" Marcia managed. "Have you ever talked to him?"

"Well, no. He wrote his name once on a piece of paper, but he doesn't talk. He moans though, sometimes, like a man having a good time, when he watches me."

Amber gripped Marcia's hand harder, as Marcia's head swam. "Listen," she said. "Can we go down to the kitchen? I can't sleep up here tonight."

"All right, dear," Betty said and they went down together to sit at the little table, drink tea, and talk. At first Betty talked about Mikhael, how she had first seen him and how she had discovered his desires.

"He likes stockings, girls. The old-fashioned kind."

Then, the conversation drifted, to stories about New York City, then about bad boyfriends. Betty told them about living in a commune back in the day.

After a while they talked about nothing much. Then the sun rose and none of it seemed quite real anymore.

For ten dollars extra a month Marcia could have cabled a TV into the house satellite feed, but she couldn't imagine sitting alone in her room watching the shows she wanted to see, the ones she *needed* to see. Just looking at all the fake haunting shit on YouTube made her hands shake so hard, she couldn't tap the keyboard. She staked out the common rooms in the student union that had televisions and she watched ghost shows at all hours of the day and night—"Hauntings," "American Ghosts," "Ghost Hunters," and others, all about people investigating possessions and haunted houses, and none of it really gave her any comfort or taught her anything useful about the spirit in Elysium House.

Nor did she sense Mikhael in her room again. Amber had struck up a friendship with Betty, and Marcia's once lover now spent most evenings over tea with the landlady, then joined Betty in her room. Neither of them invited Marcia and she fought feelings of hurt and betrayal, though she understood why Amber might seek the older woman's company. In her gloomiest moments, Marcia imagined them in bed together, mouth to mouth, hands busy, and Mikhael watching, his spirit summoned by the heat of their fucking.

Mikhael. Marcia wondered if *he* watched *her*. Did *he* lay immaterial and unsensed in her bed at night? The idea of sharing space with a ghost seemed silly and unreal, *and yet.* She guessed at least some of the people on the ghost shows must have experienced something much like what she had seen and felt.

How many more people in the world must have experienced things even stranger and gone on about the business of living? *Was everyone haunted?*

Marcia thought about it all the time.

She thought about Mikhael all the time.

On the first day of February, she brought two bottles of wine back to her room. Elysium House felt empty. Marcia heard no voices, saw no cars parked in the driveway or on the street. Alone. Exactly the opportunity she wanted.

Was that a breeze on the stairs? She felt as though someone ascended beside her, and she spoke his name aloud.

"Mikhael?"

Only the muffled sound of her own feet on the steps answered her.

She had barely reached the first landing when she felt the whisper at her ear, heard the words like a voice around a corner, a radio signal tattered by sudden white noise.

"I am here."

He had *never* spoken to Betty, she thought with a surge of pride and confidence.

She shivered with his touch, unmistakable, an electrical bristling of every fine hair on her body, and she led him up the next flight, holding tightly to the rail. She couldn't breathe, and could hardly open the door and fall inward to sit on the bed, terrified and happy.

The door blew shut behind her.

"Can you talk to me?" she asked.

Nothing answered but she felt a cool breeze around her and smelled strong incense—the kind you might smell in church. Invisible fingers touched her breasts.

She saw him then for an instant, immaculate and golden, his hair curled in the fashion of another age, his mustache ridiculous but beautiful. He had mahogany eyes and long, dexterous fingers. Then he moved toward her and dissipated.

"Oh god," she panted, feeling the push of something cold and desperate, not so much against her skin as pressing an inch or so beneath it, the invasion eerie but not unpleasant.

She shed her blouse a little self-consciously. Mikhael's vaporous apparition had vanished but she still felt him wrapped around her. She tasted him, exotic and rich, and a scent like pine smoke and pipe tobacco swirled around her. As she lay the garment aside, she felt him again, warmer than her own breath. She heard sounds of approval inside her head, and felt the urgency of thin, invisible fingers under her skimpy satin bra, but she teased him. Standing, facing him, the air moved around her, brushing the ends of her hair, her eyelashes. She unfastened her skirt and his hands lay upon hers with encouraging pressure. When his long, cool stroke against her panty-shielded pussy teased her, she bowed.

She almost came, her breath gone, flowing. *Someone was licking her*, she thought and suppressed a laugh. She abandoned caution and felt a sense of elation and experience beyond her material senses, like she might leave her skin and join Mikhael wherever the hell he was. She sat back on the edge of the bed and unfastened her garter.

"He likes stockings," Betty had told her and Marcia wore real silk, smoky enough to contrast sharply against the tan cream of her thighs. She felt the invisible current surge around her as he rolled the first one down her leg.

Sorcerer, she thought, necromancer, words from fairy tales, but this was *real*.

Halfway through removing the second stocking, she felt Mikhael's lips, vivid as snow, exploring the arch of her neck, kissing invisibly just under her ear and along her jawline. She lay back on the bed, surrendering to him, and felt his pine ghost breath against her nose and mouth, tasted spice and smoke as he kissed her with fierce, chilly lips.

Cold hands raised her hips, helping her with the panties until she lay bare except for the bra, feeling as naked as she ever had in her life, wondering what would happen next, hoping that Mikhael would fuck her. She practically tore the bra off and opened to him, terrified but excited, the sense of something icy pushing past her skin overwhelming.

Her clit swelled as though someone licked her and she began to buck, feeling his arms along her sides, his breathy hands on her bare breasts. She thrust up as the ghost tongue-fucked her, as vivid as any real lover. Even better than Amber.

Sorcerer.

She came, the room vanishing and reforming in fiery gold streaks. She imagined the dead seminary students like shadows around her, watching her naked and coming, coming, grinding against Mikhael's tongue, his fingers. She bit her pillow to stop her scream and lay a long time, perspiration musky on her body, transcended, halfway to things no one knew, to knowledge and wisdom, and love.

* * *

The early weeks of February passed like remembered days of someone else's life. Marcia woke in the morning, ate meals without flavor, and half slept through her classes. Her grades plummeted.

In her room, she felt Mikhael's presence constantly, though she did not see him or feel his touch. Nor did she try to invoke him again. Amber and Ms. Garrity hardly spoke to Marcia now, almost seemed to avoid her, and Marcia wondered if old Betty guessed what Marcia had done. Did Mikhael even visit the landlady anymore? Did he visit Amber? Marcia hoped not, for both her own dark vanity and her jealousy, and because she honestly didn't know if what she had experienced might not be a curse. She didn't wish that on her friend. That thought repeated in her mind as Amber brushed aside her greetings and smiles. Yes, maybe Mikhael's touch had cursed her.

The world felt thin. School began to seem like a play where her fellow students and the teachers spoke their lines like actors. The debates and finer points of theoretical governance seemed boring and meaningless. None of it mattered to her now.

Instead of studying government, she began to dig deeper through the university's archive records, most of them digitized and easy to search, but a surprising number still maintained on yellowed card stock in massive, polished wood cabinets. She found collections of tracts from the Oswald Unitarians, but when she requisitioned the copies, nothing in them proved helpful. The church had been an enlightened voice of open-minded deism as far as she could tell from the arcane essays, though she found surprising traces of Gnosticism, an emphasis on the world of matter distinct from God and his angels. Like any church, there had been branches of belief even within the splinter sect. The scandal that ruined the seminary was related to some arcane difference of opinion that had caused the main ecclesiastical body—in Philadelphia—essentially to excommunicate the priests and students associated with the local denomination. As far as Marcia could tell, the whole sect had vanished entirely by World War II.

Still, her instincts kept her searching and she finally found a link in a dusty catalogue that drew her full attention. *Final Repository of Documents,* the description read, *of the Oswald Unitarian Church.* The date the university received the documents was May 1910, six months after the murders of the last students. She collected favors from a friend in the history department and, after running the gauntlet of permissions, scheduled a visit on Tuesday to the university's auxiliary archives, way out on the north side of town.

The church records filled half a dozen boxes. An indifferent graduate student delivered them to her in a reading room furnished in 1950s industrial elegance. She spent hours going through the boxes. No one had opened them in a long time. A single sheet of rubbery paper from an ancient copying machine lay on the top of each one, faintly detailing the contents. Marcia had the place to herself, but she treated the old books and photographs with a scholar's reverence. She realized almost at once that this trove was exactly what she had been looking for—the papers and records that had been taken out of the seminary after the murders. Handling the material, she felt closer to Mikhael. These ledgers and annotated bibles had belonged to his peers, to his teachers, maybe even to him.

In the fourth box, she found something she had been specifically looking for, a beautifully handwritten roster of the seminary's students beginning in 1885 and continuing through the fatal year 1910. She saw handwritten names in columns with admission dates and graduation notations, and a second line indicating if the student had been assigned to a congregation after leaving the school. Starting at the end, looking for Mikhael, she read the names of the last year's students.

The last four boys were William, Morris, Abner and Joseph.

No Mikhael among them. She looked at the previous year and the one before that. No Mikhael, with or without a *K*. Maybe Betty was wrong about his name, but the ghost *had* answered to it, Marcia was certain.

Maybe Mikhael had been a teacher. She searched deeper and found records detailing the faculty, their years at the seminary, the congregations they had served before and after. As far back as the rosters went, she found no one named Mikhael.

Who were you?

Dust in the last box made her sneeze, and her eyes itched. She felt unaccountably tired. A wave of futility swept over her. She needed to know more about him but this path seemed hopeless, a chronicle of mundane lives, esoteric nonsense, a dead end.

With numb hands, she repacked the last box, listless until she picked up the last item, a plain little book. It opened and she saw elegant handwriting covered the pages. She thumbed through them and read a single word written as though in fire, a name.

His name.

The book appeared to be a diary, or a chronicle; it contained handwritten prayers and apparently a record of life in the seminary. She saw what might have been several people's handwriting, or possibly the same person's, but sometimes written in haste or in different states of mind. The early pages were dated 1908 and 1909, but the later ones ran on in a stream, with no breaks between the paragraphs.

...invocato de deo incarnato...within and apart from the firmament...days and nights of hunger... He is here.

Mikhael venhit.

Mikhael comes.

"I told you he isn't what you thought, Marcia." Ms. Garrity had been drinking. The gray-haired lady's words were clear but the inflections betrayed her. She and Amber sat on the sofa in the landlady's room and stared at Marcia accusingly. They wore house robes, Amber's ruby and Betty's smoky black and, as far as Marcia could see, both women were naked beneath their wraps.

Marcia showed them the diary. She'd stolen it from the archive and doubted anyone would ever miss it. She'd read it—the legible parts anyway—then she'd gone looking for Betty.

"You think he's something you can control," Betty went on. "Something you can call like you'd call up your boyfriend. You probably think he's in love with you…"

"Is that what you believed?" Marcia asked. "A long time ago?"

She saw rage pass through Betty like a brushfire, then it was gone, leaving cold ash behind. "We can share him," she offered. "All three of us."

"Is he what the diary says he is?"

"An angel?" Betty slumped. "Who the hell knows? But he might be."

Betty's choice of words made Marcia laugh. The journal she'd found was written by all four of the last seminary students. One of them, Morris, had been one of the heretics—part of the splinter sect of the deviant Unitarians, and he'd converted the others, probably the last teachers at the seminary too. "They summoned him," she told Betty and Amber. "Like Faust summoning the devil. It says here"—Marcia tapped the book—"that he's an angel."

"Maybe so," Betty smirked. "But he has the devil's appetites."

The room grew chill, colder than Marcia had felt before from Mikhael's presence, but unmistakably him. She saw that the other two women felt it too. Betty and Amber on the sofa, Marcia standing over them, all rooted by a common feeling, the imminence of miracle.

"Bring him," Betty said, and took off her robe. She really had taken good care of herself, Marcia saw. Small breasts that had hardly sagged, with carmine nipples that, as Marcia watched, stiffened and reddened exactly as though someone was tweaking them. A breeze blew Betty's soft gray hair like a veil around her as she rose in place to kiss the ineffable.

Amber too. She'd shed her robe entirely. Marcia had seen her friend nude many times, but never like this. Amber embraced something unseen. She flushed and—on her neck and shoulder—she bruised with Mikhael's bites, blue and purple flowers blooming on her ivory skin.

Betty put her hand on Amber's pussy, fingers sliding in, and Marcia saw Mikhael's hand too riding like a glove on Betty's hand, shining. Amber cried and pulled Betty to her, *pulled Mikhael to her.*

Marcia's pussy ran like a river. Her clothing could not come off fast enough, blouse torn, panties and skirt in a single roll. Amber went down on Betty, eating her like a cat lapping cream. Marcia remembered what that felt like; shivering and naked now, she moved nearer to them, reaching out to touch a shoulder, a breast, feeling Mikhael's aura around them like musky oil.

The spirit ran from Betty and Amber onto Marcia.

She understood the caress, Mikhael's hands tender but absolute and claiming, chill then warming, as he ran them down her shoulders, her arms, over her breasts, tweaking. Just as the essence of Mikhael's grace reached her pussy, Amber turned and began to lick her.

Marcia felt two tongues, one on her clit, the other impossibly deep inside her. She was dimly aware that Betty had produced a dildo and was working herself to a climax. Marcia reached out and found Amber's pussy and began to finger her, her hand gloved now with Mikhael's essence.

They came, all together, Betty crying like a bird, Amber moaning and Marcia calling Mikhael's name, worshipping him.

She found herself on a sort of plateau; the orgasm had been absolute, but Marcia knew Mikhael was not finished with her. As though Betty and Amber understood it too, they moved away from the sofa and knelt, watching Marcia.

Awaiting Mikhael.

Mikhael venhit.

She saw him shining then, standing beside her, tall and lean. How could she not have seen his radiance before? The other times, she had seen him as a man, golden curls, mustached, with deep-brown eyes, but now she saw him whole, in his truth. The golden curls were scales of a sort, the mustache a whipping tendril, and the depthless, dark majesty of his eyes opened into starry nighttime skies.

What was he?

Tatters of sanity blew through her brain in the gale of Mikhael's storm as he took her in his arms. She gasped, feeling the pressure of his torso, his hips thrusting, but she felt no hardness there. The length she had expected was missing.

She remembered then and giggled a little, her sanity lost. Angels have no cocks, no pussies. That much at least was true.

She stepped back to look at *him*—she still thought of him as male—and saw in the space where his legs came together, where his cock should be, a light, a pulsing radiance that drew her closer, on her knees before him.

Mikhael rested his taloned hand on her head, blessing her, then he lifted her up, spread her legs so she was open to him. She felt helpless in his grip, ready for whatever he would do to her. The angel pressed against her cunt and flowed into her, changing her flesh to joy, bringing her to divine climax all over, mind and body exploding into light, into knowledge that passed understanding. The final orgasm ripped through her, eternal, cresting and transforming her, until it consumed even her soul.

Divine ecstasy rolled off her skin, out of her mouth, her eyes, her nose and pussy. She didn't care that her screams tore at the walls and the foundation of Elysium House, didn't care that Betty and Amber curled tight at her feet, insane with the waves of their own divine pleasure. *This was the end of their world.* Marcia understood that. *And the beginning of a new one.*

She wanted to worship him as he had gifted her, to bring him to a climax that would obliterate wood and stone, lay waste to cities and the works of man. Mikhael would come as she had. She stroked where his cock would be, she bit at flesh she could not see, clawed with each growing orgasmic wave, drawing unseen blood under her nails, pulling him closer to join her in that white-hot bliss he'd bestowed.

Yes, Mikhael would come, she would see to it. He was close, so close even as her lips and tongue worshipped the space where his cock would be, where such divinity swelled beyond flesh.

He would come, and when he did—he was so close, she could feel it—the world would know his joy, his pleasure.

His glorious, burning fire.

392.4
Car

The Mating Chamber

author: Rose Caraway

category: Mating Customs

subject:
1. Shackles   2. Breeding   3. Matriarchal

The Mating Chamber

Rose Caraway

The cold morning breeze whipped through her tightly coiled black hair, across the swell of her small, dark breasts and licked between her exposed thighs. The sun rose above the jagged eastern horizon, warming the valley with its toasty golden rays. Dozens of women dressed in short robes absorbed the thin heat of New Spring; all brimming with sexual anticipation as they watched the most honored Hunters of Patriia assemble. At the queen's signal, the Hunters parted the crowd and in single file, walked toward the Hill, their captives' thick chains clanking heavily with each step. A collective rumble sounded from the entrants who looked on the shapes of the ten shrouded individuals in tow: this year's captured Donum. Even Patriia's youngest daughters ineligible for motherhood stood in awe, their games temporarily forgotten as they observed the procession of shackled men.

As the Hunters paraded the Donum, the women behind Shresha gathered in tighter, pressing and pushing against her, but she firmly stood her ground just enough to lift her nose to each of the men as they slowly walked by. A spicy, masculine brew drifted on the breeze. She wrapped her arms around her middle and pressed her thighs together as lust surged through her blood. An undeniable, physical confirmation that she fiercely desired a man to impregnate her.

The valley-dwelling Patriians were a formidable Matriarchal race that had no use for men except for once every year during the dawning of New Spring, when ten elected Hunters returned with breedable men to honor their Goddess, Shaiia. Handpicked by Queen Teshii herself, Shresha and nearly a hundred other women waited in the frosted grass. They were this year's entrants selected as potential mothers and all vying for their chance to bear Patriia's next daughter.

The Hunters were forced to slow and then eventually stop as women crowded in around them. Shresha suddenly felt closed in, and the air seemed too thick. Too many women shoved at her back, stepped on her unprotected feet. It felt like she was trying to hold back a herd of wild beasts. She jabbed her elbows into someone's ribs, forcefully shoved a woman off her poor foot and was fighting for space when an immense shadow fell over her. The frenzied chaos, halted. Shresha looked up and up. Her jaw slack, her mouth open. The last shrouded Donum had stopped just in front of her and looked as tall as a mountain. He towered over all the other men in line. With the tenacity of a spring flood desire rushed through Shresha's body. She wanted this man. She knew that beneath the shroud stood a Dalkivian. The excited whispers around her backed her suspicions.

The Dalkivian were an elusive race. A high-chinned breed of man, hardy and rumored to have hair that was the color of the sun—a glacial titan. No Patriian Hunter had ever brought one into their valley. A heavy jangle of chains at the massive man's wrists brought Shresha's attention to his hands. She gawked at their pale color but found herself enamored by their size! She could almost feel them caressing her flesh, could imagine how his thick fingers would move between her thighs and fuck her with nice slow thrusts. Those incredibly large hands promised a kind of power that Shresha shamelessly found herself wanting to experience even more than motherhood.

It would take a moment to grow accustomed to a man's body, she knew that, especially one of this size, but she didn't care. She would willingly spread her legs wide for this man. With giddy desperation, she wanted to inspect the rest of his body, to see the *other* more fabled part of him, but the formless shroud prevented her even the slightest hint of what was hidden beneath it. The precession made its way toward the Hill again and several throaty growls of frustrated longing sounded from the disappointed women.

The Hunters led their captives and neatly gathered behind Queen Teshiie, who stood at the top of the Hill patiently holding her wooden box. Teshiie was an older woman, well beyond the years of childbearing, but she watched as the Hunters settled the Donum into place with a look that suggested she wasn't too old to still appreciate what was hidden beneath the shrouds. After the line settled, the queen spoke in a loud authoritative voice that easily carried over the crowd of eager young women.

"Daughters of Patriia! It is New Spring and we have gathered once again with our most eligible women to celebrate our land's sacred tradition!" Queen Teshiie lifted the black wooden box high above her head. The older woman smiled with great pride when the entrants threw their hands into the air at the same time, cheering in exultation. With careful reverence, the queen set the ancient box on its dais and added an extra flourish of her hands eliciting another round of excited cheers from the crowd. Caught in the moment, Shresha felt the sting of tears. That old box held her destiny. Silently she prayed to Shaiia for the thousandth time that morning and wiped the tears from her eyes. Instead of listening to the queen, she scanned the ten waiting Donum. Goose bumps returned hot and rough over her skin. Though she could have all of them if she won—that wonderful bounty of unexplored male flesh made her pussy slick with the need to conquer it—she knew there was only one man she truly desired.

The big Dalkivian.

The women nearest her deliberated as though at market deciding on the best cut of meat, openly discussing their thoughts on what the size of each man's cock would be, especially the tallest one. Queen Teshiie lifted her hands to quiet them.

"Settle down. Settle down, hush now, please. We have quite an exceptional selection this year and just like all of you, I want to see them revealed!" The women crowed good-heartedly at their queen. The older woman enjoyed the playful jeering and patiently patted the air. The old queen's bright shining eyes looked on the mothers-elect. "That's more like it. Now then, our Hunters have safely returned with an exceptional bounty and I think it particularly worth mentioning that Captain Shrom, our most honored Hunter, should be applauded for returning from the harsh Great Northern Glacier and successfully bringing back our very first Dalkivian!"

Shrom stepped forward with a wide smile, her towering trophy standing behind her with no slack allowed in his chain. It occurred to Shresha that the man might be resisting but quickly dismissed the idea. The Mage always administered a tonic that made them easier to control. Shrom bowed deeply, accepting her due praise.

"Before we begin, let us honor last year's blessed mother—Darniisha!"

The crowd erupted in a loud chorus as the woman removed her short robe and then walked up The Hill and proudly presented her three-month-old twin daughters, Zetsha and Rushii. Darniisha was a squat little woman and even from where she stood, Shresha could see the beautifully feathered lines that pregnancy had tattooed into her thighs and belly. This time Shresha felt tears of envy threaten to fall. There were so many entrants. Her heart plummeted.

As Darniisha returned the awarded Key back to the queen the crowd stilled and quieted itself on its own accord. The Key of Patriia would be passed on to the next woman that would bear a daughter to honor Shaiia.

"Before we begin, I must remind all of you that when I call your name, I want you to calmly approach the box, take *one* piece of parchment, keep it folded in your hand until all entrants have drawn. Then, when I say, you may unfold it." The queen's eyes narrowed as she then warned all of them, "Remember, motherhood is the greatest honor you will ever be blessed with and anyone flippantly disregarding that honor will be punished."

Shresha swallowed the lump in her throat as a heavy feeling came over her. She had witnessed a total of four stonings. She squeezed her eyes tight, sent another hasty prayer to the Goddess and waited as the queen began calling names. One by one, women strode up to the old black box, reached inside and plucked a folded paper from it.

The minutes passed.

Shresha's eyes darted left and right as more and more women around her excitedly held a folded piece of parchment to their chests...

"Shresha!" The queen announced.

...And she wondered which one held the Key...

"Shresha!"

She didn't think she could bear the gut-wrenching disappointment...

"Shresha! For Patriia's sake child, get up here!" The queen laughed. She could count fifty-seven daughters born under her reign, but the excitement never grew old for the old woman.

Shresha's cheeks burned when the women around her snickered. On rubbery legs she approached the black box.

"Go ahead, child."

Shresha nodded.

She slid a hand inside. Her fingers lowered into the cool depths. Licking her lips, she pinched her trembling fingers on a swatch of thick paper and then carefully withdrew her hand. Queen Teshiie smiled approvingly as Shresha clutched it to her chest.

"Neptsha!" the queen shouted for the next entrant and Shresha jumped. She scurried back down to her place in the crowd, her heart hammering in her ears the entire way.

"Desh!"

"Shawnii!"

Name after name, until the very last was called, and then the queen finally closed the lid. She slid her eyes shut as much in prayer as to build tension. After what seemed an eternity she opened her eyes again and shouted, "Open! Open them and let's welcome this year's new mother!"

A great dry rustle filled Shresha's ears along with the heavy thumping of her heart. At some point she'd closed her eyes tight, listening for it; the scream, the laughter, the cries from the woman that had won, but none came. Her head began to throb. She strained to hear it; the utter joy that wouldn't be hers. But there were no shouts, no screams of celebration.

"What are you waiting for?" a sour-faced girl beside her barked. Her own unfolded parchment revealed nothing but a blank page. Shresha looked down; she'd been clutching the folded page to her chest so tightly that her knuckles ached. She was sure that there would be no point in opening it. "If you don't open it, I am going to do it for you!" the girl bleated, and started to grab for the folded sheet, but Shresha took a wobbly step back. She held her breath and slowly unfolded one corner, and then another until all that was left was one last fold. She hesitated.

"Open it you stupid thing!"

"Ishii!" The queen had come down from the Hill. "Go ahead, child."

With trembling fingers, she slowly unfolded the last corner. Time stood still as she revealed the drawn image of the Key of Patria.

"You won!" Suddenly her hand was shoved into the air with such force, Shresha had to stand on tiptoes to prevent her arm from being yanked from its socket.

"You won! She won! Shresha won!"

She was stunned, her brain assaulted by doubt as she tried to believe that her wish had just come true. Her heart raced, ready to burst from her chest. Her pussy felt swollen, hot with a single, solitary need. A sharp burning lance of desire had suddenly struck through her very core. Shresha was unaware that the queen had saved her arm from the spastically jumping Ishii and escorted her to the top of the Hill. The crowd issued thunderous cheers for her, for the daughter she would soon bear, and so loudly that she checked the sky to see if the Goddess Shaiia Herself had suddenly appeared.

"All right...hush...settle down." Now there was a low hum of eager whispers. Shresha's stomach churned as the women eyed her with envy. Could they know why the pyre of lust burned so hotly inside of her? Did they notice the wetness glistening on her thighs because she wanted to be with a man more than become a mother?

Only when the queen was certain that the crowd was under control, did she address the Hunters. "Captain Shrom? If you please."

On the lead Hunter's command and in dramatic unison, the other Hunters withdrew their knives, curved blades glinting. With quick, calculated cuts the shrouds fell away, presenting Shresha with ten naked men. The Dalkivian was the only pale-skinned man there. Once again the hot lance of desire made her insides burn like kindling at the magnificent sight of him.

He stood there, tall and pale and *mighty*. Piercing glacial blue eyes. Chin, high and proud. She looked closer at his face.

Was he fighting the effects of the Mage's tonic? The Dalkivian was bigger than the other nine men; maybe he needed more. Shresha's body vibrated with a mixture of emotions just then and she decided that the man's resistance was only imagined. She wasn't in the most reliable state of mind at the moment. It simply couldn't have been possible that the Mage had miscalculated. Resisting or not, this was a man the Goddess Shaiia Herself might elect to breed with. His hair was a gloriously tousled mane as gold as the summer sun. Even his bearded foreign jaw stirred her blood. Shresha's eyes lowered. Two big square muscles made up his chest, both dusted with light brown hair. Two columns of smaller but no less impressive muscles led her down his waist and there her gaze stalled in unexpected surprise. Nestled in a light brown patch of coiled hair the man's cock hung, thick and long and *unsheathed!*

Queen Teshiie gently tapped her shoulder. "Have you made your choice?"

None of the other men existed; they paled in comparison and quite simply held no intrigue. The queen may as well have already ordered their disposal. Shresha could find no reason to consider the others because this impressive pale Northerner was all that she wanted. She cleared her throat.

"Yes."

"Well? Which one?" The queen winked. Several loud suggestions were volunteered from the crowd.

"I, I choose the Dalkivian." It came out in a whisper more than anything else, but the crowd could see the shapes of the words her lips had formed and enthusiastically sounded its approval.

"Captain Shrom, this woman has chosen the Dalkivian. Make him ready."

Shrom inclined her head slightly as she accepted a small object from the queen.

"The Ring of Destiny!" Shrom held up a familiar stone

ring—charmed by the Mage as well—to ensure that a female baby would be conceived. Captain Shrom abruptly turned and in one practiced motion threaded the Dalkivian's thick cock through the loop until it rested securely at his base.

"This Key will unlock the chains of your chosen Donum. And as this key opens his locks, so too shall he open your womb..."

Shresha couldn't hear much after that. The Dalkivian's massive shoulders rolled once and his hands flexed again. Those intense eyes of his continued to gleam as though he were fighting an internal battle.

She was overwhelmed, her breath came in quiet shallow bursts and her knees trembled.

Guards stood just outside the locked doors of the Mating Chamber, but inside there was only Shresha and her chained Donum. She took a sip of water then set the heavy cup back on its tray, saving the rest for later. She would need it. Ten days they would be locked inside the chamber. Every night and every morning, the Mage would come to re-administer the tonic in order to keep the Dalkivian a malleable lover.

As his great shoulders rolled, his arms worked, muscles bunching in his chest. Shresha stared while recalling the lessons taught to her about the process of preparing a man. She absently chalked up the fidgety movements as normal behavior.

Stepping forward, she traced an exploring finger over the man's lips and when they parted, all she could think at that moment was what it would be like to kiss them. So she did. With both hands she pulled his neck bringing his mouth to hers. His lips parted more, almost instinctively. A low rumble issued from his throat that made Shresha's belly flutter with delight. Though still cuffed, he tried to reach for her, or was it the Key he wanted? The Mage's tonic ensured that his body would function but his mind would only be open to commands made of him. She wrapped her arms around his neck, bringing his full lips closer. "Kiss me, Dalkivian."

He did.

"My breasts. Squeeze them," she moaned as that hot lustful spike shot through her when his pale hands pushed aside the thin fabric of her robe and then closed over her dark breasts, but she noticed that the chains inhibited his mobility. She needed to make him more available to her.

"Wait a moment." She pulled the necklace from around her neck. The Dalkivian mumbled something incoherent and the deep tenor of his voice made her toes curl. He flexed his fingers, tried to reach for her again but she stopped him.

"No, you must obey me, Dalkivian. I will unlock your bindings, but then I want you to get on the bed."

With a twist and a click, two heavy shackles fell to the floor in a clatter, directing Shresha's gaze downward.

"I didn't know your kind were unsheathed. This is a pleasant surprise Dalkivian..." Shresha touched the long exposed organ with a finger and smiled when it twitched and swelled. She knelt, unlocked the shackles from around his ankles, and then there came the distinct silky-metallic sound of a Patriian broadsword being drawn from the mounted panoply on the wall. Shresha was hoisted all the way to her feet and then the long cold blade of her ancestors was held firmly against her neck. The Dalkivian was fast, she gave him credit for that, but she would have plenty to say to the Mage when he returned.

"What is happening?" It was a drunken whisper fighting for control and Shresha couldn't deny the sudden impatient temper that flared within her blood at his question. She wasn't in the mood for explanations. The blade at her throat didn't concern her. But it did offer a delightful challenge. A big, strong quarry to submit. She let him gain a little confidence first.

"You were chosen by Shaiia to be my Donum and give me a daughter," she calmly stated.

"Give you a...I've heard of your kind, but I didn't think—I'm your...captive?" A grumble came from his throat as he rubbed his temple with his free hand. The Dalkivian shook his head in an attempt to clear the groggy effects of the tonic.

"Until you are of no use, of course. That is the only reason you are in Patriia." Shresha leaned closer, against the edge of the blade and her pussy clenched at the deadly thrill of it.

"Something stung me. I, I...fell to the ground. I remember a dark woman standing over me, *grinning*!" The large man shook his head again.

"Yes, Shrom is Patriia's greatest warrior—"

All Shresha had to do was call to the guards outside. She didn't want to though. She really didn't need to either. Though he was strong, a veritable mountain of muscle standing before her, she could easily salvage the situation.

"You call yourselves *warriors?*" The man looked around the chamber now, searching for something.

Shresha smiled.

"You should be honored."

"You can't abduct men and use them this way!" He hadn't shouted exactly, only raised his voice and whatever Shresha did now, it had to be done quickly before the guards did hear him. If they came in, the Dalkivian would be killed immediately. She preferred to delay his destiny as long as possible. The talking had lasted long enough anyway. She wanted this man. Now. Ten days suddenly seemed to tick by before they had even begun. With efficient grace, Shresha grabbed the same hand the Dalkivian held the sword with, shot a quick palm against his nose with her other hand, smashing cartilage, then looped her arm across his throat and at the same time stepped around, thrust her hips behind his and then tossed him to the stone floor, hard.

She mounted him and dug her fingers into the fleshy part of his thumb, stripped the sword from his grip, then held the deadly blade to *his* throat. The look of astonishment in his crystalline eyes made Shresha smile in savage triumph. "I can have you anyway I want, Dalkivian. You are all mine now, and have but one purpose. I plan to have you many, many times so you might as well get used to it right now. *This*...is but the first way I intend to do so." She grabbed a handful of luscious golden hair, pinned his meaty arms with her knees. She lifted the sword but still pointed its tip at him in warning and then brought his mouth to her pussy. He didn't resist. The tonic still had a strong effect on him and it was plain to see that he wasn't formally trained in combat because he didn't attempt any of the number of escapes available to someone under the blade of a sword while lying flat on his back. Shresha, though not a Hunter, was still very well trained. She knew a variety of moves that would—even when matched against a man as large as the one beneath her—ensure her success. Patriian women were cunning and precise when it came to battle. It was an essential key to keeping their land secret from outsiders.

His thick probing tongue felt hot, slick. It trembled a little while licking her.

"That's good, Dalkivian. Now, suck me a little." Shresha pushed her pussy to his mouth harder. Visions of the other men on the Hill, naked and obedient, filled her mind and to her surprise, she wanted them too. All of them. Her breath caught when the man beneath her moaned a muffled, unmistakable sound of enjoyment. Maybe she wouldn't be too harsh on the Mage after all.

The large arms pinned at his sides stirred. "You want to touch me? Do you want to stick me with one of your big fingers, Dalkivian?" His nod thrilled her. She lifted her weight just enough so that he could maneuver beneath her. The sword stayed cautiously in its raised position, creating a delicious scene for her. She felt his large hand searching for her opening, and she moved to meet it. Then a finger, long, hard and so very thick found its mark and Shresha lowered herself onto it, sucking air between her teeth. She bucked her hips, grinding against his mouth and atop his finger. Glancing behind her, she found his cock standing straight and tall, the Ring of Destiny still boldly crowning its base and its blunt tip glistening, ready to penetrate her. To impregnate her. She released his beautiful hair and reached for it, stroking him at the same pace with which his finger fucked her. Another groan came from him, and it vibrated into her pussy. The next moment she felt a hot liquid gush and she made him drink her salty orgasm until her sensitive clit could take no more.

Shresha rose to her feet, boneless and panting, staring at the massive, naked man lying on the stone floor. His sexual need deliciously evident and unfulfilled. She suddenly wondered what he would taste like. Then she recalled the other men and wondered what they would all taste like. "That was good. But we are far from finished yet." She pointed the sword at him. "Get up and get on that bed, Dalkivian. I want your cock now."

The man rose to his feet, though he hesitated a moment before obeying. She watched his muscles bunch and move as he walked and then climbed onto the bed and lay down. He turned his head to her expectantly, waiting for the next command, his great cock pointing upward. She gripped the sword and walked to the bed.

She had every intention of making the most of the next ten days.

This morning, while it was just the two of them beneath the sheets, Shresha stared at the sleeping giant, feeling somewhat lazy as she studied his features. She was accustomed to seeing his expressive face during sex by now, and she found that she rather liked how peaceful he looked while sleeping too. One of his hands rested on his chest, reminding her how they sometimes snatched at her one moment and then caressed her the next. How they were coming to know how she wanted to be touched. She lifted his hand and brought it to her lips. His eyes fluttered open revealing two beautiful blue eyes. His hand closed over hers, and he gave her a brilliant sleepy smile.

She realized that today already marked their sixth day in the Mating Chamber and she also finally admitted to herself that she needed to take things a little slower. Her body ached, unaccustomed to so much sexual activity—she just hadn't been able to summon the will to stop. Over the last several days she'd made requests that the other men be brought to the Mating Chamber, sometimes five or six at a time. She had shamelessly fed her curiosity and allowed herself to become a goddess in her own mind. With so many men surrounding her, worshipping her body, her goal to become pregnant was forgotten. Shresha relished every moment in the Chamber. The position that had quickly become a fast favorite was when she had enough men for her to simultaneously hold a cock in each hand, suck on another and have the Dalkivian beneath her while yet another penetrated her from behind. In those moments of greedy bliss, Shresha thought she understood what it must be like to be the Goddess Shaiia. And strangely, the attentive Dalkivian surprised her at every turn by anticipating her needs. What had truly shocked her was when he had confessed that her pleasure brought him pleasure. In the darkness while she lay warm and cozy in his arms the night before, sleep did not come as easily as she had hoped.

Their morning meal was complete and Shresha felt refreshed and energized. She stood and reached up for a long, spine-cracking stretch and the Dalkivian knelt on the floor in front of her, his eyes just at breast level. She felt a flutter of excitement, but there also came a twinge of...*something else.*

Shresha frowned.

"What do they call you, Dalkivian?"

"Mmm?" his wet lips drew her nipples tight. Shresha let

her head fall back and grabbed handfuls of his long hair then shoved him downward. She wouldn't tolerate his not paying closer attention. As punishment for the slight infraction, she bucked and ground against his lips, tongue and teeth until the Dalkivian was out of breath. She released him, panting, and he rested his cheek against her hip. He tried to catch his breath and responded gruffly, "Behln. It's Behln."

She made her next demand, but carefully avoided eye contact. "Sit down, on the floor, Dalkivian." She refused to use his name; it was too personal. But she could still hear him saying it over and over in her mind. *Behln. It's Behln.*

She sat on his lap, facing him. While she fucked herself on his cock he stared at her breasts as they danced before his eyes. Shresha liked that he watched her body. It always resulted in his own more enthusiastic performance. She'd tested this theory by presenting him with loud rejoicing cries, and he'd responded vigorously. Now as her pussy clenched over his cock ready to release, she leaned down and took his mouth, feeding him her cries of ecstasy. He accepted them eagerly by wrapping his heavy arms around her, crushing her to his hard chest and pumping into her until he came with a great countering roar.

The Mage returned that night to administer more potion and Shresha still hadn't mentioned anything of Behln's growing resistance against it. Besides, she was becoming accustomed to him this way. She was confident in her own skills that she could easily subdue him at any time. Behln had free movement within the Chamber, but was well aware that with one word from Shresha, the Guards would kill him without hesitation. But, he never seemed to want to flee. He spoke of it and would occasionally question what was to happen after the tenth day, but Shresha quieted him with a sharp order, not to mention some very effective, distracting and energetic rounds of fucking.

She didn't want to think of what was to happen once her ten

days of mating had come to its end either. It made her...confused. All the Donum would be disposed of; they couldn't be allowed to return to their homes. For centuries her people had kept their land secret this way.

The time had come.

She felt her throat tighten with a pang of sadness while she was currently pinned against a wall of the Mating Chamber, her back digging into the sharp rigid stones. Behln huffed at her neck bruising her with his teeth. One hand cupped her ass with his two middle fingers embedded deep inside. He wiggled and fucked her with them while his cock did the same. Shresha, full to the hilt and in the throes of wild animalistic energy, grunted and groaned. She tangled her hands within his hair and yanked hard, holding on at the same time for dear life.

"Fuck me, Dalkivian! Harder! Hurt me!" she screamed, not wanting this moment to end. Suddenly he pulled her away from the wall and flung her onto the bed. He grabbed her hips and when she felt his heavy cock-tip aim for her pussy, she grabbed the sheets. In one swift movement he pounded into her. He covered her body with his, grabbed her mouth, turning her face so he could see her expression. Shresha remembered how the act of her sucking on another man's cock while he'd fucked her several nights ago had affected him, so she sucked two of his long fingers into her mouth and was immediately rewarded with an anguished and hungry groan...and then...the hardest pounding of her life.

"What's to become of me now," he asked, lazily taking her dark nipple into his mouth. She couldn't say when this had become a habit of his, but Behln always found some way to touch her while they lay together in the bed. Her nipple hardened instantly as his whiskers scraped her breast, but she looked away from his searching stare, holding the Ring of Destiny in her palm. Her heart ached a little as she clutched it tightly. When it had finally fallen away and hit the stone floor, the sound echoed throughout the Chamber. Shresha had retrieved it and then decided that she would save the ring to remember him by. Her beautiful Donum. Shresha felt the corners of her mouth turn down. It was all over and she had to find a way to accept it. With a heavy sigh she kissed his forehead and lifted his chin with her finger.

"You will bring me such great honor, Dalkivian." She searched for a reason to hate him, to make it easier for herself, but the last ten days had been so magical, so perfect, she could find no fault with this man, except that he had allowed himself to be caught.

Suddenly Behln rose onto his elbows as though he understood his fate. It seemed so cruel to rid the world of such a beautiful beast...

Through the window there came the heavy beat of drums, low and ominous. The women of Patriia were gathering once again at the bottom of the Hill, Queen Teshiie undoubtedly standing proudly at the top. For the first time in Shresha's life she understood what indecisiveness felt like. Panic seeped into her heart, made her anxious. This was how it was supposed to be, yet she couldn't bring herself to re-shackle this man and present him to be—

Suddenly she pushed away and grabbed a sword from the wall. They had used it many times during their lovemaking. Was it lovemaking? A memory buzzed over her skin as she remembered how he'd held her against a bedpost with the sword pointed at her throat, commanding her to suck his cock. It was at that moment, while she was voluntarily at his mercy, taking him into her mouth, that she thought she might love him. That she didn't ever want to leave the Mating Chamber because she couldn't imagine not having him again. The drumbeat in the distance quickened; they were almost ready for her to bring the

Dalkivian back to the Hill. Shresha thrust the sword into his hand.

"You must be quick! Take this, go through the window while there is still darkness to cover you."

At first he just sat there, unsure of something. Then he looked up at her. "Come with me!" he whispered harshly, trying to pull her to him. His eyes pleading. "I didn't think I could, but I, I've grown to want more of you. Please, come with me, we'll go together!"

"I can't. You must go, please, before they suspect something is wrong and come for you!"

What was she doing? What would the queen say when she told them all that the Dalkivian had escaped? She wrung her fingers then reached for another sword. "You must go! I can't send you to your death, not after this." A tear formed at the corner of her eye, and she felt her chin tremble. For the first time in her life, Shresha loved someone more than she thought possible. The queen would be very angry at not being able to complete the ceremony. A man that had escaped Patriia was a threat. He would be hunted relentlessly and Shresha...it didn't matter. She would fight to her death and die with love in her heart. That thought was somehow more honorable to her than having a daughter and it soothed her as she gripped the sword.

"I will wait for you, Shresha." Her name on his lips ripped a cry from Shresha's throat.

"Go, you big, you big..." the words wouldn't come. She swiped the sword at him, halfheartedly. He smiled, a sad smile, but then took her mouth with his and kissed her one last time. Without saying anything, he turned and climbed up the window ledge. In an instant he was through it, and then gone.

About the Authors

OLIVIA ARCHER is your typical California girl. That is, if your definition of "typical" includes writing porn by the pool under a hot, Hollywood sun. Her stories have appeared in *Frenzy: 60 Stories of Sudden Sex, Women in Lust: Erotic Stories* and on the website forthegirls.com.

JANINE ASHBLESS (janineashbless.blogspot.com) has had nine novels and collections of dark fantasy and horror erotica published. Her short stories have appeared in many Cleis anthologies including *Best Women's Erotica 2013* and *Thrones of Desire*. She's currently writing a trilogy about fallen angels for Cleis.

EMILY BINGHAM (queanofrope.com) is a Portland, Oregon author, whose writing has appeared in *Best Bondage Erotica 2011, Serving Him: Tales of Erotic Submission* and on cleansheets.com. She's also a fetish model for photographers across the country.

RACHEL KRAMER BUSSEL (rachelkramerbussel.com) is the editor of over fifty anthologies, including *Gotta Have It: 69 Stories of Sudden Sex; The Big Book of Orgasms; Baby Got Back: Anal Erotica; Serving Him; Going Down; Flying High; Lust in Latex; Best Bondage Erotica 2014* and others.

ANGELA CAPERTON (blog.angelacaperton.com) writes eclectic erotica that challenges genre conventions. Look for her stories published with Black Lace and eBury Publishing, Cleis, Circlet, Coming Together, eXtasy Books, Mischief, Renaissance eBooks, Seal Press and Side Real Press. Many of her stories have appeared in "Best of" collections, and on popular erotica podcasts.

HEIDI CHAMPA (heidichampa.blogspot.com) has been published in numerous anthologies including *Best Women's Erotica 2010, Irresistible, Best Erotic Romance 2012* and *2013* and *Sweet Confessions*. She has also steamed up the pages of *BUST Magazine*.

LILLIAN DOUGLAS lives and writes in the U.S. Midwest. She likes bicycles, language and sex, though not necessarily in that order.

ALLEN DUSK (allendusk.com) resides in Portland, OR. Other than writing unique blends of horror and erotica, his favorite pastimes include photography, geocaching, lusting over old horror movies and researching supernatural folklore.

TAMSIN FLOWERS writes lighthearted erotica, often with a twist in the tail and a sense of fun. Her stories have appeared in numerous anthologies and usually, she's working on at least ten stories at once. While she figures out whose leg belongs in which story, you can find out more at Tamsin's Superotica.

KD GRACE believes Freud was right. It IS all about sex, well, sex and love, and she's glad since that's what she loves to write about. When KD isn't writing, she's digging in her veg patch with her husband or walking the British countryside for inspiration.

KATYA HARRIS (Twitter @katya_harris) lives in Kent in the United Kingdom with her boyfriend, daughter and three crazy rat boys. She hopes that you like what she's written and that you'll come back for more.

KAY JAYBEE (kayjaybee.me.uk) is the author of *The Voyeur* (Xcite, 2012), *Making Him Wait* (Sweetmeats, 2012), *The Perfect Submissive* (Xcite, 2012), *Digging Deep* and *A Sticky Situation* (Xcite, 2012), *Yes, Ma'am* (Xcite, 2011), and *The Collector* (Austin & Macauley, 2012).

D. L. KING (dlkingerotica.blogspot.com) is the editor of anthologies such as *Slave Girls*, *Under Her Thumb* and *The Harder She Comes*, winner of the Lambda Literary Award and the Independent Publisher Book Award gold medal. Her stories can be found in *The Big Book of Bondage*, *Luscious* and *No Safewords*, among others.

MICHAEL LEWIS is an aspiring writer who has long hoped to balance his imagination and writing style into a format that more readers will enjoy. With his long tenure in corporate America, this represents a departure from the cost justifications and sales proposals that have shaped his writing until now.

A librarian by day, **KELLY MAHER** (kellymaher.com) thrills to write passionate tales of romantic interludes by night. Her stories have been published by Cleis Press, Black Lace Books and Ellora's Cave.

SOMMER MARSDEN (sommermarsden.blogspot.com) has been called "...one of the top storytellers in the erotica genre" (Violet Blue) and "Unapologetic" (Alison Tyler). Her erotic novels include *Restless Spirit, Boys Next Door, Learning to Drown* and the Zombie Exterminator series.

KATE MAXWELL (katemaxwell3216@yahoo.com) is a photographer and budding author of erotica living in Central Florida. This is Kate's first published work, and until now she has only shared her stories with a small circle of close friends.

CHASE MORGAN began writing erotica for his wife while away on business trips. As his muse and biggest supporter, she encouraged him to take a stab at sharing his filthy mind with the world.

LYNN TOWNSEND is a geek, a dreamer and an inveterate punster. When not reading, writing or editing, she can usually be found drinking coffee or killing video game villains. Lynn's interests include folk music, romance novels, and movies with more FX than plot.

BIX WARDEN lives in San Francisco, where she is a former board member of San Francisco Sex Information (SFSI). She has shared her true tales with the audience at SF's famous Bawdy Storytelling and her original poetry and prose with L.A.'s *Aural Sex* and Perverts Put Out at the Center for Sex and Culture.

SALOME WILDE (salandtalerotica.com) is the author of pansexual erotica, from contemporary kink to historical genre fiction. With Talon Rihai, she is coauthor of *After the First Taste of Love* (Storm Moon Press, 2012), the first novella in their Nick/Angelo trilogy, and the forthcoming boywhore novel *Turning Trick*.

KRISTINA WRIGHT (kristinawright.com) is the editor of several erotica anthologies for Cleis Press, including the Best Erotic Romance series. She holds degrees in English and humanities and her fiction has appeared in over one hundred anthologies. She lives in Virginia with her husband and their two sons.

About the Editor

ROSE CARAWAY (thekissmequicks.com) is a native Northern California writer, editor, narrator and podcaster on the hit shows *The Kiss Me Quick's Erotica Podcast* and *The Sexy Librarian Blog-cast* (rosecarawaythesexylibrarian.blogspot.com). Although her specialty is erotic fiction, she also has a passion for writing suspense, horror, fantasy and romance works. Some of her influences include Stephen King, Dan Savage, Jean M. Auel, Charlotte Brontë, Mia Martina and Anne Rice. Rose's writings prominently showcase her sex-positive approach to life, as well as her commitment to both feminism and masculinism. Being a staunch supporter of the LGBT community, she believes that people of all genders and orientations should be considered complementary and interdependent and are necessary for a truly healthy and functional society. In addition to writing, Rose's other passions revolve around keeping an active lifestyle, and a deep love of music and its many incarnations. She is immersed in the martial arts and has earned a black belt in Kenpo Karate. She also studies and practices Brazilian Jujitsu, Krav Maga and Mixed Martial Arts. If you would like to get in touch with her, just search Rose Caraway on Facebook, Twitter and most other social media sites.

Many More Than Fifty Shades of Erotica

Try This at Home!

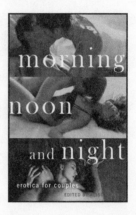

Happy Endings Forever and Ever

Dark Secret Love
A Story of Submission
By Alison Tyler

Inspired by her own BDSM exploits and private diaries, Alison Tyler draws on twenty-five years of penning sultry stories to create a scorchingly hot work of fiction, a memoir-inspired novel with reality at its core. A modern-day *Story of O*, a *9 1/2 Weeks*-style journey fueled by lust, longing and the search for true love.
ISBN 978-1-57344-956-4 $16.95

High-Octane Heroes
Erotic Romance for Women
Edited by Delilah Devlin

One glance and your heart will melt—these chiseled, brave men will ignite your fantasies with their courage and charisma. Award-winning romance writer Delilah Devlin has gathered stories of hunky, red-blooded guys who enter danger zones in the name of duty, honor, country and even love.
ISBN 978-1-57344-969-4 $15.95

Duty and Desire
Military Erotic Romance
Edited by Kristina Wright

The only thing stronger than the call of duty is the call of desire. *Duty and Desire* enlists a team of hot-blooded men and women from every branch of the military who serve their country and follow their hearts.
ISBN 978-1-57344-823-9 $15.95

Smokin' Hot Firemen
Erotic Romance Stories for Women
Edited by Delilah Devlin

Delilah delivers tales of these courageous men breaking down doors to steal readers' hearts! *Smokin' Hot Firemen* imagines the romantic possibilities of being held against a massively muscled chest by a man whose mission is to save lives and serve *every* need.
ISBN 978-1-57344-934-2 $15.95

Only You
Erotic Romance for Women
Edited by Rachel Kramer Bussel

Only You is full of tenderness, raw passion, love, longing and the many emotions that kindle true romance. The couples in *Only You* test the boundaries of their love to make their relationships stronger.
ISBN 978-1-57344-909-0 $15.95

Out of This World Romance

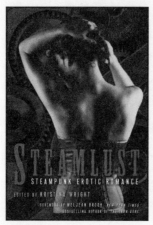

Steamlust
Steampunk Erotic Romance
Edited by Kristina Wright

Shiny brass and crushed velvet; mechanical inventions and romantic conventions; sexual fantasy and kinky fetish: this is a lush and fantastical world of women-centered stories and romantic scenarios, a first for steampunk fiction.
ISBN 978-1-57344-721-8 $14.95

The Sweetest Kiss
Ravishing Vampire Erotica
Edited by D. L. King

These sanguine tales give new meaning to the term "dead sexy" and feature beautiful bloodsuckers whose desires go far beyond blood.
ISBN 978-1-57344-371-5 $15.95

Dream Lover
Paranormal Tales of Erotic Romance
Edited by Kristina Wright

A potent potion of fun and sexy tales filled with male fairies and clairvoyant scientists, as well as darkly erotic tales of ghosts, shapeshifters and possession.
ISBN 978-1-57344-655-6 $14.95

Fairy Tale Lust
Erotic Fantasies for Women
Edited by Kristina Wright

Award-winning novelist and erotica writer Kristina Wright goes over the river and through the woods to find the sexiest fairy tales ever written.
ISBN 978-1-57344-397-5 $14.95

In Sleeping Beauty's Bed
Erotic Fairy Tales
By Mitzi Szereto

"Who can resist the erotic origins of fairy tales from Little Red to Rapunzel's long braid? Szereto knows her way around the mythic scholarship and the most outrageous sexual deviations in Pandora's Box."
—Susie Bright
ISBN 978-1-57344-367-8 $16.95

Unleash Your Favorite Fantasies

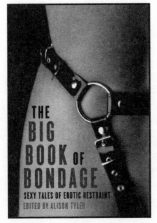

Red Hot Erotic Romance

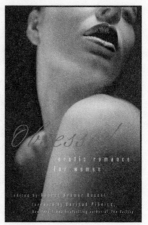

Obsessed
Erotic Romance for Women
Edited by Rachel Kramer Bussel

These stories sizzle with the kind of obsession that is fueled by our deepest desires, the ones that hold couples together, the ones that haunt us and don't let go. Whether just-blooming passions, rekindled sparks or reinvented relationships, these lovers put the object of their obsession first.
ISBN 978-1-57344-718-8 $14.95

Passion
Erotic Romance for Women
Edited by Rachel Kramer Bussel

Love and sex have always been intimately intertwined—and *Passion* shows just how delicious the possibilities are when they mingle in this sensual collection edited by award-winning author Rachel Kramer Bussel.
ISBN 978-1-57344-415-6 $14.95

Girls Who Bite
Lesbian Vampire Erotica
Edited by Delilah Devlin

Bestselling romance writer Delilah Devlin and her contributors add fresh girl-on-girl blood to the pantheon of the paranormal. The stories in *Girls Who Bite* are varied, unexpected, and soul-scorching.
ISBN 978-1-57344-715-7 $14.95

Irresistible
Erotic Romance for Couples
Edited by Rachel Kramer Bussel

This prolific editor has gathered the most popular fantasies and created a sizzling, no-holds-barred collection of explicit encounters in which couples turn their deepest desires into reality.
978-1-57344-762-1 $14.95

Heat Wave
Hot, Hot, Hot Erotica
Edited by Alison Tyler

What could be sexier or more seductive than bare, sun-warmed skin? Bestselling erotica author Alison Tyler gathers explicit stories of summer sex bursting with the sweet eroticism of swimsuits, sprinklers, and ripe strawberries.
ISBN 978-1-57344-710-2 $15.95

Bestselling Erotica for Couples

Sweet Life
Erotic Fantasies for Couples
Edited by Violet Blue

Your ticket to a front row seat for first-time spankings, breathtaking role-playing scenes, sex parties, women who strap it on and men who love to take it, not to mention threesomes of every combination.
ISBN 978-1-57344-133-9 $14.95

Sweet Life 2
Erotic Fantasies for Couples
Edited by Violet Blue

"This is a we-did-it-you-can-too anthology of real couples playing out their fantasies." —Lou Paget, author of *365 Days of Sensational Sex*
ISBN 978-1-57344-167-4 $15.95

Sweet Love
Erotic Fantasies for Couples
Edited by Violet Blue

"If you ever get a chance to try out your number-one fantasies in real life—and I assure you, there will be more than one—say yes. It's well worth it. May this book, its adventurous authors, and the daring and satisfied characters be your guiding inspiration."—Violet Blue
ISBN 978-1-57344-381-4 $14.95

Afternoon Delight
Erotica for Couples
Edited by Alison Tyler

"Alison Tyler evokes a world of heady sensuality where fantasies are fearlessly explored and dreams gloriously realized."
—Barbara Pizio, Executive Editor, *Penthouse Variations*
ISBN 978-1-57344-341-8 $14.95

Three-Way
Erotic Stories
Edited by Alison Tyler

"Three means more of everything. Maybe I'm greedy, but when it comes to sex, I like more. More fingers. More tongues. More limbs. More tangling and wrestling on the mattress." —from the introduction
ISBN 978-1-57344-193-3 $15.95

$\star$ **Free book of equal or lesser value. Shipping and applicable sales tax extra.**
Cleis Press • (800) 780-2279 • orders@cleispress.com
www.cleispress.com

Fuel Your Fantasies

Carnal Machines
Steampunk Erotica
Edited by D. L. King

In this decadent fusing of technology and romance, out-
standing contemporary erotica writers use the enthralling
possibilities of the 19th-century steam age to tease and titil-
late.
ISBN 978-1-57344-654-9 $14.95

The Sweetest Kiss
Ravishing Vampire Erotica
Edited by D. L. King

These sanguine tales give new meaning to
the term "dead sexy" and feature beautiful
bloodsuckers whose desires go far beyond
blood.
ISBN 978-1-57344-371-5 $15.95

The Handsome Prince
Gay Erotic Romance
Edited by Neil Plakcy

A bawdy collection of bedtime stories
brimming with classic fairy tale characters,
reimagined and recast for any man who
has dreamt of the day his prince will come.
These sexy stories fuel fantasies and remind
us all of the power of true romance.
ISBN 978-1-57344-659-4 $14.95

Daughters of Darkness
Lesbian Vampire Tales
Edited by Pam Keesey

"A tribute to the sexually aggressive woman and her archetypal roles, from nurturing
goddess to dangerous predator."
—*The Advocate*
ISBN 978-1-57344-233-6 $14.95

Dark Angels
Lesbian Vampire Erotica
Edited by Pam Keesey

Dark Angels collects tales of lesbian vam-
pires, the quintessential bad girls, arche-
types of passion and terror. These tales of
desire are so sharply erotic you'll swear
you've been bitten!
ISBN 978-1-57344-252-7 $13.95

* Free book of equal or lesser value. Shipping and applicable sales tax extra.
Cleis Press • (800) 780-2279 • orders@cleispress.com
www.cleispress.com

Best Erotica Series

"Gets racier every year."—*San Francisco Bay Guardian*

Best Women's Erotica 2014
Edited by Violet Blue
ISBN 978-1-62778-003-2 $15.95

Best Women's Erotica 2013
Edited by Violet Blue
ISBN 978-1-57344-898-7 $15.95

Best Women's Erotica 2012
Edited by Violet Blue
ISBN 978-1-57344-755-3 $15.95

Best Bondage Erotica 2014
Edited by Rachel Kramer Bussel
ISBN 978-1-62778-012-4 $15.95

Best Bondage Erotica 2013
Edited by Rachel Kramer Bussel
ISBN 978-1-57344-897-0 $15.95

Best Bondage Erotica 2012
Edited by Rachel Kramer Bussel
ISBN 978-1-57344-754-6 $15.95

Best Lesbian Erotica 2014
Edited by Kathleen Warnock
ISBN 978-1-62778-002-5 $15.95

Best Lesbian Erotica 2013
Edited by Kathleen Warnock
Selected and introduced by
Jewelle Gomez
ISBN 978-1-57344-896-3 $15.95

Best Lesbian Erotica 2012
Edited by Kathleen Warnock
Selected and introduced by
Sinclair Sexsmith
ISBN 978-1-57344-752-2 $15.95

Best Gay Erotica 2014
Edited by Larry Duplechan
Selected and introduced by Joe Manetti
ISBN 978-1-62778-001-8 $15.95

Best Gay Erotica 2013
Edited by Richard Labonté
Selected and introduced by Paul Russell
ISBN 978-1-57344-895-6 $15.95

Best Gay Erotica 2012
Edited by Richard Labonté
Selected and introduced by
Larry Duplechan
ISBN 978-1-57344-753-9 $15.95

Best Fetish Erotica
Edited by Cara Bruce
ISBN 978-1-57344-355-5 $15.95

Best Bisexual Women's Erotica
Edited by Cara Bruce
ISBN 978-1-57344-320-3 $15.95

Best Lesbian Bondage Erotica
Edited by Tristan Taormino
ISBN 978-1-57344-287-9 $16.95

* **Free book of equal or lesser value. Shipping and applicable sales tax extra.**
Cleis Press • (800) 780-2279 • orders@cleispress.com
www.cleispress.com

Ordering is easy! Call us toll free or fax us to place your MC/VISA order.
You can also mail the order form below with payment to:
Cleis Press, 2246 Sixth St., Berkeley, CA 94710.

ORDER FORM

QTY	TITLE	PRICE
_____	_____	_____
_____	_____	_____
_____	_____	_____
_____	_____	_____
_____	_____	_____
_____	_____	_____
_____	_____	_____
_____	_____	_____

SUBTOTAL _____

SHIPPING _____

SALES TAX _____

TOTAL _____

Add $3.95 postage/handling for the first book ordered and $1.00 for each additional book. Outside North America, please contact us for shipping rates. California residents add 9% sales tax. Payment in U.S. dollars only.

* Free book of equal or lesser value. Shipping and applicable sales tax extra.

Cleis Press • Phone: (800) 780-2279 • Fax: (510) 845-8001
orders@cleispress.com • www.cleispress.com
You'll find more great books on our website

Follow us on Twitter @cleispress • Friend/fan us on Facebook